A COURT OF WIND AND WINGS

A HADES AND PERSEPHONE RETELLING

LEGENDS OF LOVE

DANIELA A. MERA

ELAYNA R. GALLEA

This is a work of fiction. Names, characters, places, and incidents either are the product of the author's imagination or are used fictitiously. Any resemblance to actual persons, living or dead, events, or locales is entirely coincidental.

authordanielaamera@gmail.com

elayna.gallea@gmail.com

First ebook edition October 2022

Second edition November 2023

Hardback ISBN: 978-1-960343-17-8

Paperback ISBN: 978-1-960343-16-1

Ebook ASIN: B0CG6TPK7G

Book Cover Design by GetCovers

Interior/Case Laminate by Shane Nel

Map by Daniela A. Mera

Created with Vellum

Realm of the Vampires
Ice City
Winter Court
ARANTHIUM
Spring
Summer Fae Court
Nathaniel's House

To anyone who has learned to love again, even after a stormy past. Life is full of second chances. Especially when your lover is the DemiGod of Death.

PART ONE

PINING

CHAPTER 1
A FUNERAL FOR A MAN I NEVER KNEW
AIDONEUS

Present day, one week after a major attack on Lethe, the capital of The Gates of Hell

Funerals were usually not sad events for me. But there had been a select few in my life that were hard to stomach. This service was one such event with a room full of weepy people dressed in dark colors. Helena, my Ice Mer niece, and her human fiancé Erik were sitting at my side. They did not cry, but the solemn look in their eyes betrayed their deep sadness. That sadness echoed inside of me.

Less than a week ago, my brother Phelix, the Ice Mer King, sent a team of men to destroy my city. Lethe was in the process of being rebuilt, but there were casualties. All of that could be ignored for another hour or so.

One of my mother's priestesses stood at the front of the procession and spoke of the victim's life. The victim was one of many that filled out our casualty lists. They had lived a noble life that sought to protect the only family member I held in high regard. Helena was new to me, but she was important.

This funeral was distressing because it reminded me of time spent in white-washed hospitals, peering into the window of a room I wasn't allowed to enter. Magic licks under my skin at the disrespect. The King of the Daemons should be allowed everywhere.

My memory continued to wander, and the incense was replaced by the astringent scent of cleaning chemicals burning my nose--of an ache that broke my heart over and over. Machines beeping and people crying. Sitting here, in this funeral home surrounded by the sounds of weeping, wasn't better than almost crushing the asshole who prioritized Phaedra's time. Murderous rage built in my chest every time he touched her hand.

When he stroked her cheek while staring out the hospital room window to make sure I was watching.

I put my head in my hands and tried to focus on the eulogy that Erik had stood up to offer. "Jean Luc Beauchamp was a man who cared for others." He coughed into his hand, his eyes watering.

That brought me out of my own personal Hell. Erik was an impressive man. A bit too serious, in my opinion, but at least he cared for Helena. I respected the man enough to offer him the ultimate gift if he would marry Helena.

I wasn't surprised when he said yes.

Erik cleared his throat, continuing. "Every day Jean Luc spent on my ship, he cared for his fellow crew mates. Even so, I'm certain he is grateful to be reunited with his wife. Their three daughters are here with us today, and we extend our deepest regrets at his passing. He was a noble man. An honorable man. He will be--" Erik coughs again, and a tear slides down his cheek, "sorely missed."

I thought about that for a moment. Did the men who had worked on Erik's ship truly take care of each other so much? It wasn't an unreasonable thought. Indeed, those who seemed the most despicable often needed the most love.

After Erik stepped down, the priestess took his place. Her words flowed out of her, but I barely listened. After the centuries, all the blessings started to sound the same.

It did not take long for the woman to stop speaking and leave a blessing upon us all. Every person in the congregation bowed their heads as one, and the priestess prayed.

How long had it been since Fortuna gave me a blessing? I couldn't remember. I may need to arrange a meeting. But, unlike people of this world, arranging a meeting with the Divine—who also happened to be your mother—was not easy. Especially since the last time I had heard from her was right before another funeral.

When the priestess sat, no one moved. More soft sounds of tears came from behind me. It was too close, to painful. It triggered a memory long lost inside of me.

Rain.

There had been so much rain since she died. It was as if the loss of her was too much for the world to bear. I understood that. I was having a hard time bearing it myself.

The absence of my wife felt like it would split me in half. The weight was brutal and oppressive, but my heartstrings threatened to snap. Some part of me wished they would. I wouldn't mind being free of this world.

The priestess Natami stood at the front, giving the eulogy. I had thought about it once and then decided there was no way I would make it through. Natami's voice was soft as she spoke of Miranda's goodness, of the great sacrifice my wife had given the world during the Rebellion we'd spent decades fighting.

But then she spoke the words I could not forgive. Could not forget.

"Miranda's death was the only reason we were now free from the Elementals."

They slammed into me, twisting my insides. From my seat in the front pew, I shook. I couldn't listen anymore. I stood. I let the congregation think what they would. It would be me alone who would bear my mother's wrath for being so disrespectful. What did they know about the true story?

Had my wife's sacrifice helped us? Maybe.

Probably.

But it wasn't supposed to end this way. Miranda's death was someone else's fault. And now that bastard was hiding under the ocean, protected by his own little echo chamber of storming assholes with fewer brains than an amoeba.

I stormed away with thousands of eyes on me. Millions, if you counted the gods-damned new contraptions they called "cameras." I had tried to refuse them entry, but I'd been overruled by the PR team. Flinging the doors open, the cracking sound of breaking flower pots barely registered in my mind. Those damned flowers. They were periwinkles, traditionally braided into crowns and worn by beings as they passed through the Gates of Hell and entered a new realm. They had been her *favorite gift for the King of Death.*

Now, she was gone. And I hated them.

My legs moved without thought, and I sprinted down the halls then hurried out of the open doors, only to be bombarded by hoards of mourners. Dressed in black and wearing the death flower, they all started bowing, murmuring the same phrase over and over. "May she rest in the paradise of the gods."

I also wished that, but I didn't exactly want to talk about the circles of Hell during the service for my wife's death.

My blood boiling, I ignored them all and pushed through to the side of the building and into the Wedding Garden. I ran for into the bushes as though they were a Lifeline. It didn't stink of death, and security was stationed at all the entrances, protecting any stragglers from making their way in. The Warlocks also put up extensive wards to keep people from looking in. I wondered if Hecate, the leader of

Witches and Warlocks, did that because she knew me well and expected me to bolt.

The Gates of Hell was a wasteland. It was the inheritance of the Daemons.

I hated it. So much. My mother gave me these gardens in remembrance of her love. Sure, there was a small patch of periwinkles, but it was obscured by the bougainvilleas, the jacarandas, and the lilies. Trees of great variety, both tall and short, were positioned around the round oasis. In the center, there was a gazebo. I walked over, comforted by the quietness that seeped into every corner of this mysterious place.

I barely made it to the steps before I fell into a slump. Cradling my head in my hands, tears began rolling down my cheeks.

It wasn't the first time I'd cried, but it felt so final today.

I would never see Miranda again. Fortuna had taken her away and hidden her away in the threads of darkness. They wished for peace in the afterlife, but I knew the truth: my queen was gone. Forever. I could never find her, not in any corner of Hell. Dying would not resolve my problem; only complete oblivion could ease my pain. An impossible feat with my status as a DemiGod.

Tears poured out of me, and soon, I gasped for breath. I forgot I knew the kind of sadness that could crack one's soul in half. The way it could make your muscles hurt. It was the kind of sadness that made your brain scream for relief.

Slamming my fists on my thighs, I tilted my head up to the sky and let out a roar to shake the world.

It did, for a moment. My new birthright power was flowing a little too potently.

When I was done, I sensed a presence behind me.

Who could've gotten past all those wards?

I whipped around, drawing my shadows around me in a second. The entire garden darkened, and I surveyed the area, trying to find the being who would no doubt be cowering.

I found no one.

"Reyna?" I called out. She was the only person who would have the gall to interrupt me, especially on this day.

No response.

"Who's there?" I hissed. "I don't appreciate being spied on."

"I'm not spying. I'm trying to figure out why you are crying so hard?"

What the hell?

"You're shitting me, right?" Anger, hot and thick, roiled inside of me.

"No, and I would appreciate it if you stopped projecting all that rage toward me. I just wanted to see if you were okay."

The voice was definitely feminine. My head was clear enough to understand that. Was this a bombardment? Some woman searching to swoop in and find power in my grief?

Something stopped me from soaring into a terrible rage. A strange feeling within my chest. This female... whoever she was, she sounded sincere. I replayed her words in my mind.

She didn't want me to be angry at me. She was... checking on me.

A new possibility dawned. Did this mysterious woman not know who I was?

"I am not all right," I said. I doubted I ever would be again.

A long pause ensued.

"I'm sorry. My mother brought me along with her today. Did you know the queen?" she asked.

I searched for that voice. Why couldn't I see her?

"Yes. I knew Queen Miranda very well."

My throat closed.

"Then I am so sorry for your loss."

A woman appeared before me. A mighty being indeed, to be able to hide from me. She was beautiful. *I was shocked when I noticed that.*

If only that realization didn't come at the cost of heaps of guilt.

From the way the female spoke, I could tell she was young. Maybe only a century old, if that.

She relaxed, and a pair of brilliant wings unfurled behind her. They faded from pearly white, to yellow, to pink, and then it finished in a sweeping cerulean blue.

What was this Angel doing here? I thought only Raphael Zeus, my Angelic brother, came from Angel's Landing.

"Well then," she said, interrupting my thoughts. "I just came to bring you this."

She stepped forward. She was so bold and had treated me so normally that I didn't want her to see me and realize who I was just yet. My eyes traced the length of her outstretched hand and landed on a disposable handkerchief.

I almost laughed.

"For me?" I said.

"Yes. Again, I really am sorry. I don't have much experience with loss, but if you need to talk, I've been told I'm an excellent listener." She squared her shoulders a little, and something softened inside me.

"Thank you." I reached out and took the tissue. Our fingers brushed, and she flinched. Not from fear, but because I realized she still couldn't see me. Such a strange creature to be so fearless. Didn't she understand how dangerous the world was?

"Thank you, but I don't feel like speaking right now," I said. She nodded resolutely, and for a second, I thought about taking it all back. I did want to talk about Miranda's death. But I didn't need to gush everything to this woman I didn't know.

Even if I wanted to.

"Well, I'm going to go then." She turned to leave.

"Wait," I called out, and she stopped.

Turning back around, her brows rose. "You know I still can't see you, right?"

A smile tugged at the corners of my mouth. She was so honest. "Yes, I know. Before you go... would you tell me your name?"

She smiled, and my shadows retreated just a bit after coming in contact with her brilliance. "Phaedra Demtre, at your service. Actually, maybe you could help me."

"Oh?"

She nodded. "I will be moving to the capital in Angel's Landing soon to become an art dealer. If you have have any contacts, could you send them to me? My name is in all the phone books."

I smiled. She really didn't know who I was. "Of course."

And just like that, she was gone. And I felt a little lighter.

"Uncle?"

I blinked, and suddenly, everyone was gone except Helena. She was sitting at my side, looking like she had been speaking to me for a while.

"Sorry," I mumbled, rolling back my shoulders to stretch out how tense they'd gotten.

"Everything okay?" she asked tentatively. The water splashed in her aqua-chair as she leaned toward me.

Nodding, I ran a hand through my hair. "Yeah, funerals just bring up many things for me."

Helena raised an eyebrow and put a hand on my shoulder. "Aren't you the King of Death?"

I laughed. "I was born into that one."

"Well, it sounds like it sucks."

I scratched my jaw. "It definitely does. Look, I need to go to an appointment. Tell Erik I will see you for dinner later." I stood, and she rolled behind me.

She studied my face, not really looking convinced. "How's Phaedra?"

"Not good." I gritted my teeth. Phaedra was in a hospital. That's how she was. Her wounds were healed from the attack, but she wouldn't wake up and no one knew why.

"Can we see her?"

I sighed. "Maybe we can visit her later this week. I really need to get to my appointment."

Helena nodded. "All right. Stay safe, Uncle."

I hurried out of the temple and practically ran through the parking garage to find my black Fae Vertage. A long, sleek sports car in midnight black, the windows were tinted so dark that not even an immortal being could see through them. I opened the door, sliding in.

I turned on the car, and instantly, the touch screen popped to life.

"My Lord?" Toth'toros, the head of my Daemon guard, appeared on the screen. "Would you like me to order you a security escort?"

I put on my sunglasses. "Yes, actually. I'm headed to Ms. Evalde's office."

He knew that, of course. It was his job to follow my schedule.

His expression shifted just slightly as he considered my words. "Very well, my King. Anything else?"

I paused. Ms. Evalde's contact had been in my possession for over fifty years. I'd made at least half a dozen appointments, but maybe now it was time to finally go.

"Nothing more."

With the touch of a button, I programmed the destination and turned on the manual drive. I needed to work off some steam.

In a matter of seconds, I was rolling out of the parking garage and on the road to visit the best gods-damned therapist in all of Aranthium.

CHAPTER 2

I WISH I DIDN'T HATE DINNER PARTIES

PHAEDRA

57 years ago

My fingers wrapped around my coffee mug, staring out the window as the sun began its ascent into the heavens. It moved slowly as though this was the first time it had ever made the trek. With each minute, its rays pushed away the tendrils of darkness, welcoming yet another day. It was beautiful. Stunning.

I was in awe the first time I sat in my home, watching the kiss of the sun's rays envelop the city of Olimpie. This sight... How many sunrises had been stolen from me by my sheltered upbringing? Thousands, by my estimate.

Now, the sunrise was my favorite way to start every single day. There was something special about the dawn. It was always different. Fresh. New.

By the time the sun had taken its rightful place as king of the sky, my coffee cup was empty. I put the mug on the table, standing tall. Rolling my shoulders, I snapped out my wings and let them stretch behind me.

Today was another day. When I was young, I was caught in the monotony of the life my mother wanted me to live. Day in and day out, she had forced me to remain there. Stagnant.

Now, I was out from under her somewhat domineering influence. I was working, something which she fiercely disapproved of, even though my boss was someone she considered a close acquaintance. My mother didn't really do *friends*. But my boss was definitely a close acquaintance of hers.

Throwing on a pair of sleek white pants, I grabbed a specially tailored pale blue blouse and slipped it over my arms. A few buttons in the right place, and the material went around my wings like a dream. Hurrying over to the mirror, I twisted my long black hair into a chignon at the base of my neck before applying my makeup. Foundation, lipstick, eyeshadow, mascara, the works. Once my armor was in place, I took a deep breath.

Here we go.

I locked the front door, hurrying over to my balcony and grabbing my purse. My FaePhone was sitting on the charger, and I grabbed it too, swiping up while stuffing a donut in my mouth.

> Evgenia: You'd better hurry up. The boss is in a mood today.

Sighing, I typed a quick reply to the chipper Autumn Fae, who also happened to be my best friend, letting her know I was leaving before chucking my FaePhone in my purse. Evgenia took care of our boss' schedule, and she was expected to be in the office whenever he was. Which meant she was practically there 24-7.

Applying one last coat of lipstick, I stepped onto the balcony and closed the double doors behind me.

The first moment outside was always my favorite. The only thing I loved more than art was flight. The way the wind curled around me, brushing past me and rustling the feathers of my wings as though I were a long-lost friend in need of comfort. It was *everything*.

I grinned, locking the doors behind me before taking a running jump and leaping off my balcony.

The leaping portion of my routine wasn't necessary for flying, but I craved that moment of absolute and complete fear as I fell through the skies before my wings began to beat. It filled my body with a rush that kept me going through my entire day.

It reminded me I was alive. I was free. I was no longer locked in the gilded cage my mother had kept me in for my entire childhood.

And I loved it.

The wind, cool and crisp and still filled with touches of the night, brushed up under my wings. I held my breath briefly, letting myself tumble towards the earth before flapping my wings.

Once, twice.

The glorious strain on my back muscles was all I needed. I could fly with my eyes closed. And sometimes, I did.

But for right now, I had to get to work. With another quick flap of my wings, I joined the steady stream of traffic heading towards the ostentatious palace in the middle of Olimpie.

FLYING ONTO THE SEVENTEENTH-FLOOR BALCONY, I straightened my blouse and pants before re-pinning my hair. After reapplying my lipstick in the reflective glass of the balcony, I took a deep breath and pushed open the doors.

Instantly, a swarm of voices hit me. Chatter came from all around as my co-workers hurried to and fro. Raising a brow, I marched over to my desk. As expected, Evgenia was sitting in the seat across from mine, typing away hurriedly on her laptop. Her mouth was pinched, her brows furrowed as she stared at whatever she was working on. Her flaming orange hair and pointy ears spoke of her Fae heritage, as did her preference for long sweaters and tight leggings.

She looked up, her vivid green eyes becoming brighter as she saw me. "Oh, thank the gods you're here, Phaedra. I was worried you wouldn't make it on time, and I'd have to go in your stead." She twisted her hands in her lap. "You know how much I hate talking to people I don't know."

Nodding, I patted her arm. "I know, dear."

I wasn't exactly sure what had happened, but I knew Evgenia had undergone some sort of trauma when she was younger. Now, other than work, she rarely went out.

Clearing my throat, I glanced around the busy office. "Is he here?"

Evgenia nodded, her eyes widening. "Yes." She jerked her head toward his office before rummaging through her desk and pulling out a small box. "Bring these with you. They'll help."

My lips twitched up as I took the offering. "Thank you, Genie. You're the best."

She grinned, shooing me towards his office. "Remember, he's a little testy because you-know-who is supposed to visit the office tomorrow. Try not to push him too much. For all our sakes."

"I'll do my best," I replied. Suddenly, I wished I hadn't eaten that donut so quickly as my stomach twisted around. I had forgotten about tomorrow's visit.

Maybe I'd call out sick.

Pushing that thought into the back of my mind for further pondering, I straightened my back and walked over to the boss's office. Knocking once, I waited for the telltale grunt from the other side before gently opening the door.

"You called for me, sir?"

"WHAT KIND of person hosts a dinner party and decides they need new artwork *the day of?*" I muttered to myself as I flew over the streets of Olimpie.

I knew what kind.

The pompous kind. And my boss was the most pompous of them all. Nothing but the best for him. This means I'm heading to the Gallery of Angels, the highest-rated art gallery in all of Aranthium, and they had pieces of art from the most acclaimed artists, reaching as far back as the Mystanian Period.

I called the curator before leaving the office, ensuring he was ready for me when I arrived. He assured me he had several pieces he thought would work. I just needed to go in, pick one, and charge it to my boss's account.

This didn't fall under my regular job description, but since my boss argued that I had three art degrees, I was the best one to pick out art for him.

I refrained from saying that my three art degrees may have excluded me from being a glorified courier.

When I landed in front of the gallery, the flight had done wonders for my mood. I felt invigorated as I walked through the front doors. I was Phaedra Demtre, and even if my boss used me as little more than a peon running his errands, I knew who I was.

Maybe one day, he would too. Most days, I felt the weight of his lack of appreciation like a burden on my soul. I was good—

no, good was not a strong enough word. I was *great* at my job. Every day, I kept the office running and made sure everyone knew where they had to go, what to do, and I did so without him even noticing.

Maybe that is the problem, I mused.

Perhaps I was so good at my job that he didn't even notice me anymore.

“Ms. Demtre?”

A soft voice broke me out of my reverie, and my head snapped up. “Yes,” I replied, looking for the source of the voice, “that’s me.”

“Up here.”

I raised my eyes, watching the pink-haired Pixie fluttering down from the ceiling. She wore slacks and a blouse, her yellow translucent wings fluttering behind her.

“I’m so sorry,” she apologized profusely. “I was just making sure everything was lined up for tonight in the upper gallery and I didn’t hear you come in. Please accept my deepest apologies. If I had known you would be flying in, I would have been waiting for you.”

I smiled. "Not to worry. Traffic in Olimpie is a real problem. I try to fly wherever I can. I'm sure you understand, Miss..."

The pink-haired Pixie giggled. "Amberils," she filled in. "Miss Delilah Amberils."

Grinning, I extended my hand. She fluttered down and grabbed a manicured finger, shaking it. "Nice to meet you," I said.

Delilah smiled. "The pleasure is all mine. Most people never even stop to talk with me, let alone ask my name."

Just then, a deep voice shouted from the back. "Is that the Angel? Dammit, Delilah, you should have told me she was here. We can't afford to lose this client."

A harried-looking man stepped out of the backroom, wiping

his hands on his suit. His long ears pointed to the sky, his features clearly marking him as a Winter Fae. I momentarily wondered what had brought him to this side of the sea when he continued to speak. "Ah, Ms. Demtre. So good of you to come on such short notice." His voice ran over me like rancid oil, a stark difference from the booming I'd heard a few moments ago.

I raised a brow, wiping my face clean of all emotion. "Mr. Devois, I presume?"

He nodded.

"Good," I said briskly. If he was going to be rude, I was going to be all business. I had no tolerance for people who treated some species like lesser beings. As far as I was concerned, Pixies and humans were just as important as the rest of us. "I'm here for some art. Lead the way."

HALF AN HOUR LATER, I finished charging an exorbitant amount of money to my boss's credit card. He was probably going to be upset when he got the bill, but he told me to get him the best piece of artwork they had. And that's what I did. The painting I purchased was sure to cause quite the uproar at the dinner he was hosting, which I was fairly certain was the entire point. There was nothing he liked more than being the center of attention. This would keep tongues wagging for weeks, which I was sure he would enjoy.

Having paid, I tucked my copy of the receipt in my purse. "Thank you very much, Mr. Devois."

He nodded. "Please, take your time and look around the gallery on your way out."

"Thank you," I said. A glimmer of excitement fluttered to life within me. "I would like that very much."

Meandering through the gallery, I stopped and stared at several incredible art pieces. The colors used were so unbelievable; it was as though I could *feel* the emotions coming through the paintings. I might have been skilled with a makeup brush, but I had nothing on these artists. They were incredible. Breathtaking.

I could spend all day here.

But unfortunately, my phone buzzed in my pocket and reminded me of my duties. Art, it seemed, would have to wait. Sighing, I fished it out and stared at the email.

Come back to the office. Emergency. Need you.
- B

He couldn't even muster up the energy to sign the word "boss" on his emails. Huffing, I typed a quick reply, letting him know I was leaving before heading to the door.

On my way out, something caught my eye in the corner of the workroom. A painting that I was sure I'd seen before...

It was lying on the table, and several containers of paint were all around it. I took a step closer, curiosity momentarily pushing aside my sensibilities when a voice came from somewhere in front of me.

"I have it here for you, sir," Mr. Devois said in a hard tone. His voice grew louder, and something within me twisted. I shouldn't be caught standing here, eavesdropping.

Mr. Devois continued, "No one has seen it. It's a perfect match."

Sucking in a deep breath, I hurried down the hall. I turned the corner, gasping as I slammed into a hard chest.

My heart stuttered, and I stepped back.

The man I had been trying to avoid was staring at me. “Ms. Demtre,” he said, his voice as cold as ice. “I’d thought you’d already left.”

Nodding, I gripped my purse in my hands. Something about his tone frightened me, and everything within me was telling me to get away. He was dangerous. How, I didn’t know. But I knew I needed to get out.

“Yes,” I said, forcing levity I didn't feel into my voice. “I was just going, but then I got lost.”

He stared at me for a very long moment, and I fought the urge to shift on my feet. “Okay,” he said gruffly. Grabbing my arm, he wrenched me towards the door. “The exit is this way, Ms. Demtre.”

I nodded, but he didn’t let go of my arm.

He stomped towards the exit, and the Pixie squeaked in the background as we walked past.

Once we were outside, he turned to me, raising a brow. “Ms. Demtre, do you have anything to tell me?”

I sucked in a breath. What had I gotten myself into? I should have left right away. Something was dangerous here, and there was something about that painting I’d seen...

What was going on at this gallery?

“No,” I whispered.

A beat passed, then two.

“Then you’d better go,” he hissed.

I flew back to the office faster than I had ever flown before. The entire time, I couldn’t shake the feeling that something was wrong.

Soon, it would become clear that ‘wrong’ was an understatement.

That day changed my life forever.

CHAPTER 3
ACLEPSIA EVALDE PHD.
AIDONEUS

Present day

"Your Highness, can you tell me what brings you to my office today?" Asclepia Evalde asked. "I'm so glad we finally have the chance to meet, King of the Daemons."

The room around us was dark and warm. Directly to my right, a small, crackling fire had been lit under an eclectic collection of paintings depicting trees, flowers, rivers... the works. The other wall held floor-to-ceiling dark wood bookshelves stocked with first-edition novels. My eyes skimmed over the leather-bound spines, noting all the titles relating to the mind and trying to memorize the classic titles. *Withering Heights* rested next to *Anna and The Daemon Ruler*. I filed them away to read at a later date.

Every inch of this office had been calculated to put both parties at ease. Surprisingly, even the enormous window behind Ms. Evalde that overlooked Hell's Gates, the bubbling volcano, and the vast expanse of the great city—my great city—was comforting.

She wasn't a cheap therapist, so this was good.

"Lord Hades?" Ms. Evalde's deep, clinical voice repeated as she looked at me with round, golden eyes that peeked out over large-rimmed glasses. Her golden horns were the same color as her eyes.

"Hey, sorry. I'm a bit distracted by the books," I said, straightening the lapel on my sports coat.

"Oh? Do you enjoy reading?" she asked, picking up a stylus that had been made to look like a ballpoint pen. She swiped up, opening up a premier tablet that one of my companies manufactured.

"My wife loved reading," I replied automatically. "Over the centuries, the joy of it rubbed off on me. I notice you have a lot of romance novels."

"Oh yes, it's an excellent escape from stress," she replied. I raised my eyebrows, and the therapist shrugged. "Everyone needs a hobby."

"Reading is so... passive. That doesn't feel like a proper hobby," I said, my voice strained.

She studied me for a second. "So, why did you bring it up? I have many things in this office. Surely you can see the fifth-century fertility statues or the polished gemstones from the swamp witches? You work in antiquities. Why focus on my very modern book titles?" Her tone didn't strike me as irritated, just curious.

I tightened my fingers on the luxe leather armrest as a pair of lovely, dark red eyes framed by ebony hair flashed through my thoughts. "My wife always said that you could tell a lot about someone by the kinds of books they read. Hell knows why she chose me when I never read anything unrelated to work."

The therapist tilted her head, smiling slightly. "She sounds like my kind of female. I apologize if this is bold of me, but you're a public figure, so I know about her death. It was a long time ago, no?"

Here we go.

I took a long, deep breath. "A little more than three centuries ago."

The therapist nodded encouragingly when I didn't continue. I waved a hand, trying to lessen the horror of what had actually happened. "It was during The Great Rebellion, when we overthrew the Elementals. She was sacrificed in fr—She was tortured and killed, that is." I cleared my throat.

Ms. Evalde's eyes grew dark and sad. "It was one of the greatest tragedies of our time. My condolences."

I nodded, blinking rapidly to fight the unwanted moisture in my eyes. "So, it was."

A moment passed, and then I said, "Look, you can call me Aidoneus if I'm going to sit here for the next several months, pouring out my secrets."

"No problem, Aidoneus." She smiled, seeming at ease in my presence. Not something many beings could claim. I studied her, and she seemed content to allow me to continue.

After a few minutes passed, the therapist cleared her throat. "I really am interested in what you are doing here today..."

I ducked my head, raking my hand through my white hair. What was I supposed to say? I wanted to talk about Phaedra. I wanted to talk about Miranda... Both of those topics were too hard to sort through right now. I picked something safer, something that could eventually lead into... things closer to my heart. "I—er, everything said here is confidential, right?"

"Of course, sir," she replied automatically.

"Okay. All right. So, as you may know, some tabloids tend to throw around rumors about me with many high-profile women. My power isn't what it used to be, and there are some upcoming tensions I may need to deal with. Fortuna's law states that I need to get married. But, I haven't wanted anything serious since... since..."

"... Since your wife died."

My throat bobbed. "Yes."

"Does it bother you that they speculate so much about your romantic prospects?" Ms. Evalde took notes, her stylus scratching gently against her paper-like screen protector.

"It didn't use to."

"No? What changed, Aidoneus?"

A pressure built in my chest. "Gods, it is so hard to say."

She paused again, meeting my eyes. "This is a safe space."

"There's an Angel—a woman—who has been working for me for about fifty years."

"Interesting. Isn't that the last time you made an appointment?" she asked.

Damn, she was good. "Yes."

"I read she was injured in the attack, and you carried her straight to the hospital. The press says you are secretly involved. Is that right?"

I nodded. "Shit, we really went from zero to a hundred, didn't we?"

She adjusted her glasses. "Sir, I am not usually paid to make small talk. We can if you'd like. I am happy to help you however I can, but I am very good at getting to the heart of a problem."

I couldn't disagree with that. I started, "I don't know what it is about her." My words started coming out slowly, but they began pouring out faster and faster. "But I think I have feelings for her, which comes with a lot of guilt."

"And why does that make you feel guilty?"

"Well, for one, she's young. Fully grown, smart, beautiful, but young. I am... ancient. And..."

My voice trailed off. I could not finish.

"Your wife. She was your one true love."

I nodded. "Thank the gods you are good at finishing sentences."

She taps the pad again. "How do you feel about Phaedra's current condition?"

I let out a long breath. Could I say what was in my heart? Could I tell her what I was really thinking?

I decided to take a chance. "At first, I expected it to be an inconvenience. However, it has become abundantly clear that I can't live without her." My mind swims with a million moments together. Her standing in my office, anticipating my needs, touching my arm just because.

"Because you have feelings for her? Or because she is your assistant?" Ms. Evalde asked.

I shifted in my chair. "The first one." I sucked in a deep breath, and my thoughts went wild. There were so many. I was a prick. I was an idiot for having feelings for a younger woman. I was... lonely. And Phaedra was a really wonderful person.

Asclepia smiled genuinely, looking me right in the eye. There was no judgment there. There was no pity for being in love with a female who would never care for my old ass. "First, I want to start by saying that what you feel is absolutely normal. It might ease your mind to know that age gaps in relationships don't indicate anything negative if both parties are fully grown and consenting."

She stood, walking to a table where a silver cappuccino maker was perched, grabbing a small cup. "Coffee?" she asked.

I shook my head. I couldn't drink anything right now.

The therapist smiled softly, continuing, "Of course, there are dangerous, predatory people in this world."

I nodded. "Absolutely."

She continued, pinning my eyes with hers. "But I might assume that if you are in my office feeling bad about this, then you aren't one of them." She returned to her desk and took off her glasses. After setting the cup on a coaster, she folded her hands atop the onyx-coated desk. "It is also totally normal to feel a lot of guilt about experiencing those romantic feelings after an event as terrible as what happened to your wife. Let me say you aren't betraying her by moving on. Are you worried about the optics of dating someone who works at your company?"

New guilt washed over me. Assumptions were being thrown around left and right about the two of us together, and Phaedra had been asleep for all of it. I thought about the Angel, with her beautiful blue eyes and breathtaking wings. The whole world would look down on our coupling. "That could be a concern."

"Well, I'm sure if you consult your HR department, they can help you figure this all out," she said eagerly.

I blinked, regret starting to take hold of me. Aclepsia Evalde loved romance, as evidenced by the novels. She would probably be more than happy to know more about me and the Angel. Maybe it wasn't a good idea to come to here.

"There's another problem," I said quickly.

"Oh?" Ms. Evalde raised an eyebrow.

"She's... dating someone else," I blurted, clearing my throat.

"Oh," she replied, frowning. "They didn't mention that in the article about her."

I raked a hand through my hair, narrowly avoiding one of my horns. "No, they most certainly did not."

CHAPTER 4
HIGH STAKES AND LATE NIGHTS
PHAEDRA

Still 57 years ago

By the time the sun set that day, exhaustion plagued me. It was only due to the extensive lessons in Angel manners and etiquette drilled into me since childhood that I managed not to drag my wings on the floor behind me as I finally finished my work.

Upon my return to the office, I had a dozen different tasks to complete. One by one, I watched as my office mates slowly filtered out of the building, flying off balconies or taking the elevator to the main floor to jump in their cars.

Once again, I was the last one there.

Just me and the security guards. That I knew each of them by name was less a testament to my friendly demeanor. Or maybe just a testament to the number of late nights I'd worked. Tonight, even flying the short distance home seemed like a lot. I made the split-second decision to stay in the office. There was no point flying home only to turn around and come right back a few hours later. Sighing, I grabbed my purse and nodded to the security guard posted in front of the balcony doors.

"Orion," I said in greeting. "How are you tonight?"

He grinned, his gray wings rustling behind him as he pushed open the balcony door. "Not too bad, thank you, Ms. Demtre. Are you heading home for the night?"

I shook my head. "No, I'm just running to The Silver Plate for a bite. I'll be back for the night."

His smile softened. "Be careful out there, Ms. Demtre. A buddy of mine works down in the 54th Division and he mentioned that something had all the police on edge today."

"Thank you for looking out for me, Orion. I promise I'll be careful."

With that, I tucked my wings behind my back and walked onto the large balcony. The lights of Olimpie dotted the cityscape all around me, and I sighed. It was so dark that even those twinkling lights couldn't illuminate every corner of the vast metropolitan area. There was little traffic at this hour because it was the perfect time to soar toward the skyline.

There were few things that were more pleasant than flying at night. I would have remained on the balcony, staring out into the night sky for hours, except my stomach chose that very moment to let out a very unladylike rumble.

Orion laughed. "You'd better get going, Ms. Demtre. I'll be waiting for you to return. Have a nice evening."

Grinning, I waved a hand before launching myself off the balcony.

THE FLIGHT WAS everything I'd hoped it would be. I landed in front of The Silver Plate, my mouth watering at the tantalizing smells coming from the establishment.

Yes, I thought, *coming here was definitely the right decision.*

Cheaper than most places in Olimpie, The Silver Plate had the best food in all of Angel's Landing. After a long day, it was exactly what I needed. I stepped through the door, nodding at the Maitre D'. He was a Spring Fae, and his pink eyes glimmered as he looked me over.

"Ms. Demtre," he said. "It's a pleasure. Are you meeting anyone?"

I shook my head. "Not today, Charles."

"Ah," he nodded understandingly. "A table for one, then. Right this way, please."

Once I was seated with a glass of white wine in my hand, Charles hurried away with the promise of sending my waiter right over. I settled into my seat, spreading my wings comfortably behind me. The restaurant was busy, and the quiet hum of chatter washed over me. I shut my eyes, letting the stress of the day flow out of me like water as I sipped my wine.

"Did you hear about Julietta..."

"... things in the Northern Courts are worse than ever..."

"You don't care about me..."

"... police are everywhere tonight...."

Orion had mentioned the same thing. I wondered what was going on. Usually, police were present in the city, of course, but to hear them spoken about twice in the span of an hour?

That was definitely unusual. And in my experience, unusual was almost always a bad thing.

A sense of foreboding began to grow in my stomach, but moments later, the waiter appeared at my table.

I shook out of my reverie, glancing up and ordering a seafood pasta with some more white wine. I was out, so I might as well enjoy myself before having to return to the office. The Gods only knew I'd need the strength a good wine brought. The boss was always demanding the day after a dinner party.

While waiting for my food, I flagged down a waiter.

“Ma’am?”

“Can I have a newspaper, please?”

He smiled, his wings fluttering as he bowed. “Of course. They were just delivered.”

Mere moments later, I spread the paper over the table. As soon as I opened it, the main headline caught my eye. I read it once, twice, then three times.

Historic painting stolen earlier today from the Museum of Art in Olimpie.

I swallowed, my eyes quickly scanning the article as a knot grew in my stomach. Oh, my gods. Someone had stolen a priceless painting from the Museum right under the noses of the guards. Things like this never happened in Aranthium. What were the chances that an art theft would occur on the same day I was sent to the gallery by my boss?

Low. I knew that. I continued to read the article, trying to find out which painting had been stolen.

I'd been to the Museum once or twice for galas thrown by my employer, but only a few pieces had ever really caught my eye. Most of them were abstract or delighting in the beauty of the female form.

It took me a few minutes, reading past lines of text and interviews with various guards and witnesses, but finally, I found it. I inhaled sharply, staring at the newspaper in my hands.

My voice shook as I read the article under my breath. "The painting stolen from the Museum of Art today was none other than Ernesta Alfonsi’s rendition of the Massacre at the Winter Chapel. This painting, depicting a rather unfortunate act of bloodshed during the Rebellion, has resided in the Museum of

Art since its inception. Never owned by any one person, the artist specifically demanded it be kept in the public eye at all times."

That painting. I knew that painting. I *saw* that painting.

Today. On the table at the art gallery.

What was going on? Something was terribly wrong, and I couldn't help the feeling of dread that rose within me. The last time I had felt like this...

I couldn't think about that. I needed to figure out what to do now.

My stomach churned, and I lost my appetite completely. At that moment, the waiter appeared at my side. He slid the steaming plate of pasta in front of me, and bile rose in my throat.

I shoved away from the table, reaching into my purse and pulling out a large bill. Putting it down, I grabbed my bag and ran toward the restrooms as gracefully as I could manage with one hand over my mouth.

Rushing into the ladies' room, I stared at myself in the mirror as I gripped the sink. My eyes were gaunt, my face pale as I considered everything.

Okay. You'll just have to go talk to the police and tell them what you saw. Maybe it was nothing?

But my gut told me I was wrong. It had been something. And that something made me very, very nervous.

Taking a few deep breaths, I splashed water on my face until I looked... normal. My hunger was forgotten completely as I lifted my head and walked calmly to the exit. Once I was outside, I'd go to the police station and explain what I saw. Then, I could go back to work.

I gave a tight smile to the Maitre D'. His brows furrowed as I pushed open the door. A cool breeze rustled the feathers of my wings as I stepped out into the cold night air. The police station was just a few blocks away. I was about to launch myself into the air when my stomach twisted.

The wine, usually a delicious pairing with a meal, was churning in my otherwise empty stomach. I felt woozy and more than a little ill. Flying while intoxicated was not on my to-do list for today. I would have to walk. It would clear my head, and I could get my story straight.

Decision reached, I began to march towards the nearest station. I was a few blocks away when suddenly, the hairs on the back of my neck prickled.

Someone was watching me. Swallowing, I reached into my purse, grabbing a bottle of pepper spray. My mother hated that I lived in the city, but she insisted I carry it around with me at all times.

For the first time since I'd left her gilded cage, I thought she might have been right.

I gripped the small canister in my hands, slipping my purse back over my shoulder before turning around.

"Hello?" I called out, my voice echoing over the empty street. "Is anyone there?"

No response, but that cold feeling on the back of my neck got stronger. My gaze darted around as the light from the streetlights illuminated pockets of the dark road. Suddenly, I realized how foolish this decision had been. Why was I walking on empty streets at night? Even though I had attended some self-defense classes upon moving to the city, I was still just one female.

A lump of fear appeared in my throat, but I swallowed and shoved it down.

Just a bit further.

Gripping the canister, I hurried down the streets. For a few more minutes, nothing happened.

Then a sound came from above.

I looked up, my eyes widening and my heart pounding erratically as two large Angels slammed onto the road in front of me.

The ground shook with the impact of their landing, and I took a step back.

"This her, Nicolas?" one of the Angels snarled.

"Looks like it," his partner replied. Nicolas was taller than the other, looming high above me. He took a step forward, reaching into his pocket as he narrowed his eyes. "We have orders to take you in."

"Me?" My voice squeaked. "I don't know what you're talking about."

Not-Nicolas raised a brow, a wolfish smile on his face. "Oh, I think you do. You saw something today that you shouldn't have. Our boss wants to talk to you."

That knot in my stomach grew until it was an entity of its own. At that moment, I knew that there was no way I could go with these men. They were going to kill me. I was increasingly convinced of that with every second ticked by.

I cleared my throat. "Your... boss, you say?"

The Angels—goons would be a better term—nodded, exchanging a glance with each other. Not-Nicolas stepped forward, flexing his muscles. "Yes. That's what we said."

Taking another step back, my gaze darted around wildly. If I played this right, there was a chance I could get out of this situation in one piece. And then I would go to the police station and tell them exactly what happened. Obviously, I was in greater danger than I'd thought.

"Are you boys going to call him?" I asked, trying to keep my voice light.

Nicolas shook his head, his blond hair falling into his eyes. "Nope. We're going to take you to him."

I swallowed. “I see.” Shaking my head, I took a step back. My swallow was painful. I was so scared, and I was surprised when my voice came out loud and clear. “I'm afraid I'm not going to be okay with that.”

The other Angel laughed. "Did I miss the part where we asked your permission? Nicolas, did we say 'please'?"

Nicolas smirked. "No, we did not." Turning to me, he snarled. "This wasn't a question. You *will* be coming with us."

Steeling my nerves, I glanced at my feet for a moment. If I could get close enough...

I stepped forward once, then twice. When I was close enough to make out the browns of their eyes, I whipped out the canister and sprayed them both in the face. I didn't wait to see what they had to say. The moment the spray left the bottle, I dropped the can on the ground and ran. My feet slammed into the pavement as I rued my lack of exercise.

"Bitch," Non-Nicolas swore.

The dual pounding of footsteps on the pavement told me they were still coming after me. My lungs tightened as I turned the corner, my heart lifting as the blue, glowing sign of the precinct came into view.

There.

There was no way these goons would follow me into the police station. I continued to run, grateful that I had chosen to wear a pair of slacks today, when suddenly, a feeling of awareness reappeared on the back of my neck.

I kept running, but then, a large black van with blacked-out windows pulled up beside me. My eyes widened as the side door swung open. A pair of thick arms reached out, wrapping around my waist.

"No!" I yelled. “Let me go!”

It was too late. The arms held me in an iron grip, pulling me into the vehicle, and I struggled against my black-clad assailant. Apparently, the boss had sent two teams after me.

"Let me go!" I insisted. My fingers scratched my assailant's arms and face, leaving red marks as they pinned me to the ground. My wings flayed out behind me as a shooting pain wrenched through me.

"Be quiet," the man said gruffly. "We need to get you out of the city."

Get me out?

Gods, I really was going to die tonight.

"I won't go with you willingly," I spat.

“Seriously?”

In response, I screamed.

The man swore, and the van swerved as the driver yelled, "Do something Toth'toros! We need to get out of here. He will kill us if she gets hurt."

My assailant nodded. He swung over me, straddling me with his hips as black wings protruded from his back.

"Sorry about this," he said, his weight pinning me down moments before something sharp jabbed my skin.

I cried out. It felt as though fire ran through my veins. For one moment, everything was vivid. The dark clothing worn by my abductors, the horns on their heads, the leathery wings on their backs. They weren’t Angels. That much was clear.

Daemons, my mind supplied helpfully. These two were definitely Daemons.

Who was their boss? I tried to think about that question, but my limbs grew heavy and my arms weaker by the moment until I could no longer keep my eyes open.

Weariness overtook me, dragging me to a dark sea of...

Nothing.

Everything disappeared as I fell into blackness.

CHAPTER 5
A SPECIAL CATALOG
AIDONEUS

Present day

Another day, another meeting. Less than two months had passed since the attack on Lethe. Two months, and yet, sometimes, it felt like it had been just yesterday. I walked into my personal office on one of the top floors of my tower, only to discover it was still a raging mess.

That made sense since I had specifically told the staff that I didn't want it cleaned. Navigating around the boxes of antiques and mechanical contraptions from the last thousand years, I eventually made it to my desk.

"Flora," I barked, stubbing my toe on a cardboard box filled with artifacts meant to be sent to a new faction of swamp witches recently discovered near the Spring Mer lands. These witches had come out of nowhere, and yet their presence explained so much. For one, we finally knew who had made all these glass orbs, some appearing more phallic than spherical.

"Yes, King Hades." An AI popped into view on my desk. She

was my replacement while Phaedra was in the hospital—an extremely poor replacement.

"What are my meetings for today?" I asked, trying to squeeze around my desk.

"One moment," she said in an automated voice. "Pulling up yesterday's meetings."

"No, wait." I reached out as if I could grab her. "I said, 'today's meetings, ' not 'yesterday's'."

"Yes, of course, Lord Hades. Today is Tuesday, August 24—"

I cut her off before she could continue. "No! What are today's meetings?" I avoided using the word "date", hoping to prevent the same rigamarole.

"I am pulling up today's meetings, King Hades."

"Thank you," I ground out through clenched teeth, slumping into my chair.

"First meeting of the day, 9:15 in conference room 12. Meeting With King Zeus."

I spit out the nastiest word I had ever heard in all my centuries of living.

"Hey, don't kill the messenger," the AI Flora said.

I stared at her. "Sorry, Flora, that will be all for now."

She blinked out like a light, and I dragged a hand over my face. This was going to be terrible. I only tripped once while returning through the maze of boxes and artifacts, and then I slammed my hand on the elevator button and winced.

Too hard. No reason to take out my anger on inanimate objects.

I could hardly stop tapping my foot as the doors slid open. This was my private elevator, so there shouldn't have been anyone on it, but luck was not on my side. The second the doors opened, I was face to face with my shitty brother, Raphael Zeus.

"Raphael." I nodded my head.

Golden skin, his personal mark of the gods, gleamed in the

dim elevator lights. We hardly looked alike. My skin was the color of dark metamorphic rock. During the rebellion, Adrian, Phelix's father and the former Elemental God of Water, had captured me and Miranda. He spent days torturing us both, slicing me open, and stealing whatever power leaked from my wounds.

My wife had given up her very essence to weaken him, but even then, my God-inflicted lacerations never fully healed. They left pale silver streaks all over my body, smoother than the rest of my skin, and glimmered in the moonlight.

My brother leaned against one of the mirrored walls with one arm and rested his other hand on his hip. I sighed, catching a glimpse of how one pointed-shoe-clad foot was crossed in front of the other.

"Aidy," he said with an idiotic smile. He had used that nickname since we were newly formed DemiGods, and I was really sick of it after a literal eternity. He straightened, bringing up his six-and-a-half foot body—three inches shorter than my own—to its full height, and then he took a step forward.

My hand went up immediately. "You stay there. I don't want you messing with my things."

He raised an eyebrow. "But—"

I cut him off by stepping into the elevator and pressing the button to close.

"Your office looks like shit," Raphael said sardonically.

I didn't respond.

"I mean, wow. You were always untidy," he said at the exact moment I snapped, "I was never untidy."

“Still no new assistant?” Raphael asked, ignoring me completely. “What is the current one’s name? Persephone?”

“Phaedra,” I barked. “And no. I don’t need another assistant. She’ll come back to me.”

“So, the articles were true.” He smirked. "You're still whipped."

This again. I didn't want to hear it. The light above us blinked out. I could see the glow of my electric green eyes on the mirrored elevator wall. "Raphael, I am still furious with you. Straighten up, or I'll Tranpose you to Tartaro."

Raphael held his hands up. "Okay, Aidy, I get it. This is a business meeting." He pinched his thumb and forefinger together before drawing them across his lips. "I will keep it zipped about everything except the absolute essentials."

I nodded, my eyes returning to normal as the bright neon green left them, and the light slowly flickered back on.

"Good," I said, just as the elevator doors opened to the level of the tower that held all the conference rooms. "After you, shit-head," I said, gesturing for my brother to enter.

We walked through the hallway that had warm, gentle lighting. The air was neither too hot nor too cold, and I took a deep breath. There was an earthy, sweet smell in the air. It made my chest ache. I nearly stopped walking when I passed by the large corner office I had given Phaedra on her fiftieth anniversary with the company. She hadn't spoken to me much during the early years, but once she opened up, she smiled more and more each day. Seeing her smile was like getting hit by a freight train filled with summer showers and artistic energy. It made me so damn happy, I had the whole interior ripped out and she designed it all from scratch.

The door was closed, but her scent lingered.

I squeezed my jaw shut even tighter, and I heard Raphael snort behind me. I kept the "shut the hell up" on the tip of my tongue, where it belonged since I wanted this meeting to go well.

I pushed open one of the heavy modern oak doors, and the light flicked on instantly.

"You don't keep the lights on all the time?" Raphael asked.

I finally released the painful clamp on my teeth. "No, it saves energy to keep them off unless we need it."

Another huff of laughter as he walked ahead of me and trailed his hand along the gleaming wood table. He rolled out one of the conference chairs and plunked his large DemiGod ass down. "Remember when we didn't even have electricity? You didn't seem to mind burning through an entire storage room of oil for one night of partying."

I stared at him. I hated the smug curve of his golden lips and the perfect styling of his gilded hair. "Times have changed. It's become more important for me to take care of this planet for the long run. I don't want to be irresponsible and use it up for my enjoyment. I'm quite attached to Aranthium. It was a gift from our parents, after all."

"Yeah, a shitty gift from shitty parents." Raphael leaned back in his chair, and just because he knew I hated it, he kicked his feet up on the polished table. “Mom is pretty good now, though.”

I decided not to say anything. We came from different fathers, which was... *messy*. My parents, Fortuna and Aeron, had been wonderful, until they weren't. But all was resolved now. I could forgive much more easily than either of my brothers. It was in my nature.

Raph, on the other hand, had trouble with forgiveness. Maybe that was what made me want to act better today. He was a reckless idiot, but there was no need for this meeting to go so poorly. I let my corporate side come in, the kind I used for meetings with stockholders.

The trick to being successful in business, in spite of wealth, was to know what your audience wanted to hear. Once you knew that, you could strategically try to give them as much of that as possible—while keeping your own interests in mind, of course.

"Have you started styling your hair differently?" I asked, keeping my tone light. Of all my family, Raphael loved flattery the most.

His smirk had a brief flash of a genuine smile. Bingo. "Why? You decide to start giving a shit what you look like?"

I rolled my eyes. "No, I wanted to alert waste management that you were releasing too many chemicals in the air."

My golden-god brother threw back his head and barked out a laugh. He even took his damned feet off the table.

My lungs relaxed a fraction of an inch.

"So..." I raised a brow, sliding into a seat as I steepled my hands.

"So," Raphael Zeus, King of the Angels and pain in my ancient ass, said, "Aidy, I think you know why I'm here."

I studied his expression, narrowing my eyes just a little. A small bitter feeling began to uncurl in my stomach, and a great deal of acid pooled in my immortal stomach.

"No," I said slowly. "I really don't think I know why you are here. Are you finally going to help out with the disaster relief I've been bitching to you about for two months?"

Mistake, my instincts screamed as Raph's smile grew, turning wicked.

"Don't try to change the subject. You know exactly what I'm talking about. Aidoneus, it has been three hundred years."

Shit. This *is what he wanted to talk about?!*

"No," I breathed.

"Yes." Zeus said. His voice was almost gleeful as he continued. Bastard. "Three hundred years have gone by since your kingdom has had a queen, and that is a problem. You want help with the cleanup in Lethe? I'll give you something even better:

information. Why do you think Phelix was even able to attack you in the first place?"

I glared at him, an ugly emotion building in my chest. *Stop*, I urged him silently as I narrowed my eyes. *Don't say it.*

He continued, ignoring my silent pleas. "You need a wife, Aidy! The power balance is all off. Mom called and told me you needed to get married, or she will start raising hell *in Hell.* You know how bad things must be for Mom to get involved?"

I felt the temperature drop when the air conditioner came on, and my arms folded over each other. "I can imagine," I grumbled.

"You're going to ignore what I said, aren't you?" A golden eyebrow shot up toward the high heavens.

"What do you mean?" I quirked an eyebrow.

Raphael laughed. "Come on."

Suddenly, I wasn't sitting in the controlled, sleek environment of my office. My memory carried me to a place with four white walls that created a long hallway. A tacky popcorn ceiling hung overhead, and flickering fluorescent lights cast a yellow glow over everything. I stood outside of a small room, staring at the shut door. I yearned to go in, but it had been made very clear I wasn't wanted. Wasn't needed. A nurse stood at my right, frowning. I knew that look. Money and power could buy you almost everything--except entrance into a hospital room.

It hurt, even days later.

"Aidy?" Raph's voice brought me back into the present. That same bitter-sweetness washed over me.

I blinked.

"Hades," Raphael's voice was firm. "It's time to stop... whatever this shit is, and move on. I miss Miri just as much as you do—"

"Wrong thing to say, asshole." I didn't even get that mad at the ridiculous pet name he made for my long-deceased wife. My fists curled on the table, and my power surged. How dare he imply that what he felt was even a fraction as potent as what I had gone through losing my partner, the woman I thought was my mate?

I knew where this conversation was going to go. We had been here far too many times before.

"You know I didn't mean it like that." Raphael looked exasperated, like the man-child he was. It was time for this meeting to be over. "I just meant you need to grow up, Aidy!"

"Idiot," I snarled. My blood boiled in my veins, despite knowing this is what Raphael wanted. He wanted to push my buttons. To show me I needed a wife. Well, fine. Two could play this game.

Finally, an outlet for all my anger. My pain.

The lights flickered, and I slippec into my god-like state. Shadows drew near, dropping the temperature of the room.

"Seriously?" Raphael asked, clearly annoyed. Why, I wasn't sure. He started this.

Ignoring him, I didn't stop. Invisible hands wrapped my idiotic brother's neck. The second they touched his golden skin, he snapped. Golden light burst outward, and outside the conference window, swirling clouds gathered in the sky. It took mere moments for the electric bolts to begin snaking through the sky, and then lightning struck in the middle of the table. His eyes were a brilliant neon green, signifying the power of the gods.

Another flash of light hit me square in the chest, and I screamed as sparks flew off my skin. The electric jolt vibrated through my veins, making my fingertips tingle. It snapped out of whatever primal trance I had entered into.

"Enough," I thundered as I drew myself out of my volatile state. "We can't make these people suffer more because of our petty fights." I panted. The shadows evaporated, and the crackling lightning stopped.

A *crack* echoed, and the table between us wobbled for a moment before a massive fissure ran down the middle. It snapped in two, the break clean down the middle.

Raphael sighed, flicking his fingers and Transposing the table to another room. A table of the exact same model appeared before us.

Transposing, like all godly birthright powers, was based on balance. We could move whatever we wanted, but we had to replace it with something else. The broken table would be nearby for me to deal with later.

"Fine, then let this be a warning." Raph held up his hands. "No more jokes."

I nodded.

Raphael continued, "As the other half of our ruling body, this is a formal notice for you that Phelix has been removed from the Trimurti documents. We will both need to take on more responsibilities if we are to move against him. We need to be in the best shape that we possibly can be."

"And?" I ground out.

"And that is why, brother, you are going to get married. That is exactly what mom said. She told me to remind you of what she told you the last time you visited her. By the way, how long ago was that?" Zeus started picking at his fingernails.

I scowled. "Doesn't matter."

He shrugged his massive, DemiGod shoulders. "No worries. You have one month."

One month.

"No, absolutely not. That is when Erik and Helena are getting married." I crossed my arms and leaned back.

"Our niece? That's right." Zeus thought for two seconds. "Fine then. You can have two months."

I opened my mouth to interject.

"No fighting. Don't sweat it, brother. I have a catalog for

things like this. It's perfect. I made it when my first son was looking to get married. I'll arrange everything. The bride. Dowry. I'll even put my best planners on this. All you have to do is show up."

Black hair. Blue eyes. Soft, pale wings in every shade of the rainbow.

I stared at my brother, but all I saw was Phaedra.

My brother was expecting something from me that I couldn't give him.

"You already had one great love in this life, Aidy," Raph said quietly. "We aren't all so lucky with our mates."

He looked serious, and I thought of him and his queen. Separate houses hadn't been enough, so they settled on separate provinces within Angel's Landing. As soon as she had gotten her four thousand square foot "cottage", she packed her bags and started traveling the world.

My brother continued to try to convince me. "Reyna is always home when I have a problem."

He wasn't lying. His wife was a mastermind in global politics.

The warring emotions inside of me, the loneliness, the longing, all swirled in my chest and made me feel... empty. Hollow as an old log.

I was tired. So tired.

Raphael must have seen this in my face. He was a master manipulator, this golden brother of mine, and he used it to his advantage. "Aidy, dude." I flattened my lips together at the casual language. He readjusted his course. "*Brother.* Marriage doesn't always have to be about love."

"Don't speak to me about love," I snarled.

He raised a brow. "Honestly, I would be fine with just about anyone at this point. Please, just... pick someone. Anyone! I will give you the best options on the face of the planet. Think with your Little Hades, if you know what I mean." Unfortunately, I did. "I don't give a shit. Just pick someone."

He was pleading with me. There was a part of me that was inclined to believe him. I didn't need love, certainly not the kind of all-consuming love I had once had for my wife. A companion, a partner, would be enough. This was a business agreement.

This wasn't cheating on my wife. I could only do that if I loved someone else.

Soft pink mouth, upturned eyes, and long lashes. The way her round cheeks pulled up when she smiled, and the way she sang my name.

I had already betrayed Miranda's memory the moment that I gave Phaedra that office. And she didn't even love me. Hell, Phaedra had even considered my brother before she had looked at me twice. Then she started dating that absolute douchebag, Dylan.

She. Didn't. Want. Me.

Perhaps it was time to give them both up. Time to stop thinking about myself and to give back to the world I loved so much.

My eyes made a miserable trek up the table, snagging on the grain of wood before sliding across the polished leather of the office chairs. They flicked up Zeus's t-shirt and sport shorts, and then they landed on my brother's eyes.

"Fine." I hated how I felt saying that word. It was like I had laid down in front of my opponent and surrendered. But... I had no good arguments to keep the fight going.

In the moments that followed, I wished I didn't see how Raphael's lips turned up at the corners. How he congratulated me and rushed over to hug me. I didn't enjoy touching him. I was almost going to be okay... but then he wished me the best on my hunt for a high-class piece of ass.

I couldn't help myself. And honestly, I did the world a favor when I drew back my fist and punched him in the crotch.

"Women are not objects, asshole. I don't care if you are joking. Stop saying shit like that around me," I hissed down at my brother.

The prick doubled over for all of two seconds before he looked up at me and grinned. "Whatever you say, as long as you get married."

I really hated how easy it was for our bodies to heal. It would have made dealing with him more enjoyable.

Potentially more effective.

I shoved the door to the conference room open and stalked back out into the hallway.

"Bye, Aidy!" Zeus called out just as I was stepping onto the elevator.

I made a rude gesture and then smashed the button to shut the elevator doors so that I wouldn't have to look at his ugly face anymore. If I saw him again before I got married, it would be too soon.

Fortuna. Two damn months.

What if Phaedra wasn't even awake before then?

I blinked. There was no way I was marrying her, so that didn’t matter.

I hated everything.

CHAPTER 6
DON'T BREAK VASES
PHAEDRA

Still 57 years ago

Where am I?

The thoughts echoed in my mind as I tried to remember what happened. My entire body was sore. My back, my wings, my muscles all screamed as though I had flown an epic race the day before.

Wincing, I commanded my eyes to open. For a moment, nothing happened. And then, when they obeyed, I was even more confused than before.

The soft, buttery glow of sunlight filled the space where I was resting. Someone had laid me on my stomach, and my wings were splayed behind me, covering the huge bed I found myself on.

Kidnapped. It had actually happened. Someone kidnapped me.

Mother always warned me I would get into trouble, leaving

her home and the gilded cage I'd grown up in. I had scoffed, telling her that people weren't nearly as bad as she always made them out to be.

Well... It appeared as though I was wrong. In the space of one day, my life was utterly and irrevocably changed. First the incident at the gallery, then those two goons who stalked me, and now this...

Mother would never let me hear the end of this.

If I ever get out of here.

I groaned, pressing my head into the pillow. The very soft, very cloud-like pillow. What kind of kidnapper put their victim on a bed as soft as a cloud?

That was the real question. And one absolutely worth pondering. I wasn't just going to lie here, waiting for whoever had abducted me to return and finish the job. No. Absolutely not. I was going to get up and find a way out.

Resolution flooded my veins as I pushed myself to my knees and forced myself to take in my surroundings. Although everything hurt, I was in one piece. For that, I was grateful.

Black silk coverings hung in a canopy over the bed where I lay. Silk.

Who abducted someone and laid them in a soft, cloud-like bed surrounded by a silken canopy?

Probably a madman. It would be just my luck to find myself abducted by someone who had lost their mind.

Things did not bode well for me.

Pushing the silk hanging aside, my mouth dropped open as I stared at my surroundings. This was... ridiculous. Completely and utterly unexpected. After the men had dragged me into the van and drugged me, I would have expected to wake up in a tiny cell equipped with a cot, toilet and maybe, if I was lucky, a sink.

This was definitely not that.

I was in a room fit for a queen. Furniture of the darkest wood filled the space, somehow made elegant by the beautiful rugs and paintings adorning the walls. The space was massive. To call it a room would be like calling King Zeus a boy. It was just not enough.

I'd never seen anything like this. I stared, wide-eyed, at my surroundings for a minute before I remembered that despite the beautiful room, I was not a welcome guest here. Wherever "here" was, I needed to go. Patting my pockets, I soon realized my phone and purse were gone.

I was alone and defenseless.

"Get a grip on yourself, Phae," I muttered, marching over to a mantle covered in various vases. "You can't afford to let your guard down. You have to get out of here."

Growing up, talking to myself had become something of a habit. A side-effect, I supposed, of not having anyone my own age around to be with.

I studied the collection of vases in front of me. They were of various shapes and sizes—some tall and long, others wide and curvy. At the end, I settled for one that could easily be held within my grasp and looked like it could cause significant damage if thrown at someone. Grabbing the cyan vase, I tucked my wings tight behind me.

Whoever had built this room had done so with winged individuals in mind. None of the furniture was too close together, and the wide-backed couch and chairs were perfect for lounging without harming wings.

Interesting.

I slinked over to the door, pressing my ear against the wood as I held my breath.

Footsteps came from down the hall, and I pushed myself away from the door.

"... he has ordered us to treat her with dignity," a female voice said.

"Why?" This one was male, I was certain of that.

"Fortuna only knows. It's..."

Their voices trailed off as their footsteps retreated away from the door.

Interesting. Who was this he?

Taking a deep breath, I put my hand on the knob. If I was trapped in here... My chest tightened at the very thought of being locked in this room. What good was a suite fit for a queen if it meant that my freedom had been stripped away?

I couldn't be. Being unable to fly, smell the scent of fresh flowers in the air, and feel the breeze on my face as I stretched out my wings would be the worst punishment in the world.

No. If the door was locked, I would break it down. I would not be trapped.

My resolve steeled, I sucked in a deep breath and shut my eyes. Slowly, so slowly, I twisted the knob. For one awful moment, it didn't move.

But then it turned.

My breath left me in an exhale as I eased the door open a crack. It creaked, and a frisson of fear ran through me as I froze. My hand remained on the doorknob, the other clutching the vase, as I waited.

And waited.

A minute passed, then two, but no one came to the door. No one slammed it in my face. No one pulled the door open and shoved me back inside the room.

There was no one there.

Who kidnaps someone but leaves them in an unlocked room?

Raising my brows, I kept my wings tightly together as I inched the door open. Thank all the gods, it didn't make any more sound. As the door slid open, my eyes widened. This was... unexpected.

Palatial, even.

Not only that, but it was also dark. There weren't any windows, and all the doors were closed tight.

And it was empty. That was the most important part. Empty was good... right?

This was my first time being kidnapped, so I wasn't certain on that point, but it seemed like a fairly good guess.

Throwing back my head, I straightened my shoulders and took a deep breath. Adjusting my grip on my vase—there was no way I was going to walk through these halls without some sort of weapon—I tucked my wings in tight behind myself and... stopped.

Where to go?

How did one determine an escape route from a mysterious location? I had no idea where I was or how long I'd been out. For the gods' sakes, I could be anywhere in Aranthium right now.

Think, Phae.

I couldn't just stand here. Anyone could stumble upon me.

Knowing that I couldn't remain still, I made a split-second decision. The voices I'd heard seemed like they had gone to the right, so I turned left. Keeping my footsteps light as air, I thanked my mother for all her etiquette lessons. For once, I was putting them to good use.

I swallowed a snort. I could only imagine what Governess Rose would say if she saw me now. Keep your back straight. Don't let your wings touch the ground, child. Slouching is a disgrace to all Angel-kind.

Unfortunately, none of her lessons had included a manual on what to do in the event of being kidnapped. I would have to figure it out on my own.

I walked down the dark hall, turning left again and then

right. Finally, a crack of natural light appeared ahead of me. A dark curtain was open just enough to let in a sliver of light. I hurried toward it, sliding the curtain open.

A gasp escaped me. I was high in the sky—so high that I could see the clouds beneath me.

Where was I?

I could only think of a few buildings in all of Aranthium that stood this high....

None of them were a good place to be.

My wings twitched with the desire to throw open the window and fly. My fingers ran down the bottom and sides of the pane, looking for an opening.

But there was no lock on the glass, nothing that would allow it to open. It was for show, and nothing more. Disappointment rolled through me.

Swallowing the frustrated cry that rose in my throat, I dropped the curtain and hugged the vase to my chest. Stumbling backward, I took a step, then another, down the hall. I had to get out. My steps came faster and became more harried as I hurried down the halls. Seconds slipped by into minutes as I kept going.

And then I heard it.

A voice.

Deep and male, and utterly masculine. It crawled down my spine, and something twisted within me. That voice was the embodiment of power itself. It called to me in a way that I couldn't explain.

Sucking in a breath, I slowed my movements as I crept toward the voice.

You are an idiot, Phaedra, I chided myself. What kind of kidnapped victim walks toward people? You should be trying to run.

But I couldn't help it. He summoned me, and I responded. So

I inched closer to it, keeping my wings close to my back as I held my breath.

The voice was coming from a large room, and the door was open a crack.

"… I don't care what the cost is, Toth'Toros. Just make it happen."

Someone stood, and it sounded like they were pacing across the room. I pressed myself against the wall, hoping no one would walk down the hall and find me there.

Probably should have thought about that sooner.

Then again, if I wasn't supposed to be here, maybe they shouldn't have kidnapped me from the streets.

The voice started speaking again as the sound of someone sitting in a chair came from the room. "Call me with a progress update."

A phone slamming down on the receiver echoed through the room. Then a heavy sigh filled the silence. My heart cracked at the sound, and I wilted against the wall.

A minute passed as faint breathing came from inside the room. I was about to get the nerve to continue down the hallway when suddenly, a chair creaked.

"I know you're there," the voice said.

I jolted, tightening my grip on the vase. I'd been so silent, so stealthy as I had crept along… Hadn't I? Of course, there was still a chance that they weren't talking to me. Right?

A sigh—loud and obnoxious and all-together male—filled my ears. "If you're done eavesdropping on my private conversations, why don't you come talk to me, Ms. Demtre?"

Dammit.

There was no denying it. He definitely knew who I was.

I briefly considered my options. I could run, pretending I hadn't heard the voice's very obvious demand of my time. That might give me a momentary reprieve, but I was still stuck in this tower.

Or I could go into the room with my head held high, as though I hadn't just been caught eavesdropping like a petulant child.

I decided to go with option two.

Sucking in a deep breath, I inched towards the door and pushed it open. My eyes swept over the space. It was an office, that much was clear. Dark, clean lines filled the room. It was spacious and boasted a sitting area as well as a desk and bookshelves, but it wasn't cluttered. Every single piece of furniture and artwork gave off a distinctly masculine aura.

My breathing went haggard as I stared behind the desk. Black wings, the color of the deepest ink, greeted me.

"Come closer," the voice said. Power oozed from their words.

Halfway across the room, I forced myself to stop by grabbing onto the back of a chair.

"Who are you?" I asked.

The voice chuckled. "Don't you know?"

I shook my head. "I have no idea. But based on this office, am I right to presume that you are the individual responsible for my kidnapping?"

"Kidnapping?"

The black-winged individual seemed surprised by my choice of words.

"Yes," I said. "Kidnapping. Abduction, if you prefer."

"I don't," he said conversationally. "My men didn't kidnap you. They saved you."

I scoffed. "Funny. Our definitions of being saved are two very different things. Based on the fact that I woke up in a room that didn't belong to me, in a place that definitely isn't my apartment, I would say that I have most certainly been kidnapped."

"We'll have to agree to disagree," he said placatingly.

"What?" I exploded. "No! You abducted me."

He hummed, not even giving me the decency of his words, before mumbling, "semantics."

"Semantics?" I repeated, my voice flat.

"That's what I said," he replied.

"Ugh!" I huffed, red filling my vision as I glared at those black wings. Who was this man, that he dared debate my kidnapping with me when he wasn't even showing his face? The more I thought about it, the angrier I became.

Before I could think about the wisdom of what I would do, I pulled back my arm and lobbed the vase at the winged male. It went five feet to the right—because, of course, it did. The vase seemed to travel in slow motion towards the black wall, the sound of it shattering against solid stone like a bomb going off in the otherwise empty room.

I stared at the pieces of the vase as they crumbled to the ground, covering the dark hardwood.

And then the chair creaked.

My stomach twisted in knots as, finally, my kidnapper showed his face.

I stumbled back a step, my hands grasping at my side as I looked at the most beautiful man I'd ever seen. "You, you're..."

My voice trailed off as I stared at the marble skin and dark horns protruding from his white-haired head. Sharp cheekbones, brutal scars, and a sculpted body accompanied his devastating form. A fallen angel. Many beings would happily sell their souls for just one night with him. The black wings seemed to ripple as shadows gathered around him, stirring something deep in my body. "King Hades," I whispered, my mouth suddenly dry.

I've been kidnapped by Aidoneus Hades. King of the Daemons. My mother...

The thought swirled around in my mind until mirth bubbled up through me. I laughed, clutching my middle as it erupted from me. I laughed until there was nothing left within me but dry heaves, and still, my shoulders shook. I felt him watching me. The king was a beautiful, untouchable widow of the land, and I was...

"Are you done?" King Hades' voice echoed through the room, power leaking from him.

I dared a glance up. His face was cool. Impassive. As though he didn't have a care in the world.

Instantly, I straightened. This male's eyes were hard as they stared at me. "Yes," I said. Then, remembering the manners instilled in me from birth, I dipped into a low curtsey. Keeping my eyes trained on the ground, I murmured, "Apologies, Your Majesty. About the vase. I-I didn't know who you were..."

"I don't think you cared," he said blandly.

I shook, keeping my eyes on the ground. This Daemon could kill me in seconds if he wanted to. "I-I..."

"Don't make excuses. Just listen. You are here, and you aren't going anywhere."

You aren't going anywhere.

The words bounced around in my mind as my blood chilled. Being kidnapped was one thing. But hearing those words spoken out loud was another.

"Your Majesty?" My voice squeaked, betraying my feelings.

"You will work for me," he said, his voice brokering no room for discussion. Picking up the large black phone on his desk, he pressed a few buttons. "Toth'Toros, I need you to come pick up Ms. Demtre from my office."

He listened for a moment before replying, "Yes. My office. Put her to work with Elisabetta on the fortieth floor."

Then, without waiting for a reply, he turned his chair so his wings were facing me. I stared at him.

A minute passed, then two, before the king said, "You're dismissed, Ms. Demtre."

"I... What?"

He waved a hand in the air. "Go. You work for me now."

Stunned, I just stared at him.

"Oh, and Ms. Demtre?"

My mouth somehow remembered how to speak. "Yes?"

"The next time you get it in that pretty head of yours to touch one of my priceless artifacts... Don't."

CHAPTER 7
LA FLEUR GOURMET
AIDONEUS

Present day

A low melody filled the soundproof interior of my car. It was a classical piece made with an instrument from the third Aranthian period. The combination of high notes and low beats always came together to create something that made me feel... calm. Balanced. It didn't cease to amaze me that two things that seemed to be the opposite of each other could be blended into something so wholesome, so satisfying. I often turned the song on repeat.

Music had always held a special place in my life. I'd been trying to return to that on recommendation from my therapist. I tapped my finger on my steering wheel when the personalized navigation system said, *"Turn left on Cursehill Way, Your Majesty."*

Technically, I could've ordered one of those cars with self-driving features, but recently, I'd been experiencing far more anxiety than normal. Driving on its own calmed me, but driving with interesting music was like a horse tranquilizer shot straight into my brain.

"Your destination is coming up on the left."

I tapped the steering wheel to the beat of the music some more.

"You have arrived. I hope you enjoy your time at La Fleur Gourmet, High King Hades!"

Twisting the wheel, I gently pressed down on the gas and pulled into the semi-circle drive, where a valet would collect my car before turning off the music with one tap of my finger. I didn't need the Daemon female heading over to assist me to hear the weird shit I liked to listen to on repeat.

In one fluid motion, I opened my door and exited the car. Out of the corner of my eye, I saw a group of people in plain, black clothing and...

Dammit.

Cameras, bags, and ugly press passes hung around polyester lanyards. Eager paparazzi wielded their weapons of media like swords to battle. They were going to flay me alive.

I knew they would be here, but it was still a real buzzkill to see them at what was going to be yet another first date. This was my third since my meeting with Raphael. I flashed the reporters a smile, handed the valet my keys, and closed my door gently after her. One of the paparazzi sighed, mumbling something under her breath about chivalry.

All I was saying was that if they sighed over me closing a door, or not treating a being like a piece of trash, the bar was on the freaking floor. I waved briefly, and a Maitre D' came out to show me to my table.

"King Hades!" One of the reporters broke from the mob and held out a small microphone for me to speak into.

"Good evening," I said with a smile.

"Your Majesty," the Warlock with heather-purple eyes and striking white hair said. "Tell us, how was your date with Chairwoman Thistleleaf from the Summer Court? Should she expect an easy letdown if you are yet again out on another date?"

My smile remained frozen as I fought the urge to roll my eyes. There was no fun in a political arrangement where the other half of your date wasn't interested in your gender--or any gender expression that wasn't based on flowers. I doubted my brother's abilities more by the second. But that was Carolynn's business, and she had been kind enough.

I dipped my chin just a bit. "These are important... political talks, my friend. No need to get ahead of themselves. Chairwoman Thistleleaf is a competent woman, and I greatly enjoyed her company."

The Warlock opened his mouth again, but I raised my hand, cut him off, and continued my trek inside.

The inside of the restaurant was opulent. High ceilings, gorgeous reds, pinks, oranges accenting pure white and light-colored wood. It was bright and beautiful. Very flower-esqe. They did well with their branding. The woman at my side thought I didn't notice how often she glanced at me. By the time we made it to my table, she had checked me out half a dozen times, and the last time was so obvious I sent her a smile.

Her eyes went wide for a moment, and then she started gushing. "I can't tell you how excited we all were to receive the call. We made sure that your server went through a drug test and background check just to ensure your privacy."

I nodded. If I was being honest, I was a little nervous. Political date or not, I felt like a bull being paraded around in front of breeders, and that wasn't okay with me.

Unsurprisingly, the table where my arranged date would take place was empty. It was decorated with a bright floral arrangement that was strategically designed so I could still see the potential bride. A harp played in the corner, and a partition separated our table from the main dining area. In front of us was an enormous window, showcasing the beautiful nightlights of my city.

The Maitre D' pulled out the chair, and when I sat down, I noticed that her hand trailed along my arm. I pursed my lips. I didn't like being manhandled by women.

Ignoring her gesture, I shook out a napkin once before placing it in my lap.

"Your guest will be escorted in shortly, Your Majesty," the woman said, and then bowed a bit. "I'm Lilah, and my grand-mother founded this restaurant. If you need anything, please don't hesitate to ask for me by name." She smiled once more, and I nodded.

"Thank you, Lilah."

She beamed and then left me alone for a moment. My heart pounded in my chest. What if I said something stupid? I wasn't good at dating, despite the fact the world viewed me as charm-ing. It was one thing to be liked by cameras when you had a team of people helping you with your image, and another entirely to be liked by the person who would see you brush your teeth and vomit when you got sick.

I rested an elbow on the table, something my mother would've hated, and got lost in my mind. Once, when I got sick at work, Phaedra took care of me the whole night. It probably wasn't the most professional thing to ask of my assistant... but I didn't actually ask her. She just showed up in my office, and I didn't argue.

Just then, the door opened, and a strange, swampy smell filled the room. I looked up, trying not to wrinkle my nose. It wasn't exactly a stench, but the scent of stagnant water wouldn't be a best-selling perfume. The woman before me was a witch with long, sleek black hair and stunning green eyes.

I knew exactly who she was. The recently discovered swamp witch coven's queen. It was tough not to remember the shapes of some of her orbs. But, when her representative wrote to me, expressing the queen's eagerness to find a spouse, I wasn't in the mood to turn her down. She hoped a powerful union would help solidify the recognition of her witches. Unfortunately, the swamp witch queen was also keen on having children but was "willing to compromise in exchange for a quick wedding." I tried not to hold that against her.

She was indeed powerful, with sizable birth-right magic, and her witches were fiercely loyal, as evidenced by the three flanking her as she walked. As was the case with the majority of options Raphael sent me, she was very young.

My date was beautiful, in a wild sort of way. Her skin was the softest blush pink I'd ever seen, and she was dressed in a simple green gown tied at the waist with something that appeared to be hand-twisted rope. It was hard to tell if this was a designer dress, or simply something she had made. Not all political rulers cared so much about their appearance. That was something I'd inherited from my parents.

She didn't smile as she crossed over, and I noticed her shining moon-shaped earrings, which matched the coronet resting on her head.

"Queen Isolde, welcome." I stood as she approached the table. I set my napkin on the gleaming surface, walking around to pull out her chair.

She nodded slowly. "Thank you, High King Hades. These are my ladies-in-waiting, Miriam, Andrea, and Carolina." Isolde gestured to them in turn.

"It's a pleasure to meet you," I said. The three women just stared at me, looking like they wanted to kill me. I let out a nervous laugh and walked to my side of the table. "The server should be out soon."

Four sets of eyes stared at me. My cheeks were starting to hurt because of all the smiling. I was starting to sweat. Gods, this was awful. It took all of my self-control not to tap the table.

I opened my mouth to ask my date a question just as a server appeared out of nowhere.

"Your Royal Majesties." The Fae male bowed deeply. "My name is Seamus, and I'll be taking your order this evening. Chef Luisa has planned a four-course meal for your enjoyment. We hope you will enjoy the lovely bouquet." He held up a gold embossed menu with the *La Fleur Gourmet* logo on it. "We will begin with the hors d'oeuvre, a beet salad with a lemon vinaigrette and lily foam. The appetizer will be a Luisa-style onion soup with a rose water twist. We will move through our gastronomical garden to the entrée. Steak Diane with a truffle sauce so succulent you will think you've died and gone to hea—"

Isolde held up her hand. "I am vegetarian." She pursed her lips, and I could see the thick judgment in her gaze as she flicked her eyes down at his outfit. The poor waiter paled for only half a second.

"Not a problem, we have a plant-based option," Seamus said with a smile.

Isolde wasn't finished. "What kind of plants?" She raised an eyebrow.

The waiter's Adam's apple bobbed.

So what, I thought. *She is direct. That isn't such a bad quality in a wife, I suppose. Phaedra is always direct with me.*

But Phaedra's directness was laced with kindness. This though... This wasn't that. It was akin to watching someone walk across a trapeze without a net.

"I think Seamus would have to check with the chef to find out, Isolde. The first two courses sound exquisite. I'm sure you could tell us more after we have our salads," I said.

Seamus looked at me like a drowning man who'd just been

saved. "Of course, Your Highness." He turned around and left as quickly as possible.

Isolde looked at me. "He didn't tell us what dessert was."

I smiled. "I'm sure he can when he comes back." It was then I realized he didn't take our wine order either. I was really taking one for the team.

"So," I started, "Isolde, will you tell me about yourself?"

She stared at me, as did the women behind her. This would not be easy. "What you want to know?" She had an accent, and I thought it sounded nice, even though her eyes did remind me of a jungle cat assessing its prey.

I smiled pleasantly—at least, I hoped it was pleasant. "I'd love to hear about your kingdom."

She didn't even flinch as she said, "I was born and raised on Spring Mer lands. But the Mer do not always respect my people. One day we will get revenge."

I choked on my own spit. Another war? "That's very... honest of you. When is your birthday?"

That same blank expression. "In the fall."

I smiled. That wasn't really an answer. "Mine is in April. It wasn't called that when I was born—it wasn't really called anything—but it is a month of showers, and I dearly love the rain."

She pursed her lips. "It rains every day in my swamp."

At last, we were getting somewhere. "Oh? Do you enjoy that?"

She nodded. "There is a fish that comes to the surface of the waters. I kill it, and we all eat."

I furrowed my brow. "I thought you said you were a vegetarian."

"Fish are not the same. It killed one of my witches, so I killed the fish."

I blinked. "All right, well. You certainly are strong."

Wine, I definitely needed wine. Where was that server?

"If we marry, I will teach you to kill fish. You will give me a child," Isolde said. She didn't even blink.

Heat rushed to my face. We had discussed this. The ground was tremoring below us at my fury. It was humiliating to be subjected to this topic after explicitly clarifying my condition. "That won't be possible—"

She scowled. "I need an heir. You didn't know this?" She was getting angry, too.

The server was walking toward us with two salad plates. I needed a drink. The chandelier above us had already started swaying.

He reached the side of the table, and the only sound was the light clink of the plates as he placed them on the table. The poor man was sweating.

"I'm sorry," he said. He seemed just as flustered as I felt. "What would you like to drink?"

Queen Isolde said, "We have water," at the same time that I said, "Wine."

He looked between us and nodded with a weak smile, and then he was gone.

Isolde looked up at the woman on her right and sneered, "He is afraid of us. Weak man."

I blinked.

What was this?

Just then, my FaePhone started buzzing in my pocket. I knew I shouldn't answer it, but this so-called date was agony. I pulled out my phone, four sets of eyes watching me as I said, "Hello?"

A sob came through on the other end. "*Uncle, I messed it up. I need help,*" my niece wailed. I hadn't even known she had switched into her fins.

I answered so fast; I didn't even check the name. "Helena? What's wrong?"

"*Are you busy?*" She sniffled.

"Give me a half hour," I said. The spot in the middle of my chest warmed with affection for her.

The women watched me hang up.

Isolde spoke first. "Is that your lover?"

I wanted to roll my eyes, but I did not. Fortuna had better write that in the book of my life and give me extra bonuses when I passed on.

"My niece," I said gently.

She nodded. "Your family is in trouble. You must go, yes?"

I hesitated for a moment before saying, "Yes, I'm sorry."

Isolde stared at me for a long, hard second. "You are king, but you can't have a child."

My lips pressed into a flat line. "Yes."

The swamp witch queen threw a hand in the air and stood as well. "Then this dinner is over, anyway. Good day, King Hades. I hope you find a wife soon."

She walked out before me, and shame spread through my entire body. That was a dumpster fire. I waited for her to leave before I followed along. I didn't say a word to Seamus as I passed him in the hallway, but I could have sworn he looked relieved.

CHAPTER 8
DON'T FORGET THE ALMOND MILK
PHAEDRA

19 years ago

I stood open-mouthed, clipboard in hand, as I surveyed the room before me. My wings rustled behind me as the breeze came through the open window, and I mentally took stock of the crates piled before me. Even though I'd spent the last few decades working with antiques, I still felt that singular moment of awe that came over me when I encountered something ancient and beautiful.

Even as a young Angel, I'd always been drawn to things that were older than me. My mother used to call me an old soul. I simply knew that old things had value. Perhaps it was the fact that they often carried age marks or showed signs of vitality.

Thirty years ago, a few days after my abduction, the King of the Daemons suggested—rather forcibly—that I put myself to good use working with his antiques. I argued, as much as one could argue with a DemiGod, but he made it clear I would not be returning to Angel's Landing. His argument had been bolstered by the fact that bodies began turning up in Olimpie. Literally.

The bodies of every single person who worked at The Gallery of Angels were found dismembered and left around the city. The next day, the entire block that housed the gallery went up in flames.

When the newspapers had first reported on the murders, I stared at the paper clutched between my white-knuckled hands. Honestly, it was hard to believe. For a few moments, I thought it was some kind of sick joke. But King Hades arranged to have the chief of police in Olimpie call and give us a personal update about the case. At that point, it was hard to ignore.

The king assured me of my safety that very night. “No one will dare harm you in Lethe.” His eyes darkened, and the shadows swirled around him as he swore, “I would burn them before they laid a finger on you.”

A little dramatic, in my opinion, but somewhat effective.

King Hades’ statement might have been lacking in humility, but he was right. No one came for me, and I didn’t end up dismembered and in a dumpster.

After that, it was hard to ignore the fact that my stay in Lethe was going to be of a permanent variety. I threw myself into my work. Evgenia and I stayed in contact, but maintaining a long-distance friendship was hard, and we grew apart over the years.

As the familiarity of working with her faded, I tried not to mourn her absense. I never did anything half-assed, and it was a point of pride that I had become an intricate part of Hades’ staff.

It definitely didn't have anything to do with the way his nearness sent my stomach somersaulting. Clutching my clipboard, I walked around cataloging the newest arrivals when suddenly, a set of heavy footsteps came from behind me. A clunky gate, not at all like the smooth, lithe steps of a king wearing vampyrian leather.

“You’re still here.” The phrase was not worded like a question.

Sighing, I tucked my pen into the clipboard and turned around. "Yes, Dylan," I said, gesturing to the Angel standing in the doorway. "I messaged you I would be home late. This shipment just came in, and I could really use the overtime to help pay for my mother's bills..."

My voice trailed off as Dylan squinted at me. He raised a hand and fiddled with the rim of his extra-large rounded glasses. His button-down shirt was crisp, tight, and buttoned up to his neck. His expression on his face told me just how unimpressed he was with my excuses.

Well, I had been unimpressed with our sex life of late, but he didn't see me complaining.

"I thought we had a deal, Phaedra," Dylan said, running a hand through his sable hair. It flopped back over his face, never seeming to stay in one place. "You promised me you wouldn't work late anymore."

I sighed again. "It's not like we were going to do anything, Dylan. You just want to sit at home and watch TV." It had been a while since I'd been railed.

"Together," he said as if that one word was enough explanation.

I knew what he wanted to do. He wanted to sit on the couch beside each other, our wings fanned out behind us, watching the House and Garden channel. Which we would do until he fell asleep on the couch at 8:00 p.m.

I knew this would happen because it happened every night for the past decade. My boyfriend Dylan was a lot of things, including a lover of routines. Once, that stability had been just what I needed. Especially after my mother... but now?

Not for the first time, I wonder why I stay. I've already invested so much time in training him to be what I want; it's just easier to work it out instead of being alone.

Shaking my head, I turned around. "I'm sorry, I can't go just yet. I have to finish this."

"But babe, what about me?" The tone of his voice was what most people would classify as a whine.

I cringed at his pet name for me, which he *knew* I hated, and sighed. "Why don't you stay and help me? That way, I can be done earlier, and we can go home together."

He regarded me for a minute, his eyes unblinking, before he shook his head. Pecking me on the cheek, he said, "I'll see you at home."

Two minutes later, he was gone.

I felt nothing but relief.

FOUR HOURS LATER, I finally finished organizing the newest shipment of antiques.

Brushing back a lock of black hair that had fallen out of my chignon, I stood and put my hands on my hips. Everything was sorted. There was not a single thing out of order.

Perfect.

My lips tilted up into a smile as I tucked my pen back into the clipboard, sliding it onto the nearby desk. Karina, who had suddenly come into my life and claimed me as her friend, would know what to do with it when she came in.

A warm feeling of satisfaction filled me as I texted Dylan, letting him know I was on my way home. I knew he'd be angry about the late hour, but after nearly being murdered in Olimpie, I was kind of a stickler for personal safety.

The return text came moments later, and I frowned.

Dylan: We're out of almond milk. You might want to pick some up on your way home.

That was it. No "I love you." No "fly safe, Phaedra." Not even a "see you when you get home."

Huffing, I tossed my phone into my purse. I knew what Karina would say if she saw Dylan's text. It would be the same thing she'd been telling me for the past seven years, ever since Hades assigned her to help me with the antiques. My newest work friend. Karina was a firecracker of a Daemon, shorter than most, but full of life. She had suggested I take on overtime to help with the hospital bills.

Dylan didn't approve of Karina and her suggestions.

The feeling between them was definitely mutual.

I sighed. It would take me an extra hour to find a grocery store that was open at this hour, let alone one that carried the very specific brand of almond milk that Dylan wanted.

"Great," I muttered under my breath. “Looks like I won’t be getting home anytime soon.”

Slipping my purse over my shoulder, I made it halfway down the hall before I remembered I had seen the same brand of almond milk in the fridge in Hades' office yesterday.

Surely he won't mind if I borrow it. I can replace it tomorrow.

I waffled in the corridor for a minute before my stomach reminded me I hadn’t eaten since breakfast that morning. That was it. I was hungry, and my feet hurt after spending the entire day in these five-inch heels. I just wanted to get home. Having made up my mind, I traveled the short distance to Hades' office without any difficulty. One of the benefits of being a hard worker and remaining well into the night meant I didn’t cross paths with a single person.

The door to the DemiGod’s office was closed, which wasn't a

surprise. I hadn't seen the king since speaking to him after lunch, and I assumed that he had gone home. Creaking open the door, I noted the dark interior of the office. The dim light from the hallway illuminated a path to the fridge, and I slinked inside the office.

In and out.

I would replace the almond milk first thing tomorrow morning. He wouldn't even know I took it.

I was so busy trying to make sure I was moving quickly that I didn't hear the creak of the chair behind me until a voice said, "Phaedra? Is that you?"

Shit.

I froze, my wings outstretched to keep me balanced, with one foot in the air. My hunger forgotten, I tried to think of a reasonable excuse for being in here.

The problem was, I didn't have one. Although he was fair with his people, the King of the Daemons didn't allow just anyone in his office. It was his private space, his sanctuary. And there was no question in my mind that this voice belonged to the king. After three decades of working for him, I would recognize it anywhere.

A heavy knot formed in my stomach.

This was definitely a terrible idea.

I chewed on my lip, trying to figure out what to say when a low chuckle came from the direction of the desk.

“You don’t have to answer.” A chair creaked again. "I'd know it was you anywhere."

A beat passed before I sighed. “I’m sorry, sir, I was just...”

My voice trailed off as I tried to figure out how to word this tactfully. Somehow, telling a powerful DemiGod I had slipped into his office to borrow almond milk didn’t seem like a valid excuse.

Sucking in a breath, I decided my best course of action would be to avoid that entirely. Apologizing and backing away—that seemed like the best bet. Relaxing my posture so both my feet were on the floor, I cleared my throat. "My deepest apologies, Your Highness. I didn't mean to interrupt you. I honestly didn't know you were here."

Come to think of it, why *was* he here? Sitting in the dark, no less. In the nearly thirty years I'd known King Hades, I never knew him to do something like this.

Maybe something was wrong.

That thought made me uncross my arms and take a step forward. My knee met something hard—a coffee table, my mind helpfully supplied—and I cursed softly before making it the rest of the way to his desk. My hands found the light switch without issue, and soon a soft glow flooded the office.

Another creaking sound came from behind the desk, and I gasped as the leather chair swiveled.

Something was *definitely* wrong with the King of the Daemons. His marbled face was glassy, and a thin sheen of sweat covered his features. His eyes—usually an electric green so bright they reminded me of grassy meadows—were darker than usual. The king's hair was completely out of sorts, and even his wings dragged on the ground behind him.

"Hi," he slurred.

I darted forward, laying my hand on his forehead, before pulling it back abruptly. He was burning up.

"Sir!" I exclaimed.

"Do that again," he murmured, his head lolling to the side. "I've been dreaming about the way your hands feel on my skin."

Delusional. He was absolutely delusional and imagining some other woman in my place. This was definitely the fever talking.

"You need a doctor," I informed him as I reached for the black phone on his desk. Internally, I sighed. I would need to text Dylan and tell him I would be even later than I thought.

He's probably going to be more upset about the almond milk, a voice said in the back of my head.

That would be a problem for another time.

I picked up the receiver, but before I could call, a blast of green magic erupted from the king. Seconds later, the phone was nothing more than a pile of ash in my hand.

Blinking, I just... stared at him. I had no words. None. I was completely and utterly confused. And, if I was being honest, a little frightened. That pile of ash could have been me.

My brows furrowed. "What... Why did you... How sick are you?"

"I'll be fine." The delusional DemiGod shook his head. "I don't need a doctor. I just need you."

Yes. Definitely delusional.

"You could have killed me with that blast of magic," I informed him.

He shook his head. "I would never, ever hurt you." He reached for my hand, taking it in his feverish grip. His eyes pinned mine as he said, "If you were mine, I would care for you every day for the rest of your life."

That did it. There was no question about it. He was absolutely, certifiably, insane right now. I knew from trying to help my mother that there was no reasoning with people when they were in the throes of illness.

Yanking my hand out of his grip, I ignored the whimper that escaped this man—this DemiGod—and I crossed my arms. "Your Majesty, you're sick."

"Don't do that," he sighed, closing his eyes as he slumped in his chair.

"Do what?" Eyeing a jug of water on a nearby table, I walked over and poured him a glass.

My back was to him when he whispered, "Call me that. I don't... I'm not your king. I want to be many things for you, but a king isn't one of them."

I almost dropped the cup of water at that. This was... a lot. The hair on my arms stood up, and I fought the urge to close my eyes and enjoy his scent.

Too much, if I was being honest.

Grabbing my purse from where I'd abandoned it earlier, I fished out two extra-strength fever reducers. Walking over to the king, I knelt before him.

"Here," I said. "Take these." Growing up with a strict mom taught me to be prepared for anything.

He lifted a trembling hand, washing down the pills with a gulp of water, before giving me back the empty glass. His fingers brushed mine, and I swallowed as a spark rushed through me at his touch. "I'm so tired," he admitted.

There was no question in my mind about that. He looked like he was moments away from collapsing. I nodded, nibbling on my lip. "Can you walk to the couch?"

A beat passed as he seemed to think about it. "Maybe with some help."

Not stopping to think about what I was doing, I bent and wrapped my arm around King Hades' waist. He pushed himself to his feet, swaying unsteadily. He leaned against me, and I bit back a curse. The King of the Daemons was a lot of things, including *very* heavy. Somehow, we made it to the leather couch the king kept in his office, and he collapsed face down on the long piece of furniture. His black wings fanned out behind him, and he looked up at me from where his head rested on a pillow.

"Thank you, Phaedra," he said.

I grabbed a nearby blanket, pulling it up over him. "I still think you need a doctor."

"No doctor. I told you, I'll be fine." The last word was lost as he erupted into a coughing fit, and I frowned.

"You know, for such an old man, you are so stubborn," I told him.

He grinned, although the effect was diminished by the way his head lolled to the side. "I love the way you talk to me," he said. "You never take my shit."

I scoffed, gesturing at the pile of ash that used to be his phone. "Everyone is just scared of you."

"And you're not?" He actually seemed curious about the answer, and I balked. Those who stole from his tower tended to be found dead. He didn't yell when he was angry, he just sent shadows to haunt you for the rest of the day.

Funnily enough, he'd never sent them to me.

"Well," I drew out the word. "No. I don't know why. But I'm not."

My attraction to him was like a girl falling in love with a dragon. Completely impractical, impossible, and it made me feel... Confused. This man was my boss, and I shouldn't even be having these types of conversations with him. Ignoring how overheated my skin felt next to his, I picked up a pillow and brought it over.

"Lift up your head," I told the man currently regarding me with those electric green eyes.

He obeyed, and I tucked the pillow underneath him. He sighed, laying his head back down and shutting his eyes. I inched backward, but before I could get more than a few feet away, those eyes opened once more and he reached up to grasp my wrist. He pulled me on top of him, and the feel of his fevered flesh against my own did things to my body.

"Thank you for this," he whispered against my ear.

I was utterly frozen in his grasp. Shocked. Aroused. I needed to get home to Dylan. "I… Anyone would have done it," I squeaked.

"No." He shook his head. "No one has looked after me since my wife died. I always knew it would be you. My Angel."

My stomach twisted at his words. "I have a boyfriend," I reminded the king as I wiggled away.

He sighed, dropping his head back onto the pillow. "That pain in the ass doesn't deserve you. He's weak. You deserve power."

I shook my head as my heart seized, and I pushed off him. To my relief, he let me go. I thought this conversation would go differently. And I did not want to be discussing my personal relationship with my the king.

"I can't…" I picked up my purse and turned away. "I'm sorry, I have to go."

Like a coward, I didn't wait to hear what he had to say. I hurried out the door of his office, sliding it shut before I slumped to the floor.

My head fell into my hands, and I just… breathed.

I must have been far more tired than I'd thought, because the next thing I knew, a hand was shaking my shoulder. "Phaedra?"

I blinked, looking into the eyes of Toth'toros. "Thank the gods you're here," I said. Pushing myself to my feet, I gestured to the closed office door a few feet away from me. "He's sick and needs a doctor."

The Daemon looked at me, his brows furrowed, but before he could say anything else, I hurried away.

I leaped off the closest balcony, letting the night air surround me as I flew home. I was *never* going to talk about this evening again. He hadn't kissed me. I hadn't asked to lie on top of him while he was sick. There was nothing to tell Dylan about.

Except, perhaps, that I didn't love him, but that could wait for another time. When I was ready to move on. If tonight were repeated with the king, and I wasn't in a relationship...

I would be playing with fire. Fire that would scorch my soul.

It was only when I got home that I remembered the almond milk.

CHAPTER 9
A RUINED DRESS AND UNEXPECTED NEWS
AIDONEUS

Present day

Less than half an hour after my dumpster-fire of a date ended, I knocked on Helena and Erik's door. A voice called out from the other side of the door that I didn't recognize.

"It's going to be fine! Just stop crying!" the mysterious woman yelled, frustration leaking into her voice.

I didn't think it was one of my workers. My brows inched together. Was this woman making Helena cry?

I raised my watch to my face, fully intending to call security, when the door swung open wide. The Queen of the Winter Fae stood in the doorway, her mouth pinched in a scowl. I blinked.

"Your Majesty?" I asked. This made more sense—Elva, the Winter Fae Queen, was Helena's best friend. At one point, she was engaged to my late nephew.

I hadn't been devastated by his death. Fortuna certainly had fun with his soul.

"Wait, why are you here? The news said you were on a date," Elva said.

She blinked.

I blinked.

Before I had time to respond, the sound of a small child crying filtered down the hall. The Winter Fae Queen stepped aside, and I took one step inside before noticing the wet puddles on the ground leading to the TV room.

"Elva!" Helena called out. Her voice was watery enough that I skipped the rest of the hallway and Transposed by flicking my fingers. Helena was sitting in her aqua chair.

In her wedding dress.

Her expensive Le Baba Morgaine haute couture dress. I started shaking my head, but my eye was drawn by the Queen's consort, who was bouncing a baby with curls on his lap. When had they arrived?

Helena looked at me with her large, pink eyes, and her lip quivered again. "I ruined this." She picked up one shred of drenched purple-white fabric that dripped between her webbed fingers.

I sat on the light brown leather couch and took my niece's hand. "Helena, what happened?"

My eyes wandered to the red-headed consort who was getting his shirt burned by the tiny immortal. The Fae cursed, then seeming to remember who sat on his lap, covered her ears, and excused himself.

"Nathan, I told you not to let her fingers touch your clothes," Elva chided behind me.

Helena and I stared at the exchange. My niece had a sense of fascination at the family scene that I couldn't help but share. Then Helena beamed and held out her wet arms. "Give me my little princess!"

Elva, Nathaniel, and I all said "No," at the same time. Then Nathaniel bolted from the room to put out the fire on his shirt.

"Don't think I haven't noticed that you haven't told me what happened, Helena. You need to get out of your dress first. Maybe Elva can help you?"

I looked up at the Winter Queen. She raised an eyebrow and jerked her head to her daughter. The message was clear: *What about her?*

That I could help with. Gesturing to the youngling, I said, "I can hold her. Don't worry, I've got a talent for putting out fires."

Elva didn't so much as smirk as she passed me the child and led Helena to her bedroom. “Her name is Taneisha,” the queen called over her shoulder.

“Taneisha,” I repeated as the child beamed up at me.

Sitting on the couch, I stared at the small being. She was beautiful. Soft ringlets, brown skin, and piercing blue eyes made up her tiny face. She took one look at me and laughed. I would have been enamored, except at that moment, her small hand turned into talons, and she went straight for my horns.

Her laughter was infectious, and I tried to gently work her iron grip off my head. The talons clawed at my hair, and my eyes started watering as she pulled on my locks. Panic flooded me at the realization I was alone with this little rascal, and before I realized what I did, I Transposed her out for a pillow by blinking my eyes. In a second, all the pain was gone, and I twisted around to look at the little thing.

She nearly fell over as she leaned against the couch, giggling her head off.

I stretched across the ottoman, grabbing her again. Her hands came out. The talons were gone. This time, hot little flames were aimed straight at my face.

"I've dealt with more dangerous royals than yourself, little princess," I said with a pretend stern face.

She wouldn't stop grinning, and so I Transposed us again, this time on the carpeted floor. Carpet was better for toddlers, right?

As soon as she got close enough to me to burn me or tug on my clothes, we moved again. I would call someone to replace the rug after. This was... surprisingly enjoyable.

After she chased me on all fours all around the TV room, I looked up to see we had an audience. Elva and Nathaniel were looking at each other before glancing back at me. Entire conversations were passed silently, and there was an ache in my chest. I used to feel like I could communicate like that with Phaedra. Until her coma.

The small child wiggled up into my arms, nestling into my neck.

Well shit.

This felt like a real ass-kick straight to the heart.

"She went for my horns," I explained.

They nodded like they already knew exactly what she was capable of.

I slowly got to my feet, and Elva said, "Helena's in the bedroom. You can go see her."

There was a piece of me that really didn't want to let go of the little being cooing in my ear. "Are you sure?"

"No, she's Elva, and I'm Nathaniel." Nathaniel grinned at me. "Thanks for taking care of our little monster!"

I didn't even have time to groan at the terrible joke before I handed back the little creature and walked away.

When I knocked on Helena's door, it cracked open easily, as though it had not been fully closed in the first place. I applied more pressure, and the door swung open all the way. Spotting the aqua chair on the side of the bed, I made my way to the bathroom. Helena was finally out of her wedding dress, dressed in a purple turtleneck tank top that covered up to where her fins began.

The entirety of her body, save one hand holding a glass of wine, was submerged underwater. I could see the soft gray haze that her under-lids put over her pink eyes while she stared up at the ceiling.

"Helena?" I said.

Her eyes snapped over to me, and she blinked. "I'm sorry about the dress," she said, her voice coming out in a rush of bubbles, distorted by the water.

"The dress is nothing. We can get another dress." I put my hands up in a placating way, a gesture I had become more aware of with Helena. I knew how deeply she felt things, and most of the time, I could fix her problems.

She closed her eyes and blew out bubbles in the water. I leaned against the wall, waiting for her to say something else. After a few moments, she sat up, the water cascading off her hair and sloshing against the walls of the tub. She took a long drink.

"I'm a freaking idiot," she said at last.

I started shaking my head immediately. "Nope."

Her wine glass was tipped up once again, and she swallowed hard. "I am." She let out a long breath that made her shoulders sag. "Elva and the gang surprised me, and I got so excited about the wedding coming up in two weeks. I wanted to show them the dress. And then, before I knew it, I wanted to show them the venue. Nathaniel bet me an entire honeymoon to the resort in the Snow Were Territory to walk across the thin walkway that I had been such a hard ass about," Helena explained.

"I already bought you two a honeymoon," I interjected, smiling a little.

She smiled a little too. "I know. But it was the principle of it. Daddy didn't raise no fool."

I frowned. "Your father has done many terrible, cruel things, but you came out this way all on your own. A testament to your good nature."

She brushed me off, but I knew she appreciated words like that. Then she said, “Right. Anyway, I was feeling good in my legs. I was walking along just fine, but then I tripped over my own damned feet and tumbled into the fish pools. At first, I was pissed. So freaking mad that I couldn’t see straight. Then Elva’s hand appeared in my vision, and I remembered I am a lucky bitch. I have it all.

“I have you and Erik. I have a small family with Elva, and I have the sweetest little niece. But I have a niece and nephew who are still in Aqualis, with Hallie and her idiotic husband. Anger and sadness are living inside of me. And here I am trying on pretty dresses, and pretending to be a princess.” She finished her drink.

“Helena,” I paused, not sure how to proceed. “I know how you feel. But you know the goodness that will come from this event. If you can’t see it for yourself, see it for the people of our countries. Think about how humans will feel, seeing a man elevated to his worth. Think of the political advantage we will have when we move against your father. This will be fixed."

She stared at me for a long moment, but she didn’t speak.

“Where’s Erik?” I asked.

That earned me a smirk. “Holed up with insurance planners for your shitty healthcare system."

That was fair. It was one of the many things I was planning on fixing after this gods-damned issue with Phelix was resolved. Having my niece and her fiancé here had opened my eyes to things in the Gates of Hell that could be better.

“Good to hear it. Now, I don’t feel like making a bunch of seamstresses work overtime for a week.” I held up my hand, and one of the cotton balls in a glass jar disappeared just as a sewing kit appeared in my hand. Seconds later, her wedding dress was in my hand and perfectly dried.

Her eyes went wide for a second. “One day, Fortuna will give me my birthright power, and I'm going to learn how to do things like that."

I smiled. “You’ll be a fierce thing then, for sure, my niece. Now, get changed, and practice switching back into your legs. We’ll fix the tears together."

“You know how to sew?” She raised an eyebrow.

I genuinely felt offended. “I’m as old as dirt. Of course, I know basic life skills."

“But you’ve always been royalty!"

“Yes, and I still needed to learn how to stitch up a tear or sew on a button.” There was an ease in our friendliness.

Helena rolled her eyes and started squeezing out her hair. “You are as old as dirt, but I bet you know how to do much more than just sew on a button."

I grinned. "You’d actually win that bet. Now get changed."

She nodded, and I left the bathroom. When I closed the door, rain was sliding down the bedroom window. In the distance, the baby laughed.

I needed to get out of there. To clear my head.

To breathe.

THE SMELL of rain in the desert was unlike anything else I’d ever experienced. When the rain finally came after months of the smoky heat, you could feel it in your bones. It usually came right as many in the city were going to sleep. It started with a cool wind from the east, blowing in the smell of the salty water. And then the rumbling. Gods, did I love the rumbling. The laughter of the Elementals, my mother called it.

Then, like a quiet cape draped around my shoulders, the lightning came. And the rain. It was like exhaling. There was a calmness that could be achieved at no other time than when the quiet drops of rain tinkled against glass windows and darkened the pavement.

It was raining when Miranda died.

It rained the day I met Phaedra.

Rain was my mother's way of showing her love. I knew enough about the world to know it would happen with or without her bidding, and it was often hard to disentangle the two from each other. But she had told me it was her whispering "I love you" all those years ago. And I knew she meant us.

Families, lovers, and others scattered past me, and I saw no traces of the destroyed buildings from only a few months ago.

Perhaps this rain meant that everything would be all right.

I walked aimlessly, tilting my face up. I pushed away my dislike of being wet for the promise of good things to come.

There was something about letting a person into your life that was unnerving. All the carefully curated walls just sort of crumbled like godly magic. The world saw me as rich and powerful, and I was. But they didn't wish to see me for anything else. They wanted me to be an image, static and frozen. Not the man who had flashbacks to his parents. The one who had to buy suits and use the bathroom, just like everyone else.

Certainly not the kind of DemiGod who could get sick.

Absolutely not the man who cared deeply.

It was easier to say no to love, to children, to family before any of those things had a chance to reject me. After I lost Miranda, it was easier to be lonely from time to time than it was to cope with loss. But loneliness wasn't an occasional feeling anymore. It was all I felt, all the time. It hit me in my core every time that I looked at the beautiful woman with electric blue eyes.

I was so lost in my thoughts, I didn't automatically realize where my feet had taken me. Looking up, I stared at the blinking red sign of The Lethe Hospital. The best medical facility in Lethe, Phaedra was inside. I hoped she knew it was free of cost... Not that she could know that. The last time, Dylan had proved that I had no claim to her. That there was no legal reason for me to be there.

Perhaps it would be different this time.

When I walked inside the first floor, reserved for emergencies only, the receptionist froze.

"Your Majesty!" a tall Daemon female exclaimed. Everyone in the urgent care stopped and turned, even the baby that was screaming in her mother's arms.

I dipped my head, and the Daeman raced out of her office to attend to me. Her red eyes stared at me with a worried expression behind her half-moon glasses.

"Are you all right?" she asked, concern painting the entirety of her features.

Glancing down at her name tag, I said, "Yes, Camille. I'm fine. I'm here to visit an employee of mine."

Her sepia skin went a shade lighter. "Y-you know my name?"

I tapped the mirrored spot on my own chest where her name tag was and she let out a nervous laugh. It wasn't hard to tell she was blushing.

She linked her fingers in front of her. "Well, I think that's lovely. Do you mean Ms. Demtre?"

I nodded. They knew I'd been here before.

"Give me just a moment, and I will escort you up personally."

"No no, that's not—"

"I insist," she said, and batted her lashes.

I conceded. Who was I to argue? As soon as Camille was gone

from my side. I tapped my foot and smiled at some of the people around me. Perhaps the doctors and medwitches would be mad at me, but I flickered my power and healed every broken bone and minor lesion around me. Shouts of delight came up, and before I knew it, people were grabbing my hands as they walked out of the hospital.

Perhaps it really was time for healthcare reform.

Moments later, Camille was back. Her eyes were wide as she took in the suddenly empty room. “King Hades, would you follow me?”

I was at her side in a second, and she let out a shaky breath. Moments later, we were walking through a long hallway and into an elevator.

As the sliding doors closed us in, she looked at me sideways. Then she shifted her weight from one foot to the other. When she cleared her throat, my patience started to wear away. “There's actually an update on Ms. Demtre. Her condition has changed."

My heart stopped in my chest. “She’s dead?”

Just like that, the walls crashed in on me. I needed to get out of this elevator. I needed to go see my mother. Shadows swirled around me as I panicked. I needed to get to the Gates of Hell.

Desperation built within me. My emotions raged, and the lights above flickered.

Camille cried out in surprise when the elevator stuttered on its track up the building. “Gods, no! She’s awake."

I blinked, the shadows in my eyes clearing. “What?"

“Shit, I wasn’t supposed to tell you that. You were supposed to hear it from the doctor."

Hope, in spite of lived experience, sprang up inside of me. Camille was still fretting, but I drew her into a bone-crushing hug.

"Thank you, Camille," I said just as the doors slid open. I didn't wait for them.

I twisted my hands around in a flourish and Transposed directly into Phaedra's hospital room. I wasn't facing the hospital bed. Part of me was afraid that Camille had lied.

"What the hell are you doing here?" Dylan demanded.

CHAPTER 10
I QUIT
PHAEDRA

Present day

Every once in a while, throughout my long life, Fortuna blessed me with extraordinary clarity. I always *knew*, as it was happening, that I would never forget those insights. Even now, I could sort through those moments of clarity like well-worn photographs.

The feeling of absolute freedom when I flew for the first time. My first taste of freedom in Olimpie. The mouthwatering chocolate mousse that I ordered forty-three years ago after a particularly long day at work.

They weren't all good memories, of course. I remembered the day I realized what was happening with my mother. That the bad days were getting worse. I remembered the searing pain of breaking my leg after jumping off a high cliff and not extending my wings fast enough.

It was because I'd experienced all of those moments that I knew that *this*, right here, would be another moment that I would never forget.

I'd woken up a few hours ago to the realization that life was short. Even for beings like me, it was far too short.

When the doctors told me I'd been in a coma for months, disbelief washed over me.

So much time. Gone. Just like that. What did I have to show for it?

A painful headache and debt. I couldn't even comprehend the size of the hospital bill I would get after this.

It would probably take me three centuries to pay it off.

Dylan wasn't even here when I woke up to dozens of medical machines beeping at me. Nurses and medwitches alike came running into the room, fawning over me. They called the doctors, who in turn, rushed over.

Much of what they said was medical jargon, but I understood the gist of it.

I was lucky to be alive. I sustained a severe injury during the attack in Lethe, and I'd been inches away from having my heart punctured.

When most of the medical personnel left, I flagged down one of the nurses. The brown-haired Fae had a kind look on his face as he stood by my bedside.

"Yes, miss? What do you need?"

"Can you bring me a phone? I'd like to call my boyfriend."

The Fae blinked at me, a funny look coming over his face, but he brought me a phone moments later. I dialed Dylan's number, grateful that I'd committed it to heart, and listened to the ringing.

On the third ring, he picked up.

"What?" he barked, his tone anything but kind. *"I already told you people when I was there two weeks ago, I don't want—"*

"Dylan," I breathed.

He was silent for a full minute, the sound of his breathing filling the other end of the receiver. *"Phaedra, babe? Is that you?"*

"Yes," I croaked. "I'm awake. What was that about two weeks?"

"Never mind that," he said smoothly. *"I'll be right there."*

'Right there' apparently meant three hours later, because that was how long it took for Dylan to show up.

Even though the hospital was a ten-minute flight from his workplace.

I took those three hours to think about everything. When I pressed the Fae nurse about what he thought the two weeks could have meant, he reluctantly admitted I hadn't had any visitors in that length of time. What began as sadness evolved into something else. Something far more energizing and potent.

Two. Weeks.

I'd been alone for two weeks.

So many things could happen in two weeks. People could learn new skills, move across the country. Find new friends. Fall in love.

In two weeks, people's lives could be changed.

When Dylan finally arrived, I'd been ready to confront him. But then, moments after he arrived, a flash of shadows filled the small hospital room.

And here we were.

I sat on the hospital bed in a flimsy hospital gown that barely reached past my thighs and I watched as Dylan—my Dylan, the boyfriend who made me kill spiders because he hated it so much —glared at the black-winged king who was drawing shadows around himself like a cloak.

Hades hadn't looked at me yet, but he didn't need to.

I knew the moment the King of the Daemons had Transposed into my room. He had a presence about him that was uniquely his—dark and stormy and powerful. Raw and sensual. After spending years at his side, I would know him anywhere.

Why had he come?

An hour into my vigil waiting for Dylan, I'd overheard the nurses talking about Hades. They said he was supposed to be on a date this evening, but apparently, he disappeared from the restaurant. No one knew where he went.

I was still stuck on him seeing someone. *A date.*

It was irrational to be upset. I was still with Dylan. It was idiotic to cling to that one night when he was sick, when he'd... when I'd wanted to...

I hadn't even known the king was looking for a wife. I thought I knew him, this king who used shadows as shields, but apparently, I was wrong. Maybe I didn't know him at all.

Which was why, when my boyfriend repeated, "What are you doing here?", I carefully watched the King of the Daemons.

A long moment passed as the king slowly turned. His wings snapped together, and he stood tall. So tall. Like that tower he loved so much, he was a picture of poise and strength.

He made Dylan look like a small, petulant child.

In a calm, clear voice, Hades said, "I came to check on Phaedra." He gestured to me, but otherwise, he didn't move.

From my position on the bed, I could see both their profiles. They stared at each other, Angel and Daemon, their eyes steely as their jaws clenched.

"My partner?" Dylan scoffed, his tone was as hard as ice. "I told you, she doesn't need your pity."

"Who says I pity her?" Hades asked, rearing back.

Dylan tilted his head. "If it's not pity, then what is it? Because from where *I'm* standing, it looks like a boss taking an inappropriate interest in his employee."

His employee? Yes, technically, that was true, but it had been years since I'd seen myself as just Hades' employee. We had a connection.

Or so I'd thought.

Neither man spoke, and I took the opportunity to draw their attention back to me.

"Dylan," I hissed, waving my hands in the air. "What is wrong with you? Don't you know who you're talking to?"

The Angel snorted. "I'm fairly certain I'm talking to an old man who doesn't know how to take a hint." Dylan stepped forward, his hands balled into fists. "I told you, *sir*, Phaedra doesn't want you here. And neither do I. You need to leave."

"Wait, I—" I started.

"You're right." The king's words were so surprising, so unexpected, that for a moment, I just froze. Everyone did. Then Hades ran a hand through his hair, turning to me.

His expression was so conflicted, so sad, it sent a burst of pain through me. "He's right. I shouldn't have come. I'm your boss, and this was wrong. This wasn't... I'll see you at work, Phaedra." I could see the flickers of worry on his stony face shut off.

That was it?

I'll see you at work?

No.

If there was something I'd learned while walking through the seemingly endless dreamscape that had been my home for months, it was that life was too short for people who mistreated me.

"Wait," I said once more. Both men paused and looked at me. I ignored Dylan, staring at the king. "Is that all I am to you? An employee? Replaceable?"

Hades swallowed, the lump in his throat visible from here as he ran a hand through his white hair. He rasped, "Yes. That's all. An employee."

An employee.

"I see," I said after a moment. I pushed myself up, wishing I was wearing my makeup for this. But beggars couldn't be choosers. And I wasn't about to let this man walk all over me. King or not, I hadn't given him the last five decades of my life for him to treat me like this. "An employee."

King Hades wasn't even looking at me anymore. His gaze had dropped to the floor, and he shuffled from side to side.

For a very long moment, no one spoke. No one even moved.

Then, a screeching sound came from the speaker above my bed.

"Code Indigo on Level Six, Code Indigo on Level Six." a loud voice crackled over an intercom. "All personnel are required immediately for containment."

Half a dozen nurses and doctors jogged towards the nearest stairwell. In the aftermath of their departure, an awkward silence filled the room.

"Well," the king said as he moved around Dylan toward the door, his hand clenching and unclenching at his side. "I'd better be going. Phaedra, it's been... I'm glad you're all right."

Holding up a hand, I said, "Hold on a second."

King Hades paused, and Dylan turned to stare at me. My boyfriend's expression made his displeasure extremely clear. Well, too bad for him. I was going to say my piece now before I lost my courage.

Life was too short for regrets. I was tired of this girlish attraction to a man who would never by mine. I was also tired of settling for someone like Dylan just to stave off the loneliness.

"Yes?" Hades said after a moment.

I cleared my throat. "I won't be coming back to work."

He raised a white brow. "No, I assumed you would need some time to recover—"

"No," I said, interrupting the king. "You don't understand. I *won't* be coming back to work for you. Ever." Hades' mouth dropped open—something I'd never seen before—but I didn't stop. Not now. "Consider this my notice, *sir*."

"You mean..." His voice trailed off, and he turned to look me in the eyes. "What are you saying, Phaedra?"

Dylan snarled, crossing his arms in front of his chest. "I think it's pretty clear, *Your Majesty*," he sneered. "Phaedra doesn't want to work for you anymore."

"I—"

"Quiet, babe. I've got this." Dylan winked at me, and I stared at him in disbelief.

The *gall* of this man. He didn't even visit me for weeks while I was in a coma, and now he thought he could speak for me?

I opened my mouth to retort, but before I could, Dylan turned back to the king. He waved his hands in the air as he said, "No more late nights, no more working overtime. Phaedra is done. She can finally stay at home and be the wife I need her to be."

My heart pounded in my chest, and red filled my vision. My ire wasn't directed at one man. No. I had enough anger for them both.

"Wife?" I exclaimed at the same time as Hades.

"Yes," Dylan nodded, his jaw firm. "Wife."

For a moment, I felt as though I had been moved to an alternate reality. One devoid of sexual satisfaction but filled with cooking the same dinners and watching the same shows night after night. He wanted a white picket-fence life, and it would slowly suck the life out of me. First, the king was dating people. And now, this?

"Did we get engaged sometime while I was in a coma?" I asked, checking my left hand, which was—thank the gods—still as bare as the day I was born.

Dylan opened his mouth and closed it again. "No, but, I just assumed now that you're awake—"

"That was your problem," I said harshly. I was done. Anger flooded through my body, and I clenched my fists at my sides.

My head ached, but I needed to push through this. They'd left me alone for weeks. Weeks!

I was awake now, and I wasn't going to let anyone treat me that way. Not a king. Not my boyfriend. No one. I knew my worth, and I deserved better.

I sucked in a deep breath. "*Both* of your problems. You both made assumptions about what I was going to do. This wasn't the first time, but it's certainly the last. I'm done. Over it." My voice escalated, and I balled my fists in the sheets. "Life is too short for your shit.

"What?" they exclaimed in unison.

"Yes," I said. Reaching over, I pressed the red button on the edge of my bed. Moments later, a medwitch hurried into the room.

"How can I help you, Ms. Demtre?" she asked.

I met her gaze. "I don't want any visitors. Please escort these men away."

The medwitch turned, swallowing hard when her eyes landed on the king. "I-I-I..." she stuttered.

The King of the Daemons blew out a long breath. He put his hand on the medwitch's arm. "It's okay."

"Your Majesty?" she squeaked.

"I'm leaving." He turned, meeting my gaze. "For what it's worth, Phaedra, I'm sorry."

I didn't reply. He held my gaze, sighing as he ran a hand down his face. "Okay. Goodbye."

Four seconds and a puff of shadows later, the king was gone. Dylan jumped, snapping his wings back, just as the medwitch turned to him. Her face hardened. "Do I have to call security, or will you go on your own?"

Dylan turned to me, his eyes wide. "Phaedra, babe—"

"No. I meant it, Dylan. We're done. Get out."

"Baby—"

Apparently, the medwitch was stronger than she looked, because she grabbed onto my ex-boyfriend's arm and yanked him out of the room. "The lady told you to leave." She shoved him, and Dylan went stumbling out the door, which the medwitch closed behind him.

"Babe, listen to me!" he yelled, banging on the glass window with his fist.

"Go away," I moaned as my head pulsed behind my eyes. "I don't want to see you."

He continued to bang and yell, begging for me to pay attention to him.

The medwitch reached into her pocket and pulled out a phone. She raised a brow. "You want him banned?"

I nodded, suddenly unable to speak as emotion thickened in my throat.

"Hold on," the medwitch said. She punched in a few numbers, then slid it back into her pocket.

I raised a brow, but within a minute, three large security Daemons appeared behind my ex. They grabbed onto Dylan's arms, dragging him away from me.

I could hear his shouts all the way down to the street.

Only then did my did I let the burning in my eyes overflow. A few hot tears slipped down my cheeks. Interestingly enough, none of them were for Dylan.

"Can I get some tea, please?" I asked the medwitch hovering at the entrance to my room.

PART TWO

TRYING

CHAPTER 11

A LARGE SCALE DISASTER WITH DELPHINA DE LA MAR

AIDONEUS

Eight days, four hours, and thirty-two minutes had passed since Phaedra quit. I was on the floor where my personal office was located. My last meeting for the day was with the head of my personal security, Toth'toros; the regional director of the Dae Police and DaeGuard, Nyrnavox; and the Keeper of the Gate, Kharon.

No surnames, of course. Daemons did not have surnames, but they did have identification numbers that cleared up any problems on legal documents.

"Toth'toros, ID number 98-171-1005," my head of security said.

The AI Flora noted all those present, her strange hologram scribbling in the air. Once we were all checked in, we could safely record the proceedings for future revision if necessary.

"Nyrnavox, ID number 99-321-2007."

"Kharon, ID number 00-003-0001."

I steepled my hands in front of me. My attendees were squeezed into chairs that had to be cleared out before use. Phaedra spent decades making a system for me and never both-ered to teach anyone else how to handle cataloging these damned papers and new arrivals.

"High King Hades, 00-342-0000."

Leaning back in my plush leather chair, I looked at my head of personal security.

Toth'toros cleared his throat. "My Lord, there have been reports of increased Ice Mer troops along the Spring Mer borders." He shifted in his seat, trying not to knock over a stone-bead necklace in a velvet case that was still on his chair.

Leaning forward, I jotted some notes on my tablet. "This is the second complaint in three months? Is that correct?"

My head of security nodded.

"As of yet, there have been no attacks, correct?"

Another nod. Then Toth'thoros shifted again. "The warning actually came from Queen Isolde. Her witches closely monitor the lands. They do an even better job than the Spring Mer. It's impressive, the system that she has set up with them."

I pressed my lips together. I hadn't known that. She and I hadn't ended on the best of terms, but it was good to see that she was still a viable political ally. "We should send a legion to her swamp this week."

"Your Highness, with all due respect, I'm not sure that's a great idea." Nyrnavox scratched the back of his neck. His dark skin was rough, his red and black uniform was pressed in crisp lines, and his hair was shaved in a tight, militaristic cut. "We are still finishing up our final repairs. The DaeGuard is in charge of most of the heavy lifting, and while they have done incredibly well, there is a shortage of Daemon power. They are exhausted, and I promised them a month's leave."

Both of my eyebrows shot up. I stared at the director. "You did *what*? We are preparing a counterattack against King Phelix." There was a bitterness in my mouth that added an extra bite to my words.

Kharon sat back, watching the exchange between the three of us. He still insisted on wearing clothes from the second century. He was unlike any of the beings alive today, having lived nearly as long as myself. A loose black robe was wrapped around his hips and slung over his shoulders. My eyes lingered on him a moment longer before they returned to Nyrnavox.

The Regional Director bit his lip. "With all due respect, sir, these soldiers are overworked. It isn't my fault that you aren't doing your job as monarch. While our numbers are excellent, the royal army isn't what it once was. Your brother has spent the last two hundred years playing with blood-sucking parasites. He has expanded his lands so far that it's hard to get a definitive reading on exactly what the Ice Mer military looks like. After carefully reviewing all of the available information, we will not be able to carry out a siege without help."

My gut tightened. Raphael warned me of this. Since the rebellion, I avoided basing the future of my land or my people on war.

Evidently, that was a mistake.

I thought back to the gift from the Gods I was given all those years ago. It was time to pull it out once more.

Not only that, but Raphael was right. It was time to get married. Dammit. My two months were ticking away at a steady rate.

The first person I would need to reach out to would be my future queen's troops. A future queen I still hadn't picked. In total, I had met sixteen different women. The Lady of the Northern Were was high on my list. Even Queen Elva had sent me the number of one of the women on her high council.

I realized I had trailed off and snapped forward in my seat. Toth'toros and Nyrnavox were staring at me, their eyebrows slightly furrowed.

"Your Highness?" Toth'toros asked.

My gaze flicked to Kharon. "Before we reach out to my brother, it would be wise to reach out to Fortuna. She has been quiet for a long time, and we could perhaps reach an arrangement with—"

Kharon stood, pushing back his chair and knocking over a stack of seventh century books. They fell to the floor with a clatter. "Absolutely not. The Legion of the Undead is not a service that you can call on to sort out sibling rivalry," the ancient being sneered.

I sucked in a breath, but after a moment's thought, I decided to ignore his outburst. This was not the time for petty rivalries. I rubbed my hand over my face. We had reached a standstill. These men were doing their jobs. I had to do mine. I needed to pick a wife soon.

Luckily—or unluckily—I had another date this evening.

I sat up straighter in my seat. "Fine, I understand. Shall we meet again next week? I will bring an update after I finalize an engagement."

Toth'toros and Nyrnavox nodded before standing. Slowly, Kharon stood up at the same time as me.

"We will see each other then," Nyrnavox said, while Toth'toros glanced between me and the Gatekeeper before nodding and following the Director.

Once they were gone, I spoke. "What do you need, Kharon?" I wondered for a moment if Fortuna's Gatekeeper actually was an Undead himself. It would explain the hollow look in his eyes.

His hands dangled at his sides, and he looked around the room. Then he tightened his fists. "Lady Fortuna is not pleased that you haven't come to consult her about your upcoming decision."

I steeled myself and tried to make my facial expression as calm as possible by relaxing my forehead. "What are you referring to?"

He gave me a look that said he was too old for games, and honestly, so was I. I knew he was talking about my marriage. My second marriage. Sighing, I shook my head. "I—I have been busy."

Kharon shot one more look around the room. "Indeed. I could clean this up for you if you really deem it such a drain on your powers."

I shook my head. "That won't be necessary." Glancing at my watch, I realized just how late it had gotten. I needed to be at a candle-lit dinner at 8:00 pm, and it was already 7:15. Showering the day off of me sounded nice. "Now, if you'll excuse me..." I pointedly glanced at my watch, raising a brow.

Kharon shook his head. "Very well, Fortuna's son. Do not forget what I have said. If you didn't appear so busy now, I would take you over myself." He bowed stiffly, turning and taking one step before pausing. Kharon looked over his shoulder. "It is not wise to upset the Elementals, DemiGod."

My eyes narrowed at the threat. I wasn't a child, and it did not matter whether my mother wanted me to visit. It wasn't like she had sent word herself.

I followed Kharon out before taking the private elevator up to my rooms. No sooner than I had stepped through the door than Flora, the Summer AI, appeared in the entryway. "Lord Hades, I have heard from AWT."

I stared at her.

"The law firm," she said, as if I didn't know who they were.

My hands started sweating. "Yes?" I asked, trying to keep my tone even.

"One of the lawyers has successfully spoken to Ms. Demtre about a severance package."

"And?"

Flora coughed. "Ms. Demtre has refused it on the grounds of her not actually being fired."

I growled. Magic swelled in my veins, dark and cold. It curled around furniture, threatening to snap it all in half. It demanded destruction.

Thousands of years of self-control poured in, snuffing out the magic's icy intentions.

The AI was unfazed by the darkness that flickered in the room around us. AIs could not be harmed, after all.

"Did you hear from the credit company?" I demanded a touch too roughly.

The AI beamed like she was about to sing for my gods-damned birthday. "Yes, I did! They have confirmed that there is still a substantial amount of debt owed by Ms. Demtre."

I let out a long breath. "Can you give me an exact total?"

The AI's hand went out in front of her, where a holographic paper appeared. She squinted for a second as if she couldn't read well. The action seemed so lifelike; I snorted. The Summer Fae really did want us to feel like Flora was a living, breathing assistant.

Flora rattled off an exorbitant number.

I blinked. How had Phaedra even gotten that much debt in the first place?

Glancing at my watch, I saw it was now 7:25. "Thank you, Flora," I said, Transposing to my bedroom before she could answer.

With a snap of my fingers, I was out of my work suit and into a tuxedo. The plan was to go to the opera after dinner, but I had told the team of royal matchmakers from Angel's Landing that if I couldn't sit through dinner, there was no point in a show. While they had agreed, they still booked a restaurant near the Lethe Opera House.

It wasn't until after our meeting that they had informed me I would be going out with Delphina De La Mar, a Spring Mer princess. Delphina was young—younger than Phaedra, but not as young as Isolde. Not that Phaedra was that young, but if I was going to marry a woman a third of my age...

I stopped the thought before I went there. The most important thing right now was to stop letting my hormones control my actions and do my duty as a sovereign. The conversations from today swirled around my head and clumped together in one heavy and incommodious word: duty. If I wasn't capable of being rational, everything would be lost. I would not let my people down.

A screeching alarm that caught me off guard, and then Flora's voice echoed through the speakers in every room of my house. "Lord Hades, if you are hoping to make it on time to your date, you need to leave within the next five minutes."

I stared at myself in my long wood-framed mirror, and my fingers fumbled around my ebony bow tie. My thoughts hovered over to Helena, my finfolk niece. She and Delphina were the same age, and they had similar upbringings. Maybe it would be nice for her to have someone that she could relate to in the family.

Heirs were out of the question as it was—I had been rendered infertile long ago. Maybe this union made sense.

"Lord Hades," Flora's voice returned, interrupting my thoughts. Why was I considering Delphina so seriously? Is it because Phaedra was finally gone from my life forever? "Time to leave." Her voice was no longer chipper.

I quirked my head to the side. "Flora, why the hostility?"

"My creators programmed me to adjust to the needs of my user. After all the time we have spent together, I figured it was time to adjust in order to provide an improved experience."

I hesitated for one second. It felt nice to be talked to like a person again—spoken to like the insufferable ass I was being. There was no reason to be difficult right now.

"Thank you, Flora," I said again. This time, I meant it. Then I

Transposed to my car with a flourish of my hand, leaving a traffic sign in my bedroom.

Delphina De La Mar was beautiful. She rolled around in her aqua chair—designed by the same company that made my niece Helena's—with perfect ease. Long lashes were flecked with fish scales, which Delphina reassured me were 'sourced naturally.' They gave a shine to her gaze every time she blinked. Both her waist and upper body had more scales than Helena's, and her hair was thick and curly. Her skin tone was also brighter than my niece's, and it faded from a beautiful red to pearlescent white all across her body. Delphina reminded me of the tropics.

The Spring Mer princess was easy to talk to, and she made me laugh twelve times since I arrived. She was absolutely the perfect candidate for my future queen.

It turned out that she was not in direct line to the throne since she was the niece of the current queen. Delphina was brilliant, with the perfect touch of philosophy to her views about what made leaders effective.

I stared at her across the table as she ate her kelp salad. She even convinced me to try it. I picked up a piece with less dexterity than her, and it fell on my clean white shirt.

"Shit," I said without thinking, and she burst out laughing.

I unbuttoned my coat and removed the slimy plant from my person. It left a faint green stain in its place, and I covered my face with my hand.

"No one told me how absolutely charming you are," Delphina said between laughs. "You have this youthful spirit. You are wise, and yet your head is nowhere near your ass."

Grinning, I placed the kelp on my plate. "I hadn't realized that was such a strong point for me. I must tell the matchmakers to add that bit to my bio."

Delphina grinned, and I smiled back at her. "Well, I want you to know that this has been one of the best dates I've been on in a long time. It's a shame it will end after dinner." Her eyes drooped over her lids, increasing her dewy beauty.

A knot formed in my stomach. Delphina was kind, funny, beautiful, but this felt wrong. It wasn't bad enough that I was remarrying after Miranda, but I was considering marrying someone I didn't want. I swallowed hard and gave a weak smile.

Marriage wasn't just about attraction. I knew that this was supposed to be a political partnership over anything. For the hundredth time, I begged my heart to see reason.

"Delphina," I started, fully planning on flirting with her. Unfortunately, before I could say anything else, a hard lump formed in my throat, and I coughed. This couldn't continue.

When it cleared, I knew. My heart won out over my head once again. I just couldn't do it. Someone else already held my heart.

"Delphina, I'm so sorry. I can't marry you." She stared at me, and I continued. "This night has been lovely, but I cannot marry you," I finished weakly, as if I hadn't made that clear before.

Her face flooded with emotions, from confusion to hurt, then to a strange blankness.

"Your Highness, if I did something..." she started, but I interrupted her swiftly.

"Absolutely not. It's not you,"—Gods, couldn't I have used any other phrase?—"It's me."

Delphina stared at me with the exact expression someone who had just heard a bullshit explanation should have. Her lips were pursed, and she squinted her eyes. Her voice dropped in volume as she hissed, "They brought me here, paraded me around your city, and put me out to dinner with you like a brood-mare so you could... reject me to my face?"

She had a point, but I hadn't come here of my own desire. I hadn't called her, flirted with her, wanting to see her in a lovely dress. "I know you are upset, but whatever you are feeling, I can guarantee you, I feel worse."

The princess laughed again, but this time she had a very different tone. "Gods, I take it back. You are full of yourself." She shook her head, the scales in her eyelashes fluttering with anger.

Delphina didn't deserve this, but it would be worse for her to leave without understanding.

I stood and darted in front of her so she couldn't leave. Not before I could explain.

"Be careful, my lord. I would hate to *accidentally* ram you in the shins," Delphina spat.

"Please, just listen for a second," I begged. Even as I spoke, the back of my neck prickled. "I am really sorry. I promise I will make it up for you. A trip, anywhere in the world. You pick. You seem like a lovely woman, and I've enjoyed this night immensely, but you are young, and you are looking for love." I swallowed hard. "You see, my love is all used up. When my wife died, I..." Shaking my head, I took a deep breath.

The mention of my wife had my heart contracting. I hated talking about her and felt even worse for pulling that card.

"I don't want to marry. It has to be done, but this... it isn't my decision."

Delphina stared at me for a moment. "So, some part of you won't do this because of my age?" The words hit home, but she wasn't done. "Have you considered that I am being forced to do this as well? My worth largely depends on how high-ranking my future spouse will be. I mean, maybe I was delusional in thinking you would want me; your nephew also passed me up."

When she spoke, she moved like an underwater flame. Like

lava connecting with the sea and daring it to cool the molten material fast enough not to cause damage.

Shit. I ran my hand through my hair, my fingers running along one of my horns. "I..."

My voice trailed off. What was I supposed to say? Delphina was right. Age was one of the reasons I had never acted on my feelings for Phaedra. That and her shit boyfriend, Dylan.

Finally, I whispered, "Yes. I'm sorry. I am shallow, and that is one of many reasons I am not worthy of you."

She glared at me, and I could tell she wasn't fully convinced. I didn't blame her for her anger. Gods. I would be angry with myself, too.

"When you leave, tell them the truth."

She quirked an eyebrow.

"Tell them I was an asshole, and you turned me down. I won't deny it. Suitors will flock to your doorstep," I said softly. My heart ached for her, for this system, for the game of politics that crushed spirits and ruined lives. I hadn't wanted the future to resemble the past so clearly.

She nodded once, but her eyes were narrowed.

I stood out of the way and watched the crumbling remains of yet another terrible date as she rolled out of the private room. I could already hear the headlines in my head.

Difficult.

Loner.

Unable to care for another person.

But that wasn't true. I had just done it with the wrong person.

The thing about candlelit rooms was that they only seemed romantic with another person in them. Alone, they just felt like mourning. Less like a date, and more like the many times I had lit a candle for Miranda in one of my mother's temples.

I walked to the window and stared at the glowing lights of

the domed opera house. It was huge, and I should have been heading over there now with my perfectly fine prospective wife.

Cold curled in my stomach, and I wondered if I had committed a terrible mistake. This was by far the best date so far, and I blew it all up for my idiotic heart.

I scanned the city, and my eyes landed on the temple I'd spotted on my way here.

Kharon's words from earlier sounded in my head.

Sucking in a deep breath, I steeled myself before leaving the dark room.

Before I could glimpse a judgmental face, or one full of pity, I Transposed directly to my car. I hadn't used a valet this time, but I could see the camera flashes even from the parking garage.

I pressed the button to start the ignition and pulled out of my spot. Navigating my way out of the complex, I saw the paparazzi.

Delphina was there, giving an interview. To her credit, she didn't even look a little mad.

When a paparazzo saw me, he shouted, "Your Highness!"

Within seconds, the cameras started turning my direction and flashing even more rapidly.

Sighing, I shook my head. I was in for a week full of shitty headlines. With any luck, there would be another date. My heart pounded and my lungs tightened as I mentally berated myself. The drive to the temple seemed to take an eternity, but finally, I arrived.

My car was the only one in the lot.

Good. That was good. The only other beings present were the priestesses who lived on the grounds. I sat in my car for a few minutes, unsure whether to get out. Sucking in a deep breath, I tried to ease the pounding of my heart. My palms were slick with cold sweat as I reached up to pop open the door.

I had no reason to feel so nervous. Things hadn't ended so poorly between my mother and I. Even so, I had spent years dealing with grief. For a while, I had been reclusive. Alone. Placing the blame on someone was as easy as breathing for me. I needed a reason for my wife's death other than cruelty. But it hadn't been Fortuna's fault.

I pushed the door open wider, sliding out of my leather seat. The air felt colder than it had moments before. The air smelled like it always did before a thunderstorm, musty and fresh. I inhaled deeply, making a quick mental note of the amount of rain we were getting this year. The local farmers around us needed to have enough moisture.

The sound of my footfalls on the decorative stones that led up to the temple's entrance filled my ears. No matter how deeply I inhaled, my heart refused to slow down.

Finally, I reached the front. The door was open, like always, and the inside smelled like rosemary and lavender. High ceilings were all around me, and I kept walking forward to the altar at the front.

My hands were at my sides, my plan firm. I would offer a candle to the goddess, and then I would leave.

It might be good to also light a candle for Miranda, even though her soul was long gone. It was the thought that counted.

No sooner had I walked past the wooden pews than I felt one of the priestesses enter the room. I turned around, looking at the tall female Daemon with a simple white cotton dress.

"Your Highness, it is good to see you," she said.

I nodded at the priestess. "Thank you. How are things tonight?" I tried to keep my tone casual, and she smiled.

"They are good. Lady Fortuna had hoped you would come soon to consult her on your upcoming choice. A new bride is a big step. Not only for you, but for the entire realm."

I shifted from one foot to the other. The priestesses always knew so much, always spoke in ominous terms. It was always "we" and "us." I had never liked it. If Fortuna spoke to them so often, even going so far as to use them as mediums when necessary, then surely she could speak to me every couple of years.

When I looked up at the ceiling, a strange feeling clutched my chest. "You have a message for me, don't you?"

The priestess's smile widened, and she nodded. "Fortuna says you should stop punishing yourself for searching for a bride."

I froze. The same anger that seemed to be on a short leash these days flowed through my veins, hot and thick. It was shameful, but the place that my mind went wasn't Delphina, or Isolde, or any of the women.

My mind went straight to Phaedra.

"What does that mean?" I asked.

The priestess' lips tilted up. "It means that she wants you to be happy."

Despite the distance between me and my mother, all the bad in Aranthium, the shitty date, a strange hope started to blossom in my chest.

Divine intervention did not always equate to straight answers, and very infrequently did the gods spell things out for us in plain terms. Over the years, I learned that the gut reaction to such moments were usually the correct ones.

Though my choice was not attached to a massive army, there were other reasons to base marriage on. There was a certain indescribable feeling to Phaedra's magic. I'd noticed it several times while working. I'm not sure it was enough to constitute a royal wedding, but then again, none of the other women had such potent power, *and* not all of them had connections to substantial military forces.

The essential part of all of this would be my receiving a new marriage bond, which would bring a substantial reserve of power. My mind continued to race, and instead of finding reasons against my marriage, more and more the iron-clad doors which had kept me separated from that beautiful Angel opened.

The guard I had sent to check on her house at night had confirmed that Dylan never returned to the apartment. Which meant... Maybe...

"Shit," I breathed. Very rudely, I turned from the priestess, called my goodbyes over my shoulder, and headed out to my car.

The familiar hum of the car felt like the same sound that was vibrating through my chest. Power thrummed inside of me, and I tuned into my land in a way that I had not before. It had been centuries since such a stirring happened inside of me.

I knew everything about those in my employ, but Phaedra was different. She required more attention to detail. Her address was written on company documents, and I knew she never once moved in the entire time she'd been in Lethe. I'd offered to find her a new place years ago when I found out she lived in a shitty neighborhood.

She refused.

Racing down the street, I took a shortcut to 3rd Street.

My heart pounded, my palms were sweating, and then I saw the apartment.

I glanced around the street. There were no less than four questionable looking people hanging out in corners. There was a bar on the opposite end of the street, and the smell of urine and liquor had soaked into the very foundations of the buildings.

I could feel my eyes start to glow green, and a faint sheen of light shone on my car.

Gods, I was acting like a youngling.

The nerves, the power, it was all swallowing me up. Slamming the door, I got out and stretched out my wings. Taking a deep breath, I shot up.

Fifth floor, room 3018.

My feet connected with the stone ledge in front of her house.

Deep breaths, Aidoneus.

Air seared my throat and lungs. The green glow was reflected on the door. I raised my hand, and before I could talk myself out of it, I knocked.

No answer.

I knocked again, this time louder. My heart was pounding in my ears.

Moments passed, and then I heard something inside. Just as I was about to knock for a third time, the door opened.

"Hades."

Well, at least she was talking to me.

I stared at her, words escaping me.

"What the hell do you want? It's nearly 11:00 p.m.," she grumbled, her mouth pinched in a firm line.

"Phaedra," I choked out.

She was the most beautiful thing I had ever seen. There was a flush to her cheeks, and her hair hung around her face limply, as if she had spent the whole day lying down. Her wings were ruffled, and sleep made her eyes puffy. Not only that, she was wearing the least professional outfit I'd ever seen. Baggy sweatpants with a cotton shirt that hung off her shoulder. That was fair. I was barging into her home after all.

Then my eyes dipped lower.

No bra.

Shit.

My eyes grew brighter as I avoided looking down past her neck.

"Can I come in?" I blurted out. Keep it together.

She squinted at me. Then she stepped to the side and let me into her apartment.

Despite the neighborhood, she definitely tried to keep her living space clean. There was an old couch in front of a 50 inch

TV. The living room opened up to the kitchen, and I glimpsed a short hallway that I assumed led to bedrooms and bathrooms.

Gods. Don't think about her bedroom.

Phaedra closed the door and crossed her arms over her chest. "So, what do you want? Have you come to tell me you're going to stop having me followed?"

I whipped around, a strange surge of protectiveness making my blood run hot. "No."

She rolled her eyes. "Hades, I don't work for you anymore. Leave me alone."

My heart dropped. I took one last look around the apartment. There definitely wasn't anyone else here.

"Where's Dylan?" I asked, looking her straight in the eyes. I needed to know.

The corners of Phaedra's full mouth turned down. "Why does that matter?"

I wasn't going to be an asshole. I was going to do this, but I was going to do it right. "Are you still together?"

She let out an exasperated breath and looked at the ground. The seconds ticked by, small eternities in their own right.

"No," she said, the word so quiet it was barely audible.

My heart skipped a beat. The ground below us trembled, mirroring my own excitement.

I drew myself up. This was it. "As you know, I need to find a wife. The power in this land is unbalanced. War is brewing."

She studied my eyes, bit her lip, and nodded once. "I know."

"You can help me with all of those things–"

Phaedra held up a hand. "I'm going to stop you right there. No amount of money is worth running your life once more, *Your Highness*." The last words had a bit of salt on them.

"Phaedra, I don't want you to run my life." My hands shook. I just needed to say it before this entire experience got worse. "I want you to marry me."

CHAPTER 12
WAIT, WHAT?
PHAEDRA

I blinked, wondering if I had somehow ended up in another dimension in the past five minutes.

"I... what?" Not my most eloquent moment, I would be the first to admit, but I was at a loss for words. My stomach, which had been eagerly anticipating the frozen lasagna currently heating up in the oven, twisted into a giant knot.

What was happening?

In front of me, the King of the Daemons shuffled from one foot to the other. He cleared his throat, running his hand through his white hair. At any other time, I might have found his very obvious nerves endearing. Right now, however, other things were on my mind.

"I want you to marry me." He cleared his throat. "Please. I need a wife, and I want it to be you."

Did he... had he lost his mind?

That was the only reasonable response to this.

Marriage. To him. A DemiGod?

I looked down at myself. I was dressed in what could only be described as loungewear, and I didn't even have a drop of makeup on my face.

At any other time, I would feel horrified that anyone saw me like this, let alone the king.

But this...

I choked on a laugh that threatened to come bubbling up inside of me.

"You're joking, right?" I looked over his shoulder, my brows furrowed as I searched for... something. Anything that would explain this situation. "This is some kind of prank. If this is your way to get me to accept your ridiculous severance package, I'll tell you the same thing I told your lawyers: I don't want or need it."

Technically, that was a lie, but I wasn't getting into the semantics of my rather dire financial situation. No, I clearly had much more significant issues at hand.

Lord Aidoneus Hades, King of the Gates of Hell, my former boss and DemiGod blinked at me. The overhead lights shone on him, illuminating his face as he reared back. "A joke?" he echoed, his eyes wide as green flashed through them. He shook his head. "No, Phaedra. I'm serious. I want you to marry me."

Oh, my gods. I reached out, grabbing the doorframe to keep from falling over as I stared at this man. This insane man—my former boss—who had just offered marriage.

"I can't marry you," I said dumbly. "You can't be serious. You... you're... this... it's *you*."

I was barely able to speak. The king raised a brow, taking a step closer to me. The light chose that moment to shine on his marbled face, making him look like a living piece of art. "I assure you, Phaedra, I am absolutely serious." He reached for my hand, and I just stared at him as he took it in his. "Marry me."

How could I say anything? What could I say? This man was a king. A DemiGod. He was one of the most powerful beings in

Aranthium. A king leading his country through a massive conflict with his insane brother. Every night since I'd woken up from my coma, I'd spent hours combing through the news reports.

The situation was bad. The DemiGods were at war, and all of Aranthium was suffering.

This man, the King of the Daemons, was the only one standing between Phelix and his autocratic reign.

And he was asking me to marry him?

I knew what I had to say. Putting aside the two crucial facts that he was my ex-boss and the person who had orchestrated my kidnapping, I had no business being the wife of a king. Let alone *this* king.

Me.

I practically snorted as I stepped back and pulled my hand out of his grasp.

There was no question in my mind about how to answer this.

"No," I said, my gaze on his shoes. The word was soft, but I knew he heard me. Green magic sizzled around him, and shadows filled the room. I shook my head. "No," I repeated, more loudly this time. "I don't accept."

A long moment passed, and he sucked in a breath. "Phaedra," he whispered. The tone of his voice shot straight through me. My wings rustled as I inhaled.

It was then that I made a crucial mistake.

I looked up. My eyes crawled over his face. His jaw was tight, his mouth in a thin line, but it was his eyes that made my breath escape me.

They weren't hard. I'd expected them to be ice cold. Steely. Filled with anger.

But I was wrong.

His eyes were heavy, their color dark as they bored into me.

For a very long moment, he just... stared at me. Neither of us moved, and the air between us grew thick.

Then, just as I was about to raise my hand and try to explain, he turned. With a flick of his wrist, the door swung open.

His back tensed, his wings flapping as he launched himself into the air.

I stared at the empty doorway until black smoke poured into my small apartment. It was quickly followed by the smell of burnt food. I cursed, running over the kitchen and yanking open the oven door. The second the door was open, the smoke alarm sang its shrill song.

As if the black, burning air filling my apartment wasn't enough, the apartment sprinklers chose that exact moment to turn on.

Water sprayed down on me from the ceiling, soaking me within moments. My wings were sopping wet, my clothes dripping as I yanked on oven mitts and pulled my destroyed dinner out of the oven. Throwing it in the sink to the backdrop of incessant beeps, I ran to the windows and threw them open.

Between the fresh air and the towel I frantically waved over the fire alarm, the sound eventually stopped.

The silence was deafening.

I stood in the middle of my ruined apartment, my furniture now completely waterlogged and my wings dripping on the floor, and I couldn't help it. Laughter bubbled up inside me.

It was quiet at first, but the sound of mirth soon filled the entire room.

What else was I supposed to do?

How else did one respond to a night such as this? To a marriage proposal like the one I just got?

I kept replaying his words in my mind.

I need a wife.

A wife.

That much, I understood. He was a king, and things were required of him by virtue of his position.

But why me? I mean, sure. I was good at my job. Great, even. I had kept his life running smoothly for a long time. But I wasn't even sure he knew what my favorite color was. Or my favorite food. He didn't know my worst fear or my biggest secret.

He didn't know any of that, because he didn't really know me. How could he? Our relationship had been strictly professional. He was a king, and I was a nobody. He was my boss, and I was a youngling compared to him.

There was no other answer to his marriage proposal except for "no." None.

Except...

Why did I feel like I had somehow done the wrong thing?

THAT FEELING DIDN'T ESCAPE me for the next three days. I went about my life in a fog. I applied for jobs, responded to emails, and kept myself up to date on the news.

Things were not looking good in Aranthium. The death toll kept rising, more cities were being attacked, and Phelix's men were growing bolder.

War was on the horizon, and my stomach remained twisted in a knot. Unease was my companion. I stayed at home with my FaePhone by my side.

Hades never called. Every time my phone vibrated, I jumped. Grabbing the device, I would unlock it and stare at the screen.

It was never him.

I didn't even know why I wanted him to message me. To call me.

And yet, in this time of turbulence, I wanted to know how he was dealing with all this. How did he feel, knowing Helena's wedding was right around the corner?

I wanted to hear his voice.

But he didn't call, and neither did I.

SOMEONE WAS KNOCKING on my door. The sound shattered the silence of my dream, and I sighed as I pushed myself off my bed.

"Coming," I called out as I pulled on a house robe. It had slits for my wings, the fuzzy pink terry cloth covering my matching pajamas, as I stifled a yawn. I glanced at the clock on the wall.

7:26 a.m.

It was far too early, considering I'd only stumbled to bed at two this morning.

This was probably my landlord. I'd been forced to call him after what I was calling the Lasagna Incident. The sprinklers had done something to the main wall between the kitchen and the living room, and now the drywall was peeling.

With my luck, he was going to make me pay for it. The gods only knew how I'd afford that. Between Mother's care and rent, I was barely scraping by as it was.

Gripping the doorknob, I stole a look in the mirror. My hair was a mess, my eyes red and bloodshot from a lack of sleep. My clothes, while comfortable, were far from what I'd call "cute" and my skin was blotchy.

Whatever.

I had no job. No boyfriend. My mother was in a hospital far away. Even my friend Karina was busy with work.

Usually, I hated letting anyone see me without makeup.

But right now, I just couldn't muster up the strength to put on my armor.

The knocking continued.

Grumbling under my breath, I yanked open the door.

And my mouth fell open.

The King of the Daemons stood in front of me, dressed in a crisp, black suit with his horns and wings on full display. The suit accentuated the marble lining of his skin, somehow making him look more god-like than normal.

My heart beat faster in my chest. I'd hoped he would call so we could sort things out, but this... somehow, I hadn't thought he would show up.

At my door.

At seven-thirty in the morning.

"I came..." He cleared his throat. "I came to revisit our conversation from the other night."

I raised a brow. "Is that what you're calling it? A conversation? I thought you lost your mind and proposed to me?"

He blinked. "I did."

Shaking my head, I took a step back. My heart raced, and everything felt too tight. I could not believe we were having this conversation again. "I already told you I can't marry you."

As I was speaking, I was vaguely aware of a strange sensation humming through my body. It was unlike anything I'd ever felt before. It began as a gentle hum, a twisting in my stomach, but it soon flooded through me.

"Why not?" he asked, as though he had forgotten everything we had talked about.

I waved my hands in the air. "Because of *everything!* This is ludicrous!"

The DemiGod stared at me. "It doesn't seem ludicrous to me."

My skin felt too tight as a laugh escaped me. "No?"

"No."

"How does this not seem ludicrous? Look at us!" My voice rose as my heart rate sped up. "You are dressed like the king you are, and I'm wearing pajamas!"

His gaze dropped, and I could have sworn the corner of his mouth twitched. "So you are. I rather like these pajamas."

Blood rushed to my cheeks. "That's not the point!"

"No?" His voice was calm. Far too calm. "What is the point?"

"The point is we don't know each other!"

That was the crux of the matter. Of everything else, everything I'd thought about over the past four days, that was the one that stood out to me the most. He didn't know me. Not really. And I didn't know him.

The King of the Daemons took a step toward me. His voice dropped as he said, "I know you quite well. You know me very well." His eyes moved around my face, taking in every detail like he was hoping to issue a painting from memory. "I would like to know everything about you."

Too much.

It was too much.

My hands grew clammy, and that thrumming in my veins increased. I stared at the king, my mouth opening and closing as I tried to come up with a response, when all of a sudden, a blue flash erupted out of nowhere.

The entire world shook, and my stomach churned as the light blinded me.

And then, when it subsided, my eyes widened.

This was unexpected.

Something had happened. The walls of my apartment were gone, and in their place was an empty... theater? I stood on a stage with a rack of elaborate dresses and a red curtain behind me. In front of me, rows upon rows of empty seats filling the auditorium.

I stared at my surroundings, turning in a slow circle, until a Pixie flew up to me and tapped me on the shoulder.

"Excuse me, miss?" The Pixie's voice was high-pitched and filled with concern.

I stared at the small creature, whose bright blue wings perfectly matched the flowy gown that covered her entire three-inch body. "Yes?"

"How did you... um... where did you come from?" The Pixie's brows furrowed, her confusion matching my own.

Looking down at myself, I stared at my hands before raising my gaze back to the tiny winged being fluttering in front of me.

"I don't know," I said. I could barely think. Magic of some form had been used, but where did it come from? I'd never done anything like that before.

The Pixie was still staring at me, clearly waiting for a response.

"I was at home, and then... where am I?"

She looked at me like I was missing a few marbles. Quite possibly, she was correct. Maybe I was still dreaming.

I pinched myself, and pain shot through my thigh.

This was real.

"Why, you're in the Lethe Opera House, of course," the Pixie said.

I probably could have guessed that. There was only one opera house in this city. "I mean... how did I get here?"

A high-pitched laugh came from the creature. "I don't know! One moment, I was working on the finishing touches of a costume, and the next, the dress was gone, and here you were." She narrowed her bright blue eyes. "What did you do with my dress? Lady Ophelia is supposed to be singing in that dress tonight, and she needs it."

Her dress was gone.

And I was here.

In its place.

"Oh my gods," I muttered as realization dawned on me. "I think I know what happened."

I wasn't sure how, because I'd never done anything like this before, but I was fairly certain I just Transposed myself here. In the past, the king used his power to move me from one place to another on occasion, but I'd never done it myself.

I never had enough magic to do anything. Some Angels had significant amounts of magic, but to Mother's eternal disappointment, the Warlocks had reported that my powers barely registered on their scale. Nothing could be done. Magic was a gift from the gods, after all.

But to Transpose... this was no minimal amount of magic.

If I was right, then I had a lot more pressing problems than a marriage proposal. Dozens of questions flitted through my mind.

Where did this magic come from? What did it mean? Not only that, but how did I control it?

All pressing matters. Ones that I would deal with as soon as I got back to my apartment.

Taking my leave of the Pixie, I promised to get her dress back to her as soon as possible. The moment I stepped out of the National Theater, I launched into the air.

The King of the Daemons and I were going to have a little talk.

I MADE it back to my apartment in record time. I could thank the anger coursing through my veins and the strong wind currents for that. Landing on my balcony, I flung open the door to my apartment.

Balling my fists at my side, I went over the speech I had prepared on my flight over. I was going to tell the king exactly what I thought about his marriage proposal—namely, that it was ridiculous—and demand he tell me where this magic had come from.

The doctors had told me my waking from the coma was miraculous. Now, I was starting to think that this magic had something to do with it.

Ready to give my speech, it took me a moment to realize that my apartment was empty.

Well, empty wasn't the right word.

A mannequin stood in the middle of the living room, adorned in an elaborate ball gown. The fabric was a study in pink, with shades ranging from fuchsia all the way to a light coral. Honestly, it was rather garish, but I supposed it would look pretty with the lights from the theater.

Pinned on the bodice was a white slip of paper.

I stalked closer, grabbing the note.

Come to the Tower. Room 1645. Bring the dress.

• *Aidoneus.*

That was it. Short and to the point. There wasn't even a question. I suppose being a king meant that Hades was used to people just doing whatever he ordered, but if he thought I was at his beck and call, he had another thing coming. I would not be summoned like a dog.

I took my time getting ready. I showered, washed my hair, and applied makeup until my face was flawless. This day was important. I could feel it in my very soul.

I got dressed, digging out a formal suit that I rarely wore. It was black and hugged my curves, but it was appropriate for the workplace. It went to my knees, and there was a small slit that ran up the side that allowed for movement. I paired this with a white blouse that tied at my neck. Of course, it had ties at the side to help accommodate my wings.

Once I was dressed and ready, I threw the ball gown in a garment bag. Brushing back my hair one last time, I took a glimpse at myself in the mirror. I looked ready to go to war. That was how I felt. My makeup was my armor. My suit was my shield. The five-inch heels I strapped on my feet were my weapons.

I was ready for whatever would come my way. Throwing open the door to my balcony once more, I took in a deep breath before launching myself in the air. I didn't take the time to enjoy the flight.

I had a meeting to attend.

CHAPTER 13
AWT LAW FIRM
AIDONEUS

"So, Ms. Demtre used godly power?" the Daemon beside me asked. We were in conference room 2B, waiting for Phaedra to come. One of my favorite partners from AWT, Andrea Themis, was seated at my side. The Daemon's birthright powers completely blinded her at birth, but she wasn't weak. She was able to smell lies, and used her ability to become an "even shrewder lawyer." Her words, not mine.

I nodded. "Yes. We were... discussing the ongoing issue, and then she Transposed right out of the room."

Andrea was free of outward judgment, left with only the facts to work with.

"You are referring to the issue of marriage," she attempted to clarify, and picked up a pen.

I rolled my shoulders back. "I wouldn't call it an 'issue'—"

"Your Majesty, you just called it the 'ongoing issue,'" Andrea said.

I laughed nervously. "So I did."

The thick black sunglasses she used glinted in the conference room lights. Sunglasses indoors had become a familiar sight for me, as they put Andrea at ease. Thick straight across bangs brushed the tops of the frames. She wore the same tailored black suit every day, seeming to favor the expensive boxy cut. The area was perfumed with the smell of sandalwood and something sweeter.

One of the best things about Ms. Themis? She didn't ask frivolous questions like the obvious "Why are you intent on marrying your millennia-younger assistant?"

"This... *non-issue* is unlike anything I've ever seen before. However, I've been doing research. There is a ritual in the ancient texts that talks about how the Elementals stripped powers from people as punishment. I think the same would apply here. So, from my perspective, there are two options for reclaiming the godly power."

I blinked, taken aback. I knew the rituals she was referring to. They were horrific.

"What? I really don't think that's necessary."

I wasn't interested in reclaiming the power. I just wanted to know how it got there.

"You seem to have two options, sir. You can take the Angel into custody and work through the non-issue at your discretion until these new powers are returned, or you can marry her and join yourself to what could potentially be a very powerful female."

I tilted my head to the side. Something warm rippled over my skin—Fortuna knew about this. She must have. Mother sent me to Phaedra's house because she knew that Phaedra's powers had grown more potent, somehow.

Did she do this?

My eyes scanned the grains in the wood. The second option sounded much better. The way Andrea put it, it was a good reason for a marriage. We would need to give that to the press. The truth was far more humbling—I wanted Phaedra, and I would've married her even if she had no birthright power. She drew me in like a moth to a flame. But I was older than her, unable to give her what she needed.

Even so, I knew what I wanted. My eyes flicked back to Attorney Themis. "I am partial to the second option," I said decisively.

She nodded. "I figured. You smell like a Hell Hound chasing after a mate in heat."

Very blunt.

I folded together my hands on the table in front of me, my knee shaking unsteadily beneath the table. My mind felt cluttered. There weren't really coherent thoughts, just a stream of images of Phaedra rejecting me that had my stomach bunching up. I rubbed my thumb across my pointer finger on my opposite hand.

Once.

Twice.

A sharp inhale from the woman at my side broke me from my empty thoughts.

Then I felt it.

The presence of power, like lightning on the wind. An electric current filled the entire room, making my skin tingle.

The smell of... flowers. Of springtime.

The door to the conference room burst open, and the lights above us flickered.

I immediately surged to my feet.

The most beautiful woman walked in wearing a suit I hadn't seen her wear since her first day at Hades' Antiquities Inc. She held a large, heavy garment bag, and her mouth was pinched in a firm line. Water droplets covered her from head to toe, casting transparent dots on her white top.

My eyes flicked away.

"Phaedra," I breathed.

She was glaring at me. I could feel it. However, that glare was nothing compared to the anger that rippled off her in freshwater waves when her sights landed on the attorney. I could have sworn I heard a growl come from her.

"Andrea." Phaedra nodded her welcome, which the AWT partner returned. Her angry eyes landed back on my face. "You brought a lawyer?" She threw the garment bag on the ground and pointed a finger at me. "Get. It. Through. Your. Head. *I will not marry you.*"

I stared at the red nail polish on Phaedra's nail as I opened my mouth to speak. I had to say something. Anything to make her understand why this was important. Before a word could slide past my lips, Andrea spoke.

"Ms. Demtre, thank you for coming. Please sit, both of you." Her voice was calm. That was good. We needed calm. Anger and frustration and other emotions did not have a place here. Not right now.

Tugging on my suit coat, I ran a hand through my hair and sat my ass down. There was no point in being a dumbass at this moment. Themis's words from earlier were sinking in. This was no longer about what some people might deem inappropriate attraction.

Somehow, Phaedra was exhibiting god-like power, and I needed to tie myself to her or send her away to Hell.

She did not love me—she would never love me—but she deserved the best option.

This was a business deal, nothing more.

I avoided Phaedra's eyes while I pushed the leather folder containing our prenuptial agreement toward her. She stared at it like it was a pile of snakes.

Which, to be honest, it was. I'd had it prepared before her little incident this morning with the dress, and now I was grateful. If the media caught wind of Phaedra's power before she got it under control, things could go from bad to worse.

She needed my help, and whether she wanted it or not, I was going to do everything I could to help her. Because if she didn't agree to marriage, the other option was far less cordial. My stomach churned just thinking about it.

Slowly, so slowly, Phaedra's hand reached toward the folder. Her eyes scanned across the words on the first of twenty pages. There were a lot of assets to cover, but overall, this was just covering the major details of our roles.

As Phaedra read, Attorney Themis offered light commentary. "Pages one through four are essentially an introduction of assets. Prenups require full disclosure. Since you have worked for the company, we already have extensive records on what you brought when you came here and entered King Hades' employment."

Phaedra blinked. Andrea had been made aware of the dangerous circumstances that required us to extradite the Angel from Olimpie.

However, when Phaedra opened her pink mouth, she did not make a comment on that. "So, you know about my assets?"

Andrea nodded. Phaedra's face continued to blossom with more and more shades of scarlet and pink, though I could not tell if it was from embarrassment or anger.

Phaedra skimmed the papers, and Themis prattled off the rest of the contents of the document.

I cleared my throat, pretending Phaedra was a rare antiquities dealer, and I flashed her a smile. She did not return it. Her face was twisted with mistrust, with the severity of a person whose private life had been cracked open like an egg.

"Phae—Ms. Demtre," I said. "Do you understand the severity of what happened today?"

The second I spoke, I knew the words were the wrong things to say. Phaedra might have been mad before, but now...

Now everything shifted. Phaedra's face went lax, and her eyes grew wide. It wasn't like her to take shit, especially not when she felt bombarded. Once, an art auctioneer tried to get her to pay an extra ten thousand for a stolen Siren vase, and she had his license revoked.

"What do you mean?" she asked.

Leaning forward, I met her gaze and said, "You used power that you should not have."

The blood drained from her face. "But-but I've always had magic. It was small, to be sure. But maybe—"

Andrea interrupted, "Ms. Demtre, I know this is a lot to take in. But there are no scenarios in which a regular being is able to use powers that are explicitly indicative of divinity. There are no exceptions, no anomalies."

"I didn't ask for this!" Phaedra exploded. She glared at Andrea, and I was glad her anger was off me. "It's not like I stole these powers. They just appeared."

The lawyer continued, clearly used to dealing with anger. "I understand, Ms. Demtre. Still, it is a problem. We can search for the cause of your sudden surge in powers. They could be a result of your coma, or when the king helped heal you after the explosion."

The attorney's eyes flicked to me, and I wondered if she was right. But I had healed hundreds of thousands of people in my years. Never had this happened before. The gears in my mind started turning. There was no logical explanation for this.

When Phaedra just stared at the leather folder, Andrea continued, "If you do not join hands with divinity, those divine powers will be removed from you by employing a very ancient ritual."

The words hung in the air like icicles. They were sharp, cold, threatening to break off and come shooting down at any moment. The Diachorismos Ritual stripped souls of their magic. It was a harsh ritual, one that left people as husks of themselves.

I should know. My brothers and I used it on our parents. It was the key move in our rebellion to send them back where they had come from.

It was part of the reason I had lost Miranda.

My entire body broke out in a cold sweat. I wanted to open my mouth, to tell them under no circumstance was that an option. But... I couldn't move. My mouth refused to cooperate. I, too, was bound by the laws of the Divine.

After a moment, the lawyer spoke again, "So, as you can see, Hades proposing to you is actually more generous than the alternative." Though I knew Andrea couldn't see Phaedra, she dipped her head like she was peering into the Angel's very soul.

The threat hung in the air, and the contents of my stomach continued to sour while I clenched my fists.

Did Phaedra know what that ritual was? What it did? She worked for me long enough, and it was written about briefly in history books. The thing of divine legends.

Finally, Phaedra's eyes went to my own. "So, this is your choice? I said no, and now you are going to force me to be around you?" Her voice sharpened, her eyes narrowing as she spat, "Is there really no one else you want to make miserable?"

Her words cut deep, and my chest tightened.

I ground my teeth together. "When I brought you here all those years ago, it was to save your life. The reasons haven't changed. If you would prefer to continue acting like a child, then I can arrange for other options."

My old assistant's face hardened. All the anger leached from her skin, and in its place was a hard shell. Her eyes were like ice, her mouth pinched in a straight line. "I. See."

On the inside, I was screaming. This was absolutely not how

this was supposed to go. Something inside of me demanded that I take it all back, to pretend I'd never said anything. Send Andrea from the room.

But my options were running out.

I needed to try to salvage this somehow.

"Phaedra, I am not trying to threaten you," I started, and she scoffed. "I'm serious. This is not meant to be a bargaining chip over you. This was just something that happened."

A long moment passed as we studied each other.

I straightened my back. Phaedra still glared at me, but some of the heat faded away.

When she didn't speak, I continued. "I know about your debts. And your mother." The heat returned. Her eyes were hard, and I swallowed. "I know you can't really afford to be without a job, let alone paying rent for that shitty apartment yourself. So," —Phaedra's eyes flickered and her magic cast a glow all around us. Dammit. I needed to get to her before she used that magic to strangle me—"I am going to pay off all of your debt. I'll buy you a house all for yourself. I'll give you enough money to never worry about another thing in your life. Just, please, marry me."

A hum filled the room as thick tension hung in the air.

A minute passed.

Then two.

Then, her eyes returned to their normal color.

"Go on," she ground out through clenched teeth.

I blew out a breath. At least she was listening. "This doesn't need to be a normal marriage. We just need to tie our magic together. Transposing without wanting to is a problem. I can train you. I am prepared to give you everything I've mentioned and more. And..."—I couldn't let my voice break on this one. I clenched my fists beneath the table, pressing half-moons into my palms—"You are free to do whatever you wish. With whomever you want."

Maybe the last part was excessive, but this must be too good to refuse.

Her head dropped, and my heart sank along with it. Maybe she really was going to refuse.

Silence wrapped around the room. There were more words to say, but they would have to wait.

It was up to her. I'd wait as long as she needed.

Phaedra stared at me, her gaze hard. The ticking clock on the wall, an old grandfather clock from two centuries past, was the only sound as minutes went by.

Then she broke the silence.

"Are all of these things mentioned in those papers?" she asked Andrea, her eyes flicking over me as if I wasn't even in the room.

The attorney nodded. "Yes. If there is something you don't feel is clear enough, I'd be happy to change it. I have also spoken to a colleague if you want another to represent you. It might be nice to have another set of eyes on them. Or… at least one."

Phaedra laughed. The sound was like a splash of cold water, intense but not unpleasant. Some of the tension inside of me thawed.

"Yes. Please bring in the other attorney. I don't like feeling like I'm on unequal footing with the King of the Dead," Phaedra said as she shot me a glare.

Maybe being ignored was better.

Andrea Themis nodded. "Flora." The familiar AI blinked into view. Her white dress was wrinkle-free, and she wore an accommodating smile. "Can you please send up Attorney Diego Garcia. He's the Warlock that's been waiting in the third-floor lobby."

"Of course, Attorney Andrea Themis," said the AI with an overly sweet voice. Then she blinked out, and we were left in relative silence.

The clock continued to tick.

"Attorney Garcia will arrive in approximately three to five minutes," Flora's voice said through the conference room speaker.

And so we waited. My eyes flicked over to Phaedra, and she seemed to be purposefully avoiding my gaze while staring at the papers. It looked like she wasn't even reading because her eyes weren't moving.

My chest moved up and down, but the air that passed through me was silent. It was completely honed into the sunshine scent that had soaked the room.

Themis pulled out a tablet that she commanded with her voice and gently tapped a finger on the crystal screen.

I just sat there.

Within the promised few minutes, the second attorney opened the wooden door.

"Afternoon all," a tall white-haired man with umber skin and bright purple eyes said. His suit was a deep blue, appropriate for the time of day. The Warlock gave a short wave with one hand, gripping an old-fashioned leather briefcase in the other.

I was not familiar with this man, but he seemed friendly. That was good. We needed all the friendly we could get right now.

The new lawyer took a seat next to Phaedra and smiled wide. "Ms. Demtre, my name is Diego. I'm here to make sure that all of your needs are met."

My eyes narrowed when Phaedra returned that smile and shook his outstretched hand. A reminder that she wanted nothing really to do with me.

That hurt more than it should have, a signal to screw myself. She might agree to marry me, but under no circumstances did she want me as her husband. There appeared to be next to no hope that would change.

"Ms. Demtre, would you like a few minutes alone to discuss your case with Attorney Garcia?" Andrea asked.

Phaedra cast me a sour look before looking at Andrea. "Since you already know about me and my *finances*,"—the word was bitter—"I see no reason for all of this except to run up a large bill for His Majesty, King Hades."

Diego's annoyingly bright smile didn't falter, and anger bubbled up in my veins.

I leaned back to cross my arms. "Surely there is more you want?" I blurted out.

The Angel stared daggers at me. "From you? What more could I ask for than a forced arranged marriage?"

"So, you don't want the house? We can take it out."

"You're such an asshole," she snapped.

Tension thickened in the room, but I didn't deny it.

"Fine," I said. She was right. I was being an ass, but I couldn't seem to stop. "Tell me about what role you're comfortable playing? How many public events can we go to each week? What kind of story do you want portrayed to the public?"

A long moment passed, and I looked expectantly at Phaedra.

She took a deep breath, seeming to be finally considering my words. "I can't handle more than two events a week."

Two a week. I could handle that. Honestly, I would take anything she would give me.

"All right," I said, my voice a little softer. "What else?"

Phaedra caught her lip between her teeth and chewed. When she released the poor lip, the pink grew more intense. "Hades, I used to be your assistant. Do you still expect me to handle your personal life for you?"

Oof. She had a point.

"You won't be an assistant," I said firmly. "You'll be my wife. Big difference."

She rolled her eyes. “Okay, then, who have you hired to replace me?”

Blood rushed to my face. “I’ll hire someone before the nuptials.”

Phaedra scoffed. “Hire someone today.” She pressed a finger down on the agreement and looked at Diego. “I want that in writing.”

Diego nodded, taking notes furiously on a tablet.

“Consider it done, Phaedra,” Andrea said pleasantly. “What else?”

Phaedra looked right at me. “I will get my own house, but surely we must live together before then. What will that look like?”

I shrugged. “My penthouse has twelve rooms. Pick whichever you’d like.”

Andrea nodded. She tapped her pen on the table, not even looking at us as she asked, "And what about the issue of sexual intercourse?"

I choked on my own spit. “What?” I barely got out.

Attorney Themis continued without pause. “Intimacy clauses aren’t uncommon in prenuptial agreements, but they are hard to enforce in the legal systems.”

I could barely think. My mind was stuck on the two words. Images flashed through my mind, and suddenly, the room felt very, very hot. Phaedra on the table, the floor, my bed. Looking up at me with a heady gaze. I pulled at the collar of my shirt. "Did someone turn up the heat in here?" I mumbled.

No one answered me.

“Write in whatever intimacy clause you want,” Phaedra said decisively. “Physical intimacy won’t be occurring.” She glared directly at me, as if daring me to counter her.

My jaw tightened as I ground my teeth together. Keeping the words I wanted to say inside, I tuned out everything. I was done.

Phaedra could have whatever she wanted. I just didn't want to hear about it.

I picked a spot on the wall, a knot in the wood that was a rich chestnut brown. The clock ticked a steady beat, and I focused on that.

My mind wandered as the three of them chattered away.

"Your Highness, we are ready to sign," Themis said. She held a pen in my general direction.

I blinked and checked my watch. It had been three hours. Phaedra was staring at her lap, her expression unreadable.

"Yes, of course," I said and took the pen. A new stack of papers was presented to me. Yellow sticky notes are on each page that needed to be signed and initialized.

Once I finished, I looked up. Phaedra still avoided my gaze, but if I was signing these, then she would, too.

Slowly, I pushed them over to her, and watched as she signed her name next to mine six times.

My insides exploded. All the tension rang out around me, and the ground beneath us rumbled. A tremor passed through the entire city.

The light above us flickered.

I was screaming in my head.

She was going to marry me.

Phaedra would marry me.

My heart raced and my palms grew sweaty. A bolt of electric green lightning shot down from the sky, illuminating the sky.

Phaedra's eyes widened, and she glared at me. "What the hell was that?"

"That's everything," Andrea said brightly, skipping over Phaedra's comment.

"Thank you, Andrea." I stood, and moments later, the lawyers followed suit. Collecting their papers, they murmured in a corner of the room.

While they were going over paperwork, I had been thinking. A lot. If Phaedra was going to be a royal—be my wife—then she needed to be trained. She had Transposed the dress, but who knows what other powers were lurking inside of her.

Mine, a voice inside of me said. I promptly ignored it.

"Phaedra, a moment before you go," I said just as she stood. Loping across the room, I picked up the garment bag. "Transpose this back."

My words were deep, but there was no green glow emanating from me. It turned out I did, in fact, have a few shreds of self-control left.

The woman who just agreed to be my bride glared at me. "I don't know how."

"Well, you brought it here. Which, by the way, a dress for that short a distance isn't as impressive as you might think." I said, eying the gown.

She looked up at me. All five feet and two inches of her form minus the wings. "I am using godly powers and you say it's not that impressive."

I stepped toward her, invading her personal space. "Transpose it back," I challenged.

She glared. "Can I do it some other time? I would very much like to be anywhere else now."

I shook my head, but some twisted part of me enjoyed this. It was an awkward interaction, but at least she was here. Talking. To me. Not to the others. "Give it a try. You need to train. Why not start now?"

"I already said I can't." She shook her head, her words sounding like fire. "Wasn't me agreeing to marry you enough? What else do you want from me?"

I wanted everything. I wanted her not to hate me. To want me. To love me.

But it seemed that wasn't going to be the case.

Sighing, I shook my head. "Fine. You win. Don't do it."

She was going to hate me for eternity. *That* was going to be a delight.

Phaedra glared at me. "In that case, why don't you let me have some peace? As I'm sure you can imagine, this has been a very long day."

The dismissal was clear. Tense silence ensued before I looked over at the attorneys. "Thank you both for your time. It seems that I have a busy afternoon ahead of me, and now I need to take this back to the Lethe Opera House."

Andrea dipped her head. "Of course. It was our pleasure." She slipped her hand into the crook of Diego's arm, and they left the room.

Phaedra stared at me for a moment before following the attorneys silently. No "thank you", nothing.

The door snicked shut behind her. Hugging the garment bag tighter to me for a moment, I Transposed it with a snap of my fingers. A single tube of lipstick laid in its place. I stepped over the lipstick, feeling annoyed, and went up to my office.

I needed to find a new assistant.

CHAPTER 14
GIVE HIM A CHANCE
PHAEDRA

Three hours of my life had passed by in a blur. Paperwork, especially regarding marrying a king, was exceedingly tedious.

Three hours. Somehow, it didn't seem like long enough. Not when it changed the entire trajectory of my life.

But it was fine. Everything was fine.

I was going to be queen consort, and I had godly power. I was an Angel about to wed the King of the Daemons.

That was fine, right?

I couldn't even fool myself. I was a terrible liar. Nothing was fine. Everything was wrong. My entire life had turned on its head.

My head spun as I tried to sort through everything that had just happened. Had I really had a conversation with the King of the Daemons about sex?

My cheeks flushed just thinking about it. I'd spent so many years off limits to him, if I let him touch me, I would always care about him more than he cared about me. And that made me feel lightheaded and a little sick to my stomach.

I needed a break. From everything. Walking down the corridors of the tower, I nodded at the various employees as I passed them. My presence here wasn't unusual, and none of them stopped to question me.

I still could not believe this was my life. Mere hours ago, I was searching for a new job, and now I was engaged.

Not just to anyone. To *him*.

Good gods.

I needed to think about this.

Before I even realized where I was going, my feet had taken me down seven flights of stairs. I stood in front of a familiar door, and the smallest of smiles crept over my face as I turned the knob.

The moment the door swung open on silent hinges, I let out a deep breath.

It was still here.

Slipping off my heels, I picked them up with one hand and stepped inside. My feet sank into the plush carpet, and I flicked on the light-switch. Soft, buttery light filled the room, and I slipped the door shut behind me.

The light filtered down to the only thing in the room, and I extended a hand, running it down the long, black surface. It gleamed in the soft light, and I couldn't help the smile that crept onto my face as I studied the grand piano that had been my secret for the past thirty-two years.

"I've missed you," I whispered as I walked all around the piano.

Pulling out the bench, I slipped onto it before drawing up the lid. The moment the black and white keys appeared, tension left my body. I studied the keys for a moment before placing my fingers on the the shiny black lacquer.

Home.

This felt like home.

When I was younger, my mother made me practice piano for hours on end. To be the best, she told me repeatedly, one had to put in the time. Hard work would always beat a natural talent in the end.

As a child, I resented my time spent at the piano, fingers banging away on the keys for hours at a time, but I grew to love the music. The way it made me feel. Calm. Like myself.

Not many things did that anymore.

The moment my fingers landed on the keys, I played. Scales at first. One scale. Then another. I kept playing the repetitive motions until the only thing in my mind was music. No marriage. No Hades. Nothing.

Then, and only then, did I switch to music. The song that flowed from my fingers was not one I had ever played before. It was deep. Dark. Mournful.

So many things had been stolen from me in the past few months. I lost time after the attack. Memories. My job. My boyfriend. And now, since that godly magic appeared this morning, apparently I had also lost my freedom. The choice that Hades gave me wasn't really a choice at all.

I poured all of my frustrations, my pain, my anger, and my hurt into my music. Every last ounce of emotion went into my music.

I played for minutes. Hours. I lost track of time as music flowed from my fingers. It filled the room, conveying every single emotion I felt within me.

Eventually, the music shifted from being dark and deep and lonely. Now, a new harmony joined the darkness. Something lighter. Higher.

It sounded like hope.

For the first time since that power had erupted from me, I felt like maybe there was something here I could control.

Aidoneus wanted me to marry him? Fine. I'd do it.

He wanted a wife? I would give him a wife. I would be present, ready to make appearances, hold on to his arm in front of the press, and whatever else he needed from me in public. But that was all he would get.

If Hades thought I was going to be anything more than a figurehead, he was wrong. He wanted me to marry him because of my power. I would do it. I would let him train me until I could manage this on my own. Then I'd find my own way out of this.

Eventually, my vision blurred. I lifted a hand off the keys, interrupting the flow of music, and touched my cheek. My fingers came away damp. At some point, I started crying. Reaching into my handbag, I pulled out a handkerchief. A relic from a time long ago. Just like the man I agreed to marry.

Tidying myself up, I reapplied my makeup before reaching back into my purse. I slid out my phone, staring at it for a very long time. So many things happened to me recently, and I knew who I wanted to talk to.

Before I could talk myself out of what was probably a bad decision, I unlocked my phone. Scrolling through my contacts, I found the one I wanted.

My finger hovered over the button for *Angelic Long Term Care*, but eventually, I tapped it.

The picture changed, and the image on the phone shook.

Regret instantly filled me, and the desire to hang up was strong. Why was I doing this? Chances were high she wouldn't even recognise me. The last time we spoke, she referred to me as her best friend Clarice for the entire conversation. Things became very awkward when she delved into the accounts of a sexual encounter I had less than zero desire to learn about.

What was I thinking? This was a terrible idea.

My finger was just about to tap the bright red button when a mustached face appeared on the screen in front of me.

"*Oh, Ms. Demtre*!" A chipper Summer Fae wearing bright blue scrubs and a stethoscope smiled at me through the FaePhone. "*What a pleasant surprise! We haven't heard from you lately.*"

I blinked. After the day I'd had, this man's enthusiasm was edging on being excessive. But I already made the call. Now, I would see it through. Clearing my throat, I avoided his gaze. "Yes, I'm sorry about that. I've been... indisposed."

The male nurse nodded. "*Not to worry. You're calling now. I assume you'd like to speak to her?*"

"Is this... is she..." I couldn't seem to form the words needed, but thankfully, the man on the other side of the phone seemed to understand.

"*It's a good day, Ms. Demtre. A perfect day.*"

Thank the gods.

My lips tilted up into a smile. "Then yes, please," I said, tightening my grip on the silver rectangle. "I'd love to talk to her."

"*Perfect,*" the nurse said. "*She should be in the garden. I'll just place you on a brief hold while we get her ready.*"

I nodded, and the screen in front of me went black. Placing the phone on the piano, I tapped my fingers on my knees as I looked around the room.

Other than the grand piano where I currently sat, the room was completely empty. I discovered the room a few decades ago. The space was rather large, filled with dusty boxes dated as far back as the last century. When I moved them, I discovered the instrument. A hidden treasure.

My hidden treasure.

I cleared out the room, this small space tucked away in the middle of the tower, and waited for someone to tell me about the grand piano and where it belonged.

Only days, and then weeks, went by and no one said anything. It was as though the room didn't exist.

When I realized that this room had somehow become a forgotten space in this massive tower, I made it my own.

Claimed it, in a way. It became my refuge over the past thirty years, and I sought it out on multiple occasions.

It was my safe place.

Leaning my head against the wall, I shut my eyes and took deep breaths. One after the other, until my head was cleared.

"Ms. Demtre, we're ready for you."

I snapped my eyes open. The black screen was gone, and in its place was a very familiar face.

"Hello, Mother," I whispered. My vision blurred once more, and I sniffled as I wiped the tears away with the back of my hands. "How are you?"

A pause before my mother coughed. Her long, white hair hung in a limp ponytail, and she wore a bright yellow cardigan that resembled sunshine. "*Phaedra, dear? Is that you?*"

A knot appeared in my throat. "Yes, Mother, it's me."

Our relationship had changed significantly in the past forty years. Something about illness threw things into perspective. After intensive therapy, I forgave my mother for many of the things she'd done to me. It wasn't healthy, I'd been told, to let the things of my past continue to affect my life now. Forgiving my mother hadn't been easy... her parenting skills were less than adequate, but we were in a better place than ever before.

On the good days.

She grinned, her wings fluttering behind her as she leaned toward the phone. "*It's so nice to hear your voice, darling. I've missed you.*"

I sucked in a breath. To hear my mother speak as though she really knew who I was, for once... it was almost too much. My throat clogged, and I hastily ran a finger beneath my eyes, hoping she didn't notice. "It's nice to see you, too."

"Why are you crying?"

Of course, my mother didn't miss a single thing. Her eyes were sharp, and she always watched me carefully. Or she had...

until the disease ate away at her mind. But now, during these so-called "good days", bits and pieces of her personality came through.

They provided hope and reminded me that beneath the confusion and forgetfulness, the loss of memory and mental jumps, my mother was somewhere in there. The woman who, for better or for worse, raised me. We might not have always gotten along—truthfully, we rarely got along—but she was still my mother. And I loved her.

I clung to moments of clarity like these. It was all I could do. The nurses at the care home assured me that my mother was well looked after. Which was good. For the price I was paying them, she shouldn't have been wanting for anything.

"Phaedra?" my mother repeated, and I realized I had drifted off into my own mind. *"What's wrong, darling? Why did you call? Don't get me wrong, I love hearing from you, but it just seems..."*

"Oh Mother," I interrupted, "I needed to talk to you."

She smiled, and instantly, a weight was lifted from my shoulders. *"Go on, darling. Tell me what's wrong."*

And so I did.

Rifling through my purse, I fished out my handkerchief once more as my tears flowed freely. Starting with the day I woke up from the coma, quit my job and broke up with Dylan, I told my mother everything that had happened to me.

When I got to the end, we both sat back. I fiddled with my handkerchief, the material now thoroughly soaked and streaked with black mascara, as my mother picked up a mug of tea and sipped her drink through a straw. When it was empty, she put the cup down and looked right at me.

"Well, darling, it certainly sounds like you have a lot going on."

I snorted. That was an understatement. A silence stretched between us, and I realized my mother was waiting for a response. "Yes," I replied after a moment. "I certainly do. The thing is,"—I looked down at my lap and twisted my fingers together, preparing to confess something I hadn't even thought about until I began talking to my mother—"I don't hate Hades for forcing me into this marriage."

"*You don't?*"

"No." I sighed. "I understand why it needs to be done. I get it. But I wish… this isn't how I had ever pictured myself getting married."

I had never really even considered marriage as an option for myself. It was something for other people. Not for me.

I just wasn't the type of person love happened to. I didn't think it was in the cards for me.

That was the biggest reason I had stayed with Dylan for all those years. Maybe our connection wasn't deep or passionate, but for many years, our relationship had been comfortable. Consistent. I didn't *need* him.

My mother's knowing eyes met mine through the FaePhone. "*You don't love him.*" It wasn't a question. She and I both knew I didn't.

"Yes," I conceded. "Hades was my boss. I never even looked at him in that way."

A long moment passed, where my mother and I just stared at each other.

"*Give the man a chance,*" Mother said.

My mouth fell open, and I blinked. That was not what I expected her to say. "What?"

"*Give him a chance,*" she repeated. "*You said you have to marry him, right?*"

Or be stripped of my power, and quite possibly, my life. It really wasn't much of a choice. "Yes."

"*Then give him a chance. This might surprise you. Just…*" My mother's eyes took on a faraway look, and a slight tremor passed over her features. My stomach clenched and my nails bit into my skin, but I still felt a stab of pain at the next words that came out of her mouth. "*Oh Clarice, there you are! I had hoped to see you...*"

She continued to speak, her voice growing in animation, and I sighed. That was it. Good days came, and good days went.

A single tear rolled down my cheek as my mother asked me —playing Clarice—about my day. I lied and told her I had spent the day at the bakery. Food was always a safe topic with my mother. She dove into talking about her favorite red velvet cakes, and I zoned out.

When Mother grew tired of talking, the nurse and I chatted for a few more minutes. He reminded me of my upcoming payment, and I assured him I would transfer the money on time.

Once we hung up, I stood and tucked in the piano bench.

It was time to go face reality. No sooner had I stood up than my phone beeped again.

It was an email with a calendar alert.

HELENA AND ERIK, ROYAL WEDDING

I sucked in a breath, and another popped up.

DRESS FITTING FOR FIRST PUBLIC APPEARANCE
WITH LORD HADES

Tapping the email with my thumb, several paragraphs of text with pictures illustrating the short black gown I was meant to wear filled the screen.

It was time to play the part of a loving fiancée.

CHAPTER 15
A WERE CONFERENCE
AIDONEUS

I was sitting in one of the ballrooms often used for conventions downtown. Two thousand native Weres were in attendance today. One of the main functions of my empire's antiquities dealing was not just to sell to the highest bidder. Any antiquities dealer could do that. No, we worked hard to give back pieces of history to the people who had their lands stolen through tragedy, time, or conquest.

At the front of the stage, one of my lead restorationists listed artifacts. There were dozens, and we were brokering their safe return.

"The history of the petrified wood amulets can be dated back one thousand years. The initials carved into them, TJS, Teotio Jorge Salvatore, date back to the mate of the revered pack leader..."

My thoughts wandered away. These meetings were always my favorite. It felt good to contribute to a better world, but today, my thoughts were swarming around me and eating up my thoughts. The reintegration of these artifacts would have to be left to my capable team.

In my front right pocket, my phone buzzed. It would be utterly inappropriate to even glance at it while I was here, so I tried to ignore it and pay attention.

Nancy, the head restorationist, was still speaking about the amulets. "Full moons were greeted with a day-long ceremony that included—"

More buzzing.

I squeezed my fingers together and refused to look. With any luck, it would be my new assistant, Saul Schnieder. The Warlock was competent, and he was an excellent choice on such short notice. Even so, he was still starting out, so the amount of questions he asked was often tedious. Not bad, just tedious. Regardless, he would need to wait.

To distract myself, I went through a list of tasks I had to complete before I finished work. Erik and Helena's wedding was right around the corner. I wanted to make things perfect for my niece and her chosen partner.

Wedding dress.

Caterer check.

Finalize payments to the venue.

Send someone to pick up the flowers.

My eyes drifted up to the ceiling, where half a dozen golden medallions were scattered throughout. Tension was tight in my chest as I thought about where I would be tomorrow.

Friday.

Friday weddings were my favorite; I had an entire weekend to recover from the party. All the attendees had a looseness about them that enlivened the air and heightened the experience with a desire to enjoy the day like it was some Fortuna-designated gift.

The day was flying by faster than I anticipated. I still needed to pick up my tux for the rehearsal dinner tonight and another for the wedding tomorrow.

Helena asked me to walk her down the aisle. The gesture touched me, and made me infinitely more excited about her wedding, but now...

Now, things were different.

I was attending the wedding with Phaedra by my side. It was going to be our presentation to the world. Cameras would flash in our faces. Every action and reaction would be scrutinized in hoards of tabloids, legitimate news sources, picturegrammers, bloggers, and even that new app my investors put money into that showed short videos.

Since we signed our prenuptial agreements, I saw Phaedra twice. The first time, she asked whether she'd be paying for her new wardrobe. I'd informed her I was paying for it all. Why wouldn't I? As far as I was concerned, Phaedra would never have to pay for another thing in her existence unless she wanted to.

The second time, she wanted to know when she was expected to move in.

That conversation was far more tense. I hoped she would have an opinion on the matter, but instead, the conversation was awkward and stinted. She left as soon as I told her it would be a good idea to at least move into the Tower as soon as word got out of our engagement. All in all, our conversation had been... cordial. I would take that over pure, unadulterated hatred any day.

"... Once again, we would like to thank the DemiGod with a singular gift for finding talented professionals and throwing money at them, King Hades," Nancy said, gesturing toward me.

With stiff motions, I stood straight and waved as the room applauded.

"When are you going to pick a wife?" one of the women yelled.

My smile froze in place as a few more cheered.

"Will we see a Were married to his Royal Highness?" another shouted, and the room laughed.

"What about the war?"

A rock plopped in the bottom of my stomach, but I stepped forward, angling my body toward the podium. Nancy stepped aside, and I quickly adjusted the level of the small microphone to my height.

"Thank you all for your kindness in coming here today. I don't know if my upcoming nuptials rank as highly as seeing a unified people from all corners of Aranthium." I smiled, pausing for effect, feeling the crowd go quiet. "There are many things that are happening now which are so good. The world is a place worth fighting for. Rest assured that we are doing all we can to create an army strong enough to destroy King Phelix."

The room was completely silent and I could tell they were hanging on my every word. These people had suffered a lot. The Were people were once little more than thralls to their Vampire neighbors. Not only had they lost so many of their kind, they had also lost their history.

Vampires understood what many others did not. Truly conquering a people was not solely about massacring the majority. It was about taking away their culture. Destroying it, outlawing it, shaming it. Without reminders of what made a people unique, it was easy to make them believe they were whatever reductionist version of themselves oppressors created.

Recent Ice Mer attacks on the Were Territory shore had tensions running high.

These people deserved so much more than mere amulets. They deserved hope and peace.

"I promise, you will not find yourselves forced to bow before another. Your pack leaders do not need to tie themselves to me in order to become the powerful group of Weres they once were." I thought over my next words carefully. This information wasn't released yet. We weren't supposed to announce any formal engagement until tomorrow.

But... seeing these faces, those who it was my duty to protect from my brother, I wanted to give them more.

"I would appreciate it if the cameras stopped rolling for a moment," I said, holding up my hands. One by one, cameras blinked out while the room filled with whispers. "My partner has been chosen, and a wedding date has been selected. When you see the news, and find out who it is, please keep in mind that the power that will result from our union will finally bring in a new era of peace."

As soon as the words were out, there was silence. No whispers, no claps. It wasn't a malicious silence, just a curious one. My throat had become thicker with each syllable. It was true. What Phaedra and I would create would be legendary, now that she was showing signs of increased power.

But ours would be a union without love. That thought had my chest squeezing and my eyes burning.

Thousands of faces looked up to me, all of them bearing the same fur patterns as other Were, and I felt the weight of their people.

It wasn't like I forgot my duty, but mine and Phaedra's reign would not stop at Lethe.

I leaned in. "Once more, I would like to tell you all thank you. Please know that every single one of you is invited to my niece's wedding. I hope you have a wonderful rest of the weekend."

I took a step back and saw the open smiles of everyone else on the stage. The room around us broke into a slow applause, and I waved once more.

Then my pocket started buzzing again.

My teeth ground together, and I started making my way off the stage. With the closing remarks finished, I could finally see what the emergency was. I made my way down the stage, fully intending to go through the crowd to exit.

Behind me, Toth'toros and another guard were trailing closely. Together we neared the tables, and I was bombarded with outstretched hands.

I shook and shook and shook until I couldn't feel my right hand.

"Do you really mean I can come to Princess Helena's wedding?" a Were man asked. I looked at him and nodded.

"Of course," I said.

He grinned and added a bit more steel to his handshake.

I was asked a similar variation of that question at least twenty times more before I reached the doors.

Out in the enormous hallway, I took a deep breath and pulled out my phone.

2 MISSED CALLS FROM PHAEDRA DEMTRE
3 MISSED CALLS FROM HELENA, NIECE
7 MISSED CALLS FROM RAPHAEL ZEUS

Then came the text messages.

Helena, Niece: YOU ARE MARRYING PHAEDRA?

I groaned.

Raphael Zeus: Aidy, stop ignoring me. Do you even know how much schmoozing I had to do with the Spring Mer court? If you picked a wife, you need to call me ASAP.

"Hard pass," I mumbled. Raphael didn't care about me, and I was fairly certain his form of 'schmoozing' consisted of him sleeping with some foreign dignitary.

Helena, Niece: IS SHE GOING TO BE YOUR PLUS ONE? YOU HAD BETTER BRING HER TO THE DINNER TONIGHT OR I WILL NEVER FORGIVE YOU.

I took a deep breath and texted her back.

Me: Excuse me, but I believe you already invited her. Also, how do you know?

The message was seen in seconds, and Helena's first reply was a screenshot of a news article.

High King Hades announces that his new wife has been chosen and will appear at the royal wedding. As of now, none of Lord Hades' previous candidates are in Lethe…

I groaned. Of course, it didn't matter that we stopped the cameras.

Just as soon as I started to respond, another call came through.

PHAEDRA DEMTRE

I stared at the name.

Even the shape of the letters were pretty. My thumb pressed the answer button.

"Hello?" I said.

"*I thought we weren't supposed to tell anyone about the engagement until tomorrow.*" Phaedra's clipped voice was like a jagged icicle.

I dragged a hand along my face. "Look, it's not like I had a press conference. I was just at—"

"*—The Were artifact conference. Same difference, you enormous asshole. The bloggers, Hades. You really thought that just because your* *cameras stopped rolling, everyone else's did?"* she huffed from the other end.

I absentmindedly turned around in a circle, glimpsing my bodyguards who were ushering me to a more private corner as some of the participants started to leave. "I know, I know. But I didn't mention you by name. And what does it matter? After tomorrow, the world will know anyway."

Silence came from the other end.

"Phaedra?" I asked.

I could hear her moving around. *"Look, I get it. This is going to be big news. But... Gods, I just wish you'd given me a heads up."*

I shifted my weight to one foot. "I'm sorry, you're right. But you are going to need to get used to being in the limelight. Also, Helena messaged me. She wants us to sit together at dinner tonight." She hadn't explicitly told me that, but I'm sure she would have if I'd texted her back.

My muscles twitched. Did I just ask Phaedra on a date? This would be the first time *I* was inviting someone on a date since... since Miranda. I hadn't scheduled any of my rendezvous with the other women. The thought should have left me feeling conflicted, but it just felt oddly right. Excited, almost.

Phaedra huffed into the phone. I had never been more jealous of an object simply because it got to feel her warmth. Her voice grew deeper, intending to be menacing, but all it was doing was making my blood rush through my veins. *"Fine,* Aidoneus. *But give me a heads up next time, or I'm going to make you regret it."*

My eyebrows shot up. A strange thrill shot through me at the use of my first name, even if it was coated in acid. Where did that come from? Threats? From little miss sunshine? "Oh? What could you possibly threaten the DemiGod of the Dead with?" My heart pounded in my chest.

"I think it's best you never find out," she said and hung up.

I was left there, standing stupidly in a corner while I tried to catch my breath.

Fortuna, what was I going to do once we were actually married?

I looked down at my phone and opened my messages. I needed to send one more message.

> Me: Raphael, the person I marry is none of your concern, despite your constant meddling. We both have a lot on our plates. How about this? You call me if there's a real emergency and I'll do the same.

The read receipt came on almost instantly. My brother was careless on his best days. He was barely a competent leader—petty, unorganized, and incapable of putting anything other than himself first.

Our relationship did not include friendship. I'd been burned by him too many times.

He didn't respond.

Every two years, we held Olimpie Games in a different destination around the world. It was a childhood tradition I shared with Raphael–Phelix had been too young to participate, and, frankly, he never showed much interest. Perhaps that helped him harbor more bitterness, but that was completely self imposed. When it was Lethe's turn to host, we built an enormous center with large pools.

Ever the visionary, I decided to keep the pools decorative, instead of just long rectangles. A small voice inside of me nagged me to do it. I wasn't clear as to exactly why, until Helena chose it as her wedding destination. Over the course of the last week, we froze off sections of the pools to take down the room temperature and give homage to the Ice Mer culture.

Helena grinned from ear to ear when she saw the finished product. It took a small miracle to figure out how to keep the room warm enough for our guests without melting the ice, but what good was a DemiGod if he couldn't perform a few tricks?

I walked into the enormous room that was stuffed with purple, white, and blue flowers—the colors of Erik's and Helena's wedding.

A long table was laid out with seventeen place settings. No one else was here yet, and in my hand I held Helena's completed dress. Casually, I took a stroll around the place settings. Handwritten name cards with Helena's distinctive handwriting sat at each place. I smiled, seeing ones for the Winter Court Queen and her family, as I remembered the little toddler with a penchant for destruction.

I stopped when I reached the end of the table.

Uncle Aidoneus

Then I picked up the card next to mine.

"Aunt" Phaedra

I froze. What did Helena think of all of this? I swallowed twice, trying to wet my throat. Phaedra and I weren't being deceptive, per se. But it felt like it. Slowly, I replaced the plaque on the silver-trimmed plate.

"You said 6:30 in your *email*. So, where is everyone?" a cool feminine voice said behind me.

I whipped around, and all the words in my head flew out of my mind, evaporating in the flower-perfumed air.

Phaedra was wearing a dress. I mean, that wasn't shocking. I was in a suit—this was a rehearsal dinner, after all.

But she... she looked like...

I didn't let myself finish the sentence. The dress had long sleeves which gently hugged her narrow wrists, a square neckline, and it ended just after her knees. Her stunning, multicolored wings framed her petite form. Tall, pointed black heels were strapped onto her small feet. The cut of the dress seemed to meld itself perfectly against her form, creating a silky second skin. A black second-skin, like a Selkie.

My eyes traced the lines of her, and then halted.

She was a forbidden fruit.

"So," Phaedra said again, clearly irritated. "Where is everyone?" She crossed her arms, emphasizing her full breasts.

I swallowed *again*. "I-I wanted to talk to you before everyone else got here," I rasped as I walked toward her. I set the wedding dress down on a table which I assumed would be used for gifts. The closer I drew to Phaedra, the more that springtime scent invaded my nostrils. I had to keep my eyes from rolling back in my head from pleasure.

Her pink mouth was fixed in a straight line. "So you do know how to communicate in different ways than an email?" she asked dryly.

My brows knit together. "What's wrong with emails?"

Phaedra let out an exasperated sound. "Never mind. I'm here, so talk."

I rolled my shoulders back. "I wanted to apologize again for not letting you know I would bring up our engagement, even if I did it inadvertently. Truly, I hadn't planned it."

She breathed in deeply. "I know."

I dared take another step forward. "Look, the next few days are only going to get worse. Are you prepared for that?"

She unfolded her arms and squared her shoulders, though she didn't quite meet my eyes. "Yes, sir, I get it."

Hot anger broiled inside of me. "Cut out that 'sir' shit. I never asked you to do that, not even once."

She raised one black eyebrow. "Oh? I may be engaged to you now, but once upon a time I was 'just an employee'."

Now I really was confused. "What are you—"

"Phaedra!" my niece screamed, and the Angel whipped around.

My future bride was seconds away from being drenched by Helena's aqua chair. My hand hovered over her waist. I wondered if I should hold her back, but I quickly decided against it.

"No legs today?" Phaedra asked.

Helena shrugged. "Well, I'm going to be signing the vows tomorrow. I figured you all could deal with my loudness for one more night before I enslave Erik for all of eternity." Said fiancée appeared the second that Helena started to laugh like a cheesy villain in some low-budget soap opera.

I smiled. It made me happy to see them all together.

That same feeling of *rightness* washed over me again.

It coated my insides and made me feel light. I was floating. After I greeted Erik and the thirteen other guests, I practiced walking alongside Helena as she rolled down the aisle. The entire night, I didn't let myself frown. Not once.

Not when I caught Phaedra staring at us before Fortuna's altar.

I didn't even feel a little bad when I sat next to her, eating in relative silence.

She fit here, and even if she didn't love me, this union was going to be good for all of us. Families could come in many different shapes and sizes—ours was unique. One day, Phaedra wouldn't hate me.

Hopefully.

Helena looked right at Phaedra and I from the other end of the table. She raised a glass and swayed a little. "Don't think you two are free from interrogation, you know. Erik brought a knife for me just in case I need to shank one of you," she slurred.

I chuckled nervously, but Phaedra laughed like it was nothing. My future bride raised her glass with her left hand and said, "I'll cheer for a man who holds his wife's weapons." An expert deflection.

A round of laughter broke around the table as we all cheered. Nathaniel nudged Erik suggestively in the ribs. My eyes sought out Phaedra, even though she didn't so much as look at me.

My heart pounded in my chest and my hands broke out in a sweat as I leaned over. "If you dress like that during your reign, I will gladly hold any weapon you want," I said quietly.

If she heard, she didn't show it. My attempts at flirtation were instantly squashed.

"Helena, put your glass down before you break it," Queen Elva said loudly. I glanced up to see that Helena's crystal champagne flute was still high in the air. Her expression was fuzzy with intoxication.

Everyone laughed again.

I smiled to be sure, but my eyes caught on Phaedra's empty ring finger glaring up at me.

The gears in my ancient mind started turning as I soaked up the first of many nights with my new family.

CHAPTER 16
FOR THE LOVE OF MAGIC
PHAEDRA

"Are you ready for this?" Karina stood on my right-hand side with a hot curling iron as she applied the finishing touches to my hair. She was quiet, for the most part, which I appreciated. Karina was many things, but quiet wasn't usually one of them. But right now, she seemed to sense I needed these last few minutes of peace to gather my thoughts.

I couldn't stop looking at the altar during last night's rehearsal dinner. Soon—too soon, as far as I was concerned—I would be standing up there and reciting my own vows. I kept myself together during the entire dinner, but once I came home, the shock set in. I took a long shower, only letting the stress-induced tears flow once I was under the water.

The water turned cold before I ran out of tears.

"Phaedra?" she repeated.

"Hmm?" I fiddled with the sleeve of my black silk robe. "I'm sorry. What was that?"

Karina stood before me, her hair in a messy bun as she

fiddled with mine. Even wearing a worn t-shirt and faded blue jeans, my friend still looked incredibly put-together.

I was still having trouble believing this was happening. I barely slept the past few nights, between the fear of having my powers go out of control again at the worst possible moment and dread of my upcoming nuptials. My stomach was churning, and I could barely eat anything this morning.

Karina pulled my hair away from the curling iron and raised a brow. "I asked if you're ready?"

Drawing in a deep breath, I nodded. "Yes, sorry. I was just lost in thought."

She chuckled. "I don't blame you." She sighed, the sound blissful as she fluttered her eyelashes. "If I were marrying King Hades, I would be lost in thought, too."

My friend picked up another section of hair, and I studied her through the mirror. At least one of us was happy about my upcoming wedding. I was with Karina when Hades let the news slip about our marriage. To say that she was thrilled would have been an understatement.

In fact, I believe her exact words were something along the lines of a high-pitched squeal followed by, "I knew it, I knew it, I knew it!"

Karina dropped her phone on the floor, falling on the couch dramatically as she threw her hand onto her forehead. "An age gap office romance." She sighed. "How romantic!"

Did I mention that Karina enjoyed reading romance novels? Based on the very dramatic scene she proceeded to have in my living room, she read one too many of late.

Imagine how she would have reacted if she knew it was an arranged marriage.

She probably would have a heart attack.

After a few minutes passed, she sat back up. Her black eyes were bright as they pinned mine.

"Tell. Me. Everything." Karina's voice had brokered no room for discussion.

I had told her... as much as I could. Leaving out the part where Hades was marrying me for convenience and nothing else, I explained what happened.

When I finished, Karina declared herself my personal stylist for Erik and Helena's wedding. "It's your first official appearance as the queen consort-to-be," she had said. "You need help."

Despite my numerous protests, she insisted.

And so, here we were.

Pursing her lips, Karina put the curling iron on the countertop and put her hands on her hips. She walked around me, avoiding touching my wings, as she moved my hair around my head. I couldn't see myself, but I knew Karina was talented. Whatever she was doing, it was sure to be good.

When she completed a turn around me, she nodded. "Perfect." Reaching over, Karina grabbed a bottle of hairspray. "Now, close your eyes. The last thing you need is some of this in your eyes."

I complied, and within moments, the acrid scent of hairspray filled the bathroom. Karina hummed to herself, patting my hair a few moments longer before stepping back. The chair turned beneath me, and Karina made a satisfied sound. "There. You can open your eyes."

My mouth fell into an "O" as I looked at myself in the mirror. Good didn't begin to cover it. She had done something with my hair, giving it life. It was curled and pinned around my head, with loose tendrils framing my face. It was elegant but somehow managed to be effortless at the same time.

"Wow," I managed to say.

Karina chuckled. "I hope that means you like it."

I stood, wrapping my arms around her. "I love it. Thank you."

She grinned. "You're welcome. Now, let's finish getting you ready. The King will be waiting for you."

PACING INSIDE MY APARTMENT, I fidgeted with the knee-length hem of my dress. Aidoneus insisted I move out of my apartment sooner rather than later, but I told him I wasn't ready yet.

I needed some time to pack. To get ready.

Some time to convince myself I was really doing this. I had never considered myself nervous, but right now, my stomach was in knots. All the water I had nursed for the past few minutes threatened to come up. This was it. After today, there was no turning back.

We were going to make things official and go public at the wedding.

I was just about to run into the bathroom and lose the contents of my stomach when my FaePhone vibrated in my hand. Glancing down, I read the message quickly.

Aidoneus Hades

I'm on my way up.

He insisted that we needed to arrive at the wedding "in style," so he was picking me up in a limo. This was a far cry from my preferred mode of transportation (flying), but when I'd suggested I could just meet him there, the lights had flickered around the king, and shadows had gathered around him.

I'd quickly abandoned that train of thought. The last thing I needed to do right now was make a DemiGod angry. I wasn't sure what triggered my own magic, but I didn't want to find out.

Slipping my phone into my purse, I took a deep breath and straightened my back.

"You can do this, Phae," I said. "Just ignore the press like you always do."

This wasn't going to be my first time in front of the paparazzi. One couldn't work as closely as I did with the king and not be exposed to the circus that was the media in Aranthium.

But being exposed to the media and being the object of their attention were two different things.

I would be the perfect wife for the cameras. I'd say the right things, act the right way, and be the queen consort the press wanted to see. In public.

And in private, Hades would let me live my own life. A marriage in name only. He'd assured me of that.

So why did I feel so nervous? Why did butterflies appear in my stomach when a knock rang through my small apartment?

I peeked through the small hole in the door. On the other side of the door, my fiancé stood with his arms behind his back. He was dressed in all black except for the tie around his neck.

It was blue, just like my eyes.

This was it.

He raised a fist to knock again, but I swung the door open before he could.

"Hi," I said.

His jaw fell open. "Phaedra," he said, his eyes roaming all over me. "That dress is... you look... wow. You're beautiful."

His words made my stomach twist, but not in an unwelcome way. It had been a long time since anyone had called me beautiful and meant it. Dylan wasn't exactly one for words of affection.

"Thank you." My lips tilted up as I gestured to my dress. "Do you like it?"

"I... yes." He swallowed, his eyes darkening. He paused for a moment, clearing his throat. "The dress is perfect. You look like a queen."

He pulled his arm out from behind him, and I gasped.

"You brought me something? You didn't have to do that."

Especially since I didn't bring him anything. My eyes widened, and I opened my mouth to refuse the gift when he shook his head. "Please, it's nothing."

"It doesn't look like 'nothing'. It looks like a gift."

He pursed his lips. "And that would be a problem?"

"Yes," I replied instantly. "Seeing as how I don't want a gift from you."

"Okay, then. It's not a gift."

"A vase filled with roses isn't a gift?"

He shook his head. "No."

I narrowed my eyes. It looked like a gift. It felt like a gift. And that was explicitly something I *did not* want from Hades right now. "Then what is it?"

"It's a peace offering," he said. "A replacement, if you will. For the one you broke when you threw it at me in my office."

He remembered.

That meant something to me. I wasn't sure what, but before I could dive more deeply into the thoughts, Aidoneus walked around me. He placed the vase on the side table by the door before offering me his arm.

After a moment's hesitation, I slid my hand into the crook of his elbow.

He stared at the place where our bodies touched for a moment before clearing his throat. "Come. Our chariot awaits."

CHARIOT WAS, somehow, an understatement. Leave it to the King of the Daemons to have access to a vehicle like this. We were standing in the parking garage beneath my apartment building, staring at the monstrosity Aidoneus brought with him. I'd never seen it before in all my years working for him.

The stretch limo was more like an armored truck than anything else. An armored truck that probably cost ten times my yearly salary.

Toth'toros was sitting in the driver's seat, his familiar black glasses resting on his face. He met my gaze, nodding at me before returning his attention to the phone he held in his grip.

I turned and looked at Aidoneus. "This is... overkill, isn't it?" Those butterflies made their presence known in my stomach again, but this time they were definitely more of the nervous-variety. "Why can't we just show up in something a little less..."

"Large?" he offered.

I narrowed my eyes. "Ostentatious."

"Phaedra, I'm the king," he explained patiently. "And you're my fiancé. We need to arrive in the appropriate manner. Glamor and luxury are important."

To go in this... it was making a statement. Until this moment, I hadn't fully grasped the enormity of what I would do.

There would be no going back. No matter what, the moment I stepped into this vehicle, my life would be irrevocably changed.

My heart raced, and my hands grew clammy. Everything seemed far away, and my eyes pinched in the corners. Breathing, which was something I had always thought was a natural, normal thing to do, suddenly required thought.

"Phaedra?" Hades' voice sounded like it was underwater.

"I don't..." I mumbled, just as a flash of blue light erupted out of me. Above us, a dozen *pops* rang out over the ceiling.

"Shit," Hades cursed. Large hands landed on my shoulders,

pushing me down just as a shield of green magic erupted over us. Seconds later, glass rained down.

The moment the deadly rain stopped falling, the shield dissolved into thick green smoke.

An awkward silence filled the air as Hades stared at me. His gaze was assessing, sweeping over me. "Are you all right?"

"I... I think so."

My heart was beating normally now, and I could hear again. Looking up, my eyes widened. The entire parking garage was destroyed. Other vehicles that had the misfortune of being parked down here had shards of glass sticking out of their windshields, and red emergency lights were flashing everywhere. Of all the vehicles, the only one that remained in one piece was the limo.

The rest of the parking garage looked like a war zone. But there were no soldiers, no massive machines of destruction.

This was all me.

How was I going to pay for all this? I managed to open my mouth, my eyes wide as words began slipping out of my mouth. "I... the money... Oh, my gods."

Tears welled in my eyes, and I forced myself to take a deep breath. I could not cry. Not right now. Not with a face full of makeup and a wedding to attend.

I felt myself falling into a pit of panic, my hands growing clammy once more, when Aidoneus' warm hand landed on my bare arm. His touch grounded me in a way I was unprepared to dissect. "Phaedra, look at me."

It took me a moment, but I dragged my gaze away from the destruction I'd caused to him.

"It's okay," he said. "I'll pay for it. Don't worry."

Don't worry? I was beginning to do just that when a car door slammed. Aidoneus looked over his shoulder at the suit-clad Daemon who emerged from the vehicle.

"I called for another ride, boss," Toth'toros said, eyeing the glass warily as he leaned against the vehicle. "It'll be here in five minutes."

"Good call," Aidoneus said, returning his gaze to me. His voice was almost gentle as he said, "Now, do you see why we need to do this?"

I nodded. "Yes. I understand."

The problem was, I did understand. Wherever this excess of power came from, it clearly wasn't going away. I had to learn to control it before it controlled me.

Nodding, Aidoneus pulled out his phone. He pressed a few buttons, holding the phone to his ear.

"Hello, Saul. You have to come into the office." He listened for a few moments before continuing. "All right, here's what I need you to do. Find out who owns the building..."

He walked away, his voice quieting as he cleaned up my mess.

By the time our new ride appeared, I was exhausted. Every limb was heavy, and my head pounded. We hadn't even arrived at the wedding yet. I climbed into the vehicle, buckling up my seatbelt before leaning my head against the window.

As Toth'toros started the car, I drew in a deep breath.

When the car door opened, I would no longer just be Phaedra Demtre.

I would be Phaedra, wife-to-be of Lord Aidoneus Hades. King of the Daemons. And I was beginning to believe I was way over my head.

CHAPTER 17
A WEDDING FOR THE AGES
AIDONEUS

The wedding was scheduled for 8:00 p.m., but since I was playing the part of the father of the bride, Phaedra and I needed to arrive at 6:45 p.m. to ensure all final details were taken care of.

I wasn't worried. My staff was extremely competent and used to taking care of much bigger problems than a wedding. When I checked on them this morning, everything was in order.

However, my thousands of years taught me that disaster-level problems arose at the last minute. My people planned for those, and they made sure that contingency plans were in place. Many things could go wrong, and they ranged from not having enough seats to someone unexpectedly showing up and causing a scene.

In my opinion, the worst-case scenario was the possibility of one of Phelix's soldiers showing up and disrupting the ceremony. I tripled the security at the wedding, just in case.

But somehow, I hadn't anticipated *this*.

Phaedra blowing up an entire level of a parking garage had not been in the plans. Granted, it was small, but... damn.

That set us back thirty minutes, and I shifted in my seat. As far as I was concerned, tardiness was never acceptable.

Phaedra sat across from me in a much smaller limo than the one I'd originally come to get her in. Her arms were crossed while she stared out the window, her face frozen in a state of beautiful melancholy. I didn't know what to say to her, and she hadn't spoken a word to me since she'd climbed into the car.

She was wearing black again, the color of my kingdom. But it wasn't just black. The dress I'd bought for her was obsidian. It looked black to the untrained eye, but anyone with exquisite taste—or godly power—could see the faint shimmery lines of gold that cinched her small waist and created interesting patterns all over her body.

Shining dust was painted on her cheeks, and a creative kohl line made her upturned eyes more dramatic.

Phaedra could be the subject of painting—in fact, she would be. I'd have one of the restorationists commissioned to paint her and hang it up in every art gallery around town. I hadn't told her yet. I was hoping this anger she held toward me would thaw in time. A man could hope.

We were getting closer to the wedding venue, and I wracked my brain to try to find words to say. Something. Anything to get her to look at me. Even though my mind was blank, I decided to try. Doing what I did best, I opened my mouth and hoped the words would come.

"Phaedra," I said quietly.

She didn't look at me, but she made a sound that she heard me.

"The parking garage will be resolved without any problems. I put my new assistant on it, and he's very good," I said. So far, so good.

Phaedra still didn't look at me but quietly said, "Thank you."

I rubbed my hands on my thighs. "You're welcome." And just

like that, everything came back to a crashing halt. Awkward silence filled the vehicle once more.

I tapped my fingers on my kneecaps, studying the marbled bits of my skin. I hadn't always been marred like this. The marble markings on my skin reminded me that I wasn't a quitter. I could have just stopped after I lost Miranda. But instead, I kept going.

Sucking in a sharp breath, I waited another minute before I said, "We need to talk about your training. Are you going to be all right at the wedding tonight?"

Easy, Aidoneus. I winced at the rough tone of my voice. It was far harsher than I intended.

Fortunately—or unfortunately—that got her attention. The melancholy melted away as she sent me a scathing look. "Yes," she said flatly.

I let out a sigh. "I think... that you need to move in tomorrow morning."

She opened her mouth, but I was faster. "And we'll start training as soon as the movers grab your stuff."

"You're going to stop right there, Mr. Bossy," Phaedra demanded, her voice no longer passive as she put her hands up. "You don't get to tell me how to run my life just because you're going to be my husband."

My skin heated. I didn't want her to be mad, but we had crossed a dangerous line in that garage. Things were more serious than I had expected. My voice was loud as I snapped, "I am going to tell you what to do until you stop stealing dresses and blowing things up every time you see my face!"

The look she gave me was full of stubborn resolve. Her lips were pinched, and her eyes narrowed. A faint blue glow pulsed in her irises.

"Seriously?" she ground out through clenched teeth. "You're going to throw the explosion in my face? It was an accident."

An accident that could have hurt people. Surely, she knew that.

"Phaedra, I know you realize the benefit of training. It did you good all those years ago when you first took self-defense classes," I said gently. She glared at me, raising a brow. When she didn't respond, I added, "I'm sorry I raised my voice."

Her expression didn't change, and we fell back into silence. Just then, the limo stopped. Even through the deep tint of the windows, camera flashes were visible. Only a few seconds had passed when the door on the right side popped open, and the blinding flashes grew irritating.

An artificial lightning storm was waiting for us. I slid my long legs out first before holding my hand to Phaedra. She stared at it as if I were some monster from the depths of Aranthium.

She had reasons to be afraid of me, but this refusal didn't seem to be about fear. This was about defiance.

Cameras flashed, and beads of sweat prickled the back of my neck.

"King Hades!" one reporter shouted.

"Come on, move aside so we can see your lovely bride!" another called.

The bride-to-be in question was immobile, still veiled by darkness.

"Phaedra," I said gently. Her eyes jumped from the open door to mine. Apprehension was painted on her face, and instantly, compassion filled me for this Angel who had agreed to be my wife. She didn't ask for any of this, and here I was, dragging her in front of the wolves.

I regretted being so frustrated before, but the magnitude of the situation was ulcer-inducing.

"I promise not to bring up anything else tonight. It will be all right," I said gently, just as another reporter called, "Let us meet our future queen!"

She swallowed hard, her eyes studying mine. "Promise?" she whispered so only I could hear.

"Yes. I've got you."

I will always protect you, I added silently.

She studied me before slowly scooting over and taking my hand. Her palm was clammy, and her fingers trembled in mine.

All the tension from earlier evaporated as my senses honed in on that slight tremor. Every instinct hummed: *protect her.*

Phaedra took her first step out of the car. The incessant shouting of the reporters grew louder, the flashes coming faster. As soon as she was all the way out, I pulled her close to my side. I could feel time passing without looking at my watch, and we needed to get inside. Foreign dignitaries were everywhere, but there wouldn't be time for introductions and salutations until later.

Urgency hummed beneath my skin. We needed to move. Out of nowhere, Saul appeared. His white hair was styled with short spikes, and he held a leather planner to his chest.

When had he gotten here? And why wasn't he taking care of the parking garage? I glared at him with as much heat as I could muster with all those faces on us.

He stopped a few feet away. "Sir, you need to be closer to each other. They are asking for photos of you two acting more... naturally."

An electric current ran through my body at the thought of drawing Phaedra closer to me.

I took a step closer to Phaedra, but she stared straight ahead. Her lips were drawn in a tight, strained smile.

"Phaedra," I murmured, slowly wrapping my arm around her waist. The movement was gentle, and the silky fabric whispered forbidden words as my hand slid across it. I pulled her close, and she looked up at me. I leaned close and whispered against her ear, "Pretend you like me. Please."

Her eyes were wide for a moment, the smile was replaced with a look of surprise. Her lips parted as she looked up at me, and my heart did a strange flip. I couldn't fake the smile that came on my face or the pleasure from having her close.

I'd spent so many years with her nearby, and never once had I touched her this way. We were trapped in each other's eyes for a small eternity.

"That's perfect," Saul said, and then we started moving. With gentle pressure, I pushed on the small of Phaedra's back.

I leaned in close, unwilling to give up the closeness. "Sorry about all the touching, but we have to look good for the pictures."

Phaedra didn't say anything. She just kept that tight smile on her face and walked up the carpeted walkway.

During the five minutes we spent taking pictures, I drowned out most of the paparazzi's obnoxious comments. This was normal for me.

One of the reporters asked, "Who are you wearing?"

Phaedra glanced up at me, her step faltering. Her eyes were wide, like a deer being hunted.

"You don't have to answer them unless you want to," I assured her.

She nodded, the lines around her mouth tightening, and we kept going.

Just as we neared the entrance framed by an arch of purple and blue flowers, one of the bolder reporters asked, "Hades, was there a secret office romance leading up to this?"

Several of the reporters around him laughed.

I stopped dead in my tracks, releasing my grip on Phaedra. My power snapped outward like a rubber band, and the reporter was Transposed from his spot with the others to the space right in front of me with the flick of a finger.

The Vampire's expression went from sarcastic to terrified in a second.

I looked down at the man. He was a whole head shorter than me. My power rumbled in the earth below, and the sun dipped into the horizon faster than it was supposed to. Several people screamed, and a car alarm went off in the distance.

Shadows gathered around the man, and his face went even paler than it normally was. "I'm sorry, sir. I didn't mean—"

I snarled, "Yes, I'm sure you regret it now."

A long moment passed. I stared at him, and he quivered. His fangs *shook* as he drew his lip through his teeth.

Then, a small hand landed on my arm.

"Aidoneus," Phaedra said, clasping my arm. That movement, her touch, brought me back to myself from the boiling anger in my blood.

I studied the Vampire's face, barely noticing that all the other reporters had fallen silent. "It's easy to make comments when you are behind that velvet rope." Lowering my voice so only he could hear, I growled, "You will speak to my fiancée with respect, or you will not speak at all."

He nodded quickly.

I Transposed him back with a snap.

Phaedra didn't say anything else, but she sagged slightly against me as we walked into the venue. The wedding planner, an eccentric Summer Fae named Cassandra with her hair in two neon pink buns, rushed toward us. She took small, rapid steps in her too-tight pencil skirt and six-inch heels.

"Your Highness," Cassandra chirped. She grabbed my forearm and started tugging me with her long, bejeweled nails. "You're late. We need to get you into makeup."

I coughed. "Makeup?" I looked back at Phaedra, who had gone back to crossing her arms while she stood there alone. I didn't like the sight at all.

The wedding planner clicked her tongue. "Come on, it's just powder to ensure you're not shiny for the camera."

I dug my feet in. "I am sure that I am not shiny."

The Fae looked at me with a dubious expression.

I swear, Summer Fae. Every last one of them has a flair for the dramatic.

At last, she said, "Fine, go back to your date and walk her to your seat. But you need to be in place in five minutes, or I will personally hunt you down again." With that, the wedding planner left, her heels clacking on the marble floors.

I crossed back to Phaedra's side. "It's almost time. Can I walk you to your seat?"

I held out my arm for her to take. She glared at it for a very long moment before moving forward.

I guess that's a no.

I hurried to catch up to her, and we walked side by side into the enormous hall lined with flowers. Beside me, Phaedra sucked in a breath. I glanced at her, the thought of weddings heavy in my mind. "Do you... do you want something like this?"

The wedding planner might have been verging on the brink of insanity, but this place looked beautiful. Ice coated the floor. It had been sculpted to look like gentle waves, and foam was just under our feet. Small arctic fish had been placed in spheres of ice filled with water that floated through the room.

The sea was all around us in the form of sculptures, shells, colors, and smells.

Phaedra's eyes flicked to mine, and then her face clouded. "I don't know. I never thought about my wedding," she said quickly, and then we continued walking.

Never? I wondered if that was true or if she didn't want to tell me. I mean, she had probably told Dylan all about her wedding dreams.

I hated that male with every fiber of my being. I hated him

for all the pieces of my future wife he'd gotten to hold. Her dreams. Her thoughts. Moments of her life.

I hated him because Phaedra had been in love with him.

Before I could linger on that depressing train of thought, we reached the sections that were closed off for special guests. On the bride's side was my seat, right beside Phaedra's. My fiancée sat, picking up the luxurious faux mink that had been laid out lest the guests get cold. As soon as Phaedra was seated, ushers let in hoards of guests.

Dignitaries from all over the world made their way in and sat in their assigned seats. I recognized some of them from my arranged dates, though Delphina De La Mar was notably absent. Her cousin, the heir to the throne, came in and gave us a terse nod before taking his seat.

The few Vampires that had responded to the invitations sat in the back, while several of the Were pack leaders from the conference were as far away from them as possible. Fae council members were everywhere, and the swamp witches came wearing fish-skin dresses.

Queen Isolde was one of the few who actually came up to speak to me before the ceremony started. She dipped her head, and I looked over her shoulder at the other witches who had opted to sit down instead of following her up.

"King," she said, and then her eyes went to Phaedra at my side. "You found a bride that does not mind you having no kids." I froze, and beside me, a chair scraped.

Phaedra stood up as every inch of my skin burned. I wanted to make Isolde go literally anywhere else. *What the hell, witch?*

I took a deep breath. What if Phaedra didn't really understand her meaning? Technically, what Isolde had said might not be interpreted as my sterility. It wasn't as though my condition was widely broadcast.

My fiancée looked at me curiously and then back at the

women. "Yes," she said simply. Then she held out her hand. "I am Phaedra, Your Highness." The Angel was all business, like the days when she worked for me.

Isolde nodded once more, taking Phaedra's hand and shaking it. "Good. You are a good match."

Phaedra smiled. "One might say that."

My eyes flicked to my fiancée. I *might say that.*

"Thank you for coming to the ceremony," I said to the queen.

"It is very pretty but too cold. I worry for those fish." The witch eyed the ice globes.

"I assure you, no harm will come to them," I said, placing my hand over my heart.

"Good." Her gaze returned to Phaedra. "I see power around you. It makes the air hazy. You are the right one."

Phaedra tilted her head to the side, and my eyebrows went up.

"Thank you," Phaedra said slowly.

Moments later, Isolde turned and left without a goodbye. We both watched her walk away.

"I don't think I ever met her," Phaedra started.

My skin heated, and my stomach twisted in a knot. "We met while you were... Anyway, she and I..." Gods, I was making this awkward.

Phaedra pursed her lips, and understanding came. "You dated her," she said finally. Her voice was flat.

"I wouldn't say dated," I started, but the lights started flashing. Like a proper production, a pre-recorded voice came over the speakers.

"To our esteemed guests from around Aranthium, we cordially welcome you to the royal wedding. The ceremony will begin in five minutes, so please take your seats."

The voice belonged to Helena, and I smiled.

Phaedra sat back down and drew the mink around her legs.

She looked to the altar at the front of the room, where a priestess just took her place to perform the ceremony.

Unsure of what to do, I quickly said, "I'll be right back."

Phaedra nodded but didn't respond.

I walked down the aisle to where a faint X was marked in the ice. Standing there, I waved at the groom, Erik, just as he took his place at the front of the room. The pirate looked like a deer in the headlights.

I stood at the start of the aisle for a few minutes, and then the lights dimmed permanently. A few people still shifted in their modern velvet chairs with silver legs, but most of the commotion of six hundred people sitting down had faded away.

An ethereal wave of music started pouring into the space. It was some strange child of gothic rock and ambient sound—Helena definitely picked it out. It had a heavenly quality, and the melody was languid and delicate. When I asked her about it, Helena described it as sounding like what the surface air tasted like.

The aisle was mesmerizing. Currently, it was a salt pool filled with euphotic plants like seagrass and multi-colored algae. Soft lights focused on the space at the beginning of the processional. The rays of illumination skirted past me and focused on the precious little Winter Court princess making her way down the row.

Elva and Nathaniel's child, Taneisha, was barely able to walk, but she was filled with power. With each step she took, the salt water froze with perfect clarity, appearing like glass. Such a unique gift from her parents.

Taneisha beamed at me, and I remembered my singed clothes from the day we first met. The toddler's steps were clumsy at times, but she made it to the end of the aisle in one piece and did a little twirl.

Once she made it to the front, the fountains started. Water

shot up in graceful arches, paired with pale lights. Exclamations of delight filled the room as Queen Elva and her consort Nathaniel walked down as matron of honor and best man. Once the wedding party was well on its way toward the front of the room, a soprano with a powerful exotic voice began singing notes so high that they would have been painful if not paired with the strangely moving music.

Helena stepped out onto the floor, and I stopped breathing. Her dress was purple, which complemented her gray skin perfectly. There wasn't a trace of the water damage from before left on the expensive silk and chiffon layers. Her purple and blue hair hung around her shoulders, with just a few strands braided into a waterfall around her head. In her hands, she held a coral bouquet.

My niece had come into my life in an unexpected way, but she just... fit. She came to me in a time of bitter turmoil, filled with intense loneliness. She wanted stability and a family. I wanted the same things.

My eyes burned, and a pang of tenderness sucker-punched me in the stomach. I hadn't expected to cry at this moment, but dammit. I did. We practiced this last night, but I still felt shattered.

I held out my arm, and Helena grinned at me. Her face was so full of hope that my heart cracked in half. When she had her legs, she couldn't speak, but I could read her face.

"This is the best wedding I've ever been to," I whispered to my niece as I pulled her closer.

She somehow managed to smile even brighter. Slowly, we made it up the aisle, walking at her pace. Her gait was much more natural since she'd been practicing walking on two legs for so long, and she looked every inch the princess she was.

Her father and sister didn't want to be a part of her life. They had made their positions clear. Their loss. They would pay the price for desiring power over love.

When we reached the end of the aisle, Helena looked at me. She quickly moved one of her hands, signing "Thank you," before she gathered her skirts in her free hand and stepped up the carpeted ice steps to stand before Erik and the priestess.

I blinked away the emotion gathering in my eyes.

The lights followed the couple with a gentleness that evoked love. Two jumbo-sized screens were on either side of them, giving everyone in attendance, and the whole world by extension, an insider look at the nuptials.

The way the bride and groom looked at each other had me dreading returning to my seat.

How was I supposed to sit next to Phaedra with everyone watching us just as much as they were watching my niece? How could I carry out this charade? How could I touch Phaedra, something that I had wanted to do for so long, and not get addicted to the feel of her?

When I turned around, I avoided the Angel's eyes. Her gaze scorched a hole in my head. I sat down next to her, and then I made the mistake of breathing. The air was perfumed with Phaedra's springtime scent. My heart skipped a beat.

Solution: stop breathing.

Unfortunately for me, even DemiGods needed to breathe. Moments after I took my seat, the priestess welcomed the guests. A squeal filled the air, and my gaze flitted over where the Winter Fae sat. Taneisha's eyes widened as we made eye contact, and she giggled. Even though the little one wasn't supposed to move, she darted out of her mother's grasp. Running far faster than I would have expected, the toddler launched herself onto my lap.

The entire room laughed, including Helena and Erik.

The little Fae child wrapped her arms around my neck and made sounds I was sure didn't form actual words. After a few moments passed, I snuck a glance at Phaedra and found her staring at me. Her arms were no longer crossed. Instead, they twitched at her sides. A few moments later, she patted the small child on the back.

For a second—one singular moment in time—Phaedra's hand brushed mine.

Gods.

Forcing out a tight-lipped smile, I returned to the wedding. Aranthian weddings, particularly those in places like Angel's Landing or the Gates of Hell, were more like epic stories than moral speeches. Weddings spoke to the infinite potential of a couple. In this case, Helena represented Kiara, the Primordial goddess of Fate, and Erik represented Dror, the Primordial god of Freedom.

They came together, and the priestess reenacted the stories of the creation of our universe, our planet. The tension between free will and destiny was a central theme as the couple circled each other. As she instructed the couple to cling together, I stopped seeing Erik and Helena and started seeing Phaedra and myself.

I recalled what a different priestess had told me in Fortuna's temple.

Stop punishing yourself.

Be happy.

The minutes stretched on, and soon, soft snores came from the Winter Court princess. Her soft arms were splayed around my neck, and her head was heavy on my shoulder. We reached the part of the story when Helena and Erik had to make some sort of vow, a profession of their love for each other.

Erik spoke first, angling his body so the cameras could easily see him and his bride.

"Helena," he started, signing along with his words. "My life was empty, and then you walked in. From the moment you looked up at me, your face full of fire and determination, I was never the same. So many sleepless nights have brought us to today, not all of them good." He paused for a moment, the crowd laughing as his hands caught up with the words. "But together, we have everything."

Helena grinned.

Phaedra leaned over and whispered, "Do you want help with the youngling?"

I was a little shocked by the fact that she instigated the conversation. I shook my head. "No, thanks. I've got it."

She leaned away, stirring the air around us and infusing it with our mixed scents. I tried to listen to the ceremony, but my entire body was caught up in that springtime scent. My magic thrummed in my veins as though it wanted to come out and play with hers.

A few minutes later, Phaedra leaned over again. My whole body felt like I was being dipped in warm water. Her head tilted to the side just as Helena started to move her hands around. A recording of my niece's voice spoke out loud and clear. I tried not to be aware of how close her head came to my shoulder, almost touching.

Helena dabbed a tissue at her eyes, pausing her signed vows for a moment.

I leaned into Phaedra, and our heads brushed for a moment. The movement sent shocks through me. Smelling her was one thing, but touching? My entire body felt like it was on fire. My wings stretched out, circling around Phaedra and her wings—I couldn't help it.

If she noticed, she didn't react.

"And, finally, Erik, remember that I can still kick your ass anytime I want," Helena's recorded voice said.

The room erupted in laughter while Helena grinned from ear to ear. I was caught off guard by her comment and guffawed along with everyone else.

Everyone except for Phaedra.

Helena finished her declaration of love to Erik, and then the priestess spoke once again. She pronounced them husband and wife and invited them to kiss each other.

The tall woman with white robes reached her hands out wide. "Thank you all for coming today! It is my honor as one of Fortuna's priestesses to officiate over such important weddings. I'm sure I will see you again shortly." The priestess looked directly at us, her meaning clear.

Phaedra bumped into me. My cocooned wings curled tighter on instinct. A flash of fear crossed Phaedra's face, but then her features returned to being guarded just as the sleeping princess squirmed in my arms.

The room erupted in applause, and Helena's godchild woke up quickly. Soon, the most enthusiastic applause came from Taneisha. She even went so far as to blow kisses at anyone who would look. The cameras zoomed in on her, and everyone started aw'ing in between cheers for the newly married couple.

A new song started playing over the speakers, and the burst of energizing sound electrified the room. I stood, and Phaedra followed suit. Her wings brushed against the sensitive inside of my own, and I groaned audibly.

She looked up at me with one of her eyebrows raised. I set Taneisha down, and the child bolted away to follow after Helena and Erik.

The applause, the music, the pure joy in that room made me feel like I was floating through the air. I wished I could bottle this moment and drink it like fine whiskey on a rainy day.

I stuck my fingers in my mouth and blew a loud whistle. On cue, fireworks started shooting inside the room before exploding into white flower petals that rained like glitter.

Erik and Helena laughed as they walked down the aisle. They were smiling so widely that my heart hurt.

Phaedra looked around her with thinly veiled wonder. I reached toward her, my hand hovering near hers before I realized what I was doing. She wasn't angry at me right now. I didn't want to push things. Knowing that this wasn't the right time to push her didn't stop the disappointment from roiling through me as I dropped my hand back down to my side.

Just then, the sound of high heels on ice had me turning my head.

"Lord Hades, Ms. Demtre," the wedding planner said.

Soon, we were swept away in talks about our wedding.

Our wedding.

Nothing was ever going to be the same.

CHAPTER 18
I HAVE RULES
PHAEDRA

The ripping of packing tape filled the air as I tore the clear adhesive material before slapping it onto the last box. Grabbing the black marker, I scrawled *Phaedra's Bedroom* on the top and side. Pushing on the lid of the marker, I sat back on my heels.

My apartment was empty. Boxes filled the living room, and the walls were bare. All my furniture sat in a pile, ready for the movers.

This was it. I was moving. In a few minutes, I would be leaving for good. By the end of today, I would be officially living with my fiancé.

I was *not* looking forward to that.

Last night, Hades and I danced together at the wedding. It was every bit as awkward as I'd thought it would be. Even now, I could see the flashing of the incessant cameras in my mind. I could feel the way his hands gripped my hips—tight, but not to the point of pain. More like... possessive.

The moment the song ended, I lurched away from Hades. I stayed at the wedding long enough to pass my regards to the bride and groom, inviting them for dinner once they returned from their honeymoon, and then I left, claiming an upset stomach.

It wasn't a lie. My stomach had been in knots from the moment I'd stepped out of the limo. Once I arrived home, I'd taken some medicine before climbing into bed. I hadn't even undressed before lying on my stomach and pulling the blanket over me.

This morning, I woke up bright and early. I did some yoga, made myself a cup of coffee, and started to pack.

I hadn't stopped until it was all done. Now, I sat back.

I should have felt something, right? Sadness, maybe. Anger, definitely.

But instead, I felt... empty.

It struck me as strange that I didn't feel anything about moving from the apartment where I'd lived for nearly half a century of my life. I had spent hours here with Dylan and our friends. And yet, the thing that was bothering me the most was not the fact that I was leaving my apartment but the person I was moving in with.

A therapist would probably have a lot to unpack about that statement.

A knock came at the door, interrupting my thoughts.

"Ms. Demtre?" a voice called out.

"One moment, please." Straightening my clothes, I drew in a breath. It was time. Opening the door, I greeted the movers with a grin. "Good morning, gentlemen."

A trio of Daemons in navy blue jumpsuits stared at me, wide-eyed for a moment, before one of them pushed forward and handed me a pen. "My lady... my wife... she watched the wedding last night and loved it."

He paused, and an awkward moment passed as we stared at each other.

"It was a lovely wedding," I said when it became clear he was waiting for an answer.

The man cleared his throat. "When she found out where I was going this morning, she asked if I could get your autograph."

My stomach lurched. Someone wanted *my* autograph? I was a nobody. Just another Angel living in the Gates of Hell.

Except, after last night, that was no longer true.

I wasn't a nobody anymore. Now, I was a public figure. Someone whose life was under the microscope from the moment they awoke to when they put their head on their pillow.

All because of him. Hades.

I hated him for putting me in this position. He had wrenched me out of the perfectly peaceful anonymity that had been my life. Sure, I knew of a few tabloid articles that questioned our relationship after Hades healed me after the attack on Lethe—I found them after I woke up—but that was nothing. Most people didn't even recognize me. A few weeks ago, these movers wouldn't have blinked an eye if they had been assigned to work for me.

Now I was signing autographs.

But it wasn't their fault. No. This was all Aidoneus' fault. Somehow, he had given me this power, and now I had to live with the consequences.

"Sure," I said after a moment. "I'd love to."

Pasting a grin on my face, I signed the paper and even took a selfie with the movers before making sure they had everything they needed.

As soon as I was sure everything was in order, I left the keys on the counter and headed to the balcony. Throwing my things in my purse, I took one last look at the apartment.

It was bare. Empty. Like me.

I needed to clear my head, and there was nothing better than a flight to do that for me.

WHEN I ARRIVED at the large obsidian tower that loomed over the city of Lethe, I had come to two conclusions. The first was that my wings were *very* distinctive. This was a fact I hadn't considered until halfway through my flight this morning when my peaceful flight turned into a tumultuous one as a flock of paparazzi set upon me.

Literally.

A group of Angels and Daemons, all of them reporters for various news outlets throughout Aranthium, ambushed me on my flight.

The second conclusion I reached was that my new fiancé and I were going to have a little chat. We needed to have some rules in place.

Landing with a graceful *thump* on the balcony of Hades' penthouse apartment, I drew my wings in tightly as calls from the reporters still flying behind me filled my ears.

"Ms. Demtre," one of the reporters shouted, "do you care to comment on the ongoing war with the king's brother?"

Another reporter, a woman this time, called out, "When is the wedding?"

A third voice, "In the plot twist of a century, a King is to wed his old assistant. Have you always been in love with the king?"

They continued to volley questions at me, and my chest tightened. I clenched my fists at my side, forcing myself to breathe deeply as blue sparks crackled off my hands.

Shit.

Shutting my eyes, I counted backward from ten.

I *really* needed that training.

"Ms. Demtre, what was that?"

The questions came even faster now.

"Do you have godly power?"

"Why are you marrying the king?"

"Is Hades home?"

Shaking my head, I put up a hand. "No comment."

The reporters shouted, their voices mingling, but I ignored them as I pushed open the double doors and strode into the apartment. They shut behind me with a bang, and mercifully, the reporters' voices disappeared.

I had never appreciated soundproof walls and doors more than I did at that very moment. A cool air blew down from the vents, and the blue sparks faded from view.

Thank the gods.

Turning in a slow circle, I took in the room. It had been years since I'd been here last. Seven years ago, Hades hosted a New Year's celebration up here, and he had invited all his employees.

Dylan hated parties, but I'd made him come.

The apartment hadn't changed a bit. Dark colors were everywhere. While polished and clearly picked out by a designer, all the furniture was black. In fact, everything was either black or gray.

The only pop of color in the apartment was a vase full of flowers sitting in the middle of the coffee table. A note was attached to it. I walked over, running my fingers down the expensive paper.

Phaedra, I saw these and thought of you.

Make yourself at home,

Aidoneus.

Make myself at home. That would be slightly difficult. The entire apartment screamed, "A bachelor lives here!"

Well. That wasn't the case any longer, was it?

Digging out my FaePhone, I pulled up a notes app and began to list the changes I wanted to make. New furniture, carpets, window coverings. The works.

And that was just in this room.

Humming, I walked from one room to the next. By the time the movers arrived and unloaded my boxes, I counted over a hundred items we would need to purchase or change.

I smiled.

At last, something I could do. I had been feeling oddly unsettled since I'd quit working for King Hades. I needed something to occupy my days, and this was perfect.

I was so busy making a list of things to buy for the apartment that I didn't realize anyone else was in the room until a throat was cleared behind me. Blood rushed to my cheeks, and I raised my eyes from my phone. I sucked in a breath at the sight of the electric green eyes staring at me.

I shoved my phone into my pocket and straightened my back. Keeping my tone formal, I dipped my head. "Your Highness. I'm sorry. I didn't hear you come in."

"How many times do I have to tell you?" he growled, raising a white brow. "It's Aidoneus. Please."

"Your Highness," I began again.

He snarled, and shadows gathered around him.

I swallowed and took a step back. Maybe angering a DemiGod wasn't the best idea. Lowering my eyes to the floor once more, I said, "Aidoneus, I'm glad I bumped into you."

"Not as glad as I am," he said. There was an undercurrent to his words that I chose to ignore.

"Ah, yes," I said. "As you can see, the movers have brought my things. I was hoping we could make a few changes to the apartment."

He held up a hand, his wings snapping as he stepped toward me. "Say no more, Phaedra."

"Oh..."

The king reached into his pocket, pulling out his wallet. "Take this." He handed me a credit card. "Buy whatever you want. Whatever you need to feel comfortable."

I stared at the card. This was... a lot. And honestly, it wasn't what I was expecting when I mentioned making changes to the apartment. I had spent a long time working to be able to take care of myself, and I didn't like giving up control of my life. To anyone. "I have some money saved, I can contribute—"

He shook his head, cutting me off. "Let me do this for you. Please. You're the one moving into my home."

At that reminder, my eyes hardened. Who was I kidding? I could spend his money. I was marrying the man, after all. What was his was mine, etc, etc, etc.

Taking the card, I turned it over in my hand before glancing at him. "Thank you."

He nodded, extending his hand. "You're welcome." He raised his eyes, and I was taken aback by the look of... hope in them. "Would you care to join me for lunch?"

Yes, actually. I would care very much *not* to do that. I opened my mouth to reply snarkily, but just then, my stomach let out a loud grumble. It turned out that coffee and yoga did not make a balanced meal.

Sighing, I grumbled, "Lunch sounds good, thank you."

He grinned, his hand still extended toward me.

That was not happening. Yesterday, I held his hand, but it was for the press. At home, with no cameras? No way.

I glared at the offending limb until he finally withdrew it, sticking both his hands in the pockets of his trousers.

LUNCH WAS A QUIET AFFAIR. We sat at the king's too-big dining room table while his personal chef served up a three-course meal. It was elaborate and, honestly, far too much for my taste. I liked nothing more than a simple, home-cooked meal shared in front of a fire with a glass of wine.

This meal was not that. But at least it was delicious. Hitting every point from spicy to sweet, my stomach was full when I finally sat back. Hades did the same, wiping his fingers on his napkin before he looked at me.

"Thank you for dining with me, Phaedra," he said softly. "I hope you're feeling better."

It took me a moment to remember what he was talking about. Then it all came flooding back. The stomach cramping... the wedding... the *dance*.

"I am," I replied. At that moment, an Autumn Fae came and cleared the plates. I stopped talking as the Fae carried in fresh coffee and pastries. I nodded my thanks, wrapping my fingers around the mug. Waiting until the Fae was gone, I continued. "In fact, I wanted to talk to you about something."

"Oh?" the King of the Daemons raised a brow, sipping his coffee. "What do you want to talk about?"

I bit into the pastry, letting the almond and cream cheese filling melt on my tongue before I met his gaze. I'd been thinking about this ever since the meetings with the lawyers.

Placing my hands flat on the table, I said plainly, "I want to talk about sex."

He sputtered, his eyes going wide as shadows exploded from

him. He reeled them in quickly, but his fingers tightened on his mug until his knuckles were white. "I… what?"

I felt an odd glimmer of satisfaction at his surprise.

"Sex," I said, drinking my own coffee and maintaining a casual tone. "As in, I don't want to have it. At all. In fact, I know what we need."

"Oh?" He seemed capable of only the simplest of words at the moment. Good.

"Rules. We need rules. We are meeting with the wedding planner later today, right?"

"Yes." Again, with the monosyllabic words.

"Okay." I dug out a piece of paper and a pen from my purse. "Good. Then here is the first rule: No sex. Ever."

"No sex," he mumbled.

"And no touching unless specifically required for media or public appearances."

"No touching." A *crack* sounded, and I glanced down at the coffee mug in the king's hands. A black fissure appeared in the mug, but he didn't seem to notice.

I narrowed my eyes. "Are you… okay?"

He swallowed. "Yes. Fine. There's nothing wrong with me. Do you have any other rules?"

"Not that I can think of… do you have anything you want to add?"

A long pause ensued before he raised his eyes. They had hardened, and I shifted in my seat. "Actually, yes," he said. "I do have a rule."

Honestly, I was not expecting that. I raised a brow. "That's only fair. What would you like to add?"

He met my gaze. "I want us to eat together."

"Eat together?"

He nodded. "Yes. Every meal. Here. In our home, unless one of us is traveling. Is that going to be a problem?"

I narrowed my eyes, trying to think what he could get out of this. I couldn't really think of anything, and I had to eat, so I nodded. "Okay. I can do that."

Nodding, the King of the Daemons finished his coffee. "Good." He stood, his black wings spreading out behind him, and nodded. "Then I will see you at dinner."

"What about the wedding planner?" Our meeting was in an hour.

He narrowed his eyes, and a louder crack came from the mug in his hand. "Deal with her. Pay for whatever."

He bent, slamming his empty mug on the table before stomping out of the room. Shadows trailed in his wake, and the entire floor trembled as he walked.

Once he was gone, I turned my gaze to the coffee mug.

It lay in three pieces on the table.

"If you were a flower, what would you be?" Cassandra, the peppy Summer Fae, asked from her position at the long table across from me. We were in Hades' spare office, one floor below his regular one. He was lending it to me for "as long as I needed." The entire floor was filled with antiques that were in between homes, and no one was here but us.

I was coming to the rapid realization that planning royal weddings, especially ones that were rushed, was absolutely, unequivocally not fun. We'd been at this for an hour, and so far, the only thing we'd talked about was whether or not the invitations should be embossed.

Apparently, it was a hot topic.

Now, we had moved on to flowers.

I blinked. "What kind of question is that?"

She stared at me. "An important one. You can tell a lot about a person based on their floral preferences, you know."

"Really." I didn't word it as a question, but Cassandra nodded.

"Yes! In fact, my mentor, Lilliana, once told me that the most important thing a wedding planner can do is find the best flower to represent the couple. You see when you know what kind of flower you are, you can pick everything else. The dress, the colors, the food, the invitations. It all comes down to the flowers!"

She grinned at me, the glitter she'd put on her cheeks sparkling in the afternoon sunlight as she waited.

And waited.

A minute passed. Then two.

Eventually, she realized I wasn't going to answer. "What if we... circle back to the flower question, Ms. Demtre?"

The Summer Fae looked deflated, almost sad, and for a moment, I felt sorry for her. And then I remembered she wanted to know what kind of flower I was, so that feeling evaporated into thin air.

"Yes," I replied. "That's a good idea. In the meantime, why don't we talk about dates?"

She nodded, her mouth stretching into a wide grin. "Oh, yes! Perfect. Let's see. It's the middle of the spring now... were you two thinking of an autumn wedding? Think of how romantic it would be to be married amongst the leaves and the pumpkins. Or perhaps a winter wonderland? You could—"

"One week from today," I said, interrupting her.

Her eyes widened, and her voice rose to an octave I didn't even know was possible. "One week?"

"Yes," I said. "One week. We don't want to wait, and it's not like—"

The sound of shattering glass came from the room next door, and I paused as an eerie silence filled the air.

Something was wrong.

I straightened my back, raising a finger to my lips and eying the wedding planner. The hairs on the back of my neck prickled, and something felt... off.

"Wait here."

Cassandra sputtered. "Where are you going?"

Instead of answering, I stood from the table and walked over to the tea tray that had been delivered earlier. I found what I was looking for underneath a golden platter bearing an assortment of small sandwiches.

"What are you going to do with a butter knife?" Cassandra hissed, her eyes wide.

"Hopefully nothing," I muttered, sliding the blade against my arm. Turning back around, I met the wedding planner's wide gaze. "Get under the table," I ordered. "Don't move."

The last thing I needed was a frantic Fae, making things worse for me.

"Wait!" she protested, but I had already slipped out the door.

I sucked in a breath, my eyes taking in the space quickly. The hallway before me was empty, but I definitely heard something. My heart pounded, and I forced myself to remain calm, even as I heard the sound of glass crunching behind me.

Someone was here.

The self-defense classes I took years ago had prepared me for this. I could do this. As long as I stayed calm. People who kept their wits about them and remained calm were far less likely to become victims of crimes. The instructor had told us time and again that staying calm and using common sense were the two keys to survival.

I graduated at the top of my class before going on to practice several forms of martial arts. They grounded me in a way that not many other things besides music did.

Unfortunately, as I turned on my feet toward the sound of breaking glass, I remembered something else.

You should never bring a knife to a gunfight.

That was the last thought I had as I gazed down the barrel of a gun. And the man holding the gun... he wore a mask, but his eyes...

They were dead.

My heart pounded as I fought to remain calm. It was a losing battle.

I sucked in a breath. Then another.

By the third, I remembered something.

I wasn't helpless. Power thrummed in my veins.

By the fourth breath, my fingers were sparking. The magic was spreading around me. The intruder cocked the gun, and I reached into myself without even thinking. I found the godly magic waiting like a ball within me, and I yanked on it. Hard. Electric blue light filled the hallway, crackling like lightning, and the scent of ozone filled the air.

The masked man cursed, and then the gun went off.

A ringing filled my ears, but thank the gods, it didn't hit me. Cassandra screamed, her screeching wail a backdrop to my movements as I charged towards the intruder. I must have caught him by surprise because he stumbled backward, and we tumbled into the conference room. The magic continued to pour out of me, and I didn't do anything to stop it.

I wouldn't go down without a fight.

CHAPTER 19
WELCOME TO TARTARO
AIDONEUS

The rippling magic in the air sent my entire body into high alert. I was going through a particularly large stack of artifact extradition forms one second and the next, my magic was pouring out of me faster than I had time to control.

Phaedra. She is the only other person with this kind of power.

Another burst of energy rippled through me. I immediately Transposed myself out of my office and onto the floor below by clapping my hands.

The moment I arrived on the floor, Phaedra's springtime scent filled my nose.

Where is she?

Seconds later, a scream came from down the hall. I bolted straight into the room where Cassandra and Phaedra were supposed to be meeting. Danger was in the air, and my body went directly into survival mode.

Locate the enemy. Eliminate.

"What the hell is going on here?" I roared.

My one-second assessment told me that the scream came

from Cassandra, who was hiding under the conference room table. I Transposed her out by bringing my hands together, sending her into an empty HR office.

"Aidoneus," Phaedra gritted out.

She was in the corner, blue power radiating off her in waves that assaulted my senses. The Angel was sitting on top of an Ice Mer, her wings snapped together tightly, with her forearm pressed against his windpipe. A black mask lay to the side, along with a gun that was just out of reach. The male stared up at me, his expression one of agony.

Phaedra's magic had him frozen on the ground.

Her chest heaved, and her body shuddered. It took me a moment to realize it was not from fear but pure, unadulterated *power*.

"Phaedra," I said carefully. "Are you all right?"

When she spoke, her voice was not her own. "Yes." The sound was deeper, laced with power and pain.

She pressed her forearm in closer, cutting off the intruder's windpipe. His face exploded in agony.

Phelix did this. There was no doubt in my mind. He sent someone to kill my bride-to-be the day after we announced our engagement.

Heat poured over my body, puffing up my insides and tensing my muscles.

"Don't kill him. I need to get intel first," I said.

My fiancée didn't listen. She just kept pressing down on his windpipe. The masked man's eyes rolled back into his skull.

"Phaedra," I repeated. This time, I channeled my power into it, and the notes of my normal voice grew with divine power.

That got her attention.

As if suddenly realizing what she was doing, the blue magic faded, and Phaedra removed her arm. Her eyes went wide, and she sucked in a breath. Before I could say a word, she Transposed out of the room. All of our couch pillows appeared in her place.

I slowly took two steps until I stood over to the man who had the audacity to break into *my* domain, surprised he was still conscious. I lifted my foot and placed it on the intruder's chest. He was frozen in place. I could fix that, though. Make him regret ever stepping foot in Lethe.

And I would.

Rage flooded my bloodstream, flowing through every inch of my body.

He had come into my house—been close to Phaedra.

My heartbeat pounded in my ears, and my throat had long since gone dry.

I knelt and took hold of the intruder. He would pay for what he had tried to do.

Power flooded my veins as my shadows surrounded us. We descended through the tower, slipping past the people who lived beneath my rule. When we landed, we were not together.

The magic of this place—my domain—swept over the Ice Mer, removing any dangerous object from his person.

My tower had sixty-six floors—but the public was only aware of sixty-five of them. Deep down, at the bottom of the obsidian construction, was an extra floor. It wasn't the only subterranean floor, but it was as far below the earth as heaven was from the earth. Once, there were whispers of this place, but even those had stopped.

Tartaro was eternal, and it was a realm of nightmares.

Back in the days before kings wore crowns and humans stood on two feet, this floor held the entirety of my realm. It was not glamorous like the rest of the Tower. There was no polished rock, and there were no elevators.

The only way to enter was by Transposition, which limited

the ability to meet here to a very limited group: myself, my brothers, and Phaedra.

As I used my magic to reach this vast chasm of space under Lethe, the familiar dank scent of decay wrapped around me like an old friend. Mist thick enough to get lost in parted for me, showing deference to the reigning DemiGod.

This place was not merely ancient. It was a dungeon of eternal torment. The place where the old Gods' bodies—the Elementals and the Primordials—lay encased in rocks veined with black opal.

This was where the first Daemons were born. The red and yellow eyes were necessary to see in the darkness.

I inhaled deeply, looking for the intruder. The chase was part of the torture.

Warmth spread through my entire chest.

Somewhere down here was an Ice Mer who had traded legs for fins. Intel on the soldiers told me that my brother's so-called "Elite" didn't go on a single mission without the option of eliminating themselves in case of failure. I was sure the protections surrounding Tartaro had removed the pill the intruder likely intended to swallow. Good. Instant death was too good for a man like this.

I could sense his energy in the air around me. The beauty of Tartaro was that it never allowed anyone to actually die. People could exist here, remaining on the precipice of death for eternity, and never fully be freed from their agony.

The Ice Mer, with his fins, was likely gasping for breath at this very moment, his lungs rejecting the air.

In this place, returning to the brutality I had been raised on was easy. It was generally frowned upon by modern society. Not here. I allowed myself to be a monster here.

Strolling through the mists, a darkness grew inside of me. An emerald light reflected on the thick gray clouds shifting around me.

“You dared to come into my house, and now you will pay the price,” I growled into the open air. I didn’t need to shout—this was my realm. My voice carried with ease.

Beneath my feet, gems of every kind glittered. Sharp crystals jutted up from the solid rock, and most were covered in thick grime.

No response.

Several minutes passed. Growing tired of the tediousness of walking, I Transposed to the concentrated point where I felt the life energy of my enemy. My power was stronger in this place. I needed no flourish.

Wet sounds echoed off the hard surfaces of this place that was darker than Hell.

Slowly, I walked forward and kneeled. I was no longer wearing the modern clothes I had put on this morning. In my realm, I was transformed into something archaic and dark. Black robes covered my body, and my feet were bare. Shadows followed my every step.

Here, I was the DemiGod of the Dead, and everything bowed before me.

The mist skirted away from the Ice Mer. He was curled in a ball, his tail flopping on the ground like a dying fish. His fins were tucked close to his chest, and he convulsed against the ground. His eyes bulged from the lack of oxygen as he gasped over and over like a dying fish.

I watched him. There should have been regret, but all I could think about was the burst of power I’d felt from Phaedra. She had been afraid. This intruder frightened her. My Angel.

Prior experience told me it would be pointless to ask the male a question at this point. He wasn’t frightened enough. Not yet.

Instead, I continued to revert to my dark form. My wings stretched out, and the shadows hugged my skin, turning the marbled pattern into a shade so dark that it absorbed the godly light from my eyes.

There was no light in Tartaro. Living nightmares did not need the light.

The Mer started thrashing back and forth, clawing around as he tried to drag himself away from me.

Still, I watched. Waited.

His flesh caught on sharp crystals lining the floor, and he cried out. To his credit, he did not stop moving. Blood streaked the ground underneath him.

The gore he left on the crystal was disgusting. His pain fueled me. He was my enemy, and he tried to hurt my wife.

My fiancé, I corrected myself.

"Why were you in my tower?" I grunted out.

The being did not cry out, even though his tail was slick with blood. Phelix always instilled a high pain tolerance in those who worked for him.

Minutes passed. His gasping still echoed around him, and he stopped moving, collapsing to the ground.

Primal parts of me woke up with his presence, the threat of him in my life. I would not stop until he answered my questions. "Speak, and I will consider giving you water."

I walked over leisurely to where he had left blood on the ground. Kneeling down, I dragged my fingers through it and brought it to my nose.

The smell of fear was pungent. Fear could help me get answers. Impatience thrummed in my chest, tightening my shoulders.

"Your blood does not lie. You are afraid of me. That is wise. One does not meet the King of the Daemons, the Unseen One, and walk away without marks." I drew myself up to my full height. The Ice Mer whimpered in spite of himself. "Now, you will speak."

More seconds ticked by, and he just stared. I lashed out with power, slicing a shadow whip across his front. Sprinkles of warmth landed on my body, undoubtedly his blood.

This time, he screamed.

"Tell me!" I roared.

He did not speak. He would not break.

My anger fueled me to the point of breaking.

"If you do not fear the shadows, perhaps you will fear this." I extended my arms to either side of myself, and the mist lifted as the area around us burst into flame.

White hot fire licked the crystals, making them shine like diamonds.

The male convulsed, sweat covering his bloody body. The flames drew near to his skin, and he screamed more.

"Speak," I commanded.

He drew his lips together, even as tremors of pain wracked through his body.

"You tried to kill my fiancée, and I will not release you from here until you tell me why. You already know, don't you, that you cannot die here." I flapped my wings, drawing myself above the flames. The heat mirrored the hot power pulsing inside of me.

The male rolled around in pain, his flesh charring, healing, and then scorching all over again.

Hours passed, the cycle continued, and he didn't speak.

Eventually, I grew tired of this torture. This wasn't what I enjoyed. I was done with this man.

So, I did the one thing I excelled at. I made him a deal. "You have my word as a DemiGod. I will kill you once you tell me. I will not send you back to him to live out yet another series of torture."

He knew who I spoke of. My brother Phelix was not above cruel punishment.

The Ice Mer croaked out as barely intelligible, "Go to hell."

"So, you can speak," I mused. There was a part of me, deep down, that despised the way I enjoyed these meetings. But he deserved this. He tried to hurt me so I would hurt him.

I flew up higher, and the flames grew hotter. More screaming echoed off the walls, but now the pain was joined by the worst of those who had been imprisoned down here for centuries, if not longer.

"Behold your Fate!" I bellowed.

The wailing and gnashing of teeth sounded like pain personified. As the fire grew, I flew higher. This realm would not harm me, but I wanted to emphasize the difference between the two of us. I appeared to be tame, but my brother's soldier was little more than an ant compared to me. He would give out eventually. I knew it in the depths of my being.

Minutes went by.

The Ice Mer writhed. Screams continued to eek from the depths of my realm. My shadows flooded from me until the being was barely visible.

And then he opened his mouth.

"Water," the male croaked.

A smile spread across my lips. He had broken. They always did.

Snapping my fingers, the flames winked out, and the incessant cries stopped. I Transposed both of us to a murky lake within Tartaro.

Once the worthless male was in the water, I healed his wounds. He thrashed around, sending the water sloshing over the sides of the lake as he inspected his newly healed tail.

"Prepping the prized lamb for slaughter?" he asked slowly, his voice full of spite.

I leaned against a rock formation that was taller than me, creating a few spell lights to float above us. My brother's soldier stared at me, searching my face. I wondered if he was looking for traces of his blood on my skin. It didn't matter, he couldn't see it with my skin this dark.

"I wouldn't call you prized," I sneered. "Now, you are going to tell me what I wish to know."

He held up his side of the bargain.

So did I.

IT HAD BEEN a long time since I'd last visited Tartaro. The experience with the Ice Mer left me feeling hollow. Not drained, per se. But empty.

The hollowness, accompanied by the buzzing in my skull, was the worst part of visiting Tartaro. Power licked my insides, begging me to give in, to become like the gods of old. It was worse when I went down there. The old gods were lost to themselves.

I couldn't let that happen to me.

Phaedra came home hours ago. I'd been gone for more than half the day, but I imagined she must have still been there. After all, where else would she have gone? I shoved the feelings of my impending insanity away as I changed back into my suit and pushed open the front door to my apartment. Our apartment.

"Phaedra?" I called.

No response.

I rubbed the back of my neck and rolled my shoulders. My skin faded back to its scarred marble. "Flora?"

The AI materialized. "High King Hades, what can I do for you?"

"Can you make an announcement that I've arrived on all speakers?"

She nodded, and seconds later, a cheerful, "Lord Hades is home!" chimed throughout the entire penthouse.

"Thanks, Flora," I said as she blinked out with a bright, "You're welcome!"

Each step felt strange like I could feel their impact rattle around on my insides. I made my way to my kitchen, thinking about the last conversation I'd had with Phaedra.

No to sex, yes to eating together.

At least she didn't get the sex part on the prenup, a voice said.

"Inappropriate," I murmured as I opened the refrigerator and pulled out an array of food Eugene had left me. My personal chef was good, but I wondered if Phaedra actually enjoyed the food.

All the ingredients to make spicy quinoa bowls were there, and that was about all the energy I had to make after my day.

Before opening up the hermetic glass containers, I went to the sink and washed my hands. Still no Phaedra.

"Flora," I asked, and the AI blinked to life at the breakfast nook. She was sitting down like a proper guest. It was disconcerting, to say the least. "Is Ms. Demtre home?"

She nodded. "Yes, my King."

Then she was gone.

I bit my lip as I opened up one of the ebony hardwood cabinets, pulling out two white bowls.

Phaedra promised to eat with me.

It took me less than five minutes to heat up the bowls with my own magic and assemble the mixture of raw and cooked vegetables with shrimp. If I heated it myself, I could say I made it.

I laughed at the thought. Cooking had been a necessity in

the early days, and I found I didn't have the stomach to hunt every day like Phelix and Raphael. There was something about roasted potatoes that no red meat could ever quite measure up to.

I selected a chipotle dressing and drizzled it on top of my bowl. The pitcher hovered over Phaedra's as I wondered if she would actually like some, too.

I decided against it, and I put the pitcher back on the counter.

"Flora, announce that dinner is ready."

The Fae didn't appear, but her cheery voice rang through the house.

A minute passed, and still, there was no Phaedra. I tapped my fingers against the marble counter and bit my lip. Then, I walked over to the other side of the counter and sat down.

Forks.

I forgot the forks, so I stood and retrieved them.

Still no Phaedra.

Heat spread in my chest, but I tried not to hold this against her. She didn't wait on my beck and call anymore. I grabbed a bottle of wine and poured two glasses. She liked wine. I remembered that from the New Year's party she had attended a few years ago. She liked other things, too.

I made a mental note to get that grand piano Phaedra loved brought up here. When I discovered she played it, I ensured no one touched it. It would be a great surprise for her after our wedding.

I glanced over my shoulder to the hallway where the rooms were.

No movement.

Shifting the bowls and adjusting the forks so that they were in the right spot, I still waited for her to come. I hated fidgeting almost as much as I hated tardiness. Pushing myself up from my seat, I grabbed fabric napkins and decided against them. Paper napkins were better for a casual dinner.

By now, the food was cold. Frustration bubbled up within me. I was done. *Where is she?*

I reheated the bowls and stomped over to the hallway.

Which room did Phaedra choose?

I assumed that she would be near my bedroom, but what if she was on the other side of the house?

I debated for a second, wondering if I should just Transpose into all of them. But what if she was taking a bath or something?

Even though it made my heart race, it was a bad idea. We did set boundaries, after all.

Just as I was stewing, one of the doors behind me opened. I whipped around, my eyes widening. The door belonged to the room directly adjacent to my master.

Something akin to champagne bubbles started popping under my skin as I stared at Phaedra. She was wearing a pair of leggings and an oversized sweater, clearly comfortable in my apartment.

I liked that.

"Dinner is ready," I said dumbly.

"I heard," she said too quickly. "I was showering."

I raised my eyes, noticing her damp hair for the first time. Phaedra had an odd expression on her face.

My eyebrows drew together. "What's wrong?"

She blinked. "Um, you-you have... blood on you. At least, I think it's blood."

My face blanched.

"What?" I darted past her and into my room. When I reached the bathroom, I turned on the lighted mirror. Sure enough, blood speckled my face. Ice Mer blood.

"Shit," I hissed as I turned on the sink and started washing it off.

My hands were still scrubbing over my face when I felt another presence in the room.

"Ha-Aidoneus," Phaedra corrected herself.

I looked up, grabbed a bottle, and popped the lid off.

"Phaedra," I said.

She twisted her hands in front of her and then glanced at the container I had just set on the counter. "La Mar," Phaedra said, reading the bottle. "You use Spring Mer face products?"

I tensed as I turned off the tap and reached for a fluffy, antimicrobial towel. I patted my face gently, turning to face her. "They say that marine products do wonders for aging." I laughed, but she did not. I set the towel back on the rack, pumping some face lotion onto my palm.

"I think we should talk," she said quietly. The words tumbled in her mouth like she couldn't bear to have them trapped inside her anymore.

All of my attention was honed into her face. "All right."

She shifted her weight from one foot to the other. "After today, I was thinking..."—she toyed with a strand of hair—"I don't really want to get married."

"Phaedra—"

"I know we have to get married." Blue sparks flitted off her hands, and she chuckled darkly. "Clearly. I'm not going to fight you on that."

"Thank you."

"The fighting is actually what I mean."

I remained silent, and she continued. "You came to help me today, and you are helping me with money. I think this whole process would be easier if we could at least agree to be friends."

My ears popped from the internal pressure. Friends. Friends were much better than having her despise me. I didn't have to think about the answer. "I don't see why not. We worked together really well for a long time. I'm going to admit that this is sooner than I thought."

But thank the gods for that.

I'd take friends. I could work with being friends. Hatred was cold and icy, but friendship...

Friendship held promise.

Phaedra looked at her hands and crossed her legs. "Yes, I know. Me too. But I had reporters on me all day, and afterward, with Cassandra, and then..." she trailed off. "This would be easier if I had help."

Help. She was struggling with this life. Got it. "I can be helpful."

Phaedra smiled, and I tried to commit the sight of her in my bathroom to memory. She was looking around the spacious area. I had a steam shower, and the whole room had heated floors.

"Yours is nicer than mine," she said absentmindedly as she stepped over to one of the glass doors and opened it. What was she doing? Testing it for squeaky hinges? Please.

I laughed. She just saw blood on my face, and now, she was wandering around my bathroom like she owned the place. "You are welcome to use mine whenever you want."

I tried not to picture her in my shower without any clothing. Blood rushed to my cheeks, and I pulled my gaze away.

Gods, the things she did to me. Half an hour ago, I felt like shit, and now I felt very much back in my own skin.

Phaedra made a funny sound and walked back out into my bedroom. I followed her, sweat collecting in my palms. She went over to my bookshelves, which were filled with books, artifacts, and gifts that spanned several millennia.

Every step she took brought her closer to my bed. My heart pounded harder. I curled my fists.

"This might be the largest bed I've ever seen," she said. "Not that I need to know about that."

I blinked. "It's for the wings." I groaned internally, running a hand through my hair. "Your bed is the same."

She crossed her arms. "But not *this* big. Clearly, this was manufactured for two people," she said in her bossy tone. Then, when she realized what she said, she put her hands up. "Not that I need to know about that, either."

My mouth pressed in a tight line as I blinked slowly. "Why don't we go eat?" I said. I wasn't going to be able to do this for much longer. "I'm starving."

She rubbed her left wrist for a second before looking at me. "Before we eat, can I ask you about the blood?"

I pursed my lips. Questions meant dialog, and that was important. So, even though this was a topic I really didn't want to deal with, I said, "Yes."

She nodded. "Okay, so... that was the Ice Mer, obviously. Is he dead?"

I bit my lips. She was direct. I respected that. I didn't want to lie to her. "Yes."

Phaedra nodded slowly. "Good." She paused, fiddling with the bracelet on her wrist. "He wanted to kill me because I am marrying you, right?"

I nodded. She sat on the bench in front of my bed for a moment. I looked up at the ceiling, taking a very deep breath.

"I wanted to kill him. Before you got there," she said slowly.

My eyebrows went up. "I saw. Your powers are really impressive."

My Angel hummed. "All I could think about was that when I marry you, I will finally be free from my debts. But I couldn't enjoy that feeling because that asshole wanted to kill me. I'd felt so much anger. So much power. It felt... overwhelming."

I took a step toward her. "I understand that."

She looked up at me and narrowed her eyes. Gods, she was

beautiful when she got mad. “Which part? The anger or the weight of debt?”

I shrugged. “Both.”

Phaedra glared at me. “You haven’t been poor a day in your life.”

I smiled wanly. “Yes, but wealth is still a relatively new concept. When I was born, the earth was very different.”

It was her turn for her eyebrows to shoot up. She crossed her arms, looking a little uncomfortable. “Sometimes I forget just how old you are.”

More internal groaning. That was clearly the wrong thing to do. The last thing I wanted was to remind her of why we shouldn’t be friends...

Or more than friends.

Gods, I was so screwed.

“How about we go eat?” I asked, trying to salvage the evening.

She nodded, and we made our way out of my room and into the kitchen. I heated the bowls for the third time.

Phaedra looked down. “Did you make this?”

“In a way,” I said evasively.

She sat down and picked up the dressing.

“This is my favorite,” Phaedra declared, drenching the bowl. That was a little excessive, in my opinion. Then she dug in and took her first bite. A moan promptly left her lips.

My entire body woke up at that sound.

“This is so good!” she exclaimed.

I grinned. Something inside me eased at the knowledge that she liked my cook’s meals. “Really?”

She nodded enthusiastically, and I joined her.

It *was* good.

For the next few minutes, we ate in silence.

Phaedra was the one to speak again. "Can I ask yet another question?"

I nodded. "Of course."

She took a sip of wine, looking at the glass like it was a godsend.

"At Helena's and Erik's wedding, why did he sign, too? She can still hear, right?"

I sucked my lips in, biting down for a second. "I think it's more about the gesture. He expressed interest in learning how to say the vows as a gift to her. She's been learning to sign as well."

Another sip of wine. "Neither of them are very good."

I glanced at her and drew my eyebrows together. "Do you sign?"

She shrugged. "Not really. But I got into watching sign language videos on ViewTube. It's really beautiful, and it calms me down. There's a Spring Mer that makes videos about it, actually. I should set up lessons..." Phaedra trailed off.

I swallowed hard, wishing this wine was something stronger. I could use a whisky. "You don't need to do that. You're not an assistant."

"Oh."

There was disappointment in her voice.

I leaned over again, getting drunk on all this closeness. "However, if you want, I think you should do it. I'm sure they'd both be appreciative. It doesn't have to be done in an assistant kind of way. You're a part of the family now, and family helps each other out."

She looked up at me with a strange expression.

"Okay," she said slowly. "I will."

I stood up, feeling weary. "Well, spare me your old man jokes, but I try to be in bed by 10:00 p.m. So, if you'll excuse me."

Phaedra nodded, a strange expression tinting the planes of her face pink. "Of course."

I walked back down the hall to my room, but as I passed her door, I couldn't help myself. I reached my hand out and brushed my fingers over the wood. This was a new space for her, but I would do everything possible to make it comfortable. Safe.

Once my door was closed, I went about my routine mechanically. The faint sounds of the TV filtered through the door, serenading me softly as I went to sleep.

It was nice to have someone else in the house. The peace between us was... good. It was really good.

CHAPTER 20
THERE'S NO WAY YOU'RE PAYING FOR THAT
PHAEDRA

"Come on," I muttered under my breath as I pressed the "on" button on my laptop. "Please work."

The rectangular piece of junk in front of me refused to cooperate. The black screen was mocking my efforts. I'd been trying to get it to turn on for the past hour.

Nothing was working.

I sighed, getting up from my stool and triple-checking I did, in fact, plug the laptop in.

Sure enough, the black cord trailed from the outlet to the computer.

So why wasn't it working?

I checked my watch. There was less than an hour before Cassandra was supposed to video call me. After the... incident three days ago, she sent me a message explaining she felt more comfortable meeting away from the Tower.

I didn't blame her.

But assassination attempt or not, we had a wedding to plan. So here I was, setting up my laptop for a video call. This was the third one in as many days.

Part of me would be happy when the wedding planning was over.

But the other part wondered what I would do after. I couldn't very well be an assistant if I was married to the king.

I needed to do something. Sitting still wasn't in the cards for me. There was only so much redecorating I could do before I went mad.

That was a problem for another time. Right now, I needed to deal with this. Unplugging the laptop, I tried yet another outlet. No luck,

Great.

"Um... Fiona?" I paused, waiting for something to happen, but nothing did. "Florence?"

Still nothing. "Felicia?"

That wasn't it.

Gnawing on my lip, I tried to remember the name of Aidoneus' AI. "Francesca?"

Nope.

I huffed. This was a waste of time. Usually I loved technology, but clearly, this wasn't my day. Pushing myself up from my seat, I slipped into my room and rummaged through the closet.

I yanked on my favorite pair of heels—a pair of navy blue pumps with a tiny bow at the front—before slipping my phone into my pocket and hurrying to the front door. Glancing in the mirror to ensure everything was in place, I smiled at my reflection.

I might have felt like a mess inside, getting ready for this wedding, but at least I looked the part of a competent bride. No hair was out of place, and my makeup was perfectly applied.

In and out, I promised myself. This morning, Aidoneus mentioned he had to check on his soldiers and get an update on his brother. I wasn't an expert in logistics, but I assumed that meant he would be gone for the entire day. Which meant his office was up for grabs.

Getting into Aidoneus' office was surprisingly easy. Not a single person stopped me, although I heard the whispers behind me as I walked past the cubicles of various employees sorting and tagging antiques. People who had, until I was injured, been my colleagues.

When I got to the large double doors that marked the king's office, I glanced at Saul. He stood from his desk and bowed at the waist.

"His Highness isn't in, Ms. Demtre," he said.

I nodded. "I know."

He looked at me expectantly, and I sighed. "I just need to use his computer. Mine died, and I have a meeting that I need to attend."

Saul straightened. "Of course." He opened the door, walked over to the desk, and unlocked the computer. "Here you go, ma'am. Do you need anything else?"

I blinked at him. Usually, it was me doing things like this. "Ah... no, thank you."

The Warlock nodded. "I'll be right outside if you need anything."

He slipped out the door, leaving me alone in this large office. I hadn't been here since the day of the first attack, but I was unsurprised to see that things were exactly the same.

Aidoneus was *very* stuck in his ways. It took me years to convince him to move the Tower into the digital age.

A quick glance at the clock on the wall—analog, of course—told me I only had a few minutes before the meeting. I slipped into the leather seat behind the desk, adjusting my wings so they fanned out behind me.

I logged onto his computer (which still had the same password as when I worked here) and typed in *Speed Video-calls.* A small ad on the side of the browser showed off an eyeshadow palette in the colors of my wings.

I blinked. A strange feeling bubbled in my stomach. It had only been two days since the public found out. How were there already things like this?

When I logged into the video chat, Cassandra was already waiting for me.

"*Phaaaaeeeedraaaa,*" she screeched, her eyes widening as her mouth opened into a delighted grin.

This Fae was so much. I wondered how much coffee she drank every morning.

Forcing a smile on my face, I met her gaze. "Hello, Cassandra." Making sure my actions were out of view from the camera, I discreetly reached over and turned the volume down to the lowest level. "How are you?"

"Oh, I am just fabulous!" She grinned at me before flipping the camera on her tablet. Instantly, dozens of floral arrangements of every color filled the screen. "Just look at these marvelous flowers! Aren't they spectacular?"

I didn't have to fake my enthusiasm when I agreed with her. They were stunning. Cassandra began showing me various flower arrangements, and soon, time slipped by. Eventually, we decided on a bouquet made of dark red, almost black, roses. They seemed to fit the mood.

She grinned. "I am so happy with your decision, Phaedra! I will make sure the florist has everything ready for your big day."

"Thank you."

"Of course!" The wedding planner tapped a few buttons on the screen. "There, I've just placed the order. Your fiancé will get the invoice, but he's covering everything. It won't be a problem..."

She prattled on, but I wasn't listening anymore.

No, my eyes had been pulled to the email that had just arrived on the computer.

It popped up instantly, covering the entire screen.

My eyes widened, and my mouth fell open as I scanned the email. Once. Twice. The numbers at the bottom...

I clicked out of the email, returning to the video call.

"Cassandra, sorry to interrupt."

She stopped talking immediately. "Not a problem! What can I do for you? Do you have a question about the cake tasting tomorrow? The chef is preparing a dozen different flavors, but he can add more if you want—"

"No, thank you. I want to talk about the flowers."

"Oh." Her brows knit together.

I prattled off the absurdly high number on the invoice. "Is that correct?"

Cassandra nodded. "Yes, ma'am. There are costs associated with a wedding, as I'm sure you know. Add in the fact that you are getting married so quickly and the fact that people are already calling it the wedding of the century, and it's a little expensive."

"A little?" I choked. "Cassandra, I've seen vehicles that cost less than this floral bill."

She smiled at me. "Don't worry about it, dear. Your fiancé, His Highness,"—a little giggle—"is paying for everything. All you need to do is show up and look pretty on your big day."

Fury bubbled up inside me, and blue sparks erupted from my fingertips. The scent of singed wood filled my nose, and I looked down.

Shit.

There were two handprints burned into the mahogany desk.

"Ah, Cassandra, I have to go. I'll talk to you later."

She began to protest, but I had already clicked out of the

meeting. Pulling out my FaePhone, I scrolled through the contacts until I found the one I was looking for. I typed a quick message before pushing myself to my feet.

I couldn't sit still. Not right now.

Pacing around the office, my mind kept running over the bill. How many others just like that one was Aidoneus paying for this wedding?

By the time the clock read 3:00 p.m., I gave up pacing. Now I was sitting on the couch, my bare feet stretched out in front of me as I scrolled through my FaePhone.

"Phaedra?" my fiancé's voice came behind me, and I jolted. I sent him a message earlier that I needed to see him, but there had been no reply. I didn't even hear the door open.

Jumping to my feet, I rued the fact that my heels were sitting on the other side of the table.

"Uh, hi," I squeaked, looking him over. He looked... Well, he looked very dapper. I would have thought he'd just showered if I hadn't known he had spent the entire day with his troops. His hair was perfectly gelled, and he wore a crisp black suit. His wings were nowhere in sight, but his horns stretched towards the sky.

"Hi." He smirked.

A strange feeling fluttered to life in my stomach, but I squashed it. Friends didn't feel like that about friends. Especially friends who were being forced to marry each other.

I coughed. "I didn't hear you come in."

He raised a brow. "No, I see that." His gaze landed on my shoes. "Your message sounded urgent?"

I nodded, hurrying around the table and slipping my feet into my shoes. "Yes. We need to talk about our wedding."

Aidoneus's eyes widened for a split second before he pulled a calm facade over his face. "Oh?"

"Yes," I said. I pulled out my phone and clicked until I found the document I had compiled. Opening it up, I zoomed in on the total number and held it in front of his face. "Did you know about this?"

He blinked. "Did I know about what?"

"This!" I stomped my foot. "The cost of everything. This is *insane*, Aidoneus."

"Is it?" Aidoneus looked at me, his mouth twitching. "I thought most women loved weddings."

"Well, I am not like most women."

A moment passed, and I felt his eyes crawling over me. "No," he mused, "you most certainly are not, my Angel."

I ignored the nickname, forcing myself to stick to the issue at hand. "The idea of spending so much money on *one day* while we are still rebuilding parts of Lethe after your brother's attack is unconscionable."

My fiancé tilted his head. "What do you want to do?"

I crossed my arms, drawing in a deep breath. I'd spent all morning going over all our different options. Only one thing really made sense. "I don't think we should have a big wedding."

He opened his mouth to speak, but I held up a hand.

"It's wasteful, and I don't want to start my life as your wife by making extravagant decisions." Especially since I knew exactly how heavy the weight of debt could be.

A long moment passed before the king nodded his head thoughtfully. "That's fair," he said. "But Phaedra, we need to marry."

"I know," I replied. And I did. I'd resigned myself to the fact that I was getting married, whether I wanted to or not. "And we will. Today."

"Today?" His eyes widened, and green power shot like lightning through the air. Shadows curled in the air behind him. "You want to get married today."

I blinked, taking a step back from the King of the Daemons. His power rippled through the room, and he seemed larger than he had been a few minutes ago. "Yes, today."

Aidoneus ran a hand through his hair. "It's... that's really fast, Phaedra. What about the media?"

I'd already considered this. "We can invite a videographer and a photographer from Aranthium News. They can take any footage they need for the press."

My fiancé nodded, his hands tapping at his sides. "That's fair." He pulled his lip through his teeth. "Helena and Erik just got back last night. I'm sure they'd be willing to be our witnesses."

He sounded like he was really considering this. Good. This was good. I *really* didn't want a huge wedding, especially not if it came with a big bill.

My lips tilted up in a small smile. "Can you find a priestess on such short notice?"

"Yes," he mused. "But Phaedra,"—his eyes met mine—"this is big. It will change your life forever. I need to know whether you're sure. If you need to wait a few more days to get ready, that's okay with me, too. I don't want you to regret rushing into this."

Regret was a funny thing. I'd felt it a few times in my life. But right now, more than anything, I felt angry at the thought of spending so much money on a single day. As if echoing my internal thoughts, blue sparks erupted out of me, and the nearby chair burst into a flash of blue flames.

Hades' power shot out of him in a second, dousing the flames.

I sighed. "Marrying you will help me with *that*, right?"

He nodded. "Binding our power will help, yes. And I will train you."

Drawing my bottom lip between my teeth, I nodded. "Okay. I'm sure. Let's do it. Today."

A long moment passed where we just stared at each other. Then Aidoneus smiled. The look in his eyes was kind, and it softened further as he met my gaze. "How much time do you need to get ready?"

My mouth opened and closed. I had been so focused on *not* spending an inordinate amount of money on the wedding I hadn't considered that I should have been taking the time to prepare myself mentally.

I was marrying the King of the Daemons.

Today.

Cue the bile rising in my throat. Oh, my gods. I was really going to do this.

"Phaedra?" His brows were knit together, and he took a step towards me. "As my *friend*,"—he emphasized the word, and my stomach felt even worse—"you know you can tell me anything, right?"

I nodded, hoping my face wasn't betraying my lack of conviction. "Yes, I know."

He narrowed his eyes. "Are you sure?"

"Yes," I said forcefully. "I'll be fine. Shall we get married in, say, an hour? Does that give you enough time to get things ready?"

A small smile crossed his face. "An hour is great. More than enough time." He raised a hand as though to touch me, and it hovered in the air. We both stared at it for a moment before he cleared his throat. "Would you like me to Transpose you back to the apartment?"

I blinked at him. "Back?"

"I just thought... perhaps you wanted to change?" he hurried on, gesticulating wildly as he raised a brow. "But you don't have to. What you're wearing is wonderful. Truly, I would be happy to marry you no matter what you were wearing—"

Holding up a hand, I raised a brow. I had never heard Aidoneus ramble on like this. Perhaps, at another time, I would think it was funny. Something clearly set him on edge.

Maybe he is nervous, too.

The thought helped calm the roiling of my stomach, and I could take a deep breath for the first time since I'd proposed we move up the wedding.

"Yes, please. I'd like that."

He smiled, holding out his hand. "Shall we?"

Nodding, I laced my hand through his. "We shall."

Within moments, Aidoneus flicked his wrist. The office disappeared, and we were back in the apartment. I let go of Aidoneus' hand the moment my feet stabilized, and I took a step back.

"Thank you." Running my hands over my blazer, I nodded profusely. He probably thought I was crazy. "Well, I'd better get ready. I'll... uh... an hour, right?"

"An hour. Meet me in the living room?"

"Okay," I said. Before he could say anything else, I fled towards the safety of my bedroom.

One hour.

IT WAS AMAZING how much one could accomplish in an hour when they were motivated.

In my case, I had a very productive hour. I found a dress, called Mother (she was having a bad day, so it was short), then I called Karina (that call was much longer). After that, I showered, threw up, then showered again. Once all that was done, I brushed my teeth and did my makeup. After all that, I managed to drink two glasses of wine far too quickly.

When I heard voices lilting through my closed door, I was sitting on the edge of my bed. For the past five minutes, I just stared at myself in the mirror.

I looked like a bride. My wings were spread behind me, their color accentuated by the long, white sleeveless gown that hugged my body. Due to a series of rather unfortunate events that culminated in my mother's disease progressing to the point where she needed full-time care, I never had the chance to wear it to the opera like I'd originally planned.

I paired the dress with a pair of white heels, and my black hair hung down my back in loose waves.

This was it.

After this, there would be no turning back.

I would be a married woman.

"You can do this, Phaedra." I gave myself my best get-your-shit-together look in the mirror, hardening my jaw. "You already agreed to it. Just get up and do it."

Despite my less-than-stellar pep talk, it took me another ten minutes before I gathered the courage to stand. Another five before I opened the door.

I walked out of my bedroom towards the voices. When I got to the living room, I stopped. A dozen people milled around the living room, including a priestess dressed in her temple robes, Aidoneus' niece, and her new husband.

But I barely looked at any of them. My eyes went straight to my fiancé.

I wasn't the only one who had used the hour to their advantage. He'd exchanged one black suit for another, but this one was... it could only be described as the epitome of masculine elegance. Aidoneus stood near the couches, his black wings outstretched behind him as he spoke animatedly with Toth'-toros. His horns stretched above his white hair, and even from here, I could make out the glittering black of his crown.

He looked every bit the king he was.

The two men were engaged in their discussion, and it took a moment for them to notice me. But as soon as Aidoneus' eyes locked on mine, his jaw tightened, causing a feathered muscle to become oddly prominent.

"Excuse me," he said loudly. Everyone paused to watch as he strode toward me, making quick work of the distance between us.

When he came within touching distance, he met my gaze. His voice was husky, low, as he said, "You look... stunning."

Butterflies exploded in my stomach. "I... thank you." I made a show of looking him over. "You don't look half-bad yourself."

It was a lie. He looked amazing.

Aidoneus smiled, shifting from one foot to another. "Can I tell you something? Friend to friend?"

I nodded. "Of course."

He leaned in. "Don't tell anyone, but I'm a little nervous."

A small laugh burst out of me. "Friend to friend, I'm a little nervous too."

His lips tilted up. "Perhaps we can be nervous... together?"

I chuckled. "Perhaps."

He offered me his arm, and I slipped my hand into the crook of his elbow. Somehow, he made me feel at ease.

Soon, we were standing in front of the priestess.

"Please, join your hands together."

Aidoneus moved first, putting his hand in the space between the two of us. I swallowed, shutting my eyes for a brief moment. This was it.

You can do this.

I lifted my eyes to Aidoneus'. His gaze was kind and caring, making me forget my nerves long enough to raise my trembling hand. Aidoneus clasped it in his much larger hand, squeezing softly.

The priestess smiled. "Good."

She pulled a cloth from her long robes, draping it over our joined hands. Then she smiled and took a step back. Opening her arms wide, she began to speak. "My children. All marriages are a blessing from Fortuna, but in this case, there are more blessings…"

The priestess continued talking, but I barely heard her. My attention was solely focused on the man in front of me. We said our vows at the appropriate moment, signed some paperwork, and then she said, "You may kiss the bride."

Kiss. We were going to have to kiss.

I forgot about this part of weddings. How could I have forgotten about that? I made stipulations for sex, but somehow, I looked over the kissing portion. We were supposed to touch if events called for it. And marriages definitely called for kissing. I took a deep breath.

Behind us, I heard the click of the camera. Three members of the media had been invited to witness the wedding, and their photos would be sent out to all the news outlets in Aranthium.

My husband squeezed our still-joined hands as he took a step closer. "May I?"

One kiss. For the camera. I could do this.

I nodded, sucking in a deep breath. The King of the Daemon's hand cupped my cheek gently, and then his other hand slid around the back of my neck as he drew me towards him. He softly angled my face upwards.

He was so tall.

My heart was racing so fast that it almost hurt. The air

between us was charged and heavy as everything else faded away.

His mouth met mine, and that was when I realized I was in big trouble. The kind of trouble I had never, ever expected. This kiss felt good. Far too good. This wasn't just a peck. The moment his lips landed on mine, he *owned* me.

I knew I was in trouble. I let out a soft gasp, opening my mouth. He growled, his hand slipping from my cheek to the small of my back as he deepened our kiss. His tongue slipped into my mouth, and I tasted him.

And it was good. Too good. More than I had ever expected.

My head spun. I'd thought this would be pleasant at best and awkward at worst.

I couldn't have been more wrong. Aidoneus' lips were far softer than I'd ever imagined. He kissed with the ease of a man who had lived a long time but with the gentleness of someone who respected me.

And the *sparks.*

I had been kissed before. I'd done more than just kiss. But I never felt those. Honestly, until this very moment, I thought they were the things of romance novels. Not real life.

But there were so many of them that my mind lost the ability to think. Words had no more meaning. The only thing that mattered was this meeting of our mouths.

I couldn't help it. I kissed him back. How could I not?

The small gathering behind us cheered, but I didn't listen to them. I couldn't. Something deep within me was twisting. Tightening.

And then... something within me shifted. I *felt* something snap into place.

My eyes widened.

What was that?

He must have felt something because he stepped back from

me. Our chests heaved, and we stared at each other as the priestess said the final words.

My mind was spinning, the same question echoing over and over again.

What had I gotten myself into?

PART THREE

FIGHTING

CHAPTER 21

LIFE GOES ON, BUT SO DOES THE WAR

AIDONEUS

Lying in my bed, I stared up at the ceiling. The skylight was directly above me, showcasing the starry evening. My fingers were interlaced atop my chest, and the steady rhythm of my deep breaths should have been gently lulling me to sleep.

Instead, I remained here in bed. Paralyzed. Unable to move.

Phaedra was right. The bed was too big for just one person.

Phaedra. My wife.

Her name was like warm water pouring down my spine. My brain knew she was off-limits, but my body refused to reconcile itself to that fact. Mere hours ago, we kissed for the first time, but now, there was an invisible barrier around her body. She was off-limits. Untouchable.

Friends weren't supposed to want to seduce other friends.

I closed my eyes, heaving a long sigh. Since our wedding, I could feel this new space inside of me. Our union created a bond, and I felt a strange, new door that led to her within my soul. If opened, that door would allow me to access all of her. Her power, her emotions.

That door was off-limits unless she opened it for me. She likely didn't even know what it was. And, if things went according to what I imagined, Phaedra would only open for me during training.

Before coming to bed, I had turned off my phone and locked it in my drawer. Pictures of my new bride and I would be plastered over the world tomorrow. Anyone with an internet connection could watch the recording of our intimate ceremony.

We are married! SHE'S IN THE NEXT ROOM! my brain shouted at me. As if I needed a reminder.

Giving up on sleep, I slid up to a sitting position and rested my head against my upholstered headboard. Our wedding wasn't supposed to have happened like this. I was supposed to have time to work through my feelings before I was tied to her. Time to work through my feelings with Dr. Evalde before we said, "I do."

We were supposed to have time, but I threw it all out the window when Phaedra sent for me. She had been frustrated and unhappy. I would have done anything to put a smile back on her face. Before she opened her mouth, I decided to give her whatever she wanted.

My eyes fluttered closed. Getting married today made a lot of sense. I'd gotten married in front of thousands before. It was expensive, especially since we were gearing up for harder battles ahead.

Today might have been the first time I'd agreed to one of Phaedra's ideas, but it certainly wouldn't be the last. It was going to be impossible to say no to her.

There was a strange twisting in my heart. Finally, tired of my too-large bed, I stood up and walked over to one of the bookshelves Phaedra hadn't inspected yesterday. Carefully, I picked up the velvet box and opened it up. Inside was a small portrait that had been a gift from my first wife, Miranda.

I ran my fingers over the velvet box. I had held it countless times over the years. This portrait of Miranda was imprinted on my mind. I knew it by heart. Familiar yellow eyes and flowing black hair brushed into glossy curls. She had been a Daemon, and in general, was Phaedra's opposite. Phaedra was guarded, and Miranda had been an open book. Phaedra was small, Miranda had been nearly as tall as me.

My therapist, Dr. Aclepsia Evalde, told me I should resist the desire to compare the two women. But Miranda was gone—not just dead, but her soul no longer existed. It was erased. Gone. The only way she lived on now was in the halls of my own mind and the monuments I had constructed of her.

People kept telling me it was all right to move on. But what did they know? I should be thanking Phaedra for not demanding more of me than I was able to give.

I stroked a finger over Miranda's likeness and then remembered myself. Finger oils wreaked havoc on oil paint. I used my magic to remove any traces that might've clung to the sharp lines created by the paint.

Carefully, I wrapped it back up, closed the portrait box, and replaced it on the shelf.

It was then that I heard faint voices accompanied by a dramatic soundtrack. They were so quiet, barely more than a whisper. They wouldn't have woken me if I had actually been asleep.

There was only one person who would be watching television at this hour. There was only one person here.

With one quick glance back at the box representing the gaping hole in my heart, I carefully Transposed out of my bedroom and into the shadows of the living room. I blinked at the ease with which I moved. There was no struggle or strain. I just... did it with a thought.

My eyes locked onto my wife.

Smooth, Aidoneus. Hiding in the shadows is definitely less weird than just walking out of your bedroom.

Her wings were relaxed across the couch, and she was wearing a large t-shirt paired with sweatpants with far too many holes.

I hadn't been there for more than a few seconds when Phaedra's breathing changed.

"I felt that," she said quietly. She looked right at me, even though I should've been hidden.

I tilted my head to the side. "Felt me?"

She nodded.

Warm tingles erupted over my skin, giving me goosebumps. "That's normal. Now that we are joined, our powers are interconnected."

Phaedra nodded and then turned her attention back to the flashing lights on the T.V. She slowly took her feet off the couch and tucked them under her. It took me a minute to understand what she was doing.

My eyes widened. She was making space for me. That surprised me. I thought we weren't supposed to touch.

I hurried over.

As soon as my bottom connected with the leather cushion, her springtime scent washed over me. My head spun, and I felt lightheaded as if I were a young DemiGod all over again. My entire body felt like it was floating.

Being close to her was overwhelming me in the best way. And she...

She was watching television.

A glance in her direction showed that she was oblivious to my struggle. I was freaking drowning, and she was watching television like a normal person.

Holding my breath was pointless, so I just sat there. The minute stretched on.

It became two.

Ten.

I wasn't even watching this stupid movie. It was a rom-com, but clearly, Phaedra enjoyed it. For her, I would watch a hundred rom-coms. A thousand.

I would do whatever she wanted if it meant I got to be in her life.

Gods, this female made me into a love-sick fool.

"I like your pajamas," I finally said, breaking the silence between us.

She looked at me from the corner of her eye and raised an eyebrow. "I look like a homeless person."

I laughed. "But aren't they comfortable?"

She nodded enthusiastically, running a finger over the material of her shirt. "Definitely."

"Well, there you go." I let myself unravel a little, and my arms uncrossed. I laid one on the armrest, and the other rested behind the cushions on the couch.

A few minutes passed.

"Are your... gray sweatpants comfortable?" she asked, a teasing edge in her voice.

I wasn't about to pass that up. "I read once that gray sweatpants are like an Achilles' heel for women."

Phaedra barked out a laugh. "What? Where the hell did you read that?"

I looked at her and shrugged. "That's not important. Are you telling me it's not true?" My voice lowered, growing rough.

My wife laughed again, but this time, it was different. It shook a little, but not in a bad way. In a way, that told me she was as nervous about this as I was. I didn't miss the way her gaze quickly flicked up my body.

Something primal inside of me roared.

Friends didn't look at friends like that.

"They're good, I guess," she finally said. Her voice was too quiet. Even from here, I could tell that her pulse picked up, warming her body and causing the air to become thick with her springtime perfume.

It happened so fast that I didn't have time to think. The door between our bond slipped open. It was just a crack, but Phaedra flooded my insides.

She gasped, and my eyes fluttered closed. I felt *everything*.

Her power, her fear, her insecurity, her pride, and...

Behind everything else was the last thing I'd ever expected.

Desire.

It tasted like fresh rain as it coursed through her veins.

My eyes snapped open. My wife held a hand over her chest. Her breath was coming fast and shallow. Her eyes were wide as she watched me.

She felt me, too. That connection between us.

"W-what is that?" she asked.

Through the bond, I could feel her nerves, her hesitancy.

Somehow, over the past few minutes, I shifted closer to her. She was leaning towards me, too. Those inches separating us were slowly disappearing.

"That's our marriage bond," I said slowly. I didn't tell her it shouldn't be manifesting so strongly yet. That it shouldn't feel like this. So powerful. So *right*.

My bond hadn't been like this when I was just married to Miranda. Guilt stuck itself into my lower gut like a sharp stick.

Her eyes went wider, and her body pulsed the same way that mine was. She was a rainstorm in the springtime, filling every crack of my soul with her sweetness.

"I wondered if it was just a new addition to my growing powers," Phaedra confessed.

I bit my lip hard. "Maybe..." I trailed off. This was not normal. "I wasn't expecting the bond to be so strong to start. Otherwise, I would've told you more about it. Now that you're married to a DemiGod, our... powers are linked."

Technically, our entire souls could be linked, but that wouldn't happen without coming together in the most intimate of ways. Which, as my wife had made perfectly clear, wouldn't be having a place in our marriage.

Heat was coming off Phaedra in waves, and I was drowning in her closeness. This definitely was not how I remembered early marriage. My wife angled herself toward me, and conflicting emotions came through our bond.

Our instinctual attraction tied us together, but I could *feel* Phaedra's mind trying to talk her out of it.

My jaw tensed, every muscle in my body freezing. It was either that or give in to the desire coursing between us. She was already leaning in closer to me, her eyes darkening. I knew what this was. The bond was drawing us together. Its pull was addictive.

"The bond is nice," Phaedra whispered. Her eyes fluttered closed as my hand reached for hers. I shouldn't have done it, but the pull was too strong.

As soon as our skin connected, the humming between us grew louder. It was getting hard to understand where I started and she ended. We were going to get lost to each other. The power of this was unusual, overpowering, and totally unexpected.

Suddenly, Phaedra scooted all the way over and slipped her arms around my neck.

My heart caught in my throat, and for a moment, I froze. This was more than I ever thought I'd get, yet it wasn't enough. I wanted her in every way. I wanted to bring her to my bed and show her what it really meant to be married to a king.

She nuzzled the place where my neck met my shoulders, sending sparks running through me. My hands hovered over

Phaedra's back, not quite touching her yet, while I studied the top of her head.

There was so much warmth in this moment. So much trust. My heart raced, and I gave in. My arms closed around her, pulling her small body flush with mine. Her wings splayed behind her as the inches between us became nothing more than millimeters.

It wasn't close enough.

Her body was soft and pliable under me, and her warm fingers brushed up my neck and buried themselves in my hair. We were drunk, lost to the overpowering bond between us.

Just as I was about to give in to the sensation of her skin on mine, Phaedra's words from earlier flashed through my mind.

No sex. No touching.

Could I trust these emotions she was having? A part of me feared she was just feeling like this because of the power flowing between us—the marriage bond. The heat inside me turned cold instantly just as one of her hands reached my collarbone.

If it were hard for me to resist, it would be practically impossible for her.

I grabbed her hand and pulled back. Space. We needed space. I shifted her until she sat on the edge of my knees.

"Phaedra," I croaked, my voice rough. "We should stop."

Confusion and hurt flashed in her eyes. She swallowed, her pretty little throat bobbing with movement.

A minute passed as she studied me.

"Thank you for getting married today. It means a lot that you listened," my wife murmured. Her words were breathless, and the bond was still open. Her essence was still flowing into me like a steady river, and I could feel her earnestness.

I needed to be strong here. For both of us.

My hands shook as I gently picked Phaedra up, moving her back to the couch beside me. "Phaedra."

"Yes," she said breathlessly like she couldn't bear the distance I'd put between us. I could still feel her warm breath on my skin. "Aidoneus, I—"

Somehow, she tugged on her end of the bond. That intangible door was nearly halfway open, and our connection grew stronger. My head swam, and my body felt light like I'd inhaled an entire barrel of champagne.

All the resolve that had gripped me moments before started to wane.

We were in a trance. A new emotion colored the space between us. I was lonely, and she was, too. We finally found each other. We could finally be known by each other.

Desire like red roses bloomed within me. Within us. It was harder to see where I ended and where she began. Arguments against this dried up in my mind. Why shouldn't we do this? We were wed. DemiGod and wife. King and Queen Consort. We were bound together in the eyes of Fortuna.

Temperatures rose, breathing changed, and the need to be closer threatened to devour me whole. It scrambled my insides, and my eyelids grew heavy. My entire body was tight. Tense. I wanted her so badly.

But beneath that all, a trickle of regret ran through me. I wanted her so badly, but not like this. Though ending this felt like a tragedy, I reached within myself and walked over to the metaphysical door that stood between us. Drawing a deep breath, I put out a hand and gently closed it.

The inside of my soul grew quiet and cold within moments. Something whispered that I was making a mistake. But I knew I wasn't. If this were to happen, it would happen because Phaedra actually wanted it, not because of some Elemental magic.

Taking a deep breath, I opened my eyes. Phaedra stared at me, confusion budding across her devastatingly beautiful features. I slid my hands over her wrists, clasping her hands in mine. “You’re tired. This is a lot to take in at once. I think I should go back to bed, and maybe you should try to get some sleep.”

Instantly, her face fell. A pang rushed through my chest.

“Oh,” she whispered. Rivulets of messy black hair spilled over her shoulders, and her eyes were wide.

Gods. This was hard. So hard. Leaving her here, alone and waiting, was not what I wanted at all. No. I wanted to slide my hand behind her neck. I wanted to bring our lips together, our bodies, our everything.

I wanted that, but I was fairly certain she didn’t. She might have desired me, but in the light of the day, she made it clear she didn’t want this marriage.

She didn’t want me.

That thought was like dumping cold water over me, and I bolted upright, clasping my hands behind my back as I stood before my wife.

“I’m sorry,” I said quickly. Now that the spell was broken, I needed to get out of here.

Phaedra looked up at me from the couch, blinking. I could feel her testing the other side of the door, almost as if she was making sure it was shut. Whatever passed between us ended just as soon as it had begun.

“No, I’m sorry. Good night,” she said quickly, dragging a hand over her face.

I didn’t need lights to see the blush that spread across her cheeks.

I couldn’t stand her feeling embarrassed at what happened between us.

“Phaedra—” I started to speak, but then Flora’s voice came from the speakers.

“High King Hades, I have a message for you. Nyrnavox, ID number 99-321-2007, has arrived with Kharon, ID number 00-003-0001.”

Shit.

I cleared my throat and glanced at Phaedra, who wasn't looking at me any longer. She was pointedly avoiding my gaze as she braided her long black hair. My gaze dropped to the column of her pretty neck, and heat blossomed in my lower abdomen.

"Where are they located?" I asked the AI, adjusting the waistband of my sweatpants.

"The battle room, floor 45," the disembodied AI voice replied.

I nodded and then remembered Flora couldn't see me. "Right. I'll be right down, Flora."

A chirping sound came over the speakers. I looked back at Phaedra. My eyes were wide as I said, "I'm sorry. I—"

"Need to go." She smiled a bit but didn't try to meet my eyes. "No worries. See you later."

Clearly, she didn't want to talk about what had just happened. I nodded, Transposing out of the room. It was effortless. Ever since our wedding, power was at my fingertips.

I was never going to get used to how powerful I felt, how much more energy was coursing through my veins.

THE FIRST THING I did after leaving Phaedra was to turn on my phone. Unsurprisingly, there were hundreds of messages. One in particular caught my notice.

> Raphael Zeus: I suppose congratulations are in order…

I clicked off my phone immediately. I would speak to him later.

The battle floor was packed. Half a dozen DaePolice officers, in addition to Nyrnavox and Kharon, were all standing around waiting for me. Toth'toros stood in the corner of the room, but he was so still that it was easy to miss him. The television was paused, the image frozen on a reporter. Instantly, I was on high alert at the tension in the room.

I looked at every single person, trying to figure out where the hot tension coursing through the room was coming from. Some looked at me solemnly, while others didn't even meet my eyes as the chorus of "Your Highness" was repeated repeatedly.

"Good evening," Nyrnavox said, approaching me. There was a tone to his voice... something was off. I would have to dissect it later.

"Good evening." I raised a brow.

For a long moment, there came no reply.

I cleared my throat. "Does someone want to tell me what the hell is going on here?"

Everyone, including Nyrnavox, avoided my gaze.

"What's happened?" I demanded.

Kharon stepped forward. "Son of Fortuna, my lady sends her congratulations and extends an invitation for you to meet with her when this is over."

Everyone watched him with stony, intense expressions.

My stomach tied itself in knots. Something was wrong. Why wasn't anyone telling me? "What do you mean 'when this is over'?" My voice dipped into deeper registers and shadows leaked out of me. The ground trembled as I growled, "Someone had better start explaining *right this instant.*"

Nyrnavox stepped up. "My King, we know that you have been unavailable by your personal FaePhone or email due to your sudden elopement. Which, by the way, we were not notified of."

A primal snarl escaped me. "You dare presume to tell me what to do? My business is my own."

"Not when we are at war!" he snapped. "I expect you will send me updates on what assets Ms. Demtre brought to the table in this war later."

The man had been a stone for centuries, but I could feel the heat behind his words, and I ground my teeth.

"Get on with it," I bit out.

Nyrnavox took a deep breath, raising his hand. "I think it would be best if we show you." He pressed a button, and the screen, which had been previously frozen, came to life. The image of the northern female reporter changed to a very large, familiar face.

Phelix Proteus, the big hulking DemiGod and my younger brother, covered the entire screen. He was shirtless, wearing his crown. My brother was swimming in the middle of a shipwreck, his gray and green hair billowing around him. His eyes glowed green while he gripped his large trident.

"People of Aranthium," his booming voice called out. It had been a long time since I'd actually heard my brother's voice. We'd communicated via letters a handful of times over the years, and he did not even dare to show his face during the attack on Lethe last year. Even underwater, the microphones captured the rough timbre that commanded the seas.

"I would like to congratulate my brother on his new marriage. Such an odd time to get married, don't you all agree?" Phelix moved his trident across the screen as if he were testing its ability to move through the water with ease. Heat crept up my insides, and I clenched my fists.

"Two days ago, I sent a messenger to communicate with my brother. We were going to negotiate a peace offer so that we might bring an end to all this bloodshed," Phelix continued.

The curling heat turned into a flame. What messenger? He sent an assassin. I wanted to blow something up, to scream at someone. He was lying.

One of the DaePolice officers snarled from somewhere in the room. "You are the one causing the bloodshed!"

Some of the others instantly hushed him as Phelix continued, staring directly into the camera. His voice grated against me, my eyes ached from lack of sleep, and my head pounded.

"My messenger has not returned, which I could've overlooked if King Zeus had not launched against my people in the Spring Mer waters. This is the final strike. After refusing to return the heir to my throne,"—that he had tried to kill—"imprisoning, or potentially killing, my messenger, my brother, Aidoneus Hades has undoubtedly conspired with our brother Raphael Zeus. They have left me no choice but to officially declare war on the South."

Curses filled the room as my brother continued to speak.

"Up to this point, all measures taken were purely for the protection of my lands and people. I suggest you prepare for what I have in store for Aranthium." Phelix's chin tilted up, as if he were looking down at us all. Even though he was nowhere near this place, I could taste his power in the air.

It was dramatic.

It was a threat.

"When did Raphael attack?" I asked quietly. Why hadn't he told me?

No one responded before the tyrant began speaking again. "You think that you are safe from the repercussions? All of you, from the Spring Mer Lands to the Gates of Hell, have water near you. Wherever there is water, I will come, and I *will* find you."

A buzzing started in my ears as my estranged brother leaned back, drawing himself up.

"I am here to announce our war to end the oppression of tired kings and councils. It is my pleasure to declare that we have taken over the Spring Mer capital." The bastard had the audacity to smirk.

Suddenly, the camera zoomed out. He was inside of a wrecked ship—but now I realized that ship was once part of the Spring Mer castle. Behind him, dirt and debris swirled through the water. The entirety of the castle was destroyed.

Though no casualties were shown on screen, I did not doubt they were there.

"If you wish to avoid such results, I suggest that you join in the cause. I will not turn you away if you bring soldiers and supplies. Oh, and congratulations, *Aidy*. May you and your wife live a long and happy life."

The eerie sound of wood creaking under water played for a few minutes, and then the transmission ended abruptly.

Everyone turned, the weight of their gazes heavy as they stared at me.

Rage spiraled through my entire body, and my green power started glowing all around me. My fists clenched, and my wings snapped out behind me.

No one spoke. No one moved.

They were all waiting for me. Their king.

"He did send someone, but it was an assassin," I spoke through clenched teeth. Why was I even saying this? I was a king. I didn't need to defend my actions. And yet, at that moment, it felt pivotal. "The Ice Mer tried to kill Phaedra. I didn't know that Raphael sent troops to the Spring Mer lands. I thought we were in charge of that."

Once the words were out, I rubbed my pulsing jaw.

Nyrnavox shifted his weight from foot to foot as he rubbed his temples. "An assassin came into the tower, and you didn't tell me?"

I stood straighter, pinning him with a glare. "I told Toth'-toros. There was no need to tell anyone else, as I took care of it."

Nyrnavox narrowed his eyes. "No need? What did he tell you? Is the wretch still alive?"

A primal snarl rose within me as I glared at the male.

"Adjust your tone, Nyrnavox," I warned. "You are dancing dangerously close to disrespect. You may be the head of my troops, but I am *your king*." I loomed above him, my voice deepening as I stepped towards the male. Did Nyrnavox think I was the cause of this? If so, he was wrong. I wasn't careless. I didn't make decisions to hurt others.

The Daemon shrunk beneath my attention.

"The assassin is no longer breathing," I snarled. "But before he died, he told me that my brother had sent him to kill Phaedra. That was all."

Nyrnavox did not respond. He didn't move. He just glared at me.

A minute passed, the clock ticking on the wall before Kharon cleared his throat. I turned to look at the man. His expression was long-suffering, and his ancient eyes were dark. "I think that Phelix's time has come."

The head of the troops let out an exasperated breath. "I know that you are in love, but really, My King, you had to marry someone that afforded us exactly zero benefits—"

Maybe it was the heat already pulsing inside of me. Perhaps it was the fact that I was already pissed off to high heaven. I Transposed an inch away from the man who had clearly forgotten who was the king in this situation.

Flicking my fingers, I froze Nyrnavox in place with my magic as the ground beneath us rumbled.

"What I do is for the good of us all. Do not speak about what you do not know," I hissed, shadows hugging us from all directions.

Nyrnavox looked up at me, his feet still frozen to the floor. His eyes were hard as he said, "I know that we are in a war, and we do not have an army large enough to fight."

My stomach twisted in a knot. He was right.

CHAPTER 22
MULTI-FACETED AND HOT
PHAEDRA

"Let me get this straight." Karina sat across from me in the spacious kitchen, sipping an overpriced iced latte with whipped cream as she stared at me. She brought the drink with her because leaving the apartment was getting harder every day. I was bombarded by reporters, fans, and even articles of people dressing up to look like me. "You got married, had a mind-blowing kiss, and then your new husband got a work call and disappeared?"

"Yep." I wrung my hands in front of me. "And when he came back, everything was... awkward. If anything, things have just gotten worse between us."

Even as the words left my mouth, my brows furrowed. What was wrong with me? This entire marriage was a sham. A way to tame the power within me. I did not know why this awkwardness was bothering me so much.

The entire apartment was absolutely stocked with gifts. The pile that started in the living room overflowed into the kitchen. I was staring at an eight-foot crimson red tower made of the most stunning roses I'd ever seen from my new brother-in-law, Raphael Zeus.

Last night, after a very frustrating hour during which Hades attempted to teach me to Transpose something on purpose (it didn't work), he received an urgent call. He left moments later without even a "goodbye." That was the third time in as many weeks.

He had yet to return. Married life was nothing like what I had imagined.

That bond that existed between the two of us had taken me completely by surprise. I did not expect anything like this, but now I couldn't imagine living without it. This bond was like a living being that existed within me.

When he brought it up, my husband sounded surprised that our bond was this strong... What did that mean about our marriage? Our relationship?

I had spent the past three weeks trying to learn more about bonds, but the available information was surprisingly scarce.

Karina frowned. "I mean, Phaedra, I'm not a relationship expert, but it sounds like he's stressed. I watched the news, and it seems like... a lot with everything going on."

A lot was an understatement. Hades hadn't told me much, but from what I gleaned from his long hours and his extended trips, things on the storefront were not going well.

"It is." I sighed, dropping my head into my hands. "And I'm trying to help, but I feel... useless."

That was the first time I had admitted that to myself, and I was shocked to find it was true.

"Oh, honey." Karina reached across the table, taking my hand in hers. "You're not useless."

It certainly felt that way. Ever since the wedding, I hadn't been able to work. I was no closer to getting a grip on these powers, and now we were at war.

I had called my mother five times since the wedding.

None of the calls landed on good days. The last time we spoke, she reverted back to the controlling mother I remembered from my youth. She yelled at me for an hour, and I burst into tears. After we hung up, I spent the rest of the day on the couch. Aidoneus had been on the front lines, and I wallowed on the couch all day.

All in all, I would say that life since my marriage was not exactly... delightful.

I shrugged. “Maybe. I'm certainly not useful. My husband is working all hours of the day and night. He’s gone, and I'm trapped here. I'm sure you noticed the security team on your way in?”

Karina laughed. "It would be hard not to notice them. I thought they would strip-search me before Toth’toros stepped in and saved me. He was a gentleman, apologizing for their antics before he escorted me into the apartment.”

I wished I could have said I was surprised, but I wasn't. My new husband introduced me to the security team the morning after our wedding. Despite my protests, I'd been informed they were "necessary."

Now, I was under guard day and night. Helena and Karina had been the only visitors since my wedding. Helena’s drop-ins had been embarrassing, to say the least. I still had the basket of lingerie and massage oils under my bed. She clearly expected us to use them, and I didn’t have to heart to explain that our marriage was one of convenience.

"I'm sorry about that,” I muttered.

My friend laughed. "Don't be. Toth'toros is a hottie." Karina waggled her brows. "Nothing like your husband, of course. Gods above, I'm so glad you got rid of Dylan. I always hated him."

"Karina!" I gasped, clutching imaginary pearls and thinking about the red lace sheer enough to see everything. I wasn’t a virgin. I'd lived with Dylan for a long time. But I hadn't felt like my skin was on fire around him before. For one thing, Dylan's idea of a romantic night was cheap Italian food, sex, and bed before nine. For another, the man didn't even wait two minutes before checking his phone.

"Come now, Phaedra, you know it's true. The man was no good for you."

I huffed, choosing to take a long sip of my coffee. The flavored drink slipped down my throat, filling me with the sugar rush I needed to deal with this.

"Dylan was... normal." I shrugged. It was true. My old boyfriend hadn't been great, but he had been stable. "He was fine. What we had was fine."

Karina huffed. "Phaedra, no one should ever describe their relationship as 'fine'. They should be full of sparks. Energy. Emotion."

I couldn't help but flash back to the kiss I shared with Aidoneus. There were a lot of emotions in that kiss. The sparks alone were responsible for keeping me up at night. I'd woken tangled in my sheets, unsatisfied, more nights than not since my wedding.

Blood rushed to my face, and I adjusted the hem of my skirt. "This is true."

"Mhmm." Karina eyed me with the expression of someone inherently confident about all things romance. "And how is your relationship with the king?"

So direct.

It was one of the things I loved about my closest friend. Usually. At times like this, she definitely put me on edge. Evgenia, bless her, would never have asked me something so direct. Unfortunately, after more than fifty years, we had grown apart.

"Phaedra?" Karina prodded.

I sighed. "The thing is, Hades is... definitely not normal. How many newlyweds go on talk shows to talk about their weddings?"

"Other than you?" Karina postulated, humming as though she actually had to think about this. "None. I still can't believe you'll be on *Late Night Aranthium*."

Neither could I. When Hades told me his assistant had booked us on Aranthium's most popular late-night talk show, I wanted to run and hide.

Saul gave us one week to prepare.

"I know," I groaned. "Putting aside the fact that my husband is a king, he's also so..."

"Hot?"

I narrowed my eyes. "I was going to say that Hades is multi-faceted."

As my boss, he was strict. Not in a bad way. He was strict in a way that made working for him easy. I knew what he wanted, and when I did it, it made him happy. As the king, he was powerful. The strength he wielded as the King of the Daemons was impressive, to say the least. As a male, he was attractive. I would have to be blind not to admit that.

As my husband? Time had yet to tell. Three weeks was not a long enough time to know what kind of man my husband was.

"Ah." Karina grinned. "Multi-faceted *and* hot."

"What is hot? Is everything alright?" The question came from behind me, and instantly, I knew who said it.

Karina's back straightened, and blood rushed to her cheeks. "Oh, Your Highness. I'm sorry I didn't see you there."

A chuckle came as a heavy hand landed on my shoulder. "I figured as much." Hades squeezed my shoulder. "How are you, Phaedra?"

I blinked. "I'm fine," I replied.

He nodded. "Good. Karina, I hate to say this, but there are

some things I need to discuss with my wife. They are time-sensitive, and—"

"Say no more, Your Highness." Karina pushed herself away from the table so quickly that her drink trembled. Winking at me when Hades' back was turned, she slung her purse over her shoulder. "Call me, Phaedra."

The door slipped shut behind her, and I turned in my seat. My husband stood behind me, dressed in yet another black ensemble. This one was made entirely of leather. My mouth watered at the sight.

Karina wasn't wrong. Dressed like this, my husband was a certain kind of attractive. His shadows hovered in the air around him, his horns stretched high above his head.

There was no questioning his position as the King of the Daemons today.

An awkward silence filled the kitchen as we stared at each other. I kept thinking about my rules, trying to remember why the hell I made them in the first place. Right now, I wasn't sure why.

"I didn't hear you come in," I said after a moment, drawing my lip through my teeth.

Hades nodded, his eyes far away. "I just Transposed in. There is... we have to talk about something."

His tone made my stomach churn. Instantly, I knew something terrible happened.

"What happened?" I whispered.

My husband sighed, his shoulders drooping in a way I had never seen before. "You may have heard about Madea's curse?"

I began to shake my head, but I stopped as a painting bloomed to life in my memory. It had arrived in a shipment of paintings a decade or so ago. The others had been innocuous, but this one... It was so horrible, I took one look at it and started crying. Hades had taken one look at my face before ordering it to be burned. It was the only time it had happened during my time working for him.

Aidoneus' eyes traveled to the wall. "Madea was a great woman in Aranthium's history. She was one of the first Daemons, and her husband was a human. She married him, and with her help, he gained a lot of power. One day, he betrayed her and killed their two children. When kings instigated inter-clan conflicts in ancient times, they declared their intentions by killing children. It's a way to say they will do whatever they can to win. "

I stared at my husband, my jaw on the floor. "But-but Phelix already declared war. He did it on television for the world to see." My breathing was coming faster, and my head was getting lighter.

Aidoneus swallowed hard. "There was an orphanage near the borders of Angel's Landing."

"Was?" I whispered.

He nodded, running his hand over his face. "Last night, one of my spies intercepted a message about an attack. Only..."

Aidoneus shook, his shadows curling around him as if to provide comfort. Right then and there, I knew. This was the worst kind of news. The kind that made the world seem gray.

"What happened?"

"We were too late," he said a moment later, confirming my suspicions.

Too late.

An orphanage.

Bile rose in my throat.

"How many?" I whispered.

"Four dozen." Then, as if the words had taken everything out of him, Aidoneus shuddered. I pushed myself to my feet. Without thinking, I reached over and took his hand in mine. I don't know what made me do it. He just... he looked like he could use someone. Contact. A reminder he was still alive.

The moment our hands touched, I felt a spark come to life within me. That door that had remained closed since the night of our wedding cracked open, and the bond writhed within me like a living thing.

My husband was in pain, and he wanted me to comfort him.

I didn't really know what to do about that.

"I'm so sorry," I said, honesty permeating my voice. "I'm sorry it happened, and I'm sorry you had to see that."

Here I was, drinking iced coffee and gossiping with my friend while my husband was out dealing with this.

Children were murdered while I'd been relaxing at home. My biggest frustrations were that I didn't have a job. The complaint seemed trivial now. How could I care about something like that when those children were dead?

I was safe and warm, and they were gone. What kind of person did that make me?

Before I could delve further into *that* train of thought, Aidoneus nodded. "Thank you. I came back because it'll be all over the news soon, and I... I didn't want you to hear it from someone else."

He thought of me even in the midst of dealing with this tragedy. That meant a lot to me. I wasn't sure why, but I knew it was important.

"Thank you," I whispered. What else could I say? Rubbing my thumb over the back of my husband's hand, a minute passed in silence. My rules about no touching could go to Hell.

"Phaedra, those children..."

"What?" I breathed.

"They were so small. So young." Aidoneus looked at me, his eyes flashing green. "Children have so much potential. So much life to live. They are our future. And for my brother to just kill them like that..."

It was horrible.

I said as much, and Aidoneus nodded.

He murmured. "I'm so glad I came home."

Home. To me.

This man—this king—who was off limits to so many, was confiding in me. We'd had plenty of conversations in the past, but this... this was new.

Aidoneus was sharing this private part of himself with me, which made me feel... strange. Warm. Not in a bad way. In a way, that made me feel like maybe remaining friends would be harder than I thought. Because the feelings I was experiencing right now were definitely not based on friendship.

"Your brother is a monster." The words escaped me, laced with conviction.

This wasn't the first time the thought had entered my mind. It was common knowledge that the King of the Ice Mer was the least stable of the three DemiGods who ruled Aranthium. I'd been in the room when Erik admitted that Phelix had hired him to kill Helena—his daughter and heir.

What kind of bastard hired the Pirate of Death to kill their own daughter?

But this. This was a new low, even for Phelix. In war, there were casualties. These weren't the first, and certainly wouldn't be the last, but to kill children?

Monster was too kind of a word to describe his deplorable actions.

"Phelix's men are dead. They will rot in eternal torment. I have no doubt my mother has made sure of that." Aidoneus' voice sounded strange. Soft. Choked. It evoked emotions within me that I wasn't ready to unpack.

I looked up just in time to see a tear run down my husband's cheek. I squeezed his hand, taking a step towards him. Then another. When mere inches were between us, my index finger seemed to raise independently.

I wiped the tear from his cheek. "What do you need?"

A long, heavy moment passed as my husband stared at me. The air was thick, our hands intertwined, as our pulses raced.

He dipped his head toward me, his eyes filled with darkness and sorrow. "I need to forget. For a few hours."

Forget.

I could understand that.

Luckily for him, I was something of an expert at forgetting. Before I'd come to the Gates of Hell, things hadn't always been easy for me. As a young Angel, before my mother got sick, she and I had a tumultuous relationship.

My husband wanted to forget, and I could help him with that.

The perfect idea popped into my head. The night Aidoneus and I had wed, I needed to forget some things. He found me on the couch, and we'd just... been. Together.

That was the first time in my life that I could remember feeling... whole.

My lips tilted up into a small smile. "All right," I whispered. "Let's forget. And tomorrow, you give that bastard what he deserves." My husband was powerful, and there was a stability about him. "You mentioned you have acquired soldiers?"

Aidoneus nodded. "Yes," he sighed. "About thirty thousand."

I squeezed his hand, tugging him toward the living room. "Good."

He followed me willingly, our feet padding in time on the plush white carpet.

I walked him over to the couch, waiting until he was sitting before letting go of his hand. He watched me silently as I grabbed an enormous, fluffy pink blanket from the chest beside the couch. It was one of my new additions to the penthouse. A splash of spring to bring life into this dark home.

Blanket in hand, I pressed a few buttons on my FaePhone and ordered food before grabbing the TV remote. Aidoneus sat silently as I settled cross-legged on the couch, leaving a pillow between us.

Just in case.

Raising a brow, I turned to the silent statue of a man beside me. "When I was growing up, I had... a lot going on."

That was one way to word growing up with an overprotective mother, but I didn't really want to get into it.

"Oh?"

I nodded. "Sometimes, when things were a lot, I needed to forget, too."

Like that one time when I begged to be allowed to go outside and play with the neighbors. In response, my mother pulled me out of the private school I'd been attending, hired tutors, and forced me to stay inside the house for a year.

Yeah. That had been less than ideal.

Suffice it to say, she and I had our rocky moments.

Aidoneus tilted his head, his eyes watching me. "What did you do?"

I raised a brow, my lips tilting into a small smile as I pressed a button on the remote. Navigating to the channel I found a few weeks ago, I settled back on the couch. "This."

Bright colors filled the room as the sound of couples laughing filled the air. We both watched silently for a few minutes as the long-haired Were on the screen confessed her undying love for Aprici, the Vampire she had known for three days.

Within moments, it was clear that Were was in love. Or at least, she thought she was. Only time would tell.

"You watched... trash TV?" My husband's voice made it clear

he had never been exposed to the wonderful thing that was reality dating television.

I raised a brow. "Not just any trash TV." Gesturing to the television, I smiled. "*Dating in Aranthium* is the *worst* kind of TV there is. It's so bad, it's good."

"Is that so?"

"Yes, it is." I nodded. "As your friend, I am telling you, this is the perfect way to forget. Well, this and takeout. Which should be here in about ten minutes."

He chuckled. The sound was so much better than the destroyed man who had been standing in the kitchen earlier. For some unknown reason, my insides warmed at the sound.

"All right, *friend*." He emphasized the word, waving his hand at the TV before putting it on the couch beside me. "Takeout and reality TV. That's your secret to forgetting?"

"Yes." I leaned in close, mock-whispering. Somehow, we inched toward each other, and within moments, our thighs were touching. The movement sent a jolt through me, and I sucked in a breath. "And, of course, we'll gorge ourselves on ice cream after dinner."

He laughed, and I grinned. His eyes flicked down to where our thighs were touching. "Is it wrong to comment on all this touching? I just want to make sure I'm not crossing any lines."

I looked up at him and bit my lips, suddenly feeling shy. "Stupid rules were meant to be broken," I said.

He glanced at me out of the corner of his eye. "Dinner is not a stupid rule."

I laughed. "You're right. Speaking of which..." I stood back up and grabbed some green pepper tamales.

Hours later, after we had binged an entire season of *Dating in Aranthium*, the soft sound of snoring came from beside me. Empty cartons of takeout were scattered on the floor, and the empty carton of mint chocolate chip ice cream we'd shared sat on the coffee table.

The shadows had long since retreated back into my husband, and the smallest hint of a smile rested on his face. He looked... relaxed.

I stared at him for a few minutes, my stomach twisting in a sensation that was entirely odd. I felt warm but not uncomfortable. He needed to forget, and I helped him.

Maybe Karina was right. Maybe I wasn't useless after all.

CHAPTER 23
COLD BEDS
AIDONEUS

I grabbed my phone and stared at the "No Service" message in the top right corner. The last message I got was yet another request from Nyrnavox to meet. He left me a voicemail again, complaining about the lack of help with the war. The gall of the man to say such a thing. I was working my ass off, making sure that our allies were increasing daily. He had nothing to complain about.

"How did your wife feel about you leaving your bed before it was even cold?" one of the Northern Fae asked. Aed Swiftwhite had white tattoos scrawled up and around his neck, with a vicious glint in his eye.

Gruff laughter rumbled all around me. This Fae was a major pain in my ass, except for when he was running his squadron.

A nasty wind accompanied the encroaching night. I gritted my teeth and huffed a half-hearted laugh before taking a long drink of coffee and wincing. It was burnt.

"Good one," I grumbled, which won me an elbow in the ribs from another Fae Warrior.

I wasn't surprised when Queen Elva reached out with a

pledge of troops, but I was immensely grateful. Raphael was being dodgy about the whole situation, and even though these northern beings generally annoyed the shit out of me with their brutal practices and tasteless humor, I was here. We were on the eastern corner of the Winter Court, right on the border of the Ice Mer Territory.

One of my Daemon soldiers, Dagon, sat next to me. He let out a heated breath. “Gods, do they ever stop?” he grumbled.

“I wish,” another one of my officers, Naahmah, said to him before drawing his arms tighter around himself.

It was freezing in this place. We were given fur blankets and igloos to sleep in, and the mess hall was made from animal skins. After walking outside this morning, ice-covered my eyelashes. *That* was too much.

The conversation continued around me, and I looked down at my watch. At least it was still ticking. I needed to leave in an hour. Tomorrow, I had that talk show appearance with Phaedra.

Utter rubbish. But, there was little choice. My people needed to get to know their queen consort. Even though she was not crowned, Phaedra assumed the title of queen consort from the moment we said, “I do.”

More laughter erupted, and I caught the tail end of the punchline of a crude joke about sleeping with Angels.

“Just try not to get flapped in the face, is all I’m saying,” Major Swiftwhite grunted out.

Primal instinct took over as I stood, shoving the wooden bench up. The movement knocked over at least thirty Fae Warriors. They rolled up to their feet in an instant, growling at me as potato and beef stew covered their shirts. Within moments, Dagon and Naahmah were on their feet, flanking me.

I barely acknowledged them as I Transposed from my seat to stand directly behind Aed.

Grabbing his shoulder, I yanked him around. Shadows gathered around me, and the earth trembled beneath my feet. "Joke about me all you like. I am capable of outliving you and your words."

Aed snarled. "Look, Daemon King, I was just saying—"

"I know what you were saying," I said with daggers for words. Aed glared at me. I'd seen snowstorms that were warmer than his gaze. Scoffing, I continued, "I have nothing but the highest respect for your work ethic, but speak of my wife like that again, and I will personally request that you be replaced." I leaned in closer until he had to look directly up to watch my face. "And when you are no longer in the queen's employ, I will find you."

The air chilled around us, but not from my power. I stood up and smirked. His frosty power was nothing compared to mine. "Is that a threat?"

I opened my mouth at the same time that I heard, "Swiftwhite, stop being a twat. Go clean up that mess and stop picking on people twice your size." The commanding feminine voice of the new Winter Court monarch filled the now-silent tent.

I hadn't realized the Winter Queen was here. The red edging my vision receded, and the heat of my anger leached out of me. I felt like an idiot in the middle of the mess hall. The pissed-off-looking major burst out of the tent, hissing harmless curses about what a shit hole the "fish head" underwater was. He changed his tune quickly, and I appreciated that.

I turned to look at the Winter Queen. She was dressed in pure white fur that trimmed her collar and sleeves, and her hair was braided tightly across her hair. She could have been going to a dinner or straight into battle.

"Your Highness," I said with an inclination of my head. Deep down, I felt terrible. I needed to get the anger under control and stop trying to bite the head off of any person who said something out of hand. Otherwise, we might not have an army left to fight my brother.

Elva eyed me for a moment. Her mouth was straight, her eyes flat as she said, "How about you call me Elva, and I call you Aidy so I feel less weird?"

There wasn't a trace of humor in her expression that would make me think she was being facetious.

I opened my mouth, looking for the words to politely tell Elva that nicknames would not be happening when she chuckled.

"Relax, Hades. It was a joke to lighten your mood. I've been working on it with my husband. You know how it is." Queen Elva winked, and I prayed to my mother that she wasn't making an age joke.

I let out a staccatoed laugh and said, "I appreciate you speaking to Major Swiftwhite."

She nodded, stepping out of the way to avoid the soldiers mopping up the mess on the icy ground.

One of the men's heads popped up. "Can't we just leave it for the animals?"

The Fae beside him said, "Not unless the animal is you, Karn."

More laughter. Even my Daemons joined in this time.

I'd spent enough time in the last few months traveling from camp to camp between Daemon, Spring Mer, Swamp Witch, and now Winter Fae soldiers getting endless reports. Unsurprisingly, my Daemons kept to themselves enough to ensure that there was no trouble. Of course, I wasn't required to be everywhere at once, but we still lacked official pledges of support from the Snow Were, the Summer Fae, and my idiotic brother.

All in all, things were going well. I nodded at Queen Elva with a tight smile.

"Shall we walk?" I asked.

Elva drew herself up, shifting her shoulders backward. "Yes, that is why I came here."

I glanced at the entrance of the tent and saw eight new soldiers dressed in pure white, matching their queen. I gestured for Dagon to follow as we walked out of the tent.

We walked down the spell-lit walkway, passing several hundreds of igloos that the Winter Fae had made with their bare hands, toward a clearing at the end. Fae had excellent hearing, so we would need to walk quite far in order to truly not be heard.

That was inefficient, so I created a privacy pocket. The air around us became silent, even sealing out the guards that were trailing us. I noted that one of the Fae men put his hand on his weapon. Pressure built in my ears, and I fought the urge to try to pop them with my breathing.

From the grimace painted on Elva's lips, she was feeling similarly.

I cast a sympathetic smile at her and asked, "What can I do for you?"

"King Hades," she started. "I am glad to see that you haven't left for Lethe yet."

Real, tangible relief was mixed into her tone, bringing me pause. Something pricked the back of my neck, causing the hair to stand up on my body.

"Why's that?" I tried to swallow, but my mouth was bone dry.

Did something happen to Phaedra? Internally, I sought out our bond. It looked fine.

Elva cleared her throat, and then her hand disappeared into her thick fur coat. "I received this less than two hours ago." She withdrew a leather envelope and passed it to me.

My eyes flicked her tight-lipped expression one more time before I unraveled the waxed twine, keeping it shut, and slid the thick papers out. My eyes scanned the first sentence.

TRANSCRIPT: INTERROGATION OF PRISONER 18B

"What is this?" I breathed.

Elva shifted her weight from one foot to the other, the sound amplified in the small space. "According to the full report, some of my people intercepted a group of Ice Mers heading to some random stretch of open sea in the west. Most of them were killed or self-eliminated, except for one." She let out an uneasy breath, and then she met my eyes. "He offered information in place of sanctuary."

Making a clicking sound with my teeth, I tilted my head. "Impossible."

She shrugged. "The Ice Mer have a longstanding relationship with the Winter Court. I know it's shocking, but stranger things have happened."

I considered her words. Tapping my fingers at my side, I decided that a little trust could go a long way with the Winter Court Queen. "An Ice Mer was intercepted in my tower a few months ago. I still don't really know how he got there, but I was able to extract some information from him."

Queen Elva's blue eyes widened, and she shook her head as if she had misheard me. "They got into your tower?"

I nodded, running my fingers over the heavy report in my hands. "The Mer told me that he wasn't sent to kill anyone. He told me,"—I hesitated, recalling his exact words, and the moment I'd realized he'd been sent on a suicide mission—"that his King knew whose death was worth the most. But it wasn't mine."

As the words left my mouth, Elva's face paled. She glanced nervously to the side, shifting from one foot to the other. "Our report says almost the exact thing." Her gloved hands laced together as she looked at me. "Where is your wife?"

"Phaedra?" I stared at the Winter Queen. "She's at home. A security team is on her at all times."

Even as I said the words, urgency filled me. Elva's gaze was heavy, and as she studied me, I decided the team wasn't enough.

"I need to go," I said quickly.

The Winter Queen nodded. "That's a good idea. Stay with your wife. We will continue to proceed as things are." She pressed her lips in a thin line. "You should also try to see if Raphael will join us. Or your mother. We need all the help we can get."

I nodded. She was right. Something was going on with my golden-skinned brother. He and I needed to talk.

Dipping my head, I sighed. "Very well, Queen Elva. I will take my leave, but please don't hesitate to reach out with anything else." I extended my hand with the heavy envelope, ready to return it, but Elva refused me with strong gloved hands and a forced smile.

Her curly hair gleamed in the spell lights as she shook her head. "Keep it."

I let the air bubble around us down. Air rushed all around me, making me a little lightheaded for a second. It took moments to regain my composure in the middle of the frozen tundra of the North before I turned to Dagon and Naahmah. Their black leathers, paired with their dark skin, made them living shadows in this light. They were nightmares to some and friendly creatures lurking in the darkness to others.

"We need to return to Lethe. Are you ready to leave?"

They nodded, speaking in unison. "Yes, sir."

"Good. I'll notify the squadron leader, and then we will head out." I straightened the gray leather of my uniform.

The males dipped their heads, and I turned back to the queen once more. "Until we meet again," I said with a smile.

Despite the worry in my stomach, shooting sparks traveled up my arms. I was ready to go home.

WHEN I RETURNED to the apartment, the entire place smelled like Phaedra's unique brand of springtime. Thanks to the time difference between the North and South, I arrived just in time for dinner.

Transposing into the apartment, I just stared at it for a moment. The space where I had lived for centuries looked different. There were still dark colors, but now pops of earthy greens, purples, and pinks were scattered throughout. My wife had clearly been busy.

As I studied the apartment, voices filtered down the hall to the entrance.

My stomach tensed. Who was here?

"Phaedra?" I called, not bothering with the AI.

Less than two seconds passed before a cheerful, "In the living room!" called back to me.

I walked down the hall, already feeling more relaxed than in days. I needed to tell her what Elva said, but that would need to wait.

When I entered our living room, I found one of my PR agents sitting on the couch beside Phaedra.

"Hello," I drawled. It was an effort to remove traces of strain from my voice—a side-effect form working so closely with the military.

Phaedra looked up at me, and the bond between us glowed. "Hello, Aidoneus."

The PR agent, a human I'd met a few times before, tore his gaze away from Phaedra. He stood, bowing deeply in my direction. "Your Highness. I was just helping Queen Phaedra," my wife and I froze—"prepare for your interview tomorrow. She is a natural."

The man, whose name I thought was Kaden, said the last part with a little too much enthusiasm for my liking.

I returned his words with a tight-lipped smile. "Thank you." I heaved a heavy sigh, eyeing the door. "If you'd excuse us..."

The human's eyes widened. "Oh. Right. Of course, Your Majesties."

I didn't watch, but I was sure he bowed all the way out of the door.

Once Phaedra and I were alone, my shoulders loosened. My awareness stretched out from within me, and the bond between us tugged. Walking over next to my wife, I sank down into the seat previously occupied by Kaden. It was still warm, and a horrible thought crossed my mind. If Phaedra wouldn't love me, if she wouldn't sleep with me, eventually she would choose someone. The thought made me want to kill someone. Anyone.

The very idea of someone else's hands on my wife sent fire roiling through me.

As quickly as the jealousy appeared, I shoved it toward Tartaro with the rest of the trash.

Arranged. Marriage.

"What's wrong?" Phaedra asked, her voice soft. My wife was close enough to wake up every inch of me, even though I was trying to act tired.

I didn't know how I would survive an eternity of this. Being close to her and not touching her was pure torture. Sighing, I rubbed my temples. "I will tell you after the interview. Tonight, I just want to eat and rest."

"Alright." Phaedra nodded. "The chef left us with dinner already. I can heat it up if you'd like."

I smiled at her. This interaction, being together, felt so natural. So right. The air around us was soft. Intimate in a way that made me feel warm. Safe. It made me feel things I hadn't felt for a long time. This moment was soft and bright and made me wish I could bottle the moment up and preserve it for all time.

"No, my Angel. I've got it." Shaking my head, I stood, pointedly ignoring how Phaedra bit her lip at the nickname.

Seconds ticked on as I reached the fridge and pulled out the glass containers. A quick perusal told me the chef made lemon chicken and gravy with a spring mix salad. Fitting.

As I grabbed a spoon to dish it into clean dishes, Phaedra called over from the living room, "Why don't you just leave it in those?"

One second, she was in the living room, and the next, she was sitting on a stool across from me. Raising a brow, she continued, "I liked eating right out of the glassware. It makes fewer dishes, and somehow, it just tastes better."

I stared at her, nearly dropping the dishes in my hands as my mind caught up with what I'd just witnessed. "Phaedra?"

She beamed at me and stretched one of her hands to the side. "What?" she asked coyly.

"You just Transposed," I said slowly, evenly, while I set the dishes on the counter.

"Yes," she said, fighting a grin. "For teaching me, I have gotten you a gift. Do you want it now or later?"

Something fluttered in my stomach, and I wondered if this was real life. This house, her, me. "Oh?" I pretended disinterest as I forwent the plates and started heating the chicken.

"Turn around, my king," she said.

I did immediately. From behind her, she pulled out a square frame. It was made out of gleaming wood. She handed it to me, and I took it with great care.

My brows rose. "Where did you get this?"

She smiled. "I asked Cassandra." Phaedra leaned in close, pointing to the picture. "It's us, just before we said our vows."

The two of us were smiling at each other in front of the priestess, our expressions both nervous and yet... happy.

My eyes watered, and I blinked. And then I blinked again. "Phaedra..."

She grinned. "You gave me that lovely vase, which is in my room, by the way. Well, now we are even. It's a lovely picture. It deserves to be on display."

Reaching out, I cupped her cheek. She sucked in a breath, and I stroked my beautiful wife's cheek. "This is amazing. First Transposing, and now this. I can't believe it."

Phaedra pressed her lips together as I walked a few steps away, putting the picture on the counter.

"I'm so glad you feel that way. In fact, since I am getting better with my powers,"—she Transposed to my side once more, and my heart flipped—"I have something to propose to you."

"Of course, my Angel"

I turned away to grab salad dressing as she said, "I want to start working on the acquisitions floor."

For a moment, I froze. My heart stuttered, and my fingers tightened around the salad dressing. She wanted to work?

"No," I said slowly, turning back around. Even thinking about Phaedra down in acquisitions, seeing all those people, and interacting with strangers made my skin crawl.

That clearly wasn't the answer she was expecting. She chewed on her lip, crossed her arms, and tried again. "I am dying up here. I am all alone. I need to work, Aidoneus. I am a queen consort with no responsibilities, with no purpose."

A strange conflict came to life inside of me. I sucked in a breath. "Phaedra, you do have a purpose—"

"More than talk shows, decorating, and planning events, Aidoneus. I am an educated woman." A rippling of power filled the air, and she huffed. "I have multiple art degrees from the best institutes in Aranthium."

"I understand that. You are one of the best, but things are slow now because of the war. You can't just live your life. I can't either." Uneasiness bloomed within me, and I clenched my fist.

Tension grew in the room, and the air thickened.

"You are out traveling from one corner of the globe to the other. Stop treating me like I'm so fragile." she spat the words out as if she wouldn't live if they stayed inside her a second longer.

I looked up at this female. This Angel who was my wife. Phaedra was strong. She was capable and intelligent. Right now, she looked vibrant enough to outshine the desert sun. Warmth spread through me. Phaedra meant more to me than she knew. I couldn't lose her—I'd already lost Miranda. "Phaedra, I have already lost one wife. Would you ask me to lose another?"

A long moment passed, and she studied me. Her wings fluttered behind her, and she sighed.

"Aidoneus, I just need to do something," she whispered. "Please."

This conversation was far from over. I could feel it. But I was so tired. So worn out. "Can we talk more about this tomorrow? After the talk show?"

Phaedra stared at me and then the food I had in my hands. Slowly, she nodded. "All right. Tomorrow." She speared a piece of chicken with her fork, waving it around in the air. "Don't try to run away and gloss over what I'm saying."

I made a sound of agreement, and Phaedra placed the chicken in her mouth. The moment it landed on her tongue, she made a noise that I was getting sick of hearing. "Well, at least the food is good."

Rolling my eyes, I smiled. Taking my own food, I watched my wife. We couldn't shove problems under the carpet, but it was so nice to just put those aside for a second to relax. Not only that but she gave me a gift. Things were looking up.

We were definitely friends. And maybe one day, we might be more.

That thought sparked hope within me.

"So, tell me what you learned for tomorrow. Is there something I should do?" I asked as I eased onto the stool next to her. She leaned in close, starting to explain what we were going to do tomorrow.

We stayed like that for over an hour. Lost in the electric blue of Phaedra's eyes and the entrancing lilt of her voice, I completely forgot about the leather folder on my office desk.

CHAPTER 24
LATE NIGHT ARANTHIUM
PHAEDRA

"Tell me, Phaedra—is it all right if I call you Phaedra?" Amthir, the host of *Late Night Aranthium,* tilted her head as she met my gaze. A wolfish smile appeared on the Vampire's pale face, showcasing her two sharpened fangs.

We stood backstage, the sounds of the audience's murmured conversations filtering through the thick walls. Hades had just stepped away, taking a call from one of his generals.

A war was going on, and we were sitting down to film a late-night segment.

Something was wrong with the world.

I nodded, forcing a smile onto my face. "Of course. It is my name, after all."

Amthir smiled, but the look didn't reach her eyes. Her teeth were... exceptionally white. Two fangs gleamed in the artificial light—I was fairly certain they were sharper than normal. "Good. Did my assistant explain how this works?"

"Yes. She told me we would be introduced, and then—"

"Excellent." The Vampire turned, cutting me off mid-sentence. Her red hair bounced as she practically scurried onto the stage.

That was rude.

Pursing my lips, I leaned against a column and listened as Amthir greeted the audience. Stagehands rushed around me, yelling into microphones as they hurried to and fro. The roar of clapping filled my ears, and I knew it was almost time.

My stomach twisted in knots, the nerves that had been present all day getting worse. I was thankful I didn't eat anything beforehand.

A Were walked by and looked at my face before barking into the small microphone on his lapel. "Someone get me some water, asap. The queen consort looks like she's about to be sick."

Seconds later, the Were shoved a bottle of water in my hands. "Here. Drink this."

I complied, downing half the bottle in one gulp. The cool liquid soothed my insides and helped settle my stomach. "Thank you," I said sincerely.

The man nodded. "You're welcome. Nerves are normal for first-timers."

"Is it that obvious?" I straightened my knee-length pale blue dress, shifting from one foot to another. Everything, from the makeup on my face to the shoes on my feet, had been carefully picked to help me feel as comfortable as possible.

He shook his head. "Not to most."

Good. The last thing I wanted was for people to see me as weak. Nervous. There was a reason I wore so much makeup—it hid the parts of myself I didn't want others to know about. In fact, other than my mother when I was young, the only person who had ever seen me without makeup was...

Aidoneus.

I felt the moment he walked backstage. That bond within me, which seemed to grow by the day, lit up like Winter

Solstice lights. It practically quivered with joy as he approached me.

I didn't know what to make of that.

"Phaedra," Aidoneus said as he slid his hand around my waist, drawing me close. His voice was warm and caring in a way that it never had been while we'd been just co-workers.

I didn't have to fake the smile on my face as I turned. "Aidoneus."

His eyes sparkled, and he put his hand in his pocket. "Last night, your gift inspired me. I realized that I've been careless. I hope you'll forgive me."

My heart beat faster, though I wished it didn't. I couldn't keep from saying, "What do you mean?"

He withdrew two small vintage boxes with gold embossing, and my breath hitched.

"Rings," I breathed.

He smiled and nodded before popping open the red box. Inside was the most beautiful ring I'd ever seen. A stunningly blue pear-shaped stone was set in an Art Deco design. Intricate little flowers and details were carved into the gold band. I sucked in a breath.

"It's paraiba tourmaline. Rarer than diamonds, and it matches your eyes," he said softly.

I looked up at him, my eyes suddenly burning. "It's so beautiful."

He smiled. "May I?"

I nodded and offered him my hand. My skin tingled where his fingers brushed as he pushed the ring on my fourth finger. It was a perfect fit.

Shaking my head in disbelief at the three carats of pure extravagance, I looked up at him. "This is too much. You didn't even let me buy yours!"

He gave me a funny look. "I didn't realize you wanted to."

I smiled and held out my hand for the other box. I opened the black velvet and withdrew a simple gold band with floral etchings that matched my own ring.

"This is lovely, though," I murmured as I took his hand and placed the ring on his fourth finger.

Once I was done, our hands dropped to our sides, and we stared at each other for a moment. A strange happiness was flowing through my chest.

He tilted his head, looking around me for the first time. "Where is your security team?"

Waving a hand, I shrugged. "There are so many people here, and the three of them were just getting in the way. I suggested they grab some coffee before the taping."

Not to mention the fact that their presence was smothering me. I wasn't used to this. Any of it. The constantly clicking cameras. The questions. People asking for my autograph. The magic.

None of it.

Aidoneus ran a hand through his perfectly coiffed hair. "Phaedra, you can't just dismiss your security team. They are there to protect you."

Can't.

I *hated* that word. I'd heard it hundreds—no, thousands—of times growing up. My mother always told me things I couldn't do. I couldn't go out without supervision. I couldn't play with the others. I couldn't be a normal child.

I couldn't live.

My back straightened. "Is that so?" I met my husband's eyes unflinchingly. "Because it looks like I did."

His nostrils flared as he took a step towards me. His eyes sparked green, and the bond... I felt anger stirring within him. It was strange, feeling the emotions of another person.

The king had more control than I did, though, because he

didn't destroy anything in his anger. Aidoneus took a series of deep breaths until his eyes returned to their normal color. "Phaedra, my Angel, we need to talk about this."

I sucked in a breath.

There was that nickname again. I wasn't sure how I felt about it. Friends had nicknames for friends, right?

But the way he said it...

There wasn't anything friendly about his tone. No, it was all dark. Deep. Rough. Like it was just for me.

"I don't really think there's much to talk about, *Hades*." I emphasized his name and his eyes narrowed. That bond tugged on me, and frustration chipped away at the wall I was trying to construct between us. "The security team wasn't needed, so I sent them away for a few hours. It's not like I dismissed them entirely."

"You can't—"

A horn blared, cutting me off.

Less than three seconds later, a harried Daemon with a clipboard hurried over to us. "We're ready for you. Please follow me."

Ever the composed king, Aidoneus nodded. "We'll be right there."

Turning to me, he let out a ragged sigh as he laced our hands together. I didn't fight him. We were in public, and I had agreed to this. We needed to appear as a unified front for the cameras.

My husband leaned in close, whispering so only I could hear him. "This conversation isn't over."

Hand-in-hand, we walked onto the stage. Bright lights shone, illuminating a bright red half-moon couch on a living room set. It would have been a cozy scene if not for the look Amthir was giving me from the couch.

Something about her expression made me feel off.

The Vampire grinned, her fangs gleaming in the artificial

light. She stood, spreading her skirts before dipping into a curtsy that was one-inch shy of being insulting.

Amthir rose from the curtsy and gestured for us to take a seat. The couch was surprisingly comfortable, with special grooves in the back to accommodate my wings.

My husband and I sat together. He squeezed my fingers before pressing a quick kiss to our joined hands. I straightened, sparks running through me from that slight contact, and the crowd aw'd.

The Vampire's lips twitched up into what might have passed as a smile, and she took her own seat before turning to face the audience. “Ladies and gentlemen of Aranthium, I am incredibly delighted to introduce your illustrious king, Aidoneus Hades, and the woman giving hope to all assistants who dream about seducing their bosses—Phaedra Demtre!”

My husband’s grip on my hand tightened, his thumb brushing my ring. His anger was a living inferno roiling through our bond. I forced myself to keep my breathing even.

Talk shows were meant to be edgy and hard. I knew she might say something like this, but still, it stung. Forcing a smile on my face, I did the only thing I could think of: I *laughed*. “Well, it’s true that I did work for my husband before we got married, but I assure you that nothing inappropriate happened while I worked for him.”

“Is that so?” Amthir raised a perfectly manicured brow. She turned to my husband. “What about you? Did you ever feel anything for your wife while she worked for you?”

A snort rose within me, and it took everything I had to force it down. What a ridiculous question. Of course, the king never harbored feelings for me. I had been his employee and nothing more.

I waited for Aidoneus to laugh off the question.

He did not.

A very long second passed.

Then another.

Then, a third.

Every one of them felt like an hour.

I shifted uncomfortably as Aidoneus' hand grew clammy around mine.

"I..." He shook his head, clearing his throat. "Phaedra was the best assistant I ever had."

That wasn't an answer.

Apparently, Amthir agreed with me because she raised a perfectly manicured brow.

"Well," she drawled, making a face at the audience that told them exactly what she thought, "there you have it. There was definitely *something* going on in that tall black tower. Phaedra, there's nothing as exhilarating as sneaking around, right?" She winked at me, but it wasn't a friendly gesture. It was fast, like a snake striking its prey.

My skin went hot all over. "I don't think—" I began, but the Vampire shook her head. "Now, Your Highness. I have a question about the war?"

Aidoneus stiffened beside me, nodding slowly. "I thought you might," he said carefully. "As I'm sure you're aware, many things must be kept a secret in order to keep our valuable soldiers safe."

A grin spread over the Vampire's face. "As a matter of fact, the troops are exactly what I wanted to ask you about."

"Oh?"

"Yes," Amthir continued, her tone almost gleeful. "I understand you were originally looking for a wife in order to strengthen the Gates of Hell. Your first wife, Miranda, was a force to be reckoned with. She was well connected, powerful, and she really understood the role of queen consort."

Amthir paused, gesturing to a screen behind us. Seconds ago, it had a picture of a sandy beach.

I sucked in a breath, and the screen changed. My eyes widened at a picture of my old apartment. Dylan's arm was slung around my shoulders, and he was leaning in close—too close. It looked like he was licking my neck.

My mouth fell open.

Aidoneus growled, and Amthir continued. "You picked a woman who has no idea of her place. Being a royal is not about being famous. The public looks up to royalty to take care of them. Being a king or queen consort,"—a pointed look at me—"is a position endowed with duty. It is not about sleeping your way to the top."

Sleeping my way to the top? I sank further into my seat, and my eyes burned.

When Aidoneus didn't respond right away, the Vampire continued to speak. "Honestly, Your Highness, I think I speak for the entire country when I say that we were shocked that you would bind your magic to someone who doesn't appear to be able to bear the weight of the crown. Despite her three art degrees, she doesn't even bring additional troops to the table. So, High King Hades, would you care to explain to the people of the Gates of Hell why you chose such an inadequate female to rule over them?"

The words were barely out of her mouth when pure, unadulterated rage flooded the bond. My legs shook at the force of Aidoneus' anger. The second it touched me, my power flared to life. Blue sparks flew off me, matching the green ones, flitting off my husband.

The Vampire's eyes widened, and she jumped. After a second, she chuckled nervously. "I... uh... Your Highness. I wasn't aware that your wife had godly power. If you'll allow me to say how deeply..."

Her voice trailed off as Aidoneus released my hand, pushing himself to his feet. Shadows flooded out of him, creating a black wall between us and the cameras. A flash of green magic sparked from his fingertips, frying the microphones attached to the three of us.

"That was a mistake." Aidoneus' voice was deeper than I had ever heard it before. Ice laced his words. "When I remove the shadows, you will issue an apology to Aranthium. In the next breath, you are going to resign. Effective immediately."

"Sir?" Amthir squeaked.

"Did I say you could talk?" he thundered.

She shook her head.

"Once you resign, you are going to go straight home. I won't stand for this type of journalism in my kingdom. Pack a bag. You are finished. If I, or anyone who works for me, ever sees you within the borders of the Gates of Hell again, you will regret it far more than I regret coming on this ridiculous show."

The way he said those words made my insides twist. He fought for me. Protected me against this... this... this undead creature and her nasty words.

My brain might have been fine with being friends with Aidoneus, but my body was all for the way he was protecting me. Warmth flooded through me, and my core twisted. The bond... It was almost gleeful at the way my husband was defending me.

Amthir opened her mouth. "I—"

"Enough!" Aidoneus' wings snapped out behind him. In the next second, my husband's suit and tie disappeared. In its place was the black leather armor he wore when visiting troops on the front line. "Do not forget with whom you speak."

His words echoed through the soundstage, and the shadows thickened. Enormous black wings filled the studio, and his skin color deepened from its natural gray. I was glad not to be on the wrong side of his anger.

The Vampire trembled like a leaf. Her voice was quiet as she whispered, “I understand, sir.”

Aidoneus stared at her for a long minute before nodding once. “Good. Should you forget the terms of this agreement, I won’t hesitate to issue a punishment of the more permanent variety."

“No-no need for that, Your Highness,” Amthir stuttered.

“Good,” Aidoneus purred.

As quickly as they had appeared, my husband’s wings snapped out of existence. His suit and tie returned, and he smoothed down his hair. He flicked his hands, and the shadows lifted.

Amthir did exactly as she was told.

The moment she did, Aidoneus Transposed my security team and me back to the apartment. He didn’t stay.

The moment my feet touched the carpet, I walked to the bathroom. Turning on the shower, I waited until steam rose from the water. I stripped off my clothes, dumping them on the ground before walking beneath the steam.

Then, and only then, did I let the tears flow.

I stayed in the shower until my skin wrinkled and I ran out of tears.

CHAPTER 25
ONE LONG LIMO RIDE
AIDONEUS

Phaedra sat across from me in a black car with windows tinted darker than night. When I arrived home the night before, she was already asleep in her bed. But even then, her soul was so soaked in sadness that the bond had felt like a gaping hole between us.

Lunch had been a silent, awkward affair. Now, we were headed out to dinner in a public place. Saul hoped it would help patch up the damage done last night by my unstable temper. Personally, I didn't see a problem with it.

That Vampire had been acting out of line.

What really concerned me was that Phaedra still wasn't speaking. Her lovely head was tilted toward the car window, and sadness permeated the bond.

There wasn't much to see outside of passing buildings and spectators. I knew these were all sights she'd witnessed before. With her head resting against the window, my beautiful wife looked like a queen of old. A golden laurel band wrapped around her head, giving her a regal presence. But the silence was unnerving. It wasn't nerves. Those, I could handle. I didn't even think it was about the weight of her new role as a monarch.

I was fairly certain this silence was weighted. Heavy. It was about avoiding me. She hadn't looked at me since we got in the car, and our bond was quiet. Smoke the color of midnight spilled out around the gaps in place of comfortable sunshine. The past twenty-four hours had me wondering how many times I would try to break the silence before she snapped.

Rolling my head from side to side, I decided it was time for a new approach. "Phaedra." I waited to see if she would look at me. No luck. She didn't even move. "Look, that newscaster was, for lack of a better word, a bitch."

The words sounded odd coming out of my mouth—it wasn't hard to tell just how uncomfortable I felt reaching out to her.

I stared at the most beautiful statue in all Aranthium. Her eyes were glued to something outside, and her breathing was so low and quiet it was easy to miss. Hell, she barely even blinked.

"Look, I—" I started again.

The statue that was my wife came to life. It was like a thing from fairytales, though Phaedra was not some cursed maiden.

No, my wife—my queen—was the whole damned avenging warrior.

Something flickered inside of me. Words that I wasn't ready to speak, thoughts that I shouldn't be having.

Flickers of electric blue wormed their way through Phaedra's irises as she latched those dangerous eyes on me while her hair spilled around her bare shoulders. Her large ring glinted from the light pouring from her eyes.

Her arms spread wide on the leather seats as she leaned forward and snapped at me. "Do not apologize."

I didn't move an inch. Not now that the silence was broken. Not now that this vision of great and terrible power was finally speaking.

A long moment passed as the weight of the shattered silence pressed down on us. Then, Phaedra sucked in a breath and leaned back. Her fury faded just as quickly as it had come. "Don't you dare apologize," she whispered hoarsely.

"You deserve an apology," I said gently. My chin angled to the side, getting a different perspective on the distant storm painted across her face.

Her eyes snapped back to mine. "From who? From that talk show host? From you? Yes. I deserve many apologies." Her eyes grew shadowy, something entirely different from what I was used to seeing from her. "People do not apologize; if they do, they do not mean it. You are only saying this now because you want me to talk to you. To play along with this idiotic charade."

The venom-coated words were a dagger to my heart. I blinked. Things between us had been softening. I wasn't sure where this was coming from.

"Idiotic? Phaedra, I did this for your own good. Our marriage, this... everything. It was for you."

Why couldn't she see that?

Her lips twisted into a sneer, reminding me of a lioness. "My own good. What do you know about my own good? I've been alone more often than not since our wedding." She scoffed. "Some queen consort. Trapped in an apartment. Unable to help with the war. Maybe Amthir was right."

This was going downhill fast. I tugged on my suit coat and cleared my rapidly-tightening throat. "Maybe we should continue this conversation later. At a time when emotions aren't so high. We can talk about finding something for you to do. Something safe."

"Something safe." She sighed. "You just want to keep me in a box. We can't just keep putting off conversations, Hades."

We were back to that now. Damn.

Even so, Phaedra's words hit a little deeper than they should.

"I just think it would be wise to wait until we have calmed down to continue this conversation."

Maybe then, I'd be ready to deal with this.

She let out an exasperated breath, shaking her head. "Of course."

"Phaedra..."

My voice trailed off as her gaze returned to that stupid spot outside. My wife folded her arms around herself, her fingers turning her skin white from the pressure.

We turned a corner, the car swerving slightly before she twisted back.

"You know what, Aidoneus, you wanted to talk? Fine. We will talk right now. Remember that one time I told you I wanted a job?" My Angel flung her arms out to either side of her, and dread pooled low in my gut.

Shit.

Shit.

Shit.

Phaedra continued, "You said that we would talk about it later. Well, what happened later is I was paraded in front of Aranthium like a prized possession, spoken to like trash, and then bombarded with a very real accusation of not bringing anything to the table."

Her words were fire darts as they poured out of her, striking me in the chest over and over again.

"That's not a fair representation, Phaedra. I told you we couldn't live our lives like normal until after the war was over. Besides, what did that Vampire know? She'll never see another day in show business." Heat crawled up my neck and coated my skin.

The leather seat groaned under Phaedra as she heaved her weight around. "You trapped me in this, Hades. I didn't want to get married. I *want* a purpose. I *want* respect."

"You have—"

"No! You made me into a laughingstock! We don't even have that much time to train these supposedly indispensable powers to the war!"

Her voice crested, and I thought about the driver. Toth'toros was aiding in the battle room, so I had chosen someone else to drive us this evening. They were paid for discretion, right? I definitely needed to have Saul check on that later.

A mangled sound came out of Phaedra. "And now you aren't even listening." Her voice cracked on that last word, and my soul shattered wide open. She doubled over, her hair curtaining her face as she pressed her hands against her forehead.

"Don't cry," I said quickly, putting my hands in front of me. "Look, I don't know who showed you that apologies didn't mean anything, but they need to shut the hell up. I owe you a big apology, and I mean it from the bottom of my heart. Please, Phaedra, forgive me."

I pressed a hand to my chest and reached for the palm pressed to her forehead. Our fingers had barely brushed when she snatched her limb away. She flattened her back against the seat, revealing her reddened face.

Her eyes were squeezed shut as if she could keep the tears from flowing. "Yes, you owe me an apology. But I need more than that. Set me free, Aidoneus." Phaedra's eyes flew open, highlighting the silver rims of soon-to-be tears painted there. Her words were equal parts rage and desperation.

They landed in my soul and sat there. My whole body started to hurt. "Set you free? What are you saying?" My mind rushed in with a million reasons for her to stay, why she couldn't leave. None of those came out, though. All I said was, "We have a contract."

The moment the words left my mouth, I knew they were the absolute worst thing to say.

Her face grew hard, and her tears burned away by her anger before they even had a chance to fall. "A contract. A cage. I am your pretty parrot, merely repeating everything you say. To Hell with you and your contract," she hissed.

Blue rippled around us. My wife's power was no longer dark and smoky. No, now it was bright and powerful and *angry*. A bolt of sunshine-bright magic hit me straight in the chest, and a burst of pain followed suit.

I cursed. My suit coat hung in tatters off my shoulders, and there were singed holes around my torso. Both of our seatbelts were gone.

Then, as if Phaedra had absolutely no concern for her personal safety, she lunged toward the handle of the car.

My instincts took over just as she moved across the interior of the limo.

"No," I demanded. Reaching out, I grabbed her hand a fraction of a section before she reached the silver chrome handle. She attempted to yank her hand from my grasp, but my fingers drew themselves around her skin tighter.

"Hades, let me go!" she insisted.

The contact between us had the bond sparking, and my heart pounded. Primal reactions replaced sense. "No," I growled. "You just tried to get out of a moving car on the freeway."

I yanked on her wrist, and her body weight tumbled forward as I caught her off guard.

"Release me," she demanded, yanking back.

The car sped along, and the door between our souls—that bond that tied us—smashed open again. Our nearness awakened every inch of my body. Pieces of myself that I thought had died with Miranda flared to life.

"I can't," I said.

I wouldn't. Not now. Maybe not ever. She was mine, and I needed her like I needed air.

Pulling Phaedra closer, I snaked an arm around her hips. Everywhere I touched her felt like it was on fire. Her breath hitched at the movement, and the anger inside of her faltered.

Her free hand splayed across my chest. The pulse in her wrist matched my own, hot and rapid. The air in the limo was so thick that I could have dragged a knife through it. Everything was hot.

Her wings splayed out behind her, and she looked like an avenging warrior as she remained mere inches from my face. She straddled my lap, her chest heaving as she drank in air. Doing anything but holding her right now was impossible. I couldn't have torn my gaze away from her even if I tried.

The door between us wasn't just open by a crack. No, it was wide open as we poured ourselves into each other.

"Phaedra," I breathed. My voice didn't sound like my own anymore.

She placed her hand on my lips as her chest rose and fell. Her dress was low-cut, giving me the perfect view of her breasts. And gods, they were magnificent.

With difficulty, I dragged my eyes back to her face.

"I'm not a piece of property," she whispered.

I tightened my grip around her hips, feeling her settle on her weight on me. "I know."

"I don't want to be put in a cage. To be stifled."

"I know," I whispered. What else was there to say?

She leaned forward even more, cutting the distance between us in half. Her breath warmed my lips. I could lean forward and kiss her now. There was no one to stop us. We were alone.

"I'm not useless," she said.

"Never. You have never been useless."

Those lips opened, and I stared at them. Her tongue darted out, wetting the bottom of her lip. Gods, I wanted to capture those lips with mine and show her how much I wanted her. But I wouldn't push her.

"We should probably stop," she said breathlessly. But she didn't make any move to get off my lap. Instead, she raised a hand and cupped my cheek.

My heart threatened to escape my chest as sparks ran through me. My voice was hoarse as I asked, "What if I don't want to stop?"

The hand I'd slung around her hips lowered briefly before sliding up to her back. I traced the lines of her body, slowly exploring.

"I hate you," Phaedra said. Her voice lacked any conviction.

A dark chuckle slipped past my lips. "For some reason, I don't believe you."

She sucked in a breath, and confidence returned to me. The magic inside both of us glowed. I felt stronger than I had in centuries. This wasn't drunkenness from our bond. This was more. Power. Strength. Rightness.

A second passed, feeling like an hour, as her eyes searched mine. Then those eyes fluttered shut. "You're right," she breathed. "Touch me."

The moment she said the words, shadows flickered out of me. They covered us, shielding our bodies from the outside world.

Somewhere outside of the limo, the earth shifted. Clouds gathered overhead, cloaking the setting sun and rising moon.

She pressed down on my lap, rubbing her core against the bulge in my pants. "Please."

As if I would deny a plea such as hers. I brushed my knuckles over her breasts, delighting in her responding whimper. Even with clothes between us, I could feel they were as perfect as I'd imagined.

Her lips parted as I acquainted myself with her breasts with one hand while the other slipped over her hips and thighs. I trailed my fingers over her flesh, watching her pupils dilate.

Her breath stuttered, and she whimpered.

She wanted me.

No knowledge had ever felt so good.

Then she moved.

Her lips crashed against mine. She tasted like springtime showers, ripe pomegranates, and bottles of fresh blossoms.

I returned the kiss with vigor.

There was a desperation, a tension that had been locked between us, which was now coming free. Even as we kissed, I could *feel* the effects of our power in Aranthium. Magic coursed through the land, rippling across the desert and reaching far beyond. It thundered in Angel's Landing, and a storm whisked through the Capital Province.

It was so much, but it wasn't enough.

"Hades," she gasped.

In reply, I gripped her tighter. I wasn't imagining the moan as my tongue slipped between her teeth and explored.

This was better than I had imagined. It was almost too good to be real.

Almost.

The solid, ancient lines of my body met her soft, gentle curves and fit together like pieces of a puzzle. She shifted further on my lap, and her dress curved around her hips.

I trailed my hand up her thigh, her soft moans all the encouragement I needed.

"Phaedra," I growled against her lips as I felt the smooth curve of her ass. "What are you wearing?"

She broke apart from my lips, glancing down. "Underwear."

This slip of black lace could barely be classified as such.

She stared at me. "Do you like it?"

In response, I growled. "I love it."

I would definitely be fantasizing about this for years.

I went to tug it off her, wanting to see what was underneath, when a voice came from the speaker in the car.

"Your Highness, Queen Consort."

We were still in the limo. My eyes widened, and we broke apart, panting. Phaedra tried to move from my lap, but my hands dug into her waist possessively.

"Yes?" I replied, trying to keep my voice even as if it were necessary to mask what had been happening seconds before. My skin thrummed with heat and magic. Rain was falling outside, and the ground below was still trembling.

A click sounded, followed by, "There appears to be a pileup. I've called back up so that we aren't stranded alone. They can escort you back."

One of my hands slid down Phaedra's back as her breathing returned to normal. She was no longer exploring me the same way, and I could feel her pain and anger returning. When she tried to slide off of me this time, I didn't resist. She tugged down her dress and desperately tried to pat down her mussed hair.

I watched her, my gut twisting with a mix of satisfaction at seeing her affected by me and a twinge of worry. Worry she would regret this like she seemed to do with everything in relation to me.

"Are you feeling well enough to Transpose?" I asked.

She let out a long breath. "Honestly? I feel better than ever." Her tone made it clear that she didn't consider that a positive.

I turned my attention back to the speaker. "I think we've got this. We will just Transpose back."

The response came immediately. "Sir, the team is already here."

I sighed. We might as well take them with us. "Very well."

Phaedra met my eyes as I reached for the handle. I paused. "I hope you see what you are truly capable of. One day, you can have any job you want. But your power, our power combined, will bring the world to its knees."

To be honest, this was beyond my wildest dreams.

Her eyes went wide, and I opened the handle, allowing her to look outside. The sky was a thousand shades of gray, and rain poured from the heavens. All kinds of flora lined the ground around the city, the new growth overtaking the dead desert of my land. Trees burst up between cracks, and flowers tangled around light posts. Everything shook and rumbled. We caused this. Together. We were something magnificent, and our magic achieved even more than I imagined.

I held my hand out, and she hesitantly took my hand. The touch was chaste, but sparks still woke inside me. She inhaled sharply, and I knew she felt the same.

Male pride spread through me like warm water. As we slid out of the car, my wings domed above us to cover ourselves from the storm we had created. Her blue eyes were locked on mine. As other cars on the freeway spotted us, some honked, and others snapped pictures with their phones.

"Your Highness, Phaedra," a deep voice rumbled out.

Finally, I looked up to see the security team stationed behind us. Nyrnavox was standing in front of us with two Daemons. My brow furrowed. Why was he here? A knot formed in my stomach as a sense of unease grew within me.

"Good evening," I called over the rain. "We need to get to a restaurant downtown. Will you be accompanying us then?"

Even as I said the words, dread pooled in my stomach. Something was wrong. My skin grew cold.

The Daemon nodded curtly. He started walking toward us, flanked by his soldiers. The others didn't look unusual, but that didn't explain why the backup included someone as high-ranking as Nyrnavox

I stepped in front of my wife, and Nyrnavox looked directly at me. His eyes were hollow, his dark face flat. "My King, we are here to help."

Adrenaline shot through my systems, and my hand felt like pins and needles were repeatedly jabbing into my palms. Time slowed, every second feeling like an hour.

My mind screamed at me that this was wrong.

Suddenly, things began clicking into place. Feelings of wrongness. Snide tones. Danger. A black folder filled my mind's eye. The warning from the Winter Court Queen.

My blood heated, my heart raced, and I snapped, "We don't need your help."

Cursing myself for my stupidity, I stepped back. Gathering up my magic, I prepared to get us both out of here.

But I was too late. Something thorn-like shot out from Nyrnavox's outstretched hand, piercing my skin. Instantly, enough electricity to kill any normal being pulsed through me, and I dropped to my knees with a grunt.

Pain.

So much pain.

Agony the likes of which I had only felt a few times in my long life overwhelmed me as my vision blurred and refocused on the pavement. It would take more than this to kill a DemiGod, but I could be incapacitated.

I was on the ground as my body betrayed me. I couldn't move. My limbs felt like charred stumps as fire roiled through me.

Black boots walked past me. "Forgive me, My King. I told you that we needed more soldiers. I sincerely hope you know that I am doing this for the good of Aranthium."

My blood turned to ice as I strained every muscle in my body to look up. Phaedra's shocked face looked between me and the Daemon. He reached out, putting his hands on my wife. She scratched at him, kicking with as much power as she could muster in her heels. Her power flashed with that deadly blue fire.

The traitor laughed, grabbing her behind her neck.

Red filled my vision.

Phaedra jabbed an elbow, but it didn't land.

“Aidoneus!” she screamed. Then, a green flash sliced through the air, and they vanished.

I *roared.* My body shook with anger. Thunder rumbled, and the sky turned black.

One of the Daemons shouted, “What the hell?”

Head spinning, I tried to process what had happened. To move. To fight. I had to push past the poison.

My wife.

My wife.

Phaedra was gone, and in her place was the scent of rotting fish. Of the sea. Of pain.

Phelix.

“No,” I growled, searching for Phaedra. I reached for our bond, but she was gone. Wiped clean from my senses as if she'd never been there. I punched the ground as I let out a guttural roar. The taste of her was still on my lips.

With a ripple of power, the cement beneath me cracked and shattered into pieces. The cars for a mile bobbed up and down as I shot into the air. I whipped toward the Daemons, my wings snapping out around me.

I became the true king of death, the king of things lost to the depths of Aranthium.

“Where is my wife?” I demanded of the soldiers, my voice coated with death. Shadows rippled around me, and anger became the only thing I knew. Beings of all kinds were fleeing, some shouting and others screaming in the storm that had only grown more riotous.

My pulse rushed through my veins, and I could feel the magic I tried to keep a tight lock on leaking out of my pores.

The Daemons stared at me in shock.

I lashed out, bringing one of the DaePolice toward me.

"Where did that gods-forsaken bastard take her?" I demanded.

All of them just stared at me helplessly. Useless. They were useless to me. I dropped them, and they fell to the ground in a sickening splat.

Not waiting to see the damage, I continued to search.

Someone here had to know something. I would find my wife, and I would destroy everyone in my path. When I found him, Nyrnavox would rue the day he crossed the DemiGod of the Dead.

I saw a black figure running out of the corner of my eye.

The driver sprinted across broken asphalt, using his wings to vault himself over cars.

My eyes narrowed. I was in front of him in a flash. I grabbed him by the end of the neck. In the next breath, we were in my tower. We landed hard on the place where one of the conference tables had been moments ago.

The man was shouting, but he didn't fight back. "Please! I didn't know he was going to take her!"

More heat poured inside of me, and darkness the color of ink seeped into the shadows. I could feel the driver's beating heart. At that moment, I knew how easy it would be to rip the organ from his chest.

Phaedra was the only thing stopping me.

"Where is she?" I demanded, tightening my grip on his throat.

A wheezing sound came from him as he shook his head. "I don't know."

I brought our faces together, my skin transforming from marble to black. "If you know nothing, you are useless to me."

The Daemon's eyes widened. The room was completely soaked in black. I waited.

One second. Two.

With every passing moment, my anger grew.

My wife was gone, and I needed her.

I was moments away from crushing this man's throat, but something stopped me.

Aranthium was not like the days of the rebellion. The man would have a fair trial, and then I would have my time with him. Then, and only then, would he pay for his part in this.

"All I know—" he started at the same time as I said, "You have ten seconds to explain."

Releasing my grip on his throat, I dropped him on the ground. Panting, he didn't move. I dropped to the floor, rolling up my sleeves as he spoke.

CHAPTER 26
A COURT OF FISHES
PHAEDRA

Every single part of my body hurt. From the tip of my toes to my head, it felt like I'd been dropped from a thousand feet in the air. My wings... they couldn't move. None of me could move. I opened my eyes, but everything around me was pitch black.

Where was I?

I tried to push myself up, but I couldn't. It took me a moment to recognize why—something was binding my arms and legs. I was lying on my stomach, and a pounding headache raged through me.

I tried to speak, but all that came out was a mangled moan.

Moments later, I heard footsteps.

"Oh no," a disembodied voice said from somewhere above me. "This won't do at all."

A sharp prick came at the back of my neck, and then everything felt fuzzy. Dark.

I WOKE THREE MORE TIMES. Each time, I couldn’t move, and each time, they knocked me out again within moments of waking.

I didn't remember a reality without pain.

There was nothing left in my life except for the agony roiling through my veins.

Each time, I tried to reach out to someone. Anyone. No one was there. Even the bond within me felt like it was asleep.

THE GROUND beneath me was hard. My entire body was numb, but for the first time, I could move.

So I did. At first, I shifted slowly. An inch. Then two.

I paused, waiting to see if someone would come. If there would be another prick in the back of my neck.

Nothing came.

Forcing my eyes to open despite the pounding in my head, I looked around.

This was... both completely unexpected and yet utterly typical.

The ground beneath me was an equally uncomfortable and extraordinarily thick, solid, rough material. Three of the walls of my cell—because there was no mistake: this was a cell, and I really had been kidnapped—were made of the same gray material.

But the fourth wall.

That was the one that sent a frisson of fear through me.

I had never been in the Ice Mer Territory, and yet I knew instinctively that was where I was. The last wall was a large window, bringing in rays of watery sunlight. Outside the cell, seaweed blew in the current, and a large coral reef housed schools of colorful fish. A shark swam by, and three eels made their way past me.

Other than that, I didn't see a single living being.

My cell was plain. It had a toilet and a sink.

That was it.

There wasn't even a bed.

I scoffed.

Clearly, my new brother-in-law was making his feelings known about me. There was no doubt in my mind about who was behind my abduction.

It was painfully ironic that Hades first rescued me from a kidnapping all those years ago. And now, here I was. Like a cruel twist of fate, I was abducted right in front of him.

These brothers have a penchant for kidnapping.

I stood, raising my arms to the sky and trying to stretch my wings. But the walls were so narrow that I couldn't extend them fully.

Already, I felt an ache in my back. Within hours, I was certain I would feel the agony of being unable to move my wings fully.

I paced the small cell. The length was seven paces long—long enough to lie down without curling into a ball—and three paces wide.

Soon, that grew tiresome. My stomach grumbled, reminding me I hadn't eaten since before my abduction. I could have eaten in the limo, but I'd been... otherwise occupied.

Good gods, that kiss.

That was going to be a problem. There was no way that I was going to be able to live with Hades and not kiss him. Not if he did things like that with his tongue. The way his hands had roamed over me made me blush even now. Rationally, I knew there was nothing to be ashamed of. We were two consenting adults and married, for Fortuna's sake.

Irrationally, I felt like a giddy schoolgirl who had gotten her first kiss.

Or at least, what I thought a giddy schoolgirl would feel like. Mother would have had a coronary if I'd ever been close enough to anyone, male or female, to kiss. Even when she'd allowed me to attend school with the other younglings, I'd been escorted to and from the building. There had been no time for anything, kissing or otherwise.

At the thought of my mother, a pang went through my heart.

Was today a good day? Did she even know I was gone? This disease eating her memory stole her from me. I had forgiven her, but it had been too late for us.

And now...

Was it too late for Hades and me? Our kiss was not friendly, nor was it gentle. It spoke of a depth of feelings that needed to be explored. Something we could have done if this hadn't happened. Maybe I would have introduced my husband to my mother. Explained why I was so closed off. Introduced the two of them.

They were my only family.

Part of me hoped my mother was having a bad day. Then, at least, she wouldn't be worried about me.

Would anyone be worried about me?

I thought Karina would probably worry, although knowing her, she probably thought I was off enjoying my husband. It would take a few days and a dozen missed calls before she realized something was wrong.

Hades would worry.

I slumped against the ground, my wings spread as much as

they could behind me as I dropped my head into my hands. He had always cared for me as his assistant. We were friends, he'd said. Friends worried about other friends.

But would he care more? Or was I just a means to an end for him? A way to become more powerful? I honestly didn't know. How he paused when the talk-show bitch asked if he'd felt anything about me made me think that maybe, he did. The kiss was definitely a point in my favor.

But was it just the bond that made him act like that?

Thinking of the bond that lay within me, I shut my eyes. Reaching within myself, I searched for that place within myself. I could see the place where the connection between us resided, but instead of the door I had grown used to seeing was nothing but black, fuzzy darkness. Frowning, I prodded within myself.

"You won't find the bond."

I screamed.

Flinging my eyes open, my heart racing, I gasped.

The man I had never hoped to meet was swimming outside my cell in full regalia.

Long, gray, and green strands of hair flowed in the water around King Phelix, his naked upper body firm as he grasped a trident in one hand. A black crown rested on his head, and his tail swished behind him.

Pushing myself to my feet, I walked the three steps to the glass wall.

"What did you say?"

My brother-in-law sneered at me, revealing a pair of razor-sharp fangs that looked like they could cut through raw flesh. Green power sparked through his eyes as he tilted his head. "I said you won't find the bond. I took some precautions, you see. Couldn't have my brother storming down here and retrieving his bride, now could I?"

Couldn't find the bond.

For a moment, I stared at him. I hadn't even known it was possible to block a bond like ours. To do such a thing...

Phelix must have been dabbling in the darkest forms of magic.

"What have you done?" I demanded.

He smirked. "It was my father who took Aidoneus and Miranda in the rebellion. Since my brothers seemed content to exclude me, I spent a lot of time with Adrian. You are too young to remember him, but he was the greatest of the gods."

I stared at Phelix, not knowing what to say. Disappointment bloomed through me, but I wasn't going to let him know that. At the back of my mind, I'd been hoping that Aidoneus would show up at any moment and rescue me.

But maybe a rescue wasn't going to happen.

I needed to prepare to save myself. I learned a long time ago that you couldn't rely on others.

I lifted my chin, steeling myself for the possibility of not being rescued. "I see. Did you just come here to gloat, or was there a purpose to your visit?"

Phelix raised a brow. "Perhaps I just wanted to see the Angel my brother finally chose for a bride." He sneered, his eyes flashing. "I must admit, you are every bit as disappointing as I'd thought. You didn't even come with anything a wife should bring to the table. No political weight to throw around, no troops."

"How dare you—"

The Ice Mer King raised a hand, and a flash of green power came *through* the glass. " Aidoneus always had a blind spot when it came to love. I've heard rumors you have power, but I haven't observed anything in all the time you've been here." His magic wrapped around my mouth, gagging me. My eyes bulged, and I snarled.

Phelix laughed. "Just as I thought. Weak." He swam closer,

putting a hand on the glass as I struggled against the magic binding me. "You see, my brothers are going to lose this war. While you were sleeping, my men took over the Summer Fae land. It won't be long before we start to march on Angel's Landing. Soon, all of Aranthium will belong to me."

Raising my hands, I went to pull the gag off my mouth, but the magic *burned.* Tears welled, and I yanked my hands away.

Tsk'ing, the king shook his head. "No, I don't think you should do that." He sighed, rolling his shoulders. "Here's how this is going to work. The magic will dissolve once I am gone. You will be fed twice a day. If you're a good little Angel, once I have conquered Aranthium, I'll let you say goodbye to your husband before I remove his head from his shoulders."

A sob rose within me, but I tamped it down before it could come out.

I would not show weakness in front of this tyrant.

True to his word, when he was gone, the magic dissolved.

Only then did I crumble to the floor, letting the tears overtake me.

PHELIX SAID he'd feed me twice a day.

He hadn't mentioned that the rations would be pitiful or that they would mainly be comprised of raw fish. But beggars couldn't be choosers, so I ate everything I was given. Various Ice Mer delivered the meals. I thought I might make a connection with the ones delivering my food, but every time, they were different. The scant meals were placed in a box outside my cell, and once the Mer knocked on the box, I would open the small slot on my side.

I was truly alone.

I hadn't shed a single tear since that first day when Phelix had visited me. No. Tears would not help me here.

It was becoming clear that no one was coming for me.

After a week with no one to speak to, I feared I was losing my mind. Every day, I reached for the bond. Every day, it was a black, fuzzy mess. I tried to access my magic, but I was as dry as a desert. I couldn't summon my powers... I couldn't even feel them.

If only I'd received more training before my abduction. Transposing was good, but there was still so much more I couldn't understand.

I still had no bed. No blankets. Not even a change of clothes. A bar of soap was delivered on the third day, and I'd taken to washing myself at the sink above my underwear. My hair was greasy, and I couldn't get the dirt from underneath my fingernails.

Every part of me felt dirty. I wanted nothing more than to go home. When I slept, I dreamed of Aidoneus. Of our apartment. Of nights spent in front of the TV.

And every time I woke alone in this box, I screamed.

Day in and day out, I screamed until my voice was hoarse.

No one came.

CHAPTER 27
FORTUNA'S GATES
AIDONEUS

The day after Phaedra's disappearance

Twenty-four hours came and went in the blink of an eye. I hadn't slept at all, and now it was evening again. My head throbbed, and I rubbed at my temples. Anger was my constant companion.

Nearly a hundred people were down on the battle floor searching for leads on Phaedra. I'd even called Raphael, though I only got his assistant. Apparently, my brother had gotten off his ass and was off at the front lines in the swamplands. I was alone in my office, having grown so distraught and angry that I was inhibiting my team from doing their job.

Toth'toros stood near me. "Sir, perhaps it would've been better if we'd stayed with the others."

The tall Daemon was standing at attention in his full uniform. The moment I finished interrogating the driver, Toth'-toros was there. He hadn't left my side since. We'd spent every free hour since then searching for Phaedra.

"I disagree. That driver knew nothing." The throbbing intensified as I went over the information aloud, as if the head of my guard didn't already know it just as well as I did. "I told you what he said. He was notified in advance that there might be problems on the freeway. Someone paid him a large sum of money to Nyrnavox. When he saw what was happening outside, he tried to run."

The words were bitter as curses as they left my lips, leaving a sour taste behind in my mouth. Hopelessness hollowed out my insides, leaving ample space for red-hot anger to fester and burn. My wife was out there, all alone. The Gods only knew what Phelix was doing to her.

The thought of seeing her hurt again had me fisting my hands as my eyes glossed over.

The ground beneath us was alive and awake, but my power was a candle burned to the end of its wick. There wasn't enough left of me to cause any real damage. I'd nearly forgotten what life was like before Phaedra and I had married.

A small chirping sound signaling the new hour brought me back to reality.

Like a good soldier, Toth'toros stood watching. He was a trusted confidant, but sometimes speaking with him was a little like shouting in the void. The male never really gave advice. He just followed orders. He was a mass of muscle and brains and duty.

"Flora, open the curtains," I commanded. An aggravated edge permanently tainted my voice. A chirping sound filled the room, and the blackout blinds started to lift. As they inched up, the city of Lethe filled my vision. Beyond the buildings, far off on the horizon, was the enormous volcano that had existed since the beginning of time.

An idea blossomed.

I whipped around, once against facing the head of my security. "Call Kharon. We need to go to Fortuna's Gates."

Toth'toros nodded curtly. I could've sworn that there was some relief flickering behind his eyes. A twinge of embarrassment pricked at my chest. I must've looked truly pathetic these last few hours.

I snapped my fingers, needing a physical movement to Transpose a set of robes from my apartment upstairs. Within moments, my suit was gone. In its place was the oldest cloth known to Aranthium. A gift from my mother, these robes were woven with the souls of ancient evil beings that once roamed our land.

The cloth appeared midnight-black at first glance, but the colors were so much deeper than that. The fabric attracted all light and swallowed it whole. Glimmers of life sparkled along their rough surface. Raphael had a cloak of glorious light woven with the pieces of noble souls that had been freely offered. The difference between Angels and Daemons was that we did not ask the world to make sense. What could be born from the darkness? The answer was anything. Darkness was humbling, and it taught people to stay a bit closer to the ground.

Drawing in a deep breath, I inhaled the deep scent of the sacred robe. I smelled the beginning of worlds, of ash, dust, and ice—of Fortuna. Shadows curled around me as I savored the scent.

Souls found their way to Fortuna's Gates through divine intuition gifted to them by their creators. I supposed that was true of me, too. But Fortuna's Gates did not answer to me. At least, not fully. They had existed before me and would continue to exist when my body turned to dust. Time did not work the same in this godly place. This would not be an easy trek.

"Your Highness," Toth'toros said behind me. He hadn't been gone long. There was a quiet edge to his voice, a reverence from seeing his king in his true form. "Lady Fortuna awaits."

My wings eased out, completing my transition as a creature of the night. "Let us go," I said.

Toth'toros's expression turned feral, his eyes glowing. "On this night of tragedy, let all of Lethe witness its king."

Something about his voice reminded me of battles fought on fields drenched with blood. Though I wore a suit most days, the world would not so easily forget its DemiGod of Death again.

We opened one of the doors leading to the terrace in front of my office. The night air felt good on my skin. Leather wings stretched wide before we made the drop.

Instinct took over as my heart stopped, and my mind went blank. It didn't matter how many times I flew, it would never feel less exhilarating. We soared through the sky, barreling toward the tall ancient gates protected by a modern facility overseen by Kharon.

Even though summer was fading, the volcano never fully cooled. I kept it an inch from an eruption with a reserve of magic. Smoke puffed off the top of the cone-shaped mountain, painting the sky in darkness.

We swooped down, the cold air causing my hair to stand up. My entire body turned into a live wire. As we approached the entrance, I pushed my wings out harder. The muscles in my back strained against the wind as we landed.

I walked past a withering garden with Toth'toros at my right flank. As usual, there were no people in the courtyard. Mortals did not belong in this place, and very few immortals could bear it. I wasn't worried about Toth'toros. He was a Daemon, and I knew he would be fine.

"Ready?" I asked.

Toth'toros let out a breath, and I looked at him. Shadows hugged the corners of this place, and an enormous tree blocked out the moon. Its branches bore no leaves, but they were tangled and gnarled enough for there to be no need. This place was unpredictable, just like my mother. I loved her in my own way.

But even she was bound by Fate.

"Let me go in first," the Daemon said before brushing past me.

I didn't argue.

We made it to the door, but when Toth'toros pulled on the handle, it didn't move. "It's locked, my lord."

Acid pooled in my stomach. "What's going on? You called before, didn't you?"

Toth'toros nodded. "Yes." He didn't elaborate.

I strode next to him, reaching out my hand and grabbing the cast-iron handle. I tugged with all my might, but the door didn't so much as groan.

The silence shifted, no longer feeling like a warm friend. Now, it wasn't kind. It wasn't warm. It felt like a midnight assassin. Pressure mounted on my back and shoulders, and the hairs on the back of my neck prickled. Magic pressed against me, flattening me to the cold surface. Toth'toros slammed next to me seconds later. He roared in pain, and I gritted my teeth.

A chuckle sounded from behind us, and it took every ounce of strength in my body to turn around.

There, leaning against the trunk of the hideous tree, was Kharon. He was unlike any other being in Aranthium. He had been created to watch over this place, guide the dead, and attend to Fortuna. Though he lacked the leather wings of Daemons, his eyes glowed yellow. His skin was so pale it shone like a lantern. He wore black robes and sandals made of silver starlight.

"Son of Fortuna. How good of you to finally grace us with your presence." The being stepped toward me, and the jangle of coins tinkled softly in the night. Those coins were manifestations of bargains made with souls before they entered.

My unease turned to full-on nausea. It did not mix well with lack of sleep and flaming rage. "Kharon, we do not have time for this." My voice shook the earth beneath us.

Kharon's face stretched as his lips widened into a toothless smile. "If you are in a hurry, perhaps you should've come earlier."

A growl rumbled deep in my chest. "Cut the immortal bull-shit and let us in. I don't have time for this."

My wife's life is on the line.

I didn't say the final words, but the tree trembled from the power of my voice. Even in this place, I was still a DemiGod.

Kharon's smile faded. "No."

That word echoed in my chest. "What do you mean 'no'?" I demanded, clenching my fists.

Toth'toros drew closer to my side. His hands were undoubt-edly reaching for weapons.

"I wouldn't do that if I were you, Child of Tartaro," Kharon called to Toth'toros.

My head galloped like the Hounds of Hell were chasing me. Kharon always listened to my mother. If he wasn't letting us in yet, that meant that Fortuna was behind this. My eyes closed as the muscles in my jaw tensed. "What does she want?"

Another chuckle echoed off the shadow-soaked stones of this unearthly place. "So, you do remember how this works?"

I let out a slow breath. Unfortunately, I did. If Fortuna didn't let us in immediately, it was because she wanted a bargain. Kharon often brokered her deals.

Good gods. I did not have time for this.

"Yes," I replied through clenched teeth. "Now, spit it out."

Toth'toros remained silent at my side, the ever-present soldier and guard.

Kharon leisurely walked forward. "Lady Fortuna doesn't ask for much, I assure you. In fact, this time, she is nothing but generous. In payment for her help, she only asks for one simple memory."

My fingertips went cold. Fortuna never said exactly what she wanted outright. She often spoke through others, her language one of bait-and-switch, loopholes, and trickery.

"No," I said.

Kharon's expression clouded. He was a natural disaster waiting to sweep across the land. "No?" A moment passed, and his form grew.

"Shit," I breathed. "Get behind me," I commanded Toth'toros.

"Fortuna promises that the memory will help the two of you move on. If you refuse my Goddess's generosity, *DemiGod,* you will be banished from this place." Kharon's voice echoed through the yard, sending waves of sound lambasting my body. I tucked my wings in tight as my robes billowed around me. "I will ask you one last time: are you willing to sacrifice for your wife? Or will you return to a room full of machines and brainless individuals?"

I bristled. If my mother was asking for a memory, I knew exactly what kind of memory she wanted. One of Miranda.

My brain latched onto one word—sacrifice. Was I willing to sacrifice for Phaedra?

When he put it like that, the choice was already made. It was the kind of choice that tore my soul in half. Phaedra and Miranda held two halves of my heart.

But could I kill my future for fragments of the past?

I blinked back tears. The last thing that Miranda said was to live well. She would want me to be happy, to try to heal the loss that was like a gaping hole in the fabric of my world. My mother was only doing this because she wanted to fix things between us. It was a screwed-up way to go about it...

But time was running out.

My throat tightened, and my breath hitched. "I accept the deal."

Kharon's face shone so bright that I was forced to squint. A sour taste bloomed in the back of my mouth, making it hard to swallow. The light continued to grow, overtaking the shadows and causing the entire garden to transform from withering grays and blacks to vibrant green foliage, silver tree trunks, and autumn-toned flowers.

For a second, the life in death brought tears to my eyes. Kharon had sealed the deal, but he also promised me something valuable.

A string of primitive words slid out of Kharon's mouth. The syllables slowed in the air and stuck in my ears as if I were hearing them underwater. The beating of my heart grew louder and louder until...

The door clicked open.

We would still need to pass through the gates and enter the hot space under the volcano to reach my mother. It was not easy to reach Fortuna as she wove the fates of all those who lived before. But as Kharon ushered us through the entrance, I couldn't help but feel like we were finally making progress.

Hold on, my Angel.

CHAPTER 28
A TWO-LEGGED SISTER-IN-LAW
PHAEDRA

It was growing harder and harder to tell how much time had passed. A week? Maybe two.

My captors were feeding me less and less. My mind was breaking. Parts of me were withering away. Whatever dark magic Phelix used to block my bond was also taking parts of my soul.

I could barely keep my eyes open. My mind was sluggish, and thinking was a struggle.

How much longer did I have left?

Crouched against the wall, I stared blankly at the school of purple and blue fish swimming outside the walls of my prison. They looked so... calm. Peaceful, even.

I was anything but peaceful. I needed to get out of here.

Not for the first time, I reached within myself and tried to push aside the darkness covering my bond.

Nothing was there. It was empty.

I was empty.

Tears welled within me, and I allowed one single watery drop to go down my cheek. Just one. If I gave into despair, I didn't know if I'd have the strength to escape it.

A scraping sound came from the slot in the wall, and I jolted upright. Rushing over, I yanked it open. Ignoring the plate of food, I banged on the wall.

"Wait!" I yelled. "Stop! Please, whoever you are, I need to talk to you!"

There came no response.

More tears threatened to fall, but I sniffled, shoving them down.

Drawing the food into my cell, I picked at it. Dark green leaves of seaweed were wrapped around strips of raw pink fish. A silver bottle rested on the side of the plate, my water ration for the day.

For a moment, I tried to decide which one to deal with first: hunger or thirst. In the end, hunger won out.

A shudder ran through me as I put the first piece of fish in my mouth. It was slimy, and I had to choke it down. My mind drifted into a daydream, the only escape I had these days.

After this—if there was an after—I would never eat fish again. In fact, I could see myself swearing off meat altogether. I wondered what Aidoneus would think about that. He'd probably hire a vegetarian chef.

Because he cared about me.

That realization was like a dagger to my heart. My husband cared about me. Far more than I had ever given him credit for. And instead of allowing him to care for me, I'd erected barriers around my heart.

Swallowing my revulsion, I ate all the fish before grabbing the bottle. Twisting off the cap, I brought it to my lips and swallowed deeply.

Too late, I tasted the drink they'd given me. It was bitter. I threw the bottle against the wall, but already my movements were sluggish. It erupted, spraying its contents everywhere as black spots filled my vision.

"Help," I croaked before everything faded away, and I slumped onto the floor.

A SENSE of complete and utter strangeness filled me. My neck... something was different. Not wrong or painful, just uncomfortable.

Even with my eyes closed, I knew I was no longer in my cell. For one thing, my wings weren't cramped. For another, I could hear people talking for the first time since I'd been captured. I didn't realize how starved I was for interaction with others until Phelix completely stripped it away from me.

With every passing moment, that strange feeling in my throat only worsened. Drawing up a hand, I rubbed it along my neck only to find...

What in the seven circles of Hell?

My neck was no longer smooth. Instead, rough edges lined my throat to form...

Gills.

It was then I realized I wasn't breathing at all. Or at least not how I normally did. My lungs were tight, and the gills... they were keeping me alive.

I opened my eyes, and I gasped. Or I would have, except all

that happened was my mouth filled with water. I sputtered, and my lungs tightened as my body rejected the salt water that was home to the Ice Mer. I was in a room that was about four times the size of my cell, lying on my stomach on a bed made of kelp. A mirror hung on one wall, and a wardrobe took up space on another.

And then I looked down.

My clothes… someone had taken them away. In their place, I wore a small black slip. And my hair… I reached up and touched it. It was floating all around me in the water, and as I ran my fingers through the black strands, I realized they were clean.

Instantly, a shudder of revulsion roiled through me. Someone had drugged me, taken my clothes, and dressed me while I was unconscious. I hated that.

Instinctively, I reached within me to try and find that bond. My magic. Something. Anything with which to protect myself.

All I found was the black mist.

Before I could stop myself, I opened my mouth and called out, "Hello?"

This time, the water didn't rush into my lungs. It merely… sat there as if acknowledging it could drown me if it wanted.

Black magic, indeed.

Then the door swung open. The sound of chatter grew louder, and for a moment, I thought I could see merfolk in the other room. However, my vision was soon blocked as a trio of young Ice Mer swam into the room. I sat up, pulling a pillow in front of me to cover my state of undress as I stared at them. The pillow should've been waterlogged, but magic kept it full and bouncy.

The three females looked identical, from the black hair piled into elaborate buns on their heads down to the black pearls covering their busts. The only thing that set them apart was the color of their tails.

Each of their tails was bright, like the fish I'd been watching from my cell. Cerulean, magenta, and jade. At any other time, perhaps if they were in a painting and not taking part in my abduction, I would have admired them for their beautiful scales.

As it was, I was a little too preoccupied with understanding what was going on.

The one with the cerulean tail was the first to speak. "Well, well," she crooned. "I see you finally woke up."

"Of course, she woke up." Magenta laughed. "She wants to go to the party."

"What party?" I asked, blinking. Was that what the sounds were from beyond the door? "Who are you? Where am I?"

The trio ignored me, swimming into the room. Cerulean yanked open the wardrobe, drawing out a long black dress with slits in the back.

"Get the Angel standing on those strange legs of hers," she ordered. Her voice rang with authority, and instantly, the one with the jade tail swam toward me. The closer they got to me, the more the cold water rushed over my bare skin, chilling me to the bone.

Jade reached for my arm, and I tucked it away out of her reach. Cerulean hissed, her hair billowing around her like a plume of smoke as she revealed razor-sharp teeth.

"No," I said. My heart raced as I shook my head. "You can't make me do anything. I want to know what is going on. Where am I? Where is Phelix? Does he know you took me?"

The three Ice Mer burst into laughter at the sound of my brother-in-law's name. The bitter sound stung.

I hated it when people laughed at my expense. Something within me burned, and the black mist within me shifted as I clenched my fists. It was just a moment, but that singular moment was all I needed. For the first time since I'd been taken, I felt something akin to hope.

Maybe my bond wasn't gone after all. Maybe I could get out of here.

"She wants to know where the king is," Magenta tittered as she started yanking things out of the wardrobe. "She'll find out soon enough. Get the whore standing, Kintha, or I will."

Jade—Kintha—looked down at me with something that resembled compassion in her eyes. She reached out a hand, whispering, "Please. It's better if you don't anger her."

Something about Kintha's words made me pause. A vein of sincerity laced her words that made me believe her. Nodding, I gave her my hand and let her help me to my feet. My legs wobbled, but after a few moments, I was standing on my own. Kintha nodded. "Good. Wait here."

As if I could do anything else. The water ebbed around me in slow-moving currents, and I marveled at being fully immersed in water but not drowning. Now that I'd gotten used to the strange sensation of breathing through my gills, I realized that even though my wings were heavy, they weren't sodden. I wondered if the same kind of magic that gave me gills was at work on my wings.

At least I could stretch them out. I stood in the middle of the room, expanding my wings slowly as my back muscles burned and protested every inch of movement. After days of disuse, everything hurt. By the time I fully extended both wings, Kintha was back in front of me. She thrust a black dress toward me. "Here."

I raised a brow. "You want me to put this on?"

Magenta turned and sneered at me. "You do it, or we'll force you. We have our orders. You're to get dressed and be presentable in ten minutes." Her eyes crawled over my body. "We'll do our best, but we aren't miracle workers."

Cerulean cackled, and blood rushed to my cheeks. I'd been

kept prisoner for the gods-only-knew how long. It wasn't my fault I looked a little rough around the edges right now.

"Fine," I hissed through clenched teeth as I grabbed the dress. "I'll put it on."

Yanking the dress over my head, I noted the silky smooth fabric. Perfectly placed slits allowed for my wings, and the material molded to me like a second skin. Clearly, someone had taken my measurements.

How long was I out?

Magenta gestured for me to sit in the only chair. After glaring daggers at her, I complied. When I landed in the chair, the three Ice Mer got to work doing my hair and makeup. They tugged far harder than necessary, and I gritted my teeth as they worked on me. They had little regard for my wings, and I pulled them away multiple times before one of the careless trio bumped into them.

The third time Cerulean almost touched my wings, I snapped, "Don't touch me."

"Don't touch me," Cerulean mimicked cruelly as she purposefully brushed a hand over my wings.

I snarled, batting her away as I pushed myself to my feet. "Bitch," I snarled. My hands curled into fists. I wasn't about to let this Ice Mer insult me.

"Sit down," Kintha snapped as she pushed me back into the chair. She yanked on a strand of my hair, and pain pulsed through my scalp. "We only have two minutes left."

All my thoughts about Kintha being kinder than the other two went out the window.

"Hard to believe a king married her," Magenta snorted under her breath as she applied water-proof makeup to my eyelids.

I sneered. "That king will kill you all for what you're doing to me."

I hoped. If Aidoneus ever found me.

Or maybe he had decided I wasn't worth the risk?

Magenta raised a brow. “Oh, is that so?” She shook her head. “I don’t think so.”

Her words sent a frisson of fear through me. It was only amplified as stilettos were forced onto my feet. I wanted to laugh at the ridiculousness of wearing high heels underwater, but then the mean girls pulled me to my feet.

“Good luck,” Magenta crooned.

“You’re going to need it to survive this,” Kintha said mockingly.

Cerulean yanked open the door. I caught a glimpse of dozens of Merfolk swimming about with glasses in their hands moments before I felt a hand on my back.

One of them shoved me. My eyes widened, burning with salt water, and my arms splayed at either side as I stumbled out into the midst of the party. The water shifted around me as I tried to find my footing, and my breath came in bursts. I grabbed onto a small wooden table, righting myself.

It was only then that I realized that everyone had stopped talking. They were all staring at me.

A slow, watery clap came from behind me. It shouldn’t have made any sound, but the ripples of sound echoed through the water loud enough to make my brain rattle

“Ladies and gentlemen, our entertainment for the evening. The Queen Consort of the Gates of Hell, my sister-in-law, Phaedra Demtre.”

CHAPTER 29
WELCOME TO HELL
AIDONEUS

Upon entering Fortuna's Gates, a staff of pure light etched with runes hissed into existence. Kharon gripped it tightly, leading the way. We walked past the modern lobby Raphael and I had put in decades before. It had been necessary to protect Fortuna's Gate in a rapidly changing world.

The interior was a blur of steel-gray, periwinkle-white, and pristine glass. A few offices that had never been occupied lined the inside of the building. Above us, industrial-styled lights flickered. Who knew when they'd last been changed?

"Have you been taking care of this facility at all?" I asked.

Kharon glared at me over his shoulder. "It has been a long time since you've visited your inheritance," he said. "The Dead care little for mortal aesthetics."

I gritted my teeth. "I highly doubt that. At least half the circles of Hell perfectly imitate the most beautiful parts of Aranthium."

He didn't answer right away.

Fortuna's Gates drew closer with each step, and I felt the

strange magic hum in my veins. It was like fresh water in an almost-dry pipe.

Kharon's sandalled heels creaked as they connected with the tile. "Perhaps you do not see that Aranthium imitates the Underworld." He tilted his head to the side, white hair spilling over his mountainous shoulders. "You are evading my earlier comment."

I sighed deeply, deciding that I was tired of dodging his words. "You know why I haven't come."

Kharon hummed, and Toth'toros was silent at my side. "Indeed, I do. If I were in charge of judging the divine, I would say that your reasons were erroneous."

We neared a glass door that would lead us to the gates. It flew open with a speed that indicated it had everything to do with Kharon's outstretched hand and nothing to do with technology. A gust of air as cold as ice blasted my skin, and my Divine robes billowed around me.

Despite the magic filling me up and curling around my skin, a heaviness existed in the pit of my stomach. It was easy to get lost in Hell, easy to lose track of time here. I needed to get out of here and find Phaedra.

Time was running out. I could feel it.

Lightning flashed overhead, and I glanced up as if I might see my brother. It wasn't until I was gazing at the honey-colored moon that I realized a part of me had also been expecting to see my Angel laughing as if this was all some horrid joke.

But it wasn't. All I had left of her now were echoes of our kiss that lingered on my lips. Memories and dreams and fantasies.

A reminder of why I was here.

The volcano loomed before us, and Fortuna's Gate was built into its side. Jagged rocks reached up toward the heavens, creating a deadly shell around the glowing silver gates. It was fitting that they were silver. After all, it was the ultimate representation of purity, clarity, and focus.

A scale was carved into the top of the stone and filled with black opal. The bars of the precious metal were spaced out enough that a soul could see what was to come. Through the slits, I saw Fortuna's shores. The dead did not know that the gates were an illusion. Their judgment had already begun by the time they laid eyes on the gates.

A soul saw what the gates wanted them to see, and the gates took note of their reaction. But the difference was that I was not an unprepared soul, fresh from death. I was an eternal being with a lifetime of practice in turning my face to stone.

The gates seemed to writhe with excitement as I approached.

Slowly, my eyes trailed from the bottom to the top of the enormous barriers. They were three times my size. Time twisted in dizzying ways, and the pit in my stomach turned into an abscess. This place no longer felt like coming home; it felt like a gaping wound refusing to heal.

Sour and bitter flavors swirled together in my mouth, and I swallowed back the reflex to gag.

"Sir?" Toth'toros asked. He was flanking me, and I could feel the hunger inside of him. A longing. As a Daemon, he was always called to the depths.

"Speak the word, DemiGod," Kharon demanded, interrupting my thoughts.

The word. Something my mother had given to me to identify my approach.

"Must I? Surely you can open the gate alone." My jaw was tense, and I was hesitant to reveal any chink in the emotional armor I wore, which my mother could come rushing through.

Kharon's grin was feral. "You must if you wish to see Lady Fortuna. You've already made the bargain. Should you stop now, my lady will still collect payment, but you will not be permitted to see her."

Something told me Kharon would much prefer that.

I sucked in a deep breath, forming the word in my mind and heart before my tongue moved. *"Skotádi."* Darkness, gloom, night. The word my mother made for me.

At once, the gates of yore swung open. Though they should've been obsolete, they glided with ease upon ancient hinges. Glimmers of my mother's shore faded, revealing the tunnels leading to Hell. They looked real, but I knew better. This was merely another illusion.

"Prepare yourself, Toth'toros. This place is not what it appears," I cautioned the Daemon at my side.

He grinned in response and took an eager step forward. As we crossed the gates, I felt a shift. It was like being Transposed by the oldest, smoothest magic sliding across my skin and down my throat.

My deep-seated hesitance to this part of my life had me pausing. Pain flashed across my body, tearing my insides apart. I choked on the magic as I thrashed in transit. My arms flailed out, reaching for my bodyguard, only to grasp at empty air.

In the blink of an eye, I was taken from solid ground to open air. A slicing pain cut into my back.

"Spread your wings wide, my love!" a familiar voice called.

My eyes snapped in the direction of the voice. Tall as a giant, the soft curves and rolls of my mother's body bounced with joy as she cheered me on. There stood my mother, Fortuna. Her robes were pure sun-silk, glowing against her black skin and long black locks. This was how she looked when she walked the face of the earth.

Something was off about the scene, though. It was too slow to be happening in real-time.

Realization gripped me. This wasn't real... Fortuna threw me into a memory. I spread my wings wide, trying to remember how old I was here.

Young.

So young.

The wind tore against my wings, and even more pain exploded like a supernova across my back. My godling body lacked sufficient muscles to keep them spread long enough to flap, but I was saved for a few seconds before plummeting to the rocky ground.

Time resumed at a normal pace, and I was blown back when my larger-than-life mother began to clap. The ripples of air pushed me away in a rush, but it was that wind that helped me to catch the air current and soar for the first time.

"Terran!" Fortuna called. "Come watch Aidoneus fly!"

Earth-quaking heavy footfalls pierced the air as the Elemental God of Land bounded across his world.

"That's my boy! Well done!" the God roared. His skin was a deep tan, the color of sun-baked terracotta, and he smelled like rich earth.

They were too big, too powerful, and yet, once, they knew kindness. At one point in my youth, they had been good parents. But time takes a toll on all beings, even immortal ones. Morals become harder to grasp. Living became tedious and ate at the mind. Seeing my parents like this, without the sickness of the mind that would one day force them to the underworld, recolored my memories.

I cried out as the wind abruptly stopped. My wings could not support me as I dove downward. In moments, a large hand shot out to scoop me from the open air. The deft fingers that wove fate cradled me as if I were precious to her.

For a second, I was fooled. Warm tears pricked my eyes as my parents showered me with praise and bound me up with the weight of their hopes and dreams for all the things I would be able to do when I could finally fly.

The vision faded, and I hit the cold-hard stone of the wind-buffeted first circle of Hell. Pain ripped through me, and blood the color of starlight leaked from my hands and knees as I shifted back to inspect the damage. Here, the wails of those consumed in life by lust, gluttony, and greed echoed off the smooth stone around me.

I stood, exiting the cave. The shores of icy waters beat against the sharp rocks, refusing to be worn down by time and element. Toth'toros was still nowhere to be seen.

I growled in frustration. "Will you make me pass through all the seven circles?" I shouted into the abyss. "I have agreed to your bargain. Now bring me to you, Fortuna!"

No response.

Frustration bubbled in my veins, igniting that familiar fuel of magic in my insides. An idea blossomed alongside it, and I reached deep enough into the earth to shake the foundations of this realm.

Magic was different here, more antiquated and harsh. The roughness must've come from the echoes of my father's power, which I now held.

Before me, souls stumbled out of cracks and hidden spaces. Some beat their chests, others tore at their non-corporeal hair. They sought a reprieve from their torment, but those fleeting moments brought nothing more than insanity.

Guilt did not exist for them. They had earned their keep.

"God!" one of them called in a moment of lucidity. "Have you come to release us?" a Fae with patches of baldness across his scalp cried out.

His eyes were bloodshot, and his fingernails cracked and filled with dirt.

I stared down at the pitiful man, turning away.

"My affairs are not with this place," I snapped, tugging my robes closer to my body.

The Fae snarled, his humanoid expression turning beastly.

"Free me!" he roared, lunging for my skin. Seconds before he touched me, the folds of my robes lashed out and sliced at his hands. The godly magic severed the soul limbs, and they fell to the ground without a sound.

The soul fell onto his knees, howling in pain. The handful of onlookers ran away screaming.

A twinge of guilt bubbled up inside me just as my vision faded again. My sight returned as I stared up at the familiar stars. A hauntingly beautiful melody washed over me. My soul knew the tune and hummed, even as I lay in the white-powdery sand. The shores did not beat here, though they were still cold.

I sat up, and my sight swam from the sudden movement. *Another memory.*

My blood chilled, though this scene was warmer.

This was the memory Fortuna wanted to take. I knew it as strongly as I knew my own name.

In place of the dried flecks of pearlescent blood, rivulets of blood streaked my skin. My clothes were in tatters, and I sat on the ground. I stretched my arms out, placed them on either side of myself, and turned around.

A familiar golden stool and moonlight-bright loom sat before me. Its owner was surprisingly absent.

"What a lovely home you have made for me, my son," a voice that was at once young and old said. Its musical quality resonated within my bones. Fortuna strolled out, her once golden gown now faded to the color of pale starlight. "But you didn't make this. And I am unsure if it is a home or a cage." She raised one of her glossy black eyebrows.

I remembered this memory much better. It had happened mere centuries ago. We were speaking after the Rebellion. This was the first time she decided to weave in the underworld after her imprisonment.

There was a part for me to play, but I did not wish to get into character.

"Fortuna," I started, and the image slowed, as it had in the last memory. I rolled my eyes. Apparently, breaking character wasn't an option.

"It is not a cage, Mother," I whispered. The words came easily, and time did not hiccup again. "I need your help."

My voice broke on the last word. I was unexpectedly thrown into the full weight of the context of this memory. It surprised me that I still bore the heftiness of these emotions—agony, grief, loneliness, rage.

Fortuna gazed down at me. The melody had turned sharp and treacherous. "On one hand, my love, you have saved me." She held up a glorious arm parallel to the ground, and the sleeve of her gown dripped off her shoulder like a fountain. Then she raised her other arm. "But on the other hand, if you and your brothers hadn't rebelled, there would have been no need for saving."

I knew arguing was useless, but I said the words anyway. The memory demanded it. "You know what was happening in Aranthium. You were withering, and the people were suffering."

She stared at me for a long, hard second. "And what of Miranda?"

I was still sitting, but the swirling melting pot of emotions erupted. That name stole my breath, choking me with tears. I crumpled in a pile in the sand.

The song in the air changed, and compassion filled Fortuna's voice. "Aidoneus, my child, I am so sorry."

The sound of her kneeling down was loud enough to break eardrums.

I heaved and sucked in a new breath. "I need to see her. Please," I begged. Even in the ghosts of this memory, everything hurt. My soul felt like it was breaking. Tears ran down my face, and my entire body felt so broken, as though I might shatter from grief. My brain ached from tears, both shed and unshed.

My mother stiffened. "She is not here."

I froze, my body shaking with grief. "What do you mean?"

Fortuna spoke, but the sound was mechanical, as if she was citing some primordial law. "Miranda has been wiped from all existence by the curse. Her soul is gone. Destroyed. She is not here, neither in paradise nor in prison."

Heat pumped through my body, and my ears rang. "No, she can't be gone forever. Go to your loom and weave her a new fate. Give her back to me in whatever form you can!" I shouted. The heat in my body dried my tears.

My mother looked at me like she had when I used to throw temper tantrums. But I was not a child, and this was not a fit. I had lost my life in that Rebellion.

I stormed up to Fortuna's enormous knees. "Give her back!" I demanded once more.

The goddess gazed down at me, her black hair sliding down her skin like a dark waterfall. "My son, I cannot. The magic does not work that way."

She was stoic, resolute.

Betrayal was a hot knife stabbing into my flesh over and over. "Then destroy me as well. Kill me, take my essence, and cast it to the wind," I cried. New tears flowed, but these were not the same cold dribbles of grief. These were as hot as the lava that flowed through the volcano. Anger edged my vision. "Take me away and let me be with my wife."

Fortuna shook her head. "I cannot do that, either."

I roared, dropping back to my knees. Grief like I'd never thought possible ran through me. Fracturing me. I screamed until the air and strength were well and truly gone from my body, catapulting me into a place past feelings.

If Fortuna was obstinate, then there was no power to move

her. I stood up. Brushing the sand off of my ruined clothes and skin coated with the blood of my dead wife and me, I steeled myself. I took several long breaths.

I knew what came next. I knew what I would do once I left this place. After this, I faced centuries of loneliness. I would shut myself off emotionally to protect myself.

"I will never return to this place," I vowed. "If you do this, I will never return."

My mother opened her mouth, but the anger flowing through me was too potent. I held up my hand, feeling the lack of power that came from missing my other half.

"I cannot change what has happened," Fortuna began. "But I will weave you—"

In my memory, I left before she finished the sentence. But this time, something changed. I didn't leave, and neither did the grief. Everything still hurt.

Fortuna finished her sentence.

"—a new future," she called.

And then the music stopped abruptly. A few discordant notes hung in the air as deafening silence descended. The scene flashed a brilliant white. It drenched me in warmth and radiated energy. I squeezed my eyes shut, covering them with my arms, which were once again bare.

The blinding light faded, and I dropped my arms from my eyes to my sides. I was still in the same place, looking at the same being. Fortuna was not facing me. She was firmly planted in front of her loom. Music filtered around me, thick as syrup and just as sticky. The notes smothered my robes and skin.

Heartbreak filled the air. With every note, the feeling of utter despair and grief sank into my body. The music was dark. Deep. Moving. The notes were high, speaking a story of lost love and death. My heart moved with the tune produced by Fortuna. The clack of her shuttles and the reedy sound of her comb joined the notes, adding to the song. She pushed down the threads that became the percussion.

Fortuna was a lot to handle, but I knew her. Our separation for the last few hundred years couldn't erase how well I knew her mannerisms and how she spoke.

My mouth opened, but I hesitated. I was about to call her by the name the world knew her as, but the word stuck on my tongue like chalk. Now that I was looking at her, memories came flooding back.

"Mother."

The weaving stopped mid-stroke. The canvas made of waterfalls of magic, myth, and darkness was easy to see in front of her.

She didn't turn around when she breathed out one word, "Aidoneus."

Chills coated my whole body at the electricity in the air. The energy pumped into the soul-shattering grief I had been experiencing minutes before.

"Where is Toth'toros?" I demanded. He hadn't appeared with me.

Her voice was almost lazy, but there was an undercurrent of care and precision that belied her real feelings. "He has been sent back to Lethe. I needed to talk to you alone." She hesitated. "Are you ready to give me your memory?"

Her voice was strong, but she still did not face me.

I straightened my back. "If you are referring to what I just saw, then I think you are forgetting not all of that was mine."

My mother's shoulders slumped slightly, and my eyebrows shot up.

"I suppose you are right," she said.

My head tilted to the side, and I narrowed my eyes. "Why take away that memory?"

She looked at me and blinked. "So you cease being angry with me for my answer."

I swallowed. "And what would you leave me with? Without that memory, I won't know the truth about Miranda. I will come here searching again, and we will make another memory wrought with the same pain and agony. Are you ready to wait another three centuries without me?"

I took one step forward, and the sand compacted below my feet. Fortuna watched me warily. From the way her jaw clenched, I knew she had no answer.

However, she surprised me. "I'm so sorry, Aidoneus. I wish I could've done more."

At the tone of my mother's voice, warm feelings radiated from my chest. It was not always easy to love a goddess up close and personal. It was even more difficult to be the product of one so ethereal and omnipotent as Fortuna.

I came here for answers and assistance, but I couldn't recall any of the questions that had been burning my tongue to ash moments before. All I could hear was how she promised to weave me a new future. What kind of wonders could come as a result of a goddess's love for her son?

"Mom," I said quietly. "Thank you for showing me that first memory. I had forgotten that my life was not always so full of sadness."

Her head shot over her shoulder and met my gaze. The sorrow of centuries had made their mark on her usually beautiful and unmarred skin. The fabric in her lap fell.

It was tightly woven, with more dark colors than anything, but threads of brightness existed within it. The threads spoke of lightning, the moon, starlight, divine green. There were other colors, too. The red of Miranda's aura and the brilliant orange heat and lava. The obsidian circlet I wore on my coronation day.

My throat tightened.

Mother had taken out my tapestry.

"You..." I started, but my voice trailed off as my eyes fixed on a new set of rows. They were recent, their endings unfinished, and the strands still half-attached to her shuttles. Electric blue started unexpectedly out of a sea of black and white. Then it disappeared, only to reappear and intensify yards later. It wove beautiful flower patterns with rays of sunshine before it twisted around the green. Surprising flecks of seductive red twined between the two of them.

There was no denying it was Phaedra. From the first meeting at Miranda's funeral to the present day. It perfectly mirrored the rollercoaster of attraction, competition, and reluctant coworkers to friends. Then, almost something more.

One glowing inquiry rose in my mind.

"This new future you wove for me. What was it?" I asked.

My mouth was dry, and I swallowed three times, only managing to barely relieve the soreness.

She blinked, and the stars winked out for a second as if following their master. The ocean rippled with her long sigh.

"Come with me," she commanded, and we were transported to a cottage made of finely oiled wood. We were still in the middle of Fortuna's patch of paradise, surrounded by beauty, sea, and tapestries. Tapestries of every color, size, and weave lined the walls from the floors to the ceilings.

A fire blazed near an enormous high-backed velvet chair resting next to the hearth. I hadn't ever come here, though I was familiar with the clutter that preserving centuries of individual lives and collective societies could create.

Something—I assumed Fortuna's omniscience—guided her to the corner where she pulled a tapestry made of spring-time pastels and winter-blue sorrows.

Until the very end.

In one hand, she held the fabric of my life; in the other, she held what I was confident was Phaedra's. Mine was exponentially longer, but when hanging side by side, they were perfectly in sync. Every row, every color, every beat of the story was the same.

A new emotion flooded through me. This tapestry wasn't just made of the red of passion. I saw the pink of shyness, the yellow of new beginnings, the green of truth and honesty, and the blue of compatibility. It was a word I was afraid of saying.

Fortuna searched my face with her piercing eyes. "Phaedra is your match, Aidoneus. Your new future. She doesn't erase the past, but she will be in every chapter moving forward. Choose her and be happy."

My breath caught. I practically stumbled forward with my hands outstretched to brush the fibers of the two cloths. When my fingers connected with the fabric, the tapestries went soft and pliable. A chord was struck deep inside of me.

A new thought popped into my mind. An impossible, beautiful thought. "Did you give Phaedra her enhanced powers?" My neck craned to look up at my mother.

A strained expression was written upon the planes of Fortuna's face. "No, my son. That was Fate. But I was happy to weave it into reality." Her voice broke with tenderness before a teardrop the size of a bucket of water splashed down in front of me. It shattered the perfect pocket of catharsis that was strumming a tune in the air.

I had come here for a purpose. "Mother, Phelix has her. He will kill her, I'm sure of it." Fear fried my nerve endings. "I didn't come here for this. I came to find ways to rescue her. You may take the memory, for I will always remember this one. Please help me." I didn't want to sound so pathetic, but knowing what I knew now, there were no lengths I wouldn't go to.

Fortuna frowned, and paradise grew darker. "Phelix." The name was a source of many things for our mother, most of all fury. "I am going to bring your brother here."

The blood drained from my face. "I didn't even know you could do that. Don't. Phelix is—"

"Who said anything about Phelix? Madness has already taken him," Fortuna said.

Midnight blue smoke curled throughout the room as a new figure joined us in the sitting room.

My golden-skinned Angelic brother was before me, with frost, and icicles hanging off his eyelashes. Raphael was dressed in full battle armor, and he stood at an odd angle as if he had been in the middle of walking.

"What the hell?" he roared before turning around and taking in our giant mother. "Oh, hi, Mom." His eyes fell to the stretched-out tapestries and landed on me. "Aidoneus."

"Hello, brother," I drawled.

Fortuna crossed over to the now-blazing fire and sat down in her chair. "My children, I cannot give you all the answers you seek. But I know where Phelix is."

Raphael held up his large palm. "I do, too. He's right off the shores of the Realm of the Vampires."

I blinked, and our mother paused, cocking her head to the side. The only sound was the crackling of the flames.

"That is correct, Raphael," she said slowly before adding, "Well done."

My brother positively glowed. He continued, unprompted. "Once I received word from Aidy, I found a lead. Strange vampire, but then again, aren't they all? One time—" Raphael turned to me, and I could tell from his expression he was getting ready to launch into some long, unwanted story.

I raised my hand, shutting off the never-ending stream coming out of the Angel King's mouth. "Relevant info only."

He shot me a harsh glare before nodding. "I was coming to visit him when I was so rudely called home."

Fortuna's eyes fluttered closed, and she took a long sigh.

"Very well, I will send both of you back." Her eyes opened suddenly. "Aidoneus, take care of your brother."

I blinked, taken aback by her forwardness. "Yes, of course."

Fortuna nodded. "I expect to see both of you next weekend. Aidoneus, bring me your new wife. I have robes for her. They are made from the purest intentions and deadliest threats." She leaned back, fully relaxing into the velvet chair. "It is so good to finally live to see the prophecy fulfilled."

My eyebrows drew together. I had more questions for my Mother, but I needed to find my wife.

The last thing I saw before we Transposed to the bitter cold was my mother's familiar smile.

"Shit," I hissed as a gust of snow whipped at my bare limbs. She hadn't given me a change of clothes, and my magic was drained. For so many reasons, I needed my wife back. A small team of Angels stood around, and a few jumped back as we appeared.

Well, as I appeared out of thin air. I was sure that for them, Raphael hadn't been gone even a second.

Raphael laughed, back to being his jovial self. "Nice outfit. Did your mom make it?"

I punched him in the arm. Hard. "Shut up, you child, and give me something to wear."

My brother only laughed harder. "Not a chance in Hell, chicken legs."

This was not the time for his jokes. They only served to increase the anger that bubbled up within me. I didn't have time for this.

Clenching my fists at my side, I growled. "We are on a mission, behave."

Snowflakes continued to drive around us like fine powder falling from the heavens. The sun was covered, but it still gave a few sparkling rays of ghostly light that shone upon the snow.

The thick coniferous trees created a wall in front of us. I imagined it would block out whatever filtered life still managed to make it through this frozen land.

Raphael nodded. "Don't be dramatic. The entrance is just ahead." He shook his head in irritation and then started forward once more. "They are expecting us, so make all the noise you want."

I shot him a glare but followed.

He was right. We didn't need to walk far. Barely fifty paces into the woods revealed a steel door sealed tight with a lever. A trickle of acid leaked into my gut as we closed the distance.

A wave of wrongness billowed off the place.

"Raphael," I started. "I don't know who your contact is, but this feels off. Tell me his name before we go down."

The snow behind us crunched, and I whipped around, robes glowing.

A tall male wearing a pitch-black suit and pale skin just a shade too gray leaned against the trunk of a pine tree. He wore no coat, and his dark hair was combed and oiled back into a glossy hairstyle that looked like something from two hundred years ago.

Muscles were packed on each other, pulling against the fabric of his clothes as he crossed his arms. Violet eyes stared at me, swimming with faint amusement.

"His name is Garret Thorn. Welcome to my realm, Your Highnesses." The man smirked, and when he spoke, I noted the razor-sharp canines peeking out from behind his blood-red lips.

I knew this man. He had worked for me once, acquiring antiquities. He had been promptly fired when I found him stealing one night. I stood straight, towering over his already tall frame as I closed the space between us.

"Mr. Thorn," I seethed. I looked over my shoulder, glaring at my brother. "Raphael, you can't be serious. Don't trust a word out of this man's lips."

Thorn huffed a laugh. "Come now, gentlemen. I am reformed. No tricks, I promise." He splayed a gloved hand over his chest, his face molding into the very image of innocence.

Terrifying, pale-skinned, vicious innocence.

"Follow me inside so we can discuss transportation to the Ice Mer King's feast." His cold, violet eyes looked right at me. "I hear there will be one performer in particular that you may be interested in seeing, King Hades."

Burning panic flooded my veins, and I stood there, frozen. Raphael's gloved hand landed on my shoulder, heavy and warm. "Let's go inside, Aidoneus. Don't worry, I know what I'm doing."

I nodded slowly. Relinquishing my control of the situation, I prayed to Fortuna he really did.

CHAPTER 30
A BALLROOM OF DESTRUCTION
PHAEDRA

The room was silent. I gripped the table, swallowing hard. The trio of mean girls had shoved me into the middle of a sunken ballroom. Gold and silver were everywhere, from the walls to the lines covering the glass dome that made up the ceiling, but I barely paid it any attention.

My mind whirled, focusing on one word.

Entertainment.

I wished I was back in my cell. Sitting on the ground with cramped muscles eating raw fish was better than this.

"Come now, Your Highness." Phelix's voice dripped with mockery, and I shuddered. He was still behind me, but I could sense him getting closer. "Don't you want to want to greet your guests? After all, they are all here for you."

At that, a murmur went through the crowd.

I gripped the table harder, forcing myself to remain upright.

Think.

What was I going to do?

That black mist still blocked my bond, but at least now I was out of my cell. Maybe this was it. The moment I had been waiting for. If Aidoneus wasn't going to come for me, then I needed to save myself.

Steeling myself, I let go of the table and turned around slowly. The sensation of moving underwater was akin to walking through thick mud, and the action took much longer than it would have on the surface. My eyes landed on Phelix, and I raised a brow. A large golden circlet rested on his brow, and he was gripping a golden trident in his right fist.

"Your Majesty." I dipped my head toward my brother-in-law with just enough deference to acknowledge that he was a king. Just enough—but not as much as I would have a few months ago.

I already decided I would not bow before him. Phelix might have been a king, but I wasn't a nobody. I was a queen consort, and power ran through my veins, even if I couldn't feel it right now.

Not only that, but he was a murderous asshole. That alone meant that he wasn't deserving of respect. Remembering what Hades told me about the orphanage, anger pulsed through my veins.

Phelix tilted his head as a wolfish grin appeared on his face. "Welcome to my court. It was so kind of you to come all this way."

I glared at him, ignoring our audience as I stepped toward him. "Kind? You kidnapped me. Apparently, it's a familial trait." When his eyes gleamed with amusement, I clenched my fists. "Don't act like I had a choice in being here."

The Ice Mer King shrugged. "What's a little kidnapping when you're in the middle of a war?" He leaned in as though he were imparting a secret. "Remember, I can do much worse than this."

A threat lay buried beneath his words. One that sent shivers down my spine. The way he spoke...

I'd been in front of powerful beings many times before. In all those times, I had never heard someone with so much power speak so flippantly.

I knew I had to choose my next words carefully.

Holding my head up high, I gestured to the ballroom. "No matter the terms of my arrival, I am... honored you would throw such an elaborate party for me."

Phelix's eyes twinkled, and green power sparked through his irises. "Oh no, Phaedra. It was no trouble at all." He raised a brow. "Is it okay if I call you that?"

I frowned. "No, it isn't. I haven't given you permission to call me anything." Holding my head up high, I tried to channel as much queenly power into my words as possible as I said, "I demand you let me go."

"Let you go?" He smirked.

All around the room, the Ice Mer chuckled. The sound was as cool as the chunks of ice floating through the water, and I shivered.

King Phelix was clearly starved for attention because he lapped up the laughter. The sound of the crowd's amusement filled the ballroom as little bubbles of air floated around the water.

I focused on breathing through my gills.

After a minute or so had passed, the king clapped his hands.

Instantly, everyone fell silent.

"Ms. Demtre wants to go," he said, his tone dripping with derision. "But she hasn't even had any fun yet!" Slamming his trident on the floor, he raised his free hand. "We can't allow her to leave without experiencing the best my court has to offer!"

Cheers went up through the crowd, and the Ice Mer King swam closer to me.

"Besides," he crooned, lowering his voice. "You should know I don't invite just anyone to my court. In fact, one might say that only my favorite family members get this type of treatment."

Before I could respond, he raised a hand in the air. "Guards!"

Instantly, a dozen Ice Mer with tails as black as the night appeared all around me. "Make sure the queen consort is shown the attention she deserves. After all, we wouldn't want my brother's wife feeling anything less than welcome, would we?"

I shivered. Jeers and shouts filled the ballroom as violent energy came from the crowd. A rough hand grabbed onto my arm, and my stomach dropped.

"Come with me," the guard on my left growled. He tugged me along, and I half-walked, half-stumbled behind him. The water moved around me, not resisting me but not making it easy for me to follow the guard, either.

The crowd parted instantly, seeming to know where I was being taken. I stared at the Ice Mer. Dressed in their finery, their tails glimmered. They held glasses filled with a rosy liquid, and tables strewn with delicacies were scattered around the golden ballroom. The guard dragged me along, and my eyes lifted to the walls.

The moment I looked up, bile rose in my throat.

Half a dozen massive golden orbs hung from the ceiling. From afar, they looked like pieces of decoration, but as we approached, I realized the error in my ways. These orbs were not decorations. No, each orb contained a human dressed in scraps of golden cloth. Each one was moving their body seductively, spinning in slow circles as their hands twirled above their heads.

Magic must have been keeping the water out of the orbs. One of the humans looked no older than fifteen, and her blue eyes were wide as she met my gaze.

She mouthed, *help me.*

I widened my eyes. What could I do?

I dug in my heels, and the guard must have noticed where I was looking. He laughed, stopping to point at the blond human who had met my gaze. “If you’re lucky, this will be your fate. To dance for the king until your feet fall off.”

If that was a lucky fate, I didn't want to know what the male considered unlucky. Bile rose in my throat as he yanked on my arm once more.

Dozens of conversations rose all around me, and none of the merfolk were even attempting to be discreet. I heard my name and Aidoneus’, alongside updates about the war.

And then, as the Ice Mer dragged me toward the stage, I heard something that made my stomach drop.

Reaching out, I grabbed the arm of a female laughing obnoxiously with her friend. Her bright pink tail matched the tiara resting on her head. She was probably friends with the Ice Mer who dressed me.

"What did you say?" I asked, yanking her around.

The female spun, her glass sloshing as her turquoise eyes widened. "Oh, my gods!" she squealed, sounding more like an injured pig than the mean girl I instantly knew her to be. "The two-legged whore touched me!"

Instantly, the room fell silent. More guards approached me, but I ignored them.

"What. Did. You. Say?" I asked again.

She didn’t respond.

The guard pulled on my arm. "Let her go," he snarled.

I refused, tightening my grip on the mean girl. "What do you know about my husband?"

"Last warning, Your Highness," the guard hissed, twisting my arm. His nails raked my skin, leaving a flash of red behind. "I won’t hesitate to break your arm if you don't come with me."

"No," I shook my head. I turned to the female imploringly. “Please, I need to know. I heard you say something about my husband."

“I warned you,” the guard sneered. He yanked my arm, and a

searing, stabbing pain rushed through the limb. Tears welled in my eyes, and for a moment, everything went black.

When my eyesight returned, the female was further away. The guard pulled my injured arm as she smirked at me. I dug my feet into the ballroom floor, and all around me, people started laughing.

"Tell her!" someone shouted.

Another laughed. "This is the real show."

My eyes were wide, my heart pounded as the female met my gaze. She raised a manicured brow. "Fine," she sighed. "I'll tell you. If you must know, your husband disappeared the day after you left the Gates of Hell."

Disappeared.

The day after.

My heart stuttered.

"What?" I cried out. The guard holding me swam faster, and I flailed in his arms. My injured shoulder throbbed painfully. "What do you mean?"

Panic rose within me. It was one thing for Aidoneus not to come for me. After all, our marriage had been one of convenience.

But this...

The female cackled. "Most people say he's dead."

Dead.

Aidoneus was dead.

The word reverberated through my mind, and my entire body went slack. I stopped fighting as the Ice Mer guard pulled me toward a dais set in the center of the room. He threw me on the floor before a gilded throne, and something in my shoulder snapped.

I didn't even move. Laughter rose from the crowd, but I didn't even lift my head.

He was dead, and I...

I had told him we were just friends, but in those few moments between us, I'd felt like something more could have existed between us. There was a chance we could have had something real. A life together. Maybe in time, we could have built something.

We could have loved each other.

But then Phelix kidnapped me, and now Aidoneus was dead.

How did he die? Phelix said I couldn't feel the bond because of black magic, but maybe he was wrong.

Maybe it was gone because my husband was dead.

I didn't even know that one could kill a DemiGod.

A cold chuckle came from behind me, and I lifted my head off the floor to stare at the Ice Mer King. He swam over to his throne, taking his place of honor and placing his trident beside him. It rested it on the edge of the throne at an angle, the three spikes so sharp that they glistened.

Silence reigned.

The only movement was that of the humans dancing in the orbs as everyone else just... stared at me.

Eventually, Phelix cleared his throat. "I see you've heard the good news." His words ran over my skin like rancid oil, and I felt like I would be sick. "It seems someone took care of my brother for me." He clucked his tongue. "A shame, really. I was looking forward to killing both my brothers, but dead is dead. There will be the power redistribution to deal with, of course, but we can do that later."

I refused to answer him. I refused to do anything. A dark feeling roiled through me, and it took me a moment to realize what it was: grief.

I mourned for the king who had been so many things in my life. Abductor. Employer. Friend. Husband.

A weighted silence passed before Phelix slammed his trident on the ground. "Enough of this morose conversation. This is a party, am I right?" He laughed, and shivers went down my spine. "Eat, drink, and be merry!"

The words were hard and edged with shards of ice as they left his lips.

Instantly, the members of his court turned and began to chatter, their tails swishing quietly in the water as they returned to their conversations.

I remained on the floor. My fingers dragged through the grooves in the golden tile as my mind swirled over that word.

Dead.

Which meant... I actually didn't know what that meant for me.

Bad things, if my current situation was any proof.

The party whirled around me, and I lost track of time. King Phelix chatted with his guards, ignoring me completely as I remained on the dais near his feet.

For a while, I thought perhaps he forgot about me. Drink after drink was poured, and the energy in the ballroom became more frantic. Music played from hidden speakers, and the Ice Mer danced, their tails moving to the beat of the music. I pulled myself into a ball, tucking my wings around me as best I could.

Servants brought out one course after the other, serving the king and his guests.

After the third course, my stomach made a noise. Blood rushed to my cheeks, and I curled myself into a ball.

Something landed on the floor near me with a splat. I glanced up, eyeing the red piece of slimy fish.

“Eat,” King Phelix commanded.

I narrowed my eyes, wanting to refuse the food, but pains were shooting through my stomach. I must have been out for a while because I was extremely hungry.

Hating myself for obeying, I reached out and picked up the fish with two fingers. It was slippery, and I inched my fingers towards myself. Squeezing my eyes shut, I lifted the piece of fish to my mouth. Chewing it quickly, I swallowed. A shudder of revulsion ran from my spine to my feet.

"Good girl," the Ice Mer King crooned, praising me like a dog.

Bile rose in my throat, but I forced it down.

A few minutes later, another piece of fish landed on the platform near me. The message was clear.

I wasn't going to do it.

If Aidoneus was dead, there was no reason to keep me alive. They would either kill me or let me go.

"No." I shook my head. "I won't eat it."

The last word barely left my lips before a rough hand landed on my shoulder.

My brother-in-law wrenched me to my feet. "No?" He tilted his head. "Are you sure?"

Pressing my mouth in a firm line, I nodded. "Yes."

He shrugged. "So be it." He waved a hand, and for a moment, everything seemed normal.

Then, a scream came from one of the golden orbs suspended from the ceiling. I turned, my face paling, as water rapidly climbed up the interior of the orb. The blond dancer who had asked me for help screamed in terror as the water flooded her orb.

My eyes widened as it covered her feet and continued to rise.

Within seconds, her knees were covered. Then, her waist.

My heart pounded in my chest.

The water level rose to her breasts.

"Stop," I said, turning back to my brother-in-law. "You're going to kill her."

He raised a brow, gesturing to the fish. "Eat."

I swallowed, glancing back and forth between the Ice Mer King and the human who was moments away from drowning.

Could I have her death on my conscience?

Finally, I shook my head when the water was up to her neck. Dropping to my knees, I put the fish in my mouth, chewed, and swallowed. The entire time, I stared at Phelix with daggers in my eyes.

"Good dog," the king said. He waved a hand, and seconds later, the screaming stopped. Water drained back out of her orb, and the human resumed dancing.

And so, time ticked by.

The Ice Mer partied. The humans danced. My mortification grew. The king fed me. When I refused, Phelix tortured the humans until I agreed.

By the time hours passed, I wished I had never left my cell.

King Phelix threw another piece of fish before me when the waters stirred. They rushed around us, picking up tablecloths and making dresses billow. The crowd murmured, and behind me, the guards shifted.

An unnatural ripple ran through the water. Filled with power, it felt different. New.

I glanced over my shoulder. The king wasn't looking at me. He scowled at the dome ceiling.

My heart leaped. If Phelix wasn't doing this, then that meant...

Perhaps someone was coming.

Hope blossomed within me. Maybe this was it. The moment of my escape.

And then I remembered what the Mer had said.

Aidoneus was dead.

"Take the queen consort," King Phelix demanded. "Bring her back to her cell for questioning."

I barely processed the words before rough hands grabbed onto my arms.

"No!" I shouted, kicking as they began to drag me away. The guards were not gentle, and my shoulder burned. "Let go of me!"

I did not want to return to my cell. Some part of me knew that if I went back there, I would never get out again. I'd die...

Just like my husband.

The Ice Mer guards dragged me through the ballroom, and the crowd parted again. They watched me with dispassionate eyes. Those cold, unfeeling eyes lit a fire within me.

I hated them all.

"I hope you think of my face when you dream!" I screamed. “Remember that you stood by while your king tortured a queen!”

My anger grew into rage as the Ice Mer dragged me. I kicked one in the solid muscle of his upper tail. My foot hurt, but I scratched and bit at their hands. “Let me go!” I screamed.

We were halfway through the ballroom when King Phelix smashed his trident on the dais. The bang echoed through the room, and I flinched. The king cleared his throat. "*Wait.*"

The guards towing me stopped moving. I continued to kick them, trying to wrench my arms away, as Phelix laughed. "Don’t you understand why I brought you here, Your Highness?"

The guards twisted me around roughly until I faced the throne again. I bared my teeth, and my eyes burned with rage as I seethed. My chest heaved, pushing the salty water in and out of my body. I hated the acrid taste, and I hated Phelix Proteus. He met my eyes, waiting. For something.

Obviously, whatever power had been racing through the water minutes before was forgotten.

I would not give him the satisfaction of an answer.

“Aidoneus and Raphael always had their things. Their kingdoms, their wives, their armies. They had their games and their riches. Whatever was left was mine.” His gray and white beard floated around his face, and his eyes flashed green.

The color reminded me of Aidoneus and our bond, sending a searing pain through me.

My brother-in-law did not stop speaking, though. He

extended a hand, and his magic flashed through the water in a wave. The crown on Phelix's head quivered, and he sneered at me. At that moment, I saw through his disinterested act. He could pretend he was fighting this war for many reasons, but in reality, it was for selfish reasons.

Like a spoiled brat, he wanted to take back everything he had been denied.

For the first time, I noticed how much older he looked than his brothers. The glow in his eyes faded as his cruel lips twisted up. "Even though my brother is dead, Lethe still needs a queen."

I froze.

Phelix's smile grew. "Power speaks to you, I see. That's not a surprise. Never fear, Phaedra. You can still be queen. All you must do is swear fealty to me."

All the raw fish and saltwater in my stomach threatened to reappear. Dozens of eyes were fixed on me as though enraptured by this sick and twisted performance.

"No," I snarled, shaking my head.

The water clouded, and the King's eyes went green once again.

"Very well, Phaedra Demtre." Phelix raised his triton to the air. "Before you return to your cell, let me remind you just how welcome you are at my court!"

He waved a hand, and a moment later, the female closest to me threw their glasses of wine on me. Magic made their glasses move through the water like we were on land. The liquid slapped against my face, hitting me squarely in the eye. I screamed, trying to wrench free from the soldiers' grasp. More and more liquid followed until my vision blurred. I couldn't see anything.

Jeers and shouts of derision filled the ballroom, and anger festered within me. I squeezed my eyes shut and ducked my head to protect my face from more of the wine-polluted water.

That cloud of darkness within me shifted more, and once

again, I *felt* my bond. I gasped. It tasted like darkness. Like death. Like my husband.

It was just a spark, barely there, but I knew it like I knew my own name.

That sweet hope blossomed inside of me again. I wouldn't have a bond if Aidoneus were dead... right?

A voice boomed through the ballroom, "That's enough. Take her away."

The guards tightened their grip on my arms and yanked me through the ballroom again. The crowd parted, and soon, there was no one in front of us.

I stared at the doors, wrenching my limbs like a flailing fish in an effort to escape when a dark gray cloud filled my vision. Seconds later, a deafening roar came from somewhere behind me. The room erupted in a wave of heat and a cacophony of screams. I still couldn't see, but the bond within me turned into pure electricity.

It was *alive.*

It shocked my insides and cleared out the grayness from before my eyes.

Shadows replaced the watery sunlight. The guards' hands trembled, and they loosened their grips on my arms. When my hands were free, I used every bit of self-defense I had ever learned. I slammed my knee into one guard's middle, hoping that males were the same regardless of species.

I was right.

The moment my knee hit the guard's groin, he gasped. I followed it up by punching him in the jaw, knocking him right out.

I didn't have time to celebrate as I turned to the other guard. He clenched his ja, and violence sparked in his eyes even as shadows filled the space. "You won't take me down so easily, Your Highness."

I peered behind him, and my eyes widened. The bond within me sang a joyous song. Looking back at the guard, I smirked. "I won't have to."

The Ice Mer's eyes widened. "What—"

His words ended in a bloody mumble as he crumpled to the floor on top of his friend.

I looked up, ignoring the still-pulsing heart clenched in my husband's fist as I met his eyes. They flashed electric green as the rest of him was cloaked in shadows.

Aidoneus. Seeing him was like seeing the night sky for the first time in weeks. Something cracked inside me at the sight of the man I had been told was dead.

He should've been terrifying, but I wasn't afraid.

He was mine.

"You came for me," I whispered. My throat was tight.

He nodded, his expression grim. "Phaedra, I will always come for you."

Another second passed, and we just stared at each other. I didn't even know how Aidoneus was breathing underwater. He didn't have the same gills as me. But honestly? I didn't care.

He wasn't dead, and he came for me.

At that moment, it was clear. We were more than friends. Perhaps friendship had never really been an option for us.

The dead soldier's heart floated to the floor as Aidoneus opened his arms, and I walked straight into them. The moment I touched my husband's skin, the darkness inside of me cleared. Like a flash, our bond came into focus.

It writhed within me, and I felt more alive than I had in days. I gasped. "Did you feel that?"

He nodded, his voice low. "I am going to get you out of here, Phaedra."

"Okay," I whispered.

For one long moment, he just held onto me. Everything else faded away.

Then, a slow clap came from the other side of the room. Right away, my heart sank. We weren't alone, and now there was a very real chance that neither of us would make it out of here alive.

"Welcome, brother." King Phelix's voice sent chills through me. "I see you didn't do me the courtesy of dying, after all."

Aidoneus squeezed me tightly, pressing the lightest of kisses to my forehead.

Then he stepped away from me, and a shiver ran over me.

The King of the Daemons walked toward the center of the ballroom. The water parted as though it were air. As he moved, the remaining Ice Mer scurried away. They swam out of the ballroom until only a fraction of them remained.

Aidoneus flicked his hand, and instantly, he wore robes of old. They billowed in the water, adding to his majestic appearance. His wings were centered on his back, and his horns curled above him. Shadows followed his every step, slithering through the water like eels.

When he got to the middle of the ballroom, Aidoneus opened his arms wide.

"Brother," he said in a low voice. "This has gone on long enough. Put down your trident and give up your power."

Phelix laughed. "I will *never* bow down to you."

"It's not just him." Another voice came, and I turned to stare at King Raphael Zeus as he strode around a corner. His wings, like mine, seemed to be fine in the water. He wore robes of pure gold, which defied the laws of science as they billowed in the water. The Angel King glared at his brother. "This ends today, Phelix."

The Ice Mer King sneered. "How kind of you both to arrive and make this easier for me. Here I thought I would have to hunt you both down separately, and you do me the favor of showing up together."

"Enough!" Aidoneus snapped. "Make your choice. Give up your power or die."

A long moment passed before King Phelix swam toward my husband, trident in hand. "I choose death," he said. "*Yours.*"

He pointed the trident toward Aidoneus, and I screamed, tearing up my already sore throat as a blast of green magic like a lightning bolt shot out of it. Dark shadows tinged with death filled the entire ballroom, meeting Phelix's attack.

My sight faded once again just as more screams filled the air. Bolts of electric green magic lit up the otherwise dark space. It was like the aurora borealis had been brought straight to this underwater Hell.

A new thread of power wormed its way up inside of me. It was dark and sinister, unlike the magic inside me that called to life. Death lurked inside of me, waiting in the wings.

Gathering my strength, I followed the thread down to the depths of my soul where my magic lived. I took a deep breath and tunneled down further. When I reached the end of the thread, I found a cavern of blackness writhing within me like a living being begging to be let out.

Without a second thought, I let the magic free. Jets of black-green magic shot out of my fingers and toes. My body felt like it was being torn in half as the magic drained my energy. Fire coated my skin as I struggled to hold on.

CHAPTER 31
THE END OF A KING
AIDONEUS

My vision cut through the swirling mass of green. It was vibrant and breathtaking. The way it curled and attacked looked like something straight out of Tartaro. Stray rays of magic came and curled around my legs like a cat might greet its owner.

It felt like dozens of weights were tied to my ankles as I shoved myself forward. I needed to get to the source of this power.

The ballroom was set in what appeared to be a sunken city. Kelp lights were strung between tall coral columns, and the roof only covered three-quarters of the space. It was both regal and decrepit. Phelix was in front of me mere seconds ago, but now that I looked around, I couldn't see him. He was hiding, probably.

Coward.

Glancing around, I saw Raphael on the other side of the room. I nodded at him once before shifting all my attention to my wife. I needed her. That bond within me pulsed with urgency. My eyes swept the sunken city, looking for her.

There.

Black hair was fanned out on the ground.

Shit.

She must have collapsed after saving me.

Every single instinct in my body screamed. I needed to get her. Grabbing onto a chunk of broken stone, I used it to propel myself forward.

At least two hundred Ice Mer courtiers were fleeing from the place only to be replaced by Phelix's elite. Some shouted orders while the sounds of their death cries filled my ears.

My heart raced, and my muscles strained as the water distorted sound and motion. I pushed forward off of a nearby table and swam to Phaedra.

I needed her. Every nerve in my body was crying out for her.

I swam for her with all my might. At that moment, nothing else mattered. When she was within arm's reach, I scooped her into my arms and pressed her tightly to my chest. The bond between us hummed, and power flooded through me.

Without even thinking, I brushed my lips over her forehead. Her eyes were closed, but her heart still beat. Her skin was gray, and she was so small in my arms. Phaedra's wings trailed behind her as I held her unconscious form against my chest. Those gills on her neck continued to move, the magic allowing her to breathe beneath the water.

Our hearts beat as one.

Another crash came from overhead. I shoved both of us to the other end of the room.

"Does it feel good to be reunited with your wife?" Phelix's disembodied voice shouted.

I didn't reply.

A shout came from above. One of Phelix's Elite lunged through the water like a bullet. A shark accompanied him. They were both heading toward us.

I spread my wings wide. The motion was slower than I would've liked. Thanks to my godly power, I could breathe down here, but being in the water was strange. I wasn't used to it.

"Come out, Phelix!" Raphael roared from the other side of the room.

The sharks continued to approach.

Flapping my wings, I prepared to move. Hugging my wife to my chest, I whispered in her ear, "I've got you."

She didn't respond, but her wings shifted, wrapping around her like a shield.

The movement gave me hope. Shadows erupted from me, and the ground trembled. With each flap of my wings, whirlpools erupted, creating new currents.

The shark was fifty feet away now.

Then thirty.

I flapped my wings once more.

"Stay back, beast!" I shouted to our attackers through the salty medium. The shark got caught in my current, and the Elite screamed.

I sent a bolt of shadows towards them. They went skyrocketing backward, tumbling head over tail through the enormous room. Gray collided with gray when the creature slammed hard into one of the columns. Scarlet blood bloomed in the water.

Out of the corner of my eye, I saw a golden flash.

"Raphael, don't!" The words erupted from my mouth just as I turned to see my golden brother raising a fist with magic on it.

Didn't the man know that lightning and water didn't mix? As DemiGods, our power could defy the laws of nature every now and again, but this was really pushing it.

"Raphael!" I shouted urgently. "Cover me!"

He glanced at me, the strain on his face perfectly clear. The gold of his skin was glazed with green, but he still smirked. "I've got this, brother. Deal with your wife."

Nodding, I flapped my wings once more. Pushing myself backward, I shifted us until we were behind a column. A golden orb hung nearby, and I saw a black-haired human male kneeling within it. His eyes were wide as he stared at us.

I didn't have time to address that issue, but if it weren't already clear Phelix had lost his mind, that would have clinched it for me. How dare he use humans as toys?

Fresh, righteous anger bubbled up within me.

And then, a small moan came from my wife's lips. Instantly, my attention was back on her. Her eyes were still shut, her breath shallow as she rested in my arms. Pressing a kiss to her forehead, I held her tight.

"Thank Fortuna, you're alive."

Every part of me hummed as I held her close, inspecting her for wounds.

The sounds of battle erupted all around me, but I didn't heed them. Not now. My hands skirted Phaedra's arms, her torso, and her legs as I looked for wounds.

Her shoulder was off. Something was wrong with it.

I ran my hand over the injury. A flash of green came from my palm, and I watched as her skin righted itself. It would bruise, but there would be no permanent damage.

Glancing up, I saw Zeus demolishing Elite after Elite as if our brother's best forces were krill skirting through the sea.

I owed him more with every second as I inspected Phaedra for wounds. Other than her now-healed shoulder, there didn't appear to be anything else. Relief made its way through my entire body. She was going to be okay.

She was my match. My future.

My love.

I sucked in a breath as if that realization surprised me. After all the years we spent together, working, learning, weaving our way into each other's lives, she was my love. My second chance.

I caught one of her billowing locks in my hand and brushed it back.

I loved her.

Flaming-hot resolve sliced through me as my power continued to build. We were so close to having a future. I wasn't about to let it go.

A scream came from above.

Raphael destroyed the last Elite. Scarlet-painted water filled the ballroom as he grinned at me. "There, that wasn't so bad, was it?"

Always so cocky.

Shaking my head, I tightened my grip around Phaedra.

"Come out, Phelix," I called out. "I'm tired of your games."

"Where are your legions? Your power?" Raphael taunted as he drew near to me. The swagger in his step–I hadn't even known one could have a swagger underwater, but apparently, it was possible–along with the ocean's darkness, had turned Raphael's skin to burnished brown instead of brilliant gold. "You have tormented the world over a feud between brothers!"

The words did not echo around the room, but they continued to hang like signs written in a blood pact.

Silence followed.

"Come out and face us like a man, Phelix." I stepped forward, my wings curling instinctively around my Angel.

Nothing.

I decided to take a different approach. "You have always been cruel, Phelix. In the Rebellion, you betrayed us. You helped your father Adrian kill Miranda. He and Aeran were planning on destroying part of the world." At this mention of my wife, my voice did not crack.

Even though I also mentioned Raphael's father, my golden brother did not flinch. His expression was grim. We had both seen the horrors of Gods who became tyrants.

The silence prevailed.

This time, Zeus spoke. “Brother.” He sighed. “Clearly, you wish to kill us. For what? Power?” He shook his golden head. “Perhaps if you had proven yourself an effective steward of such things, you would have them.”

A wave of cold water blew through the space in response to Zeus's words. It came barreling towards me, slamming into me like a heavy weight. My back crashed into the wall, and pain fissured through me.

My arms tightened around Phaedra. I would take a million beatings if it meant she was safe.

I scanned the water, my senses on high alert. Something was happening. Power was being gathered. At first, it was nothing more than a gentle hum, but then it grew. The sea itself quivered.

My eyes shifted. Left. Right. Left.

I couldn’t see Phelix, but I knew he was here. The water tasted of his brand of power.

Phelix’s disembodied voice started to speak. “One would rule the skies, giving birth to the seraphim, One would rule the land and all things below it. One would govern the waters until he lost them.”

Bold words that our mother had prophesied.

The power continued to build. The water grew thick and sludgy, as though the power was too much. Everything was vibrating.

One of the orbs cracked. I turned, my eyes widening as water filled the orb onto the other side of the ballroom

“Help!” the human screamed.

Water rushed into their orb in seconds.

I couldn’t get to them in time.

“Please,” they begged, “help...”

Their words were cut off with a watery gurgle.

"Is this what you do?" I shouted into the water. "Enough with the games, Phelix."

Raphael nodded. "All three of us know the prophecy, brother.. Come out and face us," he shouted. His eyes were still glowing, and I was certain mine were as well.

Power rippled through the water.

Phelix did not come out. He just continued to recite our ancient lore from his hiding place. "The price for the power would be a fated queen rivaled by the dark desires of their hearts. One would love all but his wife. One would marry well and watch her die."

He paused, and I tightened my grip around my wife as though it would keep her safe.

Once, I had spent a lot of time poring over vague prophecies. After Miranda's death, I stopped. Now, the words were crystal clear. Zeus fell in love as often as the sun rose, and I had watched my wife die.

Phaedra's beating heart was pressed against my own. They beat in unison.

"Hold on," I whispered. "I'm going to get us out of here."

Even as I spoke, Phelix's magic hovered above us like a too-full balloon.

The anticipation of it exploding had my skin tingling.

My brother's voice was back in an instant. "And one would find himself wed to a woman who could suppress the power of the gods."

I froze. I always thought that Phelix's wife fit that line. She had suppressed his violent temper on more than one occasion until she died in childbirth after the rebellion.

A crazed laugh came from nearby, and a bolt of energy flew through the water. "Zeus, get down!" I yelled.

A *pop* filled my ears. My own shadows scurried around me like a shield as the power suddenly burst. The impact slammed the air from my lungs and threatened to rip the Angel I held from my arms. My heart thudded against my ribs as I somersaulted backward into the open sea.

Everything was loud. Bright. Chaos reigned. My body kept moving, head over foot, as I curled around Phaedra.

I slammed into a bed of kelp, the impact stealing the breath from my lungs. For one moment, everything was black.

Then, I wrenched my eyes open.

Shit.

The explosion had thrown Zeus to my side. The ballroom was no more. In its place were thousands of Ice Mer soldiers. Gray water was mixed with black ash, making it hard to see their faces.

My heart fell into my ass.

Before them was Helena.

How could she?

"No," I said firmly. I straightened against the army, my arms still gripping my immobile wife. "Helena, don't do this."

A feminine chuckle filtered through the water, instantly sending me on high alert. The sound was strange. Higher than my niece's normal voice. Had she been enchanted?

"Relax, Aidoneus," she said. The shell armor that had been sharpened and molded to her body glinted under the spell light. "I am not Helena. I'm her sister, Hallie."

I blinked. Of course. How could I forget about my other niece?

Hallie dipped into a half-assed curtsy, a feat for a mermaid.

"I am the new heir to the Ice Mer throne," Hallie said with a drawl that spoke of her lineage. I could hear Phelix in her every word.

Zeus swore under his breath.

I barely stepped behind Raphael, allowing his wings to hide the bulge in my arms.

Raphael raked a hand across his face. "Look, Hallie, I don't know what games your father is playing with you, but I promise, he has no intention of giving you his throne."

A ball of green appeared overhead, and I glanced up. Dressed in a full suit of armor, Phelix swam towards his daughter.

A bitter taste coated my tongue.

Now was the moment for one side to die. Us or him.

"I would not be so hasty to assume that you know my mind, brother," Phelix said to Raphael, his hair floating around him like a crown. "You see, once the three of you are dead, the power must be redistributed. I will take my place at the head of the world, and,"–he gestured to his Mer warrior daughter–"Hallie will take over my position down here."

I shook my head and continued to hold Phaedra close. A quick look around confirmed what I already suspected. I had no hope of finding a hiding space for her, so I needed her to wake up. Now. With every second that passed, the danger grew.

Reaching within me to the door between us, I sought a handle. Something to help me open it. I needed her. Alert. Awake. With me.

I needed her because life was not worth living without her in it.

My heart skipped a beat when I found the bond between us hollow. She was there, but when I peered into the cavernous blackness, I could see no signs of consciousness.

"Aidoneus. The sweet, cursed one. Now I understand why you remarried." Phelix moved the words around in his mouth while he held out his hand. Seconds later, a glowing green trident appeared in his palm. "When I watched Miranda die, and her soul be destroyed, I was sure I understood the prophecy. If your wife died, that meant that mine would throw off the tentative balance between us. She would've had more power than me. So I disposed of her after Hallie's birth."

My heart squeezed for my sister-in-law. She had been good, lovely even. And Phelix had murdered her, depriving his children of her presence.

I looked at my other niece. Hallie was close enough now that I could make out the differences between her and Helena. Her face was rounder, and her lips thinner. Her expression was pure steel.

Phelix flicked his tail and floated toward us. “Now I see I was too hasty. My wife possessed no such powers, but it seems that yours does.”

I wouldn’t have known what he was talking about if I hadn't just come from Fortuna's circle.

But I did.

The weight of the truth was both agonizing and welcome. It hurt, but knowing that I loved Phaedra made all the difference. Together, we could manage the power within her. We could use it for good, to help others. It was a heavy load. One that would require both of us to manage.

First, I needed to wake her. In order to do that, I needed to distract Phelix long enough for Phaedra to be alert. Awake.

Together, we would face my brother. There were only two possible outcomes. We would put an end to this–or die trying.

“Why didn’t you help save Miranda?” I asked, hoping the question would distract Phelix long enough for me to wake my second wife.

It worked. Phelix paused, swimming less than a hundred feet in front of me. He was so close. Far too close. Hatred bubbled in the water around him as he sneered, “Because I didn’t wish to.”

The cruelty of his words sank in almost instantly. His cruel words were like the ice floating around in the water, chilling me to the bone.

Just like him.

Phelix studied my face, violence glinted in his eyes. We had mere seconds before this was all over. His position was clear. He knew what my Angel was capable of, and now he wanted to kill my wife and steal her power, too. With it, he would be unstoppable.

I would never let that happen, even if it meant we died trying. This brother of mine had already taken so much from me. He had ruined so many things.

I shouted at my and Phaedra's bond.

There was no response.

Not giving up, I didn't stop. I pounded on the door.

Nothing.

I invaded the space with my own power. All around me, shadows curled, and magic waited in the air.

Ignoring Phelix as he blathered about what he would do to Aranthium after Raphael and I were dead, I pounded on the walls of the bond.

Come on, my love. My Angel. Hear me.

My fist rammed on solid rock as I curled my Angel to me.

Please. Wake up.

Seconds passed in agonizing slowness. Phelix gathered power around him. My heart hammered against my ribs.

Then Phaedra drew in a sharp breath.

A flicker of light appeared in the darkness.

My wife stirred in my arms, and hope took root within me.

I shouted again, and this time...

This time, the light burned brighter.

Pure joy flooded into my insides. Teal-colored magic filled me up, energizing every inch of my body. Together, Phaedra and I would make something new. Something powerful.

We would give everything we had to save the world.

That was what love meant.

Sometimes, it meant sacrifice.

My brother didn't understand love. But I was beginning to.

Sometimes, with a love like this, the only thing one could do was hold on tight and see where the world went.

Raphael, that brother of mine who was so jovial, so light, spoke beside me. "Phelix, I want you to know that if you ever felt left out, alone, I was feeling the same. But the difference was that I learned how to love and find compassion. You are incapable of that."

I turned my head, gaping at my angelic brother.

He sounded so... wise.

Evidently, Phelix did not agree. He laughed, and the sound felt like how metal tasted. "Nice to see you're still an imbecile, Raphael."

Raphael moved, opening his mouth as though to retort, but at that same moment, Phelix drew back his arm. He hurled his triton at our brother's throat. Raphael moved swiftly, turning away from the weapon, but the triton veered, following him.

A horrible gurgling sound choked out of Raphael when he hit the ground, leaving me with my still-unconscious wife.

We were out of time.

Slamming into the door between our bond, I gave it everything I had. Over and over again, I rammed into it.

It cracked.

I slammed into it.

It opened further.

Moving again, I threw my entire weight behind it.

Then, it blew open. Everything slammed into me at once, and I felt it all. The moment Phaedra pushed through back to consciousness. Her fear. Power moving through her. I felt it all like a crashing wave rushing through me.

The bond unified us.

We were two, acting as one.

And we were out of time.

"Soldiers!" Phelix called, turning around.

I squeezed Phaedra's arm. She leaned into me, murmuring softly. Relief flooded into me. My wife was awake.

It was short-lived, however, because a second later, Phelix roared, "Kill them!"

The Ice Mer burst forth from the city. Hundreds of them crowded the sea, bearing weapons of every kind. We would have a minute, maybe less before they were upon us.

"Phaedra," I said, panicked. My wings unfurled from around her slightly as I stared at her face. "Wake up. I need you."

"What's happening?" she asked quietly, her eyes blinking open.

"We have to fight."

There was no more time for words. My wings opened, and Phaedra slid from my arms.

"Trust me," I said.

She nodded.

That was it. There was no time to explain.

We would have one shot. One chance to try.

One attempt to fight, or we would die.

Together.

"Power. Now," I grunted out as I drew every drop of magic available to me.

I grabbed onto Phaedra's hand. Sparks ran through me like fire.

Gathering every single ounce of my own magic, I turned to hers. The bond between us was open, and everything she had awaited me.

Phaedra was my ready and willing partner in battle, holding out her magic for me to use.

I tunneled and tunneled, picking up all the power I could along the way.

There was no bottom. No end to the magic.

But time was running out. The Ice Mer would reach us any second.

"We have one shot," I told her.

She nodded.

The power strained within me. Anticipation thickened the water. The Ice Mer screamed as they approached.

Hallie reared up with a sneer on her face and a sword in her hand. She speared through the water, her aim clearly fixed on Phaedra as she let out a blood-curdling war cry.

The magic was overwhelming. It felt as though I had held my breath too long. If I didn't release it now, then I would pass out.

"Now!" I screamed, and our combined power burst out of us like a typhoon. Phaedra's hand was ripped from mine as a wave of energy exploded from within us. Our combined strength was like an underwater supernova of greens and blues as it swept through the seas.

As the power drained out of me, so did my sight. My consciousness ebbed and flowed like the waters around us, and black edged my vision. I fought to stay alert as I watched the aftermath of our combined power.

Screams filled the water as merfolk were blasted in every direction.

I turned to my wife, my eyes widening as I stared at her.

Phaedra floated in place, her arms stretched out at her sides. Her eyes were as wide as clams, and her wings were flayed behind her.

"Phaedra!" I yelled.

No response.

Magic flowed out of her in pulses, touching everything all around us. In every direction, kelp and coral burst from the sandy ground. The ocean around us was coming alive.

Phaedra was breathing life back into the world.

I tried to move toward her, but my body was heavy. We spent so much power so fast.

"Phaedra."

Her name was on my lips as I reached out and grabbed her hand. She turned to me and smiled. "Aidoneus."

The last thing I remembered before blacking out entirely was Phelix appearing above me and a golden ball of light wielding a trident lunging toward him.

CHAPTER 32
NEW RULES
AIDONEUS

Four days later

When I opened my eyes, the first things I saw were stars. Memories of snow and icy water were still fresh in my mind, and I bolted upright, gasping for air.

"Phaedra," I panted, thrashing around. Silk sheets slid down my bare chest and pooled around my hips. Clearly, we were out of the water.

Thank the gods.

A movement came from beside me, and I turned my head. I froze, staring at the tuft of soft yellow feathers on my bed.

This was... unexpected.

I was not alone.

The most beautiful woman in the world was lying in my bed.

Sleep smoothed out Phaedra's expression, and the world around her was gentle and vibrant.

I reached out and stroked her bare arm. She wore a plain gray tank top, and I wondered who had brought us home.

It made sense that we would stay in the same bed. We were, after all, married.

All at once, my throat dried, and my chest fluttered with emotion. My eyes burned.

We were alive. We had made it.

And...

She wouldn't have chosen to be here with me if she had been awake. I needed to respect her wishes, even if it broke my heart to do so.

"Phaedra," I said softly. A pang of regret bubbled inside me to break the illusion of the couple we could be. My arm grazed the supple skin of her arms, and it took every ounce of self-control I had not to squeeze.

She was here. In my bed. Everything within me wanted to keep her here. This Angel was my life. My second chance at love.

I loved her.

The words burned on my lips, but I clamped them together. We had just been through so much. There was no reason for me to muddy the waters of our tenuous relationship with unwanted declarations.

When she still didn't wake, I decided I should probably stop watching the moonlight spill down her hair. I would try one more time, and if she didn't wake, I would scoot over to the furthest end of the bed and try to fall back asleep.

Much to my dismay, she stirred as my marbled skin splayed across hers. Her long black eyelashes fluttered as she woke.

Eternities were born in the time it took her to look up at me.

"Aidoneus," she breathed.

My heart cracked in half. I wanted to steal this moment and never, ever give it back. My palm moved without authorization, cupping her pale cheek.

I waited for her to flinch, for her to jerk away.

She did not.

In fact, a mix of pleasure, shyness, and desire washed through me. I blinked as I stared into those stunningly blue eyes. Those emotions... they weren't mine. They tasted of the spring-time and fresh air. They were hers. Our bond was still open.

"Are you all right?" Phaedra asked softly.

I nodded, my hand still on her face. I pressed the pads of my fingers gently into her jaw, memorizing the shape of her while my thumb stroked her skin. A tiny line appeared between her brows.

"I feel so tired," my wife whispered.

I nodded, resting on one arm as I looked down over her. "I do as well. It's the power. We used so much of it."

Her throat bobbed, the movement making the graceful lines of her neck even more pronounced. This moment was perfect. Even if I never saw her like this again, I would cherish it for the rest of my life.

But I had to ask.

"Would you like to go to your own bed?" The words tasted like ash on my tongue, and my stomach curled while I waited for her response.

Phaedra blinked again and then slipped under my outstretched arm. No longer was I leaning over her shoulder. Now, she rested completely on her back, staring up at me. Beautiful wings splayed across my large bed, filling the space in the most beautiful way. I sucked in a breath. She was positioned directly under me.

"I... I would like to stay if that's all right," she said shyly, her cheeks faintly flushing. "You have become a safe place for me. I'm not ready to give that up."

Her words were like electric shots straight into my heart. She wanted to stay. I wasn't sure what that meant... for us.

But it was something. And I needed that. Honestly, I had never imagined I would find us in this position one day.

"Of course, it's all right," I said. I eased myself back down so I was no longer trapping her under me. My arm burst into flames when her hand trailed up my forearm and wrapped around my palm. She pressed my hand to her cheek.

A glassiness coated her eyes. "We are alive."

I nodded, unable to speak as she continued to touch me.

Phaedra hesitated for a second. "Is... your brother dead?"

I paused. I wasn't sure, but something inside me answered in the affirmative. The image of Raphael lunging at him was still fresh. "I think so."

"Should I feel different?"

I laughed. "So many questions. I don't know, honestly. Do you feel different?"

My wife shrugged. "Maybe?"

I smiled. "Why don't you try to go back to sleep?"

She bit her lip. "Is the war over?"

I let out a long sigh. "We will discuss everything in the morning. I don't know everything yet, either. Sleep. Please."

Phaedra nodded and closed her eyes.

Minutes passed without another word. Her breathing slowed again, and I thought she had finally returned to slumber.

I closed my eyes, content to watch over her dreams while she rested.

I would watch over her for the rest of my life if she would allow it.

"Aidoneus," Phaedra whispered.

"Hmm?"

"Thank you for coming for me."

I let out a long breath. We were together, and we had a future. But it still didn't change that Phaedra hadn't wanted me before—that we had agreed this was a marriage in name only. "I meant what I said. I will always come for you."

I felt her move closer. "I've never... had something like this before. Someone that I've trusted so much."

My eyes opened, and I turned to look at my wife. "Never?" My mind flashed to Dylan. They'd been together for so long.

Forget sleep. Now, I needed answers.

Phaedra shook her head.

I looked at her for a long moment, not sure whether or not I should ask her about her ex-boyfriend. To say it was a sore spot for me was an understatement. I opened my mouth and gathered my strength.

When I still didn't speak right away, Phaedra lifted an eyebrow. "Go on," she said gently. "Ask it."

"What was Dylan for you, then?"

The Angel scrunched her forehead a little. I watched her search for the right words. "He was comfortable. A companion. But that was all. He and I... I think we were good friends. I loved him in his own way. As a friend, I think. But I was never *in love* with him." She paused, her voice quieting. "I didn't think I would ever be in love with anyone."

Her confession lifted a weight off my shoulders. She didn't love him. She had never loved him.

A spark lit in my chest, spreading heat through my veins. Hope came to life within me.

Maybe I wasn't alone in the way I felt.

A quiet moment stretched between us as we studied each other's eyes. Part of me wanted to push the conversation. To keep going.

The other part knew just how tired she was. How tired I was. The bone-deep ache in my body was still present.

"Let's sleep," I murmured.

A single moment passed before the sheets rustled. "You

know, it should feel strange for me to be here," Phaedra said. Her voice was alert, and her tone? It made my entire body burn like the sun.

Who needed sleep, anyway? My eyes snapped open another time, and my heart raced. I wouldn't be able to sleep, regardless.

I was almost afraid to ask. "Does it feel strange?"

Phaedra didn't respond immediately, but her hand trailed up my chest. I couldn't breathe. I could barely think.

She was *touching* me. Again.

"No," she said, drawing her lip through her teeth. "In fact, I can't shake this feeling that this is right. I should feel awkward and shaky—maybe even scared or upset about everything that happened to me these last few weeks. But... you came for me. There is something I don't fully understand between us. All I can think about is how you kissed me before this happened."

My breath hitched, and I slid my legs under me to sit up. That kiss... It was the things fantasies were made of.

"Oh?" I tried not to sound as flustered as I felt.

She hummed and nodded her head.

I swallowed. "And... what do you think about... that time?" Smooth.

She didn't seem to mind when she looked me straight in the eyes and said, "As angry as I still am about a few things, I wish it hadn't been cut short."

I gaped at her. "I... feel the same way."

She smiled softly, and I continued. "I changed my mind. You're clearly capable of taking care of yourself. You can start in acquisitions as soon as you feel ready. Or whatever you want. It doesn't have to be acquisitions. Tell me what you want, and I'll make it happen."

I will do anything for you.

Seeing the joy painted across my wife's face was worth it. "Thank you!" She pushed herself up, throwing her arms around my neck. The sheer force of her hug threw me backward. My wings flattened and splayed out beneath me. I couldn't help but laugh alongside her.

Her small body shook, and her soft curves were warm on top of me, the blankets still covering our lower bodies.

My skin went tight. I was trapped in her warmth.

Phaedra pushed herself up, looking down at me with a tender expression. Her eyes were dark, and desire pulsed through the bond. Tension filled the air, and I suddenly knew this was a turning point. For us. For our future. Whatever happened in the next few minutes would change the course of our lives forever.

Any hint of exhaustion I had earlier disappeared. I was alert. Present. Here for this moment.

"Aidoneus," Phaedra whispered. "What if I wanted to change the rules?"

Change the rules.

My heart pounded, and my body reacted instantly.

Gods, if she meant what I thought she meant...

"What do you mean?" I asked carefully.

I needed her to be very clear. For both of us.

Phaedra smiled, and her face reminded me of a fox. "Dinner together is a very good rule." Ebony hair smelling faintly of roses spilled over her shoulders, hanging like a curtain over my face. "I like that rule."

I laughed. "I like that rule, too."

She grinned, raising a finger and running it over my face. "Good, then we will keep it. But the other one..."

My eyes widened. "Do you mean..." My voice trailed off, my mouth suddenly dry, and I swallowed. A beautiful woman–my wife–was speaking about feelings, and I could barely get my words out of my mouth. "I thought... you were very adamant you didn't want to have sex with me."

Phaedra's smile faded away, and my stomach dropped. Had I

gotten the wrong impression? My mind replayed the last few minutes. She had come on top of me, and we were in bed together.

Phaedra bit her lip. "I made that rule before I really knew what it would be like to be married to you."

My head tilted to the side, and I looked her right in the eye. That wasn't an answer. "And what is it like to be married to me?"

"You are kind. Attentive. You notice things, and I think you remember almost everything I've told you." Phaedra seemed to think for a moment. She smiled, drawing a hand over my arm. "You are ridiculously attractive. You shower me with gifts. Money has been one of the biggest problems in my life, but you just... fixed it."

I grinned. "I love fixing things for you. It makes me feel like I'm paying you back for all those years as my assistant."

Her lips tilted up, and she continued. "I didn't know that you would make my life better in every way. I didn't know how much I would want you."

My eyebrows shot up. "The bond—"

She silenced me with a finger on my lips. "I've thought a lot about that–I had time, you know, in my cell–and I think the bond is just... an expression of feelings that were already there. Things I didn't want to think about, feelings I hid from. I don't think you hid from those feelings."

Phaedra smiled down at me. I blinked. I could listen to her talk forever, especially about this. She drew her lip through her teeth. "So... did you have feelings for me? Before?"

"Yes," I whispered. The word shot out of me, and the confession made me feel lighter than I had in years. Finally. *Finally.* This weight was off my chest.

She tilted her head. "When?"

"Do you... you might not remember this, but we met a really

long time ago." I reached up and tucked a loose strand of hair hanging over her eyes behind her ear.

Her eyebrows furrowed. "When you had me kidnapped?"

I shook my head, sitting up. She scooted back until we were both sitting cross-legged on the bed with our wings splayed out behind us. "No. You came to Miranda's funeral."

I watched her face change as she searched her memories for a moment, and then her eyes widened. "The garden. I'd forgotten all about that. That was you?"

I nodded as memories of that rain-soaked day filled my mind. Our history was so long and beautiful. "I wasn't in love with you or anything. But you helped me feel... normal. For a minute. For me, that was the debt of a lifetime. You told me, 'Remember my name,' so I did. When you were in danger because of the fraudulent paintings, I took care of it."

I thought of the tapestries Fortuna was weaving. Our lives were intertwined.

Phaedra was watching me, and those beautiful lips of hers parted. "You... thank you."

"When you started to work for me, it was only as a favor to you. But then... you became something more. The first moment I realized it was when I went searching for you. I found you playing the piano in a storage room. The melody was so beautiful but so sad." I hesitated for a moment. "Fortuna, my mother, speaks through music. I felt like I was overhearing your pain and loss. I wanted to take care of you. It surprised me."

It was Phaedra's turn to blink. "I-I thought that was my secret room."

I smiled. "It was. But I made sure that it stayed that way."

She bit her lip. "Did you listen often?"

"Would it bother you if I said yes?"

The truth was, I had listened for hours. Some days, her music was the only thing keeping me sane.

"No," she said after a moment. "It wouldn't bother me at all."

"Good," I murmured. "I listened often."

She let out a slow breath, and I felt the emotions welling inside her. "Where was the piano supposed to go?"

I touched her hand. "In my living room. Well, now it's our living room."

Her face was so full of emotion: happy, moved, tender, grateful. It made my own heart crack.

Phaedra seemed to think for a moment. "I think we need some new rules. It seems mine weren't any good."

"Oh?"

"Yes," she whispered. "The new rule–the only rule–is that we should express our feelings however we see fit."

My heart stuttered. "What do you mean?"

With timid hands, she reached up and wrapped her fingers around my neck. Pulling me close, she whispered, "This."

Phaedra kissed me softly, and I savored the gentle movement of her lips like morning dew. But the power of the sun quickly burned away as she deepened our embrace.

I'd be lying if I said I hadn't been here before. I'd imagined this, dreamed of it. Every feeling. Every word.

And yet, this, right here...

It surpassed all expectations.

The bond between us hummed, but the immense drain from earlier had subdued it. My first coherent thought was that I hadn't brushed my teeth recently enough.

Those thoughts were promptly forgotten as Phaedra broke away. She kicked the sheets off, revealing undergarments the same color as her tank top.

Her eyes swept over me, taking in my bare chest and the black boxers that were my only clothes. A hungry look appeared in her gaze, sending warmth through me.

She moved over me once again, her thighs straddling my hips. Her kisses were sweet at first, but quickly morphed into aggressive nips and bites.

I loved every second of it.

Her fingers traced the solid muscles of my arms and chest.

"I love these," she murmured, running her nail down a slightly raised scar on my chest.

In response, I glided my fingers over her chest. She shivered, her skin feeling like the softest silk beneath my fingers.

Hooking the strap of her tank top, I lifted my gaze to hers. "Can I take this off?"

Her breath hitched, and she lifted her arms. "Yes."

The whisper of the fabric against her skin was music I wanted to hear repeated for the rest of my life. A flush darkened her skin, and for a long moment, I stared at her.

She was beautiful, perfectly made, and just for me.

Wetting my lips with my tongue, I reached forward and captured her breast with my mouth. She moaned, her back arching as she leaned into me.

I couldn't help it. I licked and sucked until she panted before moving to the other side and applying the same treatment.

Her body was a little springtime garden; I wanted to be the thunderstorm it yearned for.

When I moved on from her breasts, she was flushed all over, panting and yearning for more.

Exactly how I wanted her.

My hands dipped below her waist, and her breathing stopped entirely.

I demanded she restart her breath with another rough kiss.

The magic between us, though faint and spent moments before, was already gaining traction. It filled us up and ushered us onward down this path. Sweat beaded over my body as she pushed me, kissing me back.

"My turn," she breathed.

She kneeled in front of me, jerking my boxers down. Her breath caught as she took all of me in, the desire in her eyes evident. Her tongue darted out, and she licked her lips as she reached out and took me in her hands. Her strokes were firm, and with every passing moment, a fire burned within me.

I groaned, my head falling back. Another time, I wanted to know what it felt like to have her mouth on me.

Not right now, though. I wouldn't last through that.

Instead, I reached out and took her hips. Flipping us on the bed, I made quick work of her underwear. Her eyes looked up at me, filled with so much love and trust that I couldn't believe it.

Nestled between her legs, I stared at her. "I need to hear the words."

Her lips parted. "I want you, Hades." She lifted her hips, settling my tip at her wet core. "All of you."

It was everything I needed to hear. With a single thrust, I was home.

In all my years, I'd never imagined this would feel so good, right, *perfect*. Drawing back out of her, I entered again, harder this time.

She moaned encouragingly, her hands clawing at my back.

That was all I needed. The rhythm between us picked up until I was teetering on the edge of a cliff. My hand slipped between us, finding the place where we were joined. My hand grazed that button, and she screamed, pulling us both over the edge.

Afterward, she lay on top of me, just breathing. Her heart raced to the same tempo as my own. In place of a door that had once represented our connection, a tunnel had carved out a path between us.

"Did you feel that?" I asked.

She huffed out a laugh. "Oh, I felt it."

I grinned and released her hands to squeeze one of her thighs. "I mean the bond."

She raised herself onto her forearms, searching my face. "It's different, right?"

I nodded. "Phaedra, I need to be honest with you about something. Please know I'm not expecting you to say anything in return yet."

She raised an eyebrow. "Oh?"

I took a deep breath. "I love you," I said quietly.

Her face flooded with emotion. "Aidoneus–"

I grabbed her hand. "Wait, please." I squeezed her hand. "Don't. Don't say anything. Not yet." The last thing I wanted was for her to close herself off to me again. "You don't have to love me as well. I just... I needed you to know."

My wife smiled, but it didn't quite reach her eyes. "Thank you for telling me. Just... give me a while to process all of... this."

She gestured at our naked bodies, and a part of me deflated. I knew she might not feel the same, but it was harder than I expected to reconcile what had just happened and how she had just reacted.

Patience, Aidoneus.

We had a long time together.

I took a deep breath and nodded. "Take all the time you need," I finally said. The words felt right, even though they didn't satisfy me.

She smiled and laid back down. Her wings brushed my arm and chest, and I stared for at least another hour, waiting for her to say something else. Anything.

She didn't.

CHAPTER 33
A QUEEN RISES
PHAEDRA

My nose twitched as the smell of something strong filtered through the layers of my dream. The thoughts of entangled limbs and mangled sheets were dispersed by the aroma of caffeine.

"Mhmm," I groaned, pressing my head into the pillow. "What is that smell?"

A soft chuckle came from behind me, and I forced my eyes open.

"I brought you some breakfast." Aidoneus' soft voice rolled over me, his words still carrying traces of sleep, and I smiled at the roughness I heard there.

They reminded me of what we'd done the night before. My core twisted at the thought.

That had been... unexpected.

And yet, it felt so right.

There were so many emotions at war within me. Too many emotions. I couldn't unpack them all right now.

I turned, lifting my head from the pillow and smiling at my

husband. He stood in a pair of gray sweatpants that hung low on his frame, and he'd pulled a t-shirt over his chest. A pity.

A tray rested between his hands, laden with a carafe of coffee, two mugs, various pastries, and a small container of jam. He looked so relaxed. So unlike the powerful DemiGod I knew him to be.

Was it only days ago that we'd been battling his brother in Aqualis? It felt like years had passed, and yet, here we were.

"Did you make me breakfast?" I asked, pushing myself up.

His lips twitched. "Well, to be honest, I didn't so much make this as I just assembled it. My chef did most of the heavy lifting."

I smiled. "No matter. It smells delicious." I patted the bed next to me, and he approached me warily.

"Phaedra..." His voice hitched. "We need to talk."

Talk.

That word was ominous. It always held a heavy weight. What did he want to talk about? Last night? Even as the thought entered my mind, I wondered if he regretted it. What we'd done... I had never experienced a connection like that before. The bond between us had made everything feel like *more*.

But maybe it hadn't been reciprocated. Maybe he regretted it. He had said he loved me, but I was certain it was just the aftermath of what we had done.

Maybe in the light of the day, he had decided otherwise.

Aidoneus poured me a cup of coffee, and I accepted it with a small smile. Staring at the rising steam, I asked, "Oh? What do you want to talk about?"

He slipped onto the bed, and the mattress dipped. I slid towards him with a small squeak. Our thighs touched, and I inhaled sharply. Sparks flitted through me at the point of contact, much like they had last night.

Apparently, that wasn't going away any time soon.

He sucked in a breath, but his hand inched toward me

instead of pulling away. Aidoneus glanced over at me, and the look in his eyes...

The emotions I'd seen reflected in them last night were still there. And within me... I felt something twisting. An emotion that I had yet to unpack was waiting there for me.

Without even thinking, I slipped my hand into his. That bond between us seemed to sing at the contact.

"I'm glad you wanted to talk because I have so many questions." I squeezed his hand. "How did we get home? Is everyone okay? Your niece and her husband? The war? What's going on?"

I stopped talking, and he let out a small chuckle.

"You do have *so many questions,*" he affirmed. Tightening his grip on my hand, he ran his thumb over my skin. "I woke up an hour ago and made some calls. Let me see if I can address some of those questions while you eat."

He raised a brow, waiting while I picked through the pastries. I popped one into my mouth, letting the flavors of lemon and butter explode on my tongue. A sound of appreciation slipped out of me, and he shifted in his seat.

My husband's lips twitched, and he raised his free hand. "Let's see. We passed out after releasing all our power. Phelix is dead."

"I'm so sorry." I tightened my grip on Aidoneus' hand. "I mean it. Phelix was... troubled, but he was still your brother."

My husband nodded, his gaze distant. "Thank you." A long moment passed as we both sat with the weight of Phelix's death resting on us. Aidoneus raised his hand, running it through his hair. "Raphael's men brought us home four days ago."

"Four days?" I almost spat out my coffee. "It feels like mere hours."

He nodded. "Using so much power is... draining."

I raised a brow. "Clearly. And the war?"

"It's over. With Phelix dead, his allies have scurried back to their homes. The Queen of the Winter Fae has generously provided troops to ensure the peace efforts go smoothly." He cleared his throat, shifting on the mattress. "Helena will have to assume her birthright power. The balance is off, and the Ice Mer are in need of her. Helena will be a good leader. She and Erik are strong, and I do not doubt that they will adapt well. Helena sent me a long email detailing her plans to set up a council of Ice Mer, so she doesn't have to return to Aqualis."

Nodding slowly, I thought about what that meant. Helena was powerful, courageous, and strong, and I knew she would be a good leader for her people. Not for the first time, I admired how Aidoneus cared for his family. She was his niece, but he treated her more like a daughter ever since she arrived.

I loved that about him.

My husband continued. "That's not all, though."

The air in the bedroom shifted, and somehow, I knew the next words out of Aidoneus' mouth would be important. Whatever he was going to say would shift the course of our entire lives.

"Oh?"

He nodded. "I meant what I said last night, Phaedra. I love you."

Love.

I wasn't sure what I felt for him. When we had wed, we'd been... not even friends. And now, with what we'd done, I knew we had left friendship behind us.

But I wasn't sure what I felt. I needed time.

I opened my mouth, but he continued. "Don't say anything. Not now. But I want you to be crowned as queen. I want you by my side as my equal for the rest of our days."

"Queen?" I shook my head. "I'm already queen consort, and your people have made it clear they don't think I bring enough to the table."

Just thinking about how Amthir, the former host of *Late Night Aranthium*, had treated me made me shudder. The thing was, I knew that she wasn't the only one in Aranthium to hold the opinion that I wasn't good enough to be queen.

"Don't," Aidoneus said.

"Don't?"

He shook his head. "Don't discredit yourself. We are here, *alive,* because of you. We won because of you. This war is over because of you."

A feeling of warmth filled me with his words. "Do you really believe that?"

"Absolutely." His voice was filled with conviction. "And once you are crowned, all my people will know that, too. You are my wife, Phaedra. I want you by my side in every single way."

The way he spoke... his tone... this was a part of Aidoneus that no one else saw. That he felt comfortable to share this part of himself with me made me feel special. Wanted. Secure.

"When will this coronation take place?"

A few months would give me enough time to prepare mentally, and then maybe...

He cleared his throat. "Tomorrow."

My fingers splayed, and the mug landed on the carpet with a soft *thud*. Brown coffee spilled out over the top, and I darted to the ground. Grabbing a towel that rested nearby, I patted at the liquid, hoping it wouldn't stain the beautiful carpet.

"I'm sorry," I said, turning to look at the King of the Daemons. "I thought you said tomorrow."

He chuckled. "I did."

My eyes widened, and my stomach dropped. Tomorrow was so soon. "But what... how? Why? That's so fast, and I just..."

He shook his head. "Saul is taking care of all the arrangements. All you need to do is show up."

"But—"

His hand landed on mine, and he squeezed tightly. "Phaedra, when you were... gone, it felt like my heart had been ripped out of my soul. I was broken. Alone. And now that you're back, I don't want to wait. If there is one thing I've learned over the centuries I've lived, it's that life's too short to wait for things that are important to you. So please, say yes. When you're crowned my queen tomorrow, you will be my equal in every way."

His eyes were so wide, the passion in his voice so sincere, that I was blown away.

"All right," I said after a moment.

"All right?" he echoed.

I nodded. "Tomorrow. A coronation." A shiver ran through me at the words. "What do I need to do?"

He grinned. "Just show up. I'll take care of the rest."

"Just show up," I repeated Aidoneus' words to myself as I adjusted my long blue ball gown for the hundredth time.

It fell to my hips in a tight corset, the back lacing around my wings before loosening around my legs. From afar, I looked like a mermaid.

I loved it. I had never worn anything like this, and it felt extraordinarily fitting. My makeup was perfect—not too much and not too little. Just enough to feel put-together without being over the top. I felt beautiful. Strong.

I was ready for this. Or at least as ready as I could be for this. Being crowned queen was never something I had ever even dreamed of. And yet, it was happening in a few minutes.

Aidoneus had spoken the truth. All I'd done was show up. After our conversation yesterday, he'd been whisked away by his assistant, Saul. The two of them had left, and within an hour, Karina had arrived. Apparently, my husband called her and asked that she spend the day with me. I told her about my kidnapping—not the nitty, gritty details, but the overarching theme of being taken, then rescued—and she spent the rest of the day regaling me with trivial gossip.

It had felt like the old days before my coma, and I loved every moment. Aidoneus hadn't come back at all. He texted me, saying something important had come up and he would see me at the coronation.

That didn't upset me. I was used to being alone and having time to think. What we'd done the night before was definitely something I needed to think about. Maybe he'd sensed that I needed some time alone. To think.

Because he loved me, and I...

I was fairly certain I reciprocated those feelings. The problem was, how did I know what love was? My mother loved me as best as she could, but she was cold. Hard, even. And then the disease had stolen her. Karina loved me in that special way that friendship could fill holes within our hearts.

Dylan... he never loved me. He cared for me, absolutely, but what we'd had wasn't love. It was companionship.

But Aidoneus and I?

We definitely had passion. We had desire. That much was clear. But lust was not love.

Before I said anything to this man, the King of the Daemons, I needed to figure it out for myself.

Did I love him in return? If so, what did it mean for us?

These questions kept swirling around in my mind, keeping me company as I stood before a pair of ornate black doors lined with gold, waiting to be called into the massive ballroom. It had been six years since the last time I'd set foot in this room. It was at the base of the Tower and could seat more than three thousand people comfortably.

The sounds of murmured conversations came from behind the doors, and I knew the large room was packed. I only hoped this experience would go far better than the last time I had appeared in front of a crowd.

I twisted my hands in front of me until I *felt* a tug on the bond within me. My breath caught, and I turned just in time to see Aidoneus striding toward me. His eyes were bright, and he was wearing an all-black suit. His horns, as were his wings, were on full display, and shadows trailed his every step.

He was death incarnate, and he was my husband.

The King of the Gates of Hell.

His eyes met mine, and my knees went weak. He paused, his eyes moving down my body appreciatively as he stood a foot away from me. Those lips I'd dreamed about last night curved into a rugged smile, and he said, "My Angel, you will be a stunning queen."

Somehow, his words settled the nervous butterflies flitting about in my stomach. "Thank you," I breathed. I studied him, a wry smile on my face. "You don't look so bad yourself."

He grinned. "How did you sleep last night?"

"Not as well as the night before," I replied instantly. Blood rushed to my cheeks at the implication, but he simply laughed.

"Good," Aidoneus said. "Neither did I."

With a grin, he offered me his elbow. I laced my arm through his, and then he leaned down. Brushing his lips over mine in a kiss that was not long enough, he whispered, "The Gates of Hell are lucky to have you as their queen."

My lips tilted up, but before I could respond, he flicked his hand. A shadow went out, and the doors flung open. Instantly, the conversations ceased. The rustling of fabric filled the air as row after row of spectators rose to their feet. We waited, my arm on my husband's, until the entire room was on their feet.

Only then did we move. We walked toward the stage, and I kept my eyes on the front. Walking from the back to the stage took ten minutes, and I could feel the weight of the gazes watching our every step. Out of the corner of my eye, I saw the cameras recording the entire thing, but they didn't bother me today.

Near the front, I saw Helena and Elva, their heads bent together as their respective husbands sat on either side of them. Helena caught my gaze and grinned.

Standing on the stage stood a priestess, not unlike the one who had married us. Aidoneus leaned in, his hand on mine as he whispered, "A coronation, it seems, is not unlike a marriage. Except this time, one is binding oneself to the country."

A fitting description, I thought.

When we came to the stage, my husband released my hand. He stepped a few feet away from me as the priestess came forward. She bowed, her robes swishing about her as she held out a steady hand. I placed mine on hers, and she turned to face the crowd.

"Fortuna smiles upon us today, people of Aranthium. She has returned our king and sees fit to provide us with a queen." A cheer rose from the crowd, and I felt their love. Their adoration. It washed over me in a wave, and I smiled. The priestess continued to speak, delving into the history of the Gates of Hell, but I wasn't paying attention. My eyes swept over the crowd until...

I gasped. Sitting in the front row, watching with a small smile on her face, was my mother. Beside her sat a Fae I only recognized from video calls. The energetic nurse was grinning, wearing a fancy tuxedo, and blending in with the rest of the crowd. Mother was dressed in a simple green gown, but her eyes glimmered with understanding.

Today was a good day.

Silver shimmered in my vision, and I blinked the tears away. Yanking my attention back to the priestess, I mumbled my accord when she asked me if I would do whatever it took for my country.

Then I lifted my gaze to Aidoneus.

Did you do this? I mouthed.

He grinned. *I did.*

Warmth swept through me like the sun on a hot summer day. This must have been the reason he was gone yesterday.

He fetched my mother and brought her here so she could see this.

He loved me, and I...

I loved him, too.

The warmth grew in my chest until a flash of blue magic erupted from within me. A rumble of thunder came from above, and multi-colored petals began to fall from the ceiling of the ballroom. They rained on the crowd as gasps of delight filled the air.

The priestess chuckled. “Well, there certainly is no question about the queen’s power now, is there?”

I smiled softly.

“Shall we continue?” the priestess asked.

“Yes, please.”

Suddenly, the ceremony couldn't be over fast enough. I nodded at the right moments and said the right things until, finally, the priestess gestured to the side. Aidoneus came to stand next to me, his arm brushing up against mine, as a small Were child came forward. He held a red pillow and a beautiful black crown glimmered in the light. The Were bowed in front of me, his eyes shimmering with obvious delight. "Your Majesties"

"Thank you, Ryo," Aidoneus said in a gravelly voice. He reached over and took the crown off the pillow.

The Were bowed, scurrying off the stage.

Aidoneus turned to me, his eyes sparkling. "Do you, Phaedra Demtre, agree to rule the Gates of Hell with justice and fairness to the best of your ability?"

Drawing in a deep breath, I swallowed. "I do."

He smiled. "Do you swear to use your godly magic as gifted to you by Fate to protect those who claim you as their sovereign?"

"I do."

A cheer went through the crowd, and he stepped toward me. The bond within me felt like it was glowing, and my wings rustled behind me as I stood tall.

This was it.

"Then, my beloved wife," he said the words with such gentleness and reverence, "it is my greatest pleasure to crown you Phaedra, Queen of the Gates of Hell. My Angel." My stomach fluttered as he lifted the crown.

The moment it settled on my head, a flash of blue magic swept out of me.

A feeling of rightness filled me. The rest of the ceremony went by in a blur. The priestess spoke some more, but I barely heard it. A row of children came onto the stage. Fae, Mer, Were, and even a few humans. Each of them handed me a flower until I held a massive bouquet in my hands.

Then, finally, it was over.

Aidoneus took my arm and led me off the stage. We walked into a small room filled with bottles of water and a tray full of snacks. We slipped in, and I closed the door, locking it.

He stood silently, watching me.

I placed my bouquet on the counter before turning around. “My mother is here.”

It wasn't a question, but he nodded. "Yes."

"You did this." I stared at him, this king whom I'd married.

"Yes," he replied. "I've arranged for her to come and live in the tower. I've hired full-time care to look after her, and we'll ensure she has the best medication. Her bills are paid. You don't need to worry about that..." His voice trailed off, and he glanced at my face. "Are you mad? Should I have told you? I know that you didn't have the best childhood—"

I interrupted him, putting my hands on his chest and tilting my head until my mouth was inches from his. He sucked in a breath, and I whispered, "I'm the furthest thing from mad that there could be. I am not mad. Aidoneus, this is the most incredible thing anyone has ever done for me."

His eyes softened. "So you're not upset? I know it might be overstepping the bounds of our... whatever we are, and if you're not ready for things—"

I stopped the flow of his words with my lips. His words dried up, and his arms came around me, pressing me against him. We kissed and kissed until my entire body was tingling.

"Aidoneus, I'm not angry," I whispered against his lips. "I love you, too."

He stilled for a moment, and that bond within us pulsed with energy. "What?"

I grinned against his lips. "I said, I love you."

He groaned, his hands sweeping down my thighs as he lifted me. I was vaguely aware of him walking us backward until my bottom sat on the counter.

"Gods, say it again." His lips left mine, trailing a course down my body.

"I love you."

"Again," he growled, his mouth traveling further south.

"I love you." The words were little more than breaths of air as breathing became more difficult. My heart pounded, and warmth twisted within me.

"Again," he demanded as he lifted my dress.

My hands twisted in his hair. "I. Love. You."

Then, words were no longer needed between us. Our bodies fit together, our lips, tongues, and teeth saying the words we couldn't say aloud.

I love you.

As we joined, our bonds singing in delight, everything felt fresh. New. Exciting.

What began as a marriage of convenience evolved into something more.

I loved this man. He was mine. Hades, the King of the Daemons, loved me.

Together, we would rule the Gates of Hell.

I couldn't wait to see what would happen next.

EPILOGUE
AIDONEUS

Fifty years later

"So, do the feathers give you another layer of insulation? Or are you so warm because of the coat I bought you last Winter Solstice?" I asked Phaedra casually. She sat across from me, dressed from head to toe in white.

In the bitter cold of Were Territory, it snowed ten months out of the year. Even though it was summer back home, snow fell from the skies here. It glinted like glitter as it landed on my wife's obsidian black hair.

We sat in an enormous lodge upon invitation from the Pack Leaders. Our relationship had done nothing but blossom in the last five decades, and finally, there was true unification between the North and South.

Except for the Vampires. Those shady bastards had gone silent after helping Raphael and me win the last war.

Phaedra smiled at me. "I am warm because I love you." It was a new smile that I hadn't seen before this morning. This morning, she'd been quiet while we ate breakfast. The food was exquisite, and the log walls created a luxurious, cozy feeling that was hard to replicate in the desert. A companionable silence existed between us, and I had grown to appreciate it. Even so, today, nerves filled the air. They weren't just mine.

With Phaedra, I felt like a whole being. More than anger and power... life. Just thinking about our adventures in the last half-century together made my blood heat.

That was what *this* was. A new adventure. A year ago, we started traveling down here consistently. Neither Phaedra nor I expected it, but a new opportunity had unfolded before us that threatened to change our existence forever.

And now, today was the day we had been waiting for.

The doors to the private dining room blew open, and in breezed my brother, arm-in-arm with his wife, Reyna. Instantly, Phaedra sat up straight as the energy in the air changed. All the world's greatest powers were standing in the middle of a snowy, coniferous forest.

"Where's my new nephew?" Raphael's voice boomed. His golden skin looked as if it had been polished. He was six and a half feet of pure DemiGod.

His wife just rolled her eyes and brushed past him. "Dammit, Raphael, it's 8:00 a.m. You need to calm down. Somehow, you've managed to make this about you." Reyna stopped in front of Phaedra, her long faux fur parka brushing against her knees. She was beautiful enough to be a statue and shrewd enough to win a spot at my brother's side. Reyna's skin was dark, a lush brown, and she came from old Aranthium money.

Raphael looked wounded in the corner, and the energy in the air shifted. I really wasn't looking forward to being in front of yet another of their conjugal yelling matches.

"Zeus," I rumbled. "Please."

My brother glared at me. "Aidy—"

Phaedra interrupted us both. She smiled kindly at my brother and his wife. "We are so appreciative that you both came for this. We weren't sure if you would both make it."

Reyna flashed a perfect smile with teeth so white it put the snow to shame as her wings fluttered out behind her. "I wouldn't have missed it for the world." I smiled, content to leave it at that, but my sister-in-law continued, "Raphael, on the other hand, would've kept his lazy ass in bed all day."

My brother growled. "Ah, here we go!" He threw his hands in the air.

I let out a sigh. Phaedra and I were the ones undergoing a life-changing event, yet even now, had to babysit my insufferable brother.

Such was family life.

A chirp-like notification came from Phaedra's FaeWatch. She glanced down at it, her brows rising. Then, always the peacemaker, she stood and smiled. "Raphael, how about you and I go get my mother? We should make sure that Helena and her family are awake along the way."

Nine years after the war, Helena and Erik had adopted their niece and nephew. The four of them made a cozy family.

Raphael grinned. It was slow and sensual in a ridiculous way. I don't even think he realized he was doing it.

"As the Queen commands," he drawled while holding out his arm for Phaedra to take.

Reyna reached out a black-gloved hand and smacked Raphael hard on the back of his head. "Stop that," she snapped.

My wife and I burst into genuine laughter. It was good to be with my family. Eventually, the other couple joined in.

A familiar gray-skinned female entered the room, and my heart warmed.

"I just don't understand why it had to be this early in the morning," Helena complained to Queen Elva, who was walking at her side.

"Helena, I swear to the gods. Just go to bed earlier, and you won't be tired," Elva said with a laugh.

Dressed in an oversized cropped sweater, my niece wheeled into the room. The water from her aqua-chair sloshed quietly while she crossed the room. On the other side of my niece was her mortal-turned-eternal husband. He always looked uncomfortable at family functions—he preferred the sea—but always showed up.

Clinging to his leg was a small, little gray-skinned Merling. Giselle had Helena's eyes, but the hair color was all wrong.

Nathaniel was a little behind everyone, walking beside his daughter, Taneisha. The young princess was pushing another aqua chair that housed Ian. The two of them were always together. Apparently, Ian rarely used legs because he liked talking to Taneisha so much.

"Someone call the DaePolice. It looks like a little bitch got in here," Helena called from the other side of the room, eyeing Raphael.

"Helena, the kids," Nathaniel chided from the back.

"It's fine," Elva said quickly.

As far as I knew, Helena and Raphael never really talked about what happened in my tower. It seemed her main mode of communication with the king was to mess with him.

Raphael whipped around, and Erik growled at him.

The golden DemiGod just shook his head.

"Helena! My favorite niece!" Reyna called. She skirted around the table, throwing her arms around the purple-haired Ice Mer.

Helena's face was buried in Reyna's coat, but I still heard her say, "Well, the other one is in prison, so I better be your favorite."

Uncomfortable chuckles abounded. Ian and Giselle smiled, but they didn't laugh. Morbid, inappropriate, charming. That was my darling niece Helena.

Phaedra walked behind Reyna.

"We were just going to see if you were awake. We're going to get my mom," the Queen of Hell's Gates declared while grabbing Raphael's golden arm.

Helena waved at them. "Try not to kill anyone, asshole!"

Raphael's head whipped around at the last moment. "That only happened once!" he called back, just as Ian whispered to Taneisha, "He tried to kill Aunt Helena."

"She's joking!" I called as Phaedra pulled my brother into the hallway and shut the door.

Once Raphael and Phaedra left, an awkward pause filled the air. I wasn't always the best with personal get-togethers, and I felt even less prepared today.

The air was thick with anticipation. The only ones who seemed unaffected were Ian and Taneisha. The two preteen-equivalent beings laughed at each other as they whispered back and forth.

"Phaedra is the best one in this family, you know," Helena said after a few minutes passed.

Reyna glared at Helena, but I grinned. She was right. My wife was incredible.

"Did you forget about your amazing husband?" Erik asked as he picked up Giselle and hugged her tightly.

"I could never forget about you," Helena replied, a quiet laugh in her voice.

"Good." Erik bent, brushing a kiss over his wife's lips as he supported the Merling in his arms.

Helena glanced up at him, and his eyes flicked down to her. I had been married long enough to know that an entire conversation happened in that one look.

Erik cleared his throat, but Reyna spoke first.

"So, Erik, how is the transportation business coming? Last I heard, you were working miracles for the swamp witches in the Spring Mer land." Reyna sat down with a sweeping motion, her every movement that of a person who carried her confidence on her sleeve.

Erik nodded. “It’s good. My new crew runs a tight ship, but with an entire armada, it’s hard not to be the best.”

Reyna waited for him to continue. When he didn’t expand, she said, “I imagine. Fascinating what a human can do with a few extra years. It makes me think.”

I opened my mouth at the same time Helena said, “It makes me wonder what humans could do if we gave them more credit during their lifetimes.” My niece's eyes flashed with warning, and I breathed deeply.

The minutes passed with more idle chit-chat, thankfully avoiding any other potential outbursts until Raphael and Phaedra returned with my mother-in-law nestled between them. Age, illness, and proper care had made her soft. The hard days weren’t so hard anymore. I often enjoyed having her close.

She cooed as she walked into the room. “It’s so lovely here. Thank you, Phaedra, my sweet,” she said.

Helena leaned toward me. “What time are they getting here?”

I checked my watch. It was nearly 8:30 a.m. My heart fluttered, and my stomach somersaulted. “Any minute, actually,” I said.

Helena wagged her eyebrows. “Exciting!”

I nudged her chair with my knee. “Shut up, or I will give you legs.”

Helena laughed as Phaedra returned to my side. Part of me relaxed just at the sensation of having my wife near. Her hand sought my own, and she gave it a little squeeze.

The doors opened once again, but this time, a receptionist walked in. The female Were had feminine sideburns framing her brown face. “Your… Highnesses?” she asked with uncertainty in her voice. I got it. We were a big bunch, and the Were Territory wasn't a culture built on decorum. "The social worker has arrived. Are you ready for them?"

Phaedra and I answered at the same time. *"Yes."*

The word was eager and rang in the small room. Clouds gathered ahead, and the earth rumbled a little below. Our power was overwhelming sometimes.

It was hard to keep a rein on my emotions when the other door opened wide. Pack Leader Theodora was accompanied by a woman whom Phaedra and I had communicated with several times in preparation for this day.

The two of us stood, my wife pressed into my side.

In front of both of them was a little Were cub. He was currently in human form, but we knew well that could change with the slightest shift in emotions.

My throat grew tight at the sight of the little one wobbling as he walked. He was furry, sweet, and perfect. Our relatives moved to either side of us, creating a walkway toward me and my wife. The little pup's eyes bulged out of his head as he stared at Helena and my brother.

"Jorge," Phaedra said softly. Immediately, the little one's eyes snapped onto my queen. He let out a howl of pure joy. Just like that, his clothes ripped and flew right off his small body while he switched into a wolf and bounded toward us. His front paws landed on Phaedra and shoved her into me.

We met Jorge while visiting one of the orphanages. His parents were killed in a mining accident, and he imprinted on Phaedra the second he'd set eyes on her. The orphanage worker had hemmed and hawed, but we left and went straight to discuss his adoption with the Pack Leaders. They had heartily agreed. Paperwork had been signed, but we had to wait a little while to prepare him for leaving the orphanage.

I didn't even know I was crying until the impact knocked tears from my eyes.

"Hey buddy," I said softly and kneeled down to pick him up. While he hadn't imprinted on me at first sight, he gave his love freely. The child started licking my face, and I laughed as I fell onto my back.

In an instant, there was a naked Were toddler on top of me.

Everyone laughed.

Phaedra knelt next to me and draped a cardigan over the little one.

Theodora's voice filled the whole room. "Congratulations to the new parents."

I sat up and pulled Phaedra in close, covering her face in kisses before kissing our new son.

The entire room cheered. This was our family. Some by blood, others by choice. The Winter Queen and her husband, the children that came into our lives one way or another, my brother, my niece. It felt so good.

Raphael's voice was louder than the others as he boomed, "Mom asked me to tell you that you must bring him to her as soon as you get home. She doesn't want a priestess blessing him—she reserves that right all to herself."

I smiled up at my brother and nodded. I was okay with that.

Phaedra kissed my cheek. "Easy, my love."

I blinked. I hadn't realized that the ground beneath me was rumbling. My emotions were so fierce they nearly blinded me.

I held my wife and new son close, looking at the rest of our family. Each of them had tears in their eyes. When Miranda died, I thought my life was over. I still loved her—a part of me always would.

But my mother was right, my life didn't end with hers.

"Thank you all so much," I said softly.

Jorge threw his arms around me, and his little furry face curled into the base of my neck. He was so warm, our own little heater. His heart was beating so fast it joined the chorus of mine and Phaedra's.

I felt at home.

THANK YOU FOR READING! If you enjoyed the book, please review!

We have plans for a Romanthian novella in late 2024! Check our social media to find out more. In the meantime, if you would like to check out some of our separate series, check them out here:

Daniela: To Steal a Bride (Coming November 27th, 2023)

Elayna: A Game of Love and Betrayal (Coming March, 2024)

ALSO BY ELAYNA AND DANIELA

We also write our own series! Check them out below:

The Binding Chronicles

Elayna R. Gallea—Upper YA/NA High Fantasy Romance

The Blood Tournaments

Daniela A. Mera—Young Adult Dystopian Fantasy Romance

The Ithenmyr Chronicles

Elayna R. Gallea—Upper YA/NA High Fantasy Romance

Entangled with the Enduar

Daniela A. Mera—New Adult Fantasy Romance

The Divinity Chronicles

Daniela A. Mera—Upper YA/NA High-Fantasy Romance

The Sequencing Chronicles

Elayna R. Gallea—Young Adult Dystopian Fantasy Romance

Acknowledgments

We want to thank the readers that made this book a reality. To our ARC and Beta Readers, know that your comments and encouragement really propelled us onto finishing and publishing our novel.

To our writing group partner, Sydney Hunt. Thank you for your endless wealth of knowledge, for letting us endlessly bounce ideas off of you during our editing process.

Of course, we would be no where without the support, inspiration, and love from our incredible families. They were very cool with our THIRD joint-custody book baby.

Thank you to Elayna's family: Aaron, Britanny, and Jack.

Thank you to Daniela's Family: Josué, Jacqulyn, Grant, Érica, and Victoria.

ABOUT THE AUTHOR

Daniela A. Mera and Elayna R. Gallea became friends through teaching languages. Daniela lives between Nevada, USA and Hidalgo, Mexico, living out her own fantastical dreams one day at a time. Sign up for her newsletter to get updates and free novellas or extra book chapters!

For print version, visit:

www.danielaamera.com

facebook.com/AuthorDaniela.A.Mera
instagram.com/authordaniela.a.mera
amazon.com/~/e/B09JDDZQX7
goodreads.com/authordanieaamera

About the Author

Elayna R. Gallea lives in beautiful New Brunswick, Canada with her husband and two children. They live in the land of snow and forests, near the lovely Saint John River. When Elayna isn't reading or writing, she can be found teaching French online to her amazing students. Tap the image or click here to see more of her work!